THE DOORS BETWEEN

K. R. MENENDEZ

ISBN 978-1-63784-189-1 (paperback)
ISBN 978-1-63784-190-7 (digital)

Copyright © 2023 by K. R. Menendez

All rights reserved. No part of this publication may be reproduced, distributed, or transmitted in any form or by any means, including photocopying, recording, or other electronic or mechanical methods without the prior written permission of the publisher. For permission requests, solicit the publisher via the address below.

Hawes & Jenkins Publishing
16427 N Scottsdale Road Suite 410
Scottsdale, AZ 85254
www.hawesjenkins.com

Printed in the United States of America

"Hello, hello? Anyone there? Wow. This thing is still working. A little slow, but okay. Testing, testing, one, two. Testing, three, four. This may be the best thing I ever found. I didn't want to say that. To anyone listening, I am recording this. I have to tell you my story, which you won't believe. I barely believe it, and I am living it right now. Where to start? I'll begin with my name. Names are powerful, and you really should not tell your full name unless it's crucial. Since the end of my world is upon me, my name is...

"Sorry about that. The power went out again. So the end of my world. It sounds dramatic and desperate, and it is. One day after the Storm, which you call hurricanes, I pulled some junk from the edge of the Wamp. I had a bad feeling because of the enormous piles of stuff coming from your world to Tween. Just to let you know, I am not an alien from another planet but really just a neighbor of sorts. How can I explain...I live...I travel. Have you ever walked through a door on your way to the living room, for example, but for a split second, you thought you were in a different room, house, building, or another country? You may have just shrugged it off, thought it was déjà vu, or just your crazy imagination, or a bad gas station burrito. It is called a glimpse or a small window or hole between worlds, which disappears. The large glimpses are called rifts, and they remain open. Thousands of years ago, my people made various magical doorways to seal up the twelve rifts and to protect all the worlds. Only four magic doors still exist. The protectors of the rifts were called Doorfs, and they ruled Between for 817 years. Anyway, that was a thousand years ago. None of the people living in Between remember the old days. Well, almost no one. You see, I am the last Doorf, the last protector of the portals. My name is…

"Sorry again. The power is fading. The ruins are crumbling around me, and this will be my last chance to explain. I am almost finished reconstructing the last door. I will attempt to go through one last time and get some help. If I can't find my elf friend, all will be lost, and your world may be next. I hope someone hears this transmission and comes to my aid. I really don't know what else to say. I know, a farewell from my world, 'May the Good find you and keep you.' If anyone does hear this…or finds…I need your help! … name is…"

> When the River Drayne cuts the land in three,
> and the Junks bring trouble
> from beyond the east and west,
> When the Felds are burned,
> and the Celos crumble,
> When the Firrest is fire,
> and the Wamp no more,
> When the battle is over
> and the ways cries out,
> When between streets blood runs red,
> and the fountains scream, "All is dead!"
> When the Rocs lay in ruins,
> And the ruins rise again,
> Then the door which was, will be,
> and the door which was not will close.
> Then the end will come to begin anew,
> And the protector will race into battle,
> To seal the victory of the few,
> Then the Good shall triumph and
> Lift the flag of victory in surrender.
>
> Prophecy from the Book of Good

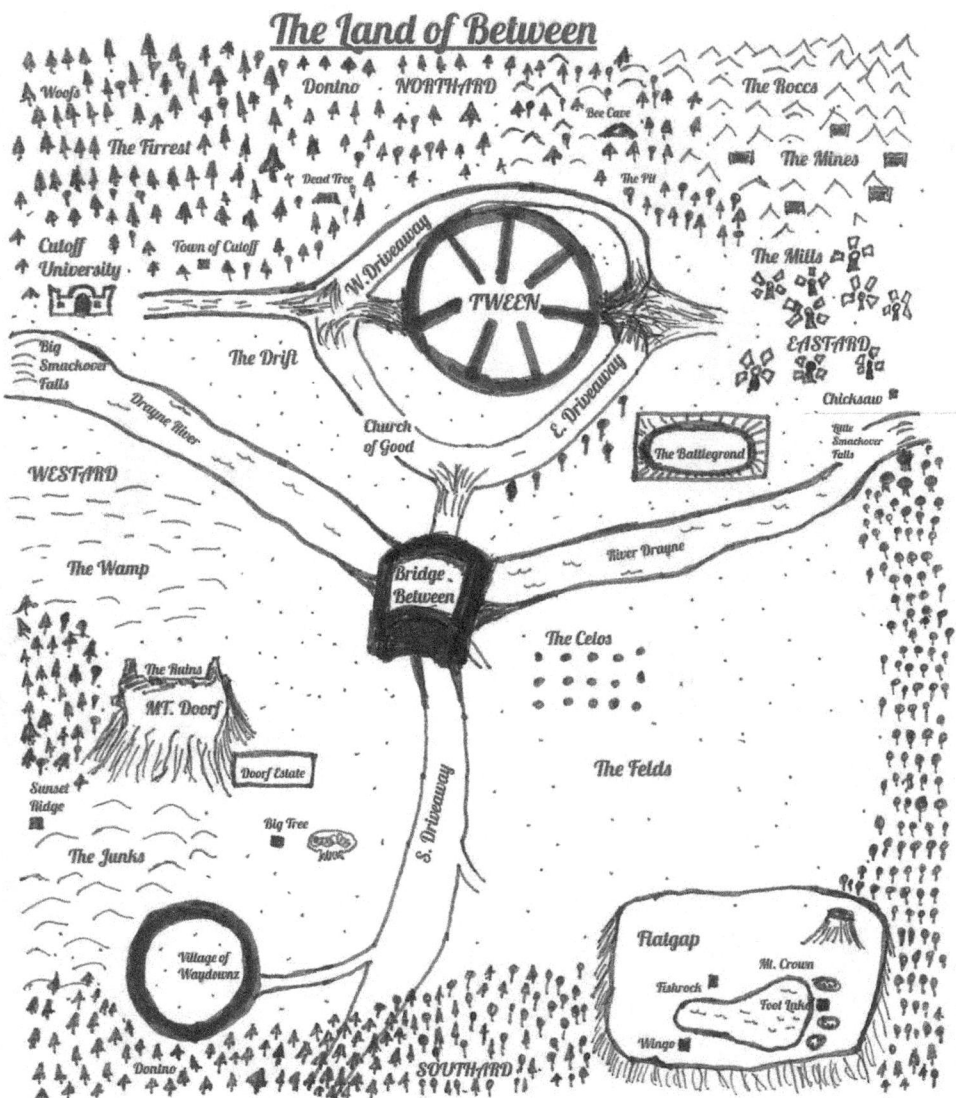

CHAPTER 1

Happy Is the Man Who Finds Wisdom

Along an ancient cobblestone road, windswept trees littered the path called the Driveaway. A severe Fourland Storm had blown from the west and east throughout the previous night. It left devastation and junk everywhere. An exhausted group of locals, the Tween Legion, had been removing the large debris from the road from sunup to now almost sundown. The Legion's main officer, Captain Jak Chico, rested on a twisted stump. His jacket and shirt were stained with sweat and earth. He poured some greenish ale into a wooden cup. He took a long sloppy drink.

He wiped his unwrinkled forehead and his curly black hair with his left hand. He knew his men admired his rank and looks. He also recognized most of the Tween women sweetly lusted for him. He smirked. He surveyed the Driveaway and all the intense labor the Legion had completed in one day. He sipped the ale this time, sloshed it around his mouth, and then spat it out. His dark complexion helped him keep cool in the hot sun. He rose to his feet and stretched his tall, athletic build. He twisted his strong neck back and forth. He wore a large hunting knife in a dark sheath on his left hip. He called to the nearest guard walking past.

"Popson, how much more do we have to do?" Chico removed the knife and picked at his left hand.

"Captain, we found bits of some junk and one maple tree. The junkman is checking out the stuff, and the Legion is working on the maple," responded the guard.

"Well, don't just sit there. Get the junker so we can finish the job. Now!" Chico barked and put away the knife.

"Yes, sir!" the guard said as he ran up the next hill.

Popson found the junkman a half mile down the road. He stood over six feet tall with square shoulders and strong arms and legs. He wore reflective goggles over his wavy brown hair. He wore a faded cowboy-style shawl over his Legion work attire. He removed some large tree limbs from the stone path with ease. He placed them in front of several mangled pieces of silverish gray metal pipes, tattered white bedsheets, and immense volumes of weathered books.

"Hey, junker. You were hard to find. The captain needs your help on the final tree. You coming? What did you find?" asked the winded guard.

The junkman called back, "Just some more garbage the storm blew in. I'll get it later." He tossed the branches like twigs. He gave a friendly smile and stuck out his hand to the guard. "Popson, right? I'm Tood. I just joined the Legion a few moons ago."

The guard ignored the handshake. "Great, junker. I know who you are. I was at the Jump and Jive last year. Let's get back before Chico puts us both on latrine duty."

Tood smiled. "No problem. Let me grab my staff."

The guard half grinned and teased, "How's your pooch doing after your big fight?"

"We made amends and—"

"I don't care. Let's go."

Tood and Popson hustled back down the road and witnessed the Legion struggling to move the massive leaf-covered obstacle.

Captain Chico called out, "Anytime this century, ladies. We do have a party to get to."

"Sorry, Captain. I found some really amazing—" Tood started.

"Junk? No kidding. The junkman found junk," Chico jeered, and the troop cackled. "If it's no trouble, could you help us with this blasted tree?"

"Yes, sir," Tood and Popson said and moved next to the winded Legion.

Chico ordered, "On the count of three. One. Two."

Tood pushed before the rest of the Legion and cleared the entire tree from the Driveaway. The soldiers had nothing to push and fell on their faces, all except for the captain.

"There you go, Cap." Tood ran back up the hill toward his prizes. "I'll see you all at Sembly. The Good bless you."

Chico stared at Tood and then at the maple and then back at Tood as he ran off.

"The Good be with you. It's at five. Don't be late," Chico muttered. He scowled at the moaning Legion laying on the ground. "Get up, you lazy Schlapinskis! Grab those sacks and let's move! Move it! Wamp scum!"

Tood removed the branches from around the junk and gave an enormous yawn. He had helped the Legion remove debris from the Mills to the Felds. His muscles burned, and his stomach screamed, but he had forgotten about it once he found the junk.

Usually after a Storm, he would find wheels, chairs, pipes, and weird contraptions from the other realms. Today, he found something he had not seen in years—a compooter! Tood carefully lifted the stiff bedsheets into his sled, stacking the heavy books on one end and the pipes on the other side. He picked up his staff and touched it to the sled. A single spark shot out, and the sled levitated and followed Tood as he ran down the Driveaway.

As Tood reached the Bridge Between, he slipped to the underside of the stone cut structure and pushed in a diamond-shaped brick. The rock wall opened to reveal a secret passage, which he and the floating sled entered undetected. Flickering lights appeared as the passage door closed to reveal an antechamber with ropes, chains, and pipes of various sizes on the wall. Opposite the hanging items was a wooden plank door with no handle. Tood placed the end of his staff on the door, and it opened to a lime-lit tunnel with a spiral slide.

The junkman leaped down the slide with the sled in pursuit. He spiraled and zoomed down the tunnel toward his house by the Ruins. As he got closer to the ancestral home, his descent slowed as the slide's angle incrementally increased. His approach activated more long cylinder lights showing his landing area covered in two layers of worn-out spring mattresses. Tood did a flip as he soared from the slide and landed safely on the farthest bed. The sled gently bumped against the back of his legs. He looked back and grinned at his prizes and moved to the door directly in front of him.

He knocked a complicated sequence, and the door opened. He heard and then saw a rattling and steaming red pot. He stepped inside a warm and wonderfully smelling tile-covered kitchen. Tood touched the sled and pushed it into the adjacent room as he moved over to a black stove and shut off the fire under the pot.

He lifted the lid and inhaled the rich aroma of vegetables and savory beef. His stomach groaned in agony. He reached for his favorite green speckled bowl and a large silver ladle. He scooped the stew into his bowl and placed it on the kitchen island opposite the stove. Tood slightly banged his head on the pans hanging over the island. He reached for some small bread loaves in a wicker basket. He picked up a spoon from the third drawer and slid a tall wooden stool under him and bowed his head in thanks. Within moments, his meal was devoured, and he went to the frigger to get a cold drink. RC Cola was his favorite, and he had an ample supply. The satisfying carbonation and caramel syrup combination slid down his throat and then erupted in a deep abdominal belch.

Tood whistled a low tone and called out, "Woof, please come to the living room." Tood reached into a jar on the top shelf and pulled out a large crusted biscuit. He walked into the living room and spotted a gigantic Siberian husky sniffing the contents of the sled. Tood tossed the biscuit at the beast. Woof snatched it midair. "What do you think? Anything good, or should I just dump it in the Junks?"

Woof swallowed the biscuit and made three yips and a bark.

Tood asked, "You want it for a new plaything? The books or the pipes?"

Woof howled low, which sounded like laughter.

"Neither. You want the wrappings. Sorry, pal, the sheets are mine. It's a new compooter. See?" Tood exclaimed with pride as he pulled out a thin black rectangular device with glass on one surface. "This is a handheld compooter like *Star Trek*, a communicator. I think I have a charging cord." He left the room with the device and came back with a long black cord.

Woof gave it a sniff, rolled his eyes, and gave another low howl.

"I can have it. The battery is dead. Oh, thanks, you are so gracious, king of the Firrest. I have to charge it. I know, I know. You like *Star Wars*." He plugged it into the nearest outlet and gently placed it under the couch. Tood exclaimed, "You can have the rest! Just let me unwrap it first."

The junkman slowly unwrapped the first layer of cloth, which exposed three leather straps holding together the bundle. Tood took out his hunting knife and removed the straps. The bundles seemed to relax and take a different shape. Tood looked at Woof. "What is this?"

The canine dug his pointed nose deep into the wrappings. He barked, jumped up, and vigorously wagged his tail.

"No, it can't be." Tood scrambled to remove the wrappings. From the seventh layer, long curly jet-black hair flowed. Tood's hands trembled as he pulled back the last wrapping. He revealed the face of an elegant young lady with olive-toned skin. A gold chain necklace with an amethyst jewel was draped on her smooth neck. She seemed to be in a deep sleep. Tood lifted her from the sled and laid her on the soft living room couch. He gently scooped a throw pillow under her head and covered her in the couch quilt. Woof gave a friendly bark, bound from the room, and went out the back screen door.

"Great. Just great," Tood bemoaned while shaking his head. He joined his canine friend on the porch. "I just wanted a compooter."

CHAPTER 2

A Soft Answer Turns Away Wrath

Tood slumped down on the swing bench on the back porch. Woof was gnawing on a large bone next to the bench. Tood reached down and rubbed the back of the beast's neck and looked toward the Big Tree, the oldest and thickest tree in Tween.

"What are we going to do with her?" Todd pondered. "She looks so familiar."

Woof gave a series of quick grunts and a low growl.

"She is not your new plaything."

Woof howled with a deeper growl. Todd responded, "I know I said you could have the rest of the wrappings, but that was before I knew…"

The beast dropped his bone and barked continuously as Tood spoke.

"I do not want her for my mate." Bark. "No, I'm not going to put her back." Bark. "A sacrifice to the Wamp monster? Are you kidding?" Bark. "Do I think she is pretty?" Bark. "Yes. I don't know if she likes cats." Bark. "You want to be her plaything?" Bark. "How would

I know about the necklace?" Bark. "Does she like to dance?" Bark. "When is her birthday?" Bark. "Why does she smell like lavender and chocolate?" Bark. "Does she like *Star Wars* or *Star Trek*?" Bark. "What is her favorite color?" Bark. "No, I don't know her name." Bark. "What do you mean just ask her?"

Woof stopped barking and padded over to the back door where a tired young lady with black curly hair stood wrapped in the Doorf family quilt.

"Woof is right. Just ask me." The young lady reached out and scratched Woof on the head.

Tood fell off the bench in surprise and stumbled off the porch. He turned to face his sleepy visitor. Woof had already shown his massive underside to her. Woof howled in glee as she vigorously rubbed his belly. She spoke to Woof with incoherent baby doggy talk.

Tood spoke to the visitor, "Miss. Miss. Miss! Would you please stop doing that."

"Oh, sorry. I just love dogs. Not a cat lover." She gave him one last long rub. "You are a big cutey, aren't you? You sweet giant mighty hunter." She stopped, blushed, and stood upright. "Sorry."

Woof was upside down and barked at Tood.

"No. No. No! We *cannot* keep her," Tood growled. "Now get up and stop embarrassing yourself in front of our guest."

The massive canine flipped in a flash, growled, but stayed with the girl.

"Don't call me Lord Doorf and come over here, now."

Woof crouched lower and growled menacingly.

"You're giving me ultimatums! You will not run off with her to the Firrest. I won't allow it."

The beast bore his teeth and moved closer to Tood.

The junkman slid forward, roared back, and growled, "Go ahead and leave, but the girl stays here!" He quickly moved into a fighting stance.

Woof accepted the challenge with an echoing growl, arched his back, and began to circle his prey. Tood countered by circling the opposite direction. The battle was imminent.

"Excuse me. Excuse me, Mr. Woof and Mr. Doorf," a sweet voice called from the back porch. The man and beast slowly turned toward her. "If you guys are about to fight over little o'me, then you might want to know my name, at the least." The visitor was swinging on the bench with her legs crossed and gave the combatants a radiant smile. "I believe I do have a say in the matter, but if you two want to duke it out, by all means, knock each other out. I would like to see who would win this brawl. Continue, please. Don't let me, a stranger in a strange world, stop you. By the way, my name is Emmy Castillo, from Charlotte, North Carolina, North Kakalacke. I see by your expressions you have no idea what I'm talking about. I do like to dance, mostly swing. So I met Woof, and I know your last name is Doorf, or was it dwarf? I'm a December baby. Anyway, I tend to ramble when I'm nervous, and is there any food? Because I am starving. I am not a Trekkie. Love all things Jedi. Oh, I love chocolate and lavender, but not together. Really cool, I mean awesome, how you understand everything Woof says. Is that normal here? And where exactly is here?"

Tood and Woof had regained their composure and were mesmerized by the sheer speed in which Emmy spoke.

"My name is Tood. Sorry about our little misunderstanding. It is nice to meet you, Emmy Castillo of North Carolina. Welcome to the land of Between. Let's go inside to talk."

Woof barked and ran up to Emmy.

"Yes, we can get her some food." Tood looked at his guest. "Do you like...how do you say it...pole tree?"

"Poultry? Yes, I love chicken."

"It's not chick-hens, but it is very delicious," Tood answered and walked to the kitchen.

Woof tugged on her sheets, and she followed him back to the living room. Emmy plopped down on the couch and snuggled up tight with the warm quilt. Woof sat directly in front of her and barked over his shoulder toward the kitchen.

"I won't forget the drinks," Tood grumbled. Then he yelled back, "Get her my robe from my bedroom!"

Woof pounced over to the bedroom and returned with a faded red lounge robe with a matching belt. He placed it on the couch next to Emmy and stared at her.

"Thank you. A little privacy, please."

Woof growled and slowly pushed the kitchen door and dragged himself in.

Emmy waited until the door closed before she removed the quilt and linens. She sniffed the robe and then slid on the comfortable oversized garment and tied it snuggly around her thin waist. She heard Tood speaking to his friend.

"Why don't you do something productive and give her a tour of the downstairs? Instead of ogling her."

Emmy jumped on the couch when she heard Woof's paws. She smiled at Woof as he entered. He awkwardly grinned back for a moment too long. The beast rolled his eyes and rumbled what sounded like "Let's go."

"Lead the way, mighty hunter," Emmy soothed as she got up and followed him.

Woof liked the sound of that, crossed the living room, and stopped in front of a wooden door with the word *torture* on the doorknob. Emmy slowly turned the knob and pushed the door open. Lights immediately revealed a room filled with ancient and modern exercise equipment. Each piece looked like it was in working order and clean, but she did not know what many things were. She spotted a treadmill, free weights, a weight bench, and a rowing machine.

"Is that a Bowflex? This is a torture room," Emmy announced as she closed the door.

Emmy looked for Woof and saw him lying down on a colorful spiral rug in front of another door. Emmy quietly stepped over Woof and opened the door. Again, the lights turned on automatically.

"Must be motion detection," she thought out loud. A large king-sized bed neatly made with some type of military uniform was arranged on the far side. There was a large dresser on the wall and two closet doors. A beautifully framed bay window was directly across from the bed, which overlooked a sunlit porch with various flowers and plants. Emmy closed the door and noticed the decorated foyer.

A central spiral staircase dominated this area, but as she moved around, she saw pictures and paintings beautifully displayed on the walls and tables. Some paintings looked oddly familiar and gorgeous, others bizarre, and still others like children's work. What caught her eye were the photographs of Tood when he was younger.

"This is Times Square in New York City. This is San Francisco. This is Chicago. Is that Walt Disney World in Florida? This is… North Carolina, Outer Banks. More questions for Tood," Emmy pondered and then stepped gently toward the stairs.

A low growl emanated from the spiral rug as she placed a toe on the first step. Emmy looked over to see gleaming blue eyes glaring at her. "Sorry. Just curious."

Woof padded over to her. She rubbed his head. The beast moved over to the last unknown door and nudged it open.

Emmy stammered and smiled. "I wasn't really going to go up there without permission, of course. The front door is also quite lovely." She quickly moved to the open door.

Woof made a low grumble, which sounded like "Whatever."

Emmy pushed the last door open to reveal a long black oval dining table with six white chairs on each side and one king chair on each end. The four walls each had a large mural of an ancient intense battle. She liked history, but she did not recognize the scenes. Woof followed her and gave a quick howl.

Tood wore a kitchen apron when he opened the top half of a rustic Dutch door. "There you are. Great. Food is almost ready. Is the robe fine?"

"Very comfy, thank you."

"Great. Emmy, grab a seat anywhere. Here are some bread loaves. Just put them on the table. Here is a glass of water. This bowl is for Woof. Could you place it over there? Thanks. Be right back." Tood closed the door.

Emmy carefully placed the items down and sat in the chair closest to the king chair and waited for Tood. Woof slurped the water from his immense bowl. She sipped her water.

Tood burst into the room wearing a "Kiss the Cook" apron. He carried the best-smelling poultry in an orange bucket in one hand and a salad bowl with all the fixings in the other. He placed them in front of Emmy. "You eat, and I'll talk."

CHAPTER 3

There Is a Way That Seems Right to a Man

The Tween Legion had quick-marched on the Driveway to the Mills about a mile from their base. Popson spotted a white something off to the left.

"Hey, Cap! I saw some junk over there. Should we stop and check it out?" Popson asked, jogging next to his leader.

"Company, halt!" Captain Chico ordered. "Popson, Chang, you are with me. The rest of you, double-time it to the barracks and meet us at Sembly at five."

"Sir, yes, sir!" the Legion called out and quickly moved away in ranks.

The three soldiers walked back to where Popson had spotted the junk.

Popson explained, "It looked like the stuff the junkman hid behind some branches."

Chang reached it first. "It is bedsheets, and it has three leather straps holding it together."

"Should we bring it to Tood? Or just leave it here?" Popson asked.

"Who? Oh, the junkman. No. Why should he have all the fun?" Chico smiled. "Let's see what we got here."

Chang and Popson kneeled next to the junk. Chang removed the first layer, and Popson cut off the straps. Both jumped back when the package took the shape of a body.

"What is this? A body? Captain Chico, what do we do?"

The captain moved in close and slowly removed layer after layer of linens. His hand pulled back when a long white mane flowed from the sixth layer. He noticed a gold chain and then pointy ears. Chico lifted the face cloth.

"Is that an…elf?" Chang screamed.

Popson muttered in near hysteria, "I thought they were a myth."

"There hasn't been an elf in Between for over two hundred years," said Chico.

"Is it alive, sir?" whimpered Chang.

Chico leaned in close to see if it was breathing. No movement and no breath came from the body. The captain carefully reached out his left hand to touch its face. The skin was incredibly soft and warm.

Brilliant green eyes popped open. A lightning-fast hand shot up and throttled the captain. The elf lifted him in the air. Chang and Popson fell back and screamed. A second later, the vice-grip hand released the captain, and the menacing eyes closed back to sleep. Captain Chico lay in a heap coughing and trying to breathe normally.

Chang and Popson came over to their captain and helped him up.

Chico shrugged off their help, rubbed his neck, and cleared his rasping throat.

"We are wrapping this thing up and locking it up in the cell. This thing is dangerous." He rubbed his temples. "Did it say anything when it had me?"

"No," Chang and Popson said. "We didn't hear anything."

"Because you were screaming." The captain shook his head. "Never mind. It was just my imagination. Let's strap it up tighter and move it quickly before anyone sees this monstrosity."

Within moments, the junk linens returned to the original shape. They moved it around the Driveaway quickly to the rear entrance to Arms. The barracks were empty. The Legion had obeyed Captain Chico and hustled to Sembly. Popson and Chang carried the body. Chico was the lookout and opened the back door to the holding area.

After Chico unlocked the ten-by-ten cell door, the guards moved the junk to the cot.

Popson and Chang rushed out, and Chico slammed the iron bar door behind them.

"So, Cap, what do we do next? Report it to Mayor Kokinkus?" asked Chang.

Chico answered, "We can't report it now with the celebration going on. It would cause too big of a commotion."

"We can't leave it here." Popson panicked. "The rest of the Legion will find out."

The captain started pacing back and forth in front of the cell and then stopped. "Here is what we are going to do. First, no one outside of this room should know about any of this." Chico paused. "If word gets out, I will personally tie raw meat to you and leave you in the Firrest for the wild dogs." Popson and Change nodded in agreement. "Second, we have to get to Sembly and the celebration. I will go to Sembly to deliver my speech. You still got my notes, Popson? Good man. You two will stand guard over the prisoner. Once I finish, I will come back to relieve you, and you will join the celebration. Any questions?"

Chang raised his hand. "What if the prisoner gets up or talks?"

Chico moved to be face-to-face with the scared guards. "There is to be no contact with it. No talking, no touching, no eye contact, no visitors. And do not go into the cell no matter what. Got it? Be vigilant and remember your training."

"Yes, sir!"

"Now get to the barracks, shower, and get dressed for the Sembly. I will watch it until you return."

Popson and Chang flew out the door to their quarters.

Chico took a deep breath and exhaled as he moved to his office next to the cell. He removed his sweat-stained jacket and shirt and placed them on his desk chair. He removed his knife and sheath and stored it in the bottom drawer. His dress outfit was hanging neatly by his coatrack. His captain helmet sat in the middle of the desk. Chico proudly dressed into his uniform. He had made a good living as a soldier, and he knew he could do even more for Tween if he were the mayor. Seven years as captain of the Legion was enough experience. He smoothed out his pants and jacket and looked with confidence into the wall mirror. He slightly glanced at the package in the cell. He sighed and rubbed his strong hands through his black curls. "A fine mess you have there, Chico."

"I have never been called a mess before, but I am covered in rags," whispered an unknown sultry voice.

"Who said that?" Chico scrambled from his office to the holding area.

"It is the thing covered in rags. What did you call me? The junk."

Chico ran to the cell door and stared at the junk. No movement was coming from the body. The captain cried out, "Who are you? How are you doing this? Get out of my head!"

"I cannot until I awaken. At the present, our minds are linked together. My thoughts are in your thick head. I must say, you have a very interesting little town here, and you have been a bad boy, haven't you?"

"What are you talking about?" Chico whispered.

"Now, Captain," the saucy voice continued. "Do not be coy. I know your thoughts. The bribes from the various leaders in Tween, that new house of yours, and the secret rendezvous with so many females. The mayor's daughter, the banker's wife, and the miner's daughter, just to name a few. It must be the uniform. Women do love a man in uniform."

Chico called, "Stop it! I get it. What do you want?"

"Release me. Now. Or there will be grave consequences."

"Never." Chico fumbled with the keys as he moved to the iron door. "I will just wake you up and break the link."

"I would not do that if I were you," the elf warned.

Chico tried to get the key into the hole and sniffed in disgust. "Why? Are you going to take over my body?"

"Exactly," the voice announced.

Captain Chico immediately dropped the keys. His head crashed into the metal bars, and his body slumped.

15

Popson and Chang eagerly reentered the holding area in full uniforms and dripping wet hair. They noticed their leader resting against the cell door with his eyes closed. Popson reached out and touched Chico's shoulder.

"Captain. Everything all right, Captain? Cap?"

Chico's eyes slowly opened, and he straightened up. "Just fine. Having a power nap. Long day, boys." He stepped away from the cell. "Chang, pick up those keys. Remember, I'll be back after the Sembly. No one in or out."

"Yes, sir!" The men saluted.

Chico grabbed his helmet and went to the door.

"Oh, Captain?" Popson called and stuck out a parchment. "Your speech, sir. You asked me to give it to you before the Sembly."

Chico stopped and turned around. "Of course. Good man, Popson. Definite promotion for you. And you too, Chang." He snatched the paper and headed to the door with Chang close behind. Chang followed him out the door and stood guard.

"Chang, what are you doing?"

"Standing guard, sir. Just like you said, sir."

"Do we normally guard the door, or do we patrol the Arms?"

"If we have a prisoner, we guard the door, sir."

Chico whispered, "Do we want anyone to know we have a guest?"

"No, sir?"

"Is that a question or an answer, soldier?"

"No, sir. I will do a patrol, sir."

"Good man. I will see you soon. Good night." Chico walked away toward Sembly as Chang began his patrol in the opposite direction.

"Good night, sir."

Chico waved as he turned the corner. The cobblestone streets echoed with the steady beat of the captain's boots as he made his way to Tween Circle. He placed his helmet on and crumbled up the parchment. He tossed it precisely into a trash can twelve feet away.

The captain smirked and commented, "I do love a man in uniform."

CHAPTER 4

The Horses Are Prepared for the Battle, but Deliverance Is of the Lord

"So you are saying, somehow, I traveled through some sorta magical portal?" Emmy said.

"Door," Tood corrected.

"Door. From my dimension."

"World."

"Sorry. From my world to Between. And you are the only one who can take me back."

"Yes."

"You don't know why I was bundled like luggage or how I got this necklace."

"Correct. No clue. Yet."

"Is there a door which goes directly from Between to my world?" Emmy asked.

"Technically, yes. It was called the Door Between. It was destroyed more than two hundred years ago when the castle was destroyed. Theoretically, we could have used it to move directly to another world, bypassing Between altogether. It no longer exists."

"Okay. You then have to locate a door's remains, put it all together, and do some mumbo jumbo to open the door. I can't go back until you find all the pieces to the doorway, which could take…"

"A week if all goes well. Or a month, if not so good. Three months if it's bad, and a year—"

"Let's not talk about that. You also have to keep me concealed from the Tweeners…"

"Tweeners? You come up with that? I like it."

"Thanks. Or they would freak out, grab pitchforks, fire, and hunt me down."

"Exactly," Tood announced as he finished putting on his uniform jacket and buttoned it. "You got the basics for now. I will be back right after the celebration, and we will talk some more. I promise."

Emmy paced as Woof watched her back-and-forth motion in the foyer.

"And now you are leaving me here with Woof to go to the assembly for the three hundredth celebration of the founding of Tween." She reached over and touched Woof's ear. "Thanks for the grub. You're a pretty good cook. Or is it a chef?"

"You're welcome. Thanks. I'm not sure. It would be suspicious if I didn't go as part of the Legion. The celebration is at Sembly, not an assembly." Tood mentioned as he grabbed his helmet and moved to the front door.

"You look very dashing, by the way, in your uniform." Emmy blushed.

"Thanks. Not bad for a hand-me-down." Tood opened the front door. "There is more chick-hens and stew in the kitchen and some drinks in the frigger."

"The what?"

"The re-frigg-er-actor. The big wooden door cabinet on the right."

"Okay."

"I left a book in the living room. It's the history of Between and the founding of the city of Tween. If you get bored, I have some RCA videos in the living room. Woof will show you." The beast barked and wagged his tail. "Emmy, please stay in the house. It is very dangerous for you out there. Woof will keep you safe. I promise I will show you around tomorrow and explain all that I can. Don't worry, you are among friends. Buenos noches." Tood shut the door.

"Buenos noches. Buenos noches? You know Spanish too. How? Another question for tomorrow," Emmy mumbled.

She meandered over to the kitchen and opened the frigger. She noticed four glass bottle sodas. "What do we have here? RC Cola? I thought they stopped making this years ago. Grandpa loved these." She snapped open the top and took a long drink. "That is so good." A little burp escaped.

Emmy closed the frigger door, and Woof was quietly sitting on his hind legs behind the door. Emmy jumped. "Flipping burgers! Whoa! You scared me! You want some food or a drink?"

Woof barked and wagged his tail. "A drink." Emmy had understood him. "Weird."

She reached back into the ice box and pulled out another cola. "Do you want me to pour it in a bowl? No." She popped the cap off and handed it out. Woof grabbed the bottle with his front paws, laid down on his back, and guzzled the bottle in seconds. A massive eruption bellowed from the canine and echoed throughout the kitchen, rattling some pans.

"Nice one! Watch this." Emmy took another long swig. She stopped drinking and opened her mouth to let out a big belch, but nothing came out. Woof howled in laughter.

"No, wait, it's coming!" She opened her mouth again, and again, only silence.

Woof howled again and then bowed his head and bellowed another gaseous eruption.

"Okay, I get it. I'm no match for you. You win. Come on, let's get to the living room."

Woof led Emmy to the living room, and she picked up the heavy history book. She sat on the couch and placed the book on her lap. She perused the first few pages until she came to a picture of a magnificent medieval castle atop a grassy hill.

She read aloud, "The Castle Doorf was created as a sanctuary for the people of Between to house and protect the rift doors, to keep the secrets of other worlds, and defend freedom against those who would use its powers for nefarious purposes.

"Nefarious does not sound good, does it, Woof?"

Woof ignored her and moved to the wall opposite the couch. He pushed a panel with his paw. The rectangular framed picture of a waterfall on the wall flipped over to reveal a forty-three-inch flat-screen television. The bookshelves against the same wall also flipped over to display shelves full of Blockbuster videos and CDs, along with a CD player and a video player labeled RCA. Emmy put the book down on the coffee table and carefully walked over to the display.

"Oh, RCA. I get it," Emmy announced. She scanned the videos and CDs and picked out a movie she recognized as *Back to the Future*. "Do you like this one, Woof?"

Woof panted as she put the video into the RCA. She sat back down on the couch, and the beast joined her and put his head on her lap. As the movie music began, she rubbed him softly behind the ears. "I guess it's you and me and Marty McFly."

Emmy woke up with a start and in confusion. She rubbed her eyes and scanned the area and thought she was back home in Charlotte. She watched the giant dog snoring on her lap and knew she had not been dreaming about this strange Between world. She could not feel her legs but could not really move Woof off her. She looked up to hear the last line of the classic eighties hit, "Roads? Where we're going, we don't need roads."

As the credits played, Emmy slid herself from under Woof's head without disturbing him. Her legs were tingling with sleepiness, but she was able to quietly stretch them out and step into the kitchen. She opened the frigger and grabbed a piece of poultry and another

RC Cola. She tiptoed through the Dutch door, past the dining room, and into the foyer. She ate the meat in silence, swigged the cola, and then placed the bottle on the table. With stealth, she climbed the spiral stairs to the top and then stopped abruptly. Piercing blue eyes glowed at her.

"Woof? How…you were just…man, you are good. I just wanted to look around, please," Emmy begged.

Woof put his head down and allowed her to pass.

"Thank you, mighty hunter," Emmy whispered as she walked past to the first upstairs door.

She pushed the door open and noticed a neat queen-size bed in an ornate wooden frame. The bed was covered with a beautiful Amish-looking comforter. It also had a dresser, end table, small desk, desk lamp, and a closet. She closed the door.

The next two rooms on the right side were the same size and shape, but the only difference was the bed comforter. The last door on the right was a large clean bathroom with two modern sinks with hot and cold running water. The white porcelain tub had four strange twisted bird feet and a large showerhead. It also had a long wooden framed mirror and several clean towels on a flowery towel rack.

Emmy walked left, down the hallway to the next door. As she opened the door, the room lights shimmered on over a large wooden desk with an office chair. There was a window in the middle and a wall covered with books, volumes, scrolls, and loose parchments. Emmy went to the desk and noticed letters and papers stuck in various mini cubbyholes above the desk. In the center was a leather-worn Bible, opened to Proverbs with several highlighted verses. She read aloud, "To understand a proverb and an enigma; the words of the wise and their riddles."

She picked up a picture frame. It was Tood and maybe a brother? She put it down and picked up one facing down. She nearly dropped it. "Is this my…my grandfather and Tood?" She put the picture down and decided to leave Tood's personal office. She now felt like she was intruding and quickly departed.

The next room was filled with musical instruments, including a full drum set, lead guitar, bass guitar, keyboard, and a microphone.

Brass instruments, woodwinds, and string instruments were neatly displayed on the walls. Stacks of sheet music and old vinyl records were in the corners. A dust-covered antique jukebox sat sadly next to the records like a wallflower.

Emmy closed the door and saw a pull-down attic door above her in the hallway. She ignored it, moved to the last room, and opened it. Again, the lights shimmered on and displayed all sorts of children's toys from various decades. Hundreds of board games and puzzles were organized against the walls on dark-stained wood shelves. Emmy shut the door and moved back to the stairs. Woof had moved, and she saw him lying on his favorite spiral rug at the bottom of the stairs. She tiptoed down the stairs, grabbed her bottle of soda, and slid back into the kitchen.

Emmy slowly drank her soda. She loved this kitchen. As her eyes adjusted to the low light, she perceived a light coming from a closed door in the corner of the kitchen. With silent steps, she moved to the kitchen's back door. She reached for the shimmering doorknob. Woof howled at her. Emmy jumped into the air.

"Hey! You scared the crap out of me! Stop that!" Emmy yelled.

Woof whimpered and moved next to his new friend.

"It's all right," she consoled him and petted him. "Why can't I go in there?"

Woof growled low and then whimpered again.

Emmy bent down and rubbed his head. "Oh, it's okay, buddy. I won't get hurt as long as my mighty hunter is with me."

Woof jumped into her arms and licked her continuously, but his strength knocked her back and into the door, which swung open. She shrieked as they stumbled together down the stairs into an organized two-car garage.

Bright automatic fluorescent tubes flickered on as they fell into the empty side. The far side of the garage was occupied but remained in gray shadows. A worn green tarp blanketed a shapely vehicle. White-walled tires rested on a hazard yellow car lift. The twenty-five-feet wide wood-paneled garage entry creaked and stirred due to the unexpected intrusion.

Emmy pulled herself up from the floor, leaning on Woof. "That was fun." Emmy giggled. "Thanks for breaking my fall." She looked around. "Whoa! Look at this place."

Woof barked and headed back to the door.

"Come on, Woof. We are still in the house. I just want to look around for five minutes. Please?"

Woof tilted his head and stuck out his tongue.

"Thank you."

Emmy walked over to the red and black tool bench. She recognized the wrenches, screwdrivers, and other equipment typically found in a professional garage. "You know, Woof, my grandfather was a great mechanic, and I used to help him with all sorts of cars in his shop after school."

Woof looked at her, unimpressed.

She spun around and tiptoed over to the dark side toward the awakening vehicle. "My grandpa could fix anything, but his pride and joy"—Emmy grabbed the tarp and smiled—"was working on his '57 Chevy Bel Air. This has the same outline."

Woof jumped to his feet and growled.

Emmy whipped off the tarp in a flourish, causing the dust to cascade like sparkles on the revealed intense hot rod. She gave a little cough but was astonished. "I knew it. This is just like Grandpa's car."

A jet-black 1957 Chevrolet Bel Air, with slick flames painted on the doors, brilliant chrome bumpers and grill, titanium rims, with three tri-power carburetors protruding from the hood, dared her to move closer.

She read the New York State vanity license plate: DR@90N 1.

"Dragon 1. Cool name. This is amazing and so beautiful. It's a little better than Grampa's." She looked at Woof. "Do you know the horsepower of this beauty? Did Tood do this? Wow." Emmy caressed the paint and moved over to the driver's side door. It trembled with anticipation.

Woof barked.

"Don't worry. I just want to sit inside for a second. I won't even close the door." She effortlessly opened the door and felt invited to come inside. A furry blur slipped past her and sat on the passenger side.

The massive canine stared at Emmy, grinned, and yipped.

"So you like how the material feels too," Emmy announced as she sunk down on the patent leather seats. "Hello, Dragon. This is so incredible." Her hands embraced the steering wheel, and she closed her eyes in hot rod satisfaction. She could almost feel the kiss of the 270 BHP surging and the V8 Super Turbo-Fire power glide ignite. "Oh yeah," she moaned.

Without warning, the door slammed shut and locked. The lights blazed, and the engine roared to life. The radio blared to Little Richard, "Oh, we're gonna have some fun tonight! We're gonna have some fun tonight! Hooo!"

Woof whimpered as Emmy panicked. "I didn't do it! I didn't do it! We have to get out of here! I thought this car was Herbie, but it's Christine! Help!"

Woof howled in despair. They were trapped.

"Keys? There are no keys!" In despair, she hit all the dashboard buttons. Nothing worked. She attempted to turn off the music, but the volume became deafening. She covered her ears.

The Chevy gloriously revved again, and the garage door slowly yawned to the cool evening. Emmy scrambled to get out, but all the doors were locked, and the windows would not move. She pounded on the side windows in vain. The mechanical beast moved with determination through the opening to make its escape to the outside world.

She yelled at Woof, "Well, technically, we are still in the house!"

The classic hot rod revved once more as it cleared the garage. It peeled out, throwing gravel and dirt everywhere. Emmy and Woof screamed in horror as the Chevy raced and sparked into the night. It zoomed straight toward the Ruins. The spark-filled valley echoed when a strange bugle charge emitted from the hot rod. Within seconds, real flames erupted and roared from the shiny engine. Dragon victoriously rocketed into the starless night and vanished.

CHAPTER 5

Let Another Man Praise You and Not Your Own Lips

"Buenos noches? Where did that come from?" Tood asked himself.

He ran down the front steps and made his way to Mt. Doorf. He pulled out his pocket watch and realized he had only fifteen minutes to make it to Sembly. He stopped running and scanned the area around him. He clicked his watch and then disappeared into the dusk with his next steps.

Tood reappeared inside a dark room, which slowly illuminated as he moved to the nearest wall. Tood pressed another diamond brick, and with a slight push, the secret passage opened to Tween Circle. He stepped out behind a large dried-out fountain. The structure had a large sphere in the center with four smaller spheres attached by smooth rods. Each small weathered circle had an engraved directional letter representing east, west, north, and south. Etched in the large circle was a large six-pointed star. Tood stepped back to admire the ancient fountain.

"Tood!" yelled a voice behind him. "What are you doing here?"

Tood turned to face Captain Chico walking into Tween Circle.

Tood saluted. "Captain. I thought you would be at Sembly already."

"I still have a few minutes. I enjoy walking around town when it's quiet." Chico smirked and looked at the fountain. "I really like this fountain. I wish it still worked. I have always wondered what it means." He sighed deeply and closed his eyes. "It just brings me peace to see it undisturbed. You know?"

Tood looked back at the Spheres and smiled. He never heard of the captain being so meditative. "You're not the only one, sir."

Tood stepped quietly over to the captain. "Hey, you want to see something that will blow your mind? I discovered it a few years ago."

"Yes, of course. And as your captain, I order you to give me all your secrets," Chico joked slyly.

"Just this one, Captain," Tood replied with a laugh. He walked over to the fountain and reached around the large sphere into a small crevice. He placed his hand inside and pulled a rusty chain. He stepped back, and the mechanisms could be heard whirring and grinding. Water burst from the top of the large sphere and showered the smaller spheres. As the smaller ones became saturated, they began to rotate around the large sphere.

"Wow!" Captain Chico's mouth opened wide.

"Just watch. There's more," Tood encouraged.

As he spoke, the water, which had collected at the base, shot a stream of water in an arc over the large sphere to the other side. The arcs became higher and higher.

Captain Chico was speechless. Once the arching streams reached their apex, lights flickered around the Center Sphere, illuminating the entire moving structure. The ring of light glowed brighter with each new pulse.

"Wahooo! I have never seen anything like this! Amazing!" Chico jumped in the air and was about to hug Tood. He stopped himself and punched the junkman hard in the arm.

Tood had been watching the fountain and did not notice the almost hug. He felt the punch and rubbed his throbbing arm. "That is some punch you got there, Captain."

"I know, sorry, but I'm so excited. The whole town needs to know about this. How did you do that?" Chico looked at Tood with admiration.

"Well, I was cleaning the statue one night and dropped my broom. When I reached for it, I saw the chain. When I pulled it, boom!" Tood pointed to the fountain.

Chico cleared his throat. "You know, Tood, the people of Tween and I do not give you enough credit for all you do for the city. That is going to change. Tonight."

"Thanks. I appreciate that, but it is just my job as the junkman," Tood shyly replied. "What do you mean, change?"

"Humble too," Chico continued. "You get rid of all the junk, clean up the town, travel all over Between, captain a battleball team, and still have time to be in the Legion. You are the unsung hero of Tween, and I'm going to show my appreciation to the whole land tonight during my speech."

"Really, Captain, that is not necessary. I'd rather be unsung and unheard," Tood stammered.

Chico moved close to Tood and placed his arm around his shoulder and looked into his eyes. "It is necessary. Let's go before they miss us too much."

Tood moved back over to the beautiful moving fountain. "First, let me turn this off." He went to the backside of the Center Sphere and pulled the chain again. Within seconds, the water stopped flowing, and the spheres rotated back into their original positions. "This will be our secret," Tood announced.

"For now." Chico smiled and stuck out his hand. "Thanks, Tood. I won't forget this."

They shook forearms in the Between tradition of friendship. They ran toward the celebration noise and music blaring from Sembly.

Captain Chico and Tood arrived moments after the official start and fanfare of the three hundredth anniversary of the founding of Tween. Colorful banners with the number 300 flew from every building, lamppost, and window in the city. Children and adults were running back and forth to various booths of numerous food dishes and skill games on both sides of Sembly. A local Vararity band played swing music on a small stage.

"You know," Chico commented to Tood as they walked down through the party. "Those games are rigged. One in a hundred chance to win. The ring toss is the worst. At least one in a thousand."

"Let's give it a try," Tood announced. "I'll pay."

Chico agreed. "It's your rocks."

They stepped up to the ring toss vendor. "Three green gems for three tosses. Hey, you're Capin Chico. It is such an honor, sir. What a great match for Arsenal. Can you sign my battleball?"

"Anything for a fan. What's your name?" Chico smirked and pulled out his pen.

"Bert Moneymaker, sir." He handed the ball over.

Chico signed and read it aloud, "To Bert, Arsenal's biggest fan. Make lots of money! Yours truly, Captain Chico. Here you go, Bert. Thanks for supporting Arsenal."

"This is great. My girl's not going to believe it."

"Bert, can we play a round now?"

"Sure, sure." Bert handed over the three rings to the captain. "This round is free."

"Thanks again." Chico aimed and got the first ring on a bottle. He did it twice more. "Well, I must be getting better." In disbelief, Bert handed over the large toy animal prize.

"Your turn, Tood," Chico challenged.

"That'll be six green gems," Bert grumbled.

"What? You just said three," Tood complained.

Bert eyed him with suspicion and anger. He spit on the ground next to the stand. "You the new junkman, right? Nine gems."

Tood slowly handed the gems over. He closed one eye and aimed. Bert laughed at him. He then nonchalantly tossed all three at once, and each one landed on a bottle. Bert's mouth dropped open.

Tood grinned, reached over, and grabbed the prize. "Thanks."

"That was great! Did you see his face? He was like, duh!" Chico commented as they walked toward the main stage. "Do you normally get that kind of hate from the citizens?"

"Sometimes, but I've adapted." He paused. "The Junk Incident with my family happened over thirty years ago. Some people don't forgive," Tood pondered.

"Or forget." Chico looked back at the vendor. He put his hand on Tood's shoulder. "You know, junkman, I'm having a party tonight at my new house. Why don't you stop by later?"

"Sounds great." Tood smiled and then handed his prize to a little girl going in the opposite direction. "We better get over to the Legion."

Chico and Tood came upon the Legion standing in rows. All the soldiers saluted their captain. He ordered them to sit down in their assigned chairs.

Tood whispered to Chico, "Where are Popson and Chang?"

"They are on a special assignment for me. By the way, come to Pepe's Grill tomorrow around nine a.m. I have something to talk to you about."

"Sure. About what?"

"Nothing but a little junk we found on the way back. No big deal. Can't talk now. The mayor is coming to the podium." Chico hushed him.

A small round man wobbled up to the front of the stage. He had a nicely trimmed beard, a black top hat, puffy red tie, and a three-piece suit with tails. He stepped up to the podium and spoke into a large circular microphone.

"People of Between, citizens of Tween, honored guests and leaders, and the future of our fair land, our children, welcome to three hundredth celebration of Tween's founding!"

New torches throughout Sembly were turned on, and the courtyard was as bright as noon. The crowd cheered in appreciation of the lights. "I am, of course, your Mayor Kokinkus of Tween and the elected governor of our fine land."

The crowd started cheering, "Kokinkus! Kokinkus! Kokinkus!"

One loud man yelled, "I love you, Kokinkus!"

"I love you too," the mayor responded, and the crowd laughed.

"All this week," the mayor continued, "we will be having celebrations in each sector of our city. The schedules have been posted outside of every postal office. We have so much to celebrate and to be thankful. I am also thankful for the most amazing sport anywhere. On Friday, it will begin. The new season of BATTLEBALL!"

The crowd chanted, "Battleball! Battleball! Battleball! Battleball!"

When the fans quieted a little, the same loud man screamed, "I love BATTLEBALL!"

"We all do, son. We all do," Mayor Kokinkus proclaimed as he regained control of the crowd. "This year, we have a new team joining the league. It's our first team from south of the River of Drayne. This team has taken a black castle on a field of green as their flag and team colors. These Wandering Knights are ready for a fight! It is the Waydownz Undivided!"

The crowd lightly clapped as a sporadic number of green and black banners popped up among the spectators.

The loud man gave an echoing, "Boo! Go home, junkers!" The crowd laughed.

"From right here in Sembly is everyone's favorite underdog. The spherical warriors will be sporting their traditional orange and blue, the Tween City Battle Club!"

More cheers rang out as banners were raised. "Let's go, Tweeners!" *Clap, clap, clap, clap, clap!* "Let's go!"

"*Go*, Tweeners!" the loud fan yelled with sarcasm. The spectators chuckled.

"My personal favorite, wearing a red hourglass on a blue field. This time, they are coming for you. The Federales Battle Institute!" The mayor raised hands in victory.

"FBI! FBI! FBI! Tick, tick, boom!" the Federales fans yelled, and the banners went flying.

Kokinkus cleared his throat. "Next is the rowdy bunch from Vararity. This was the most penalized team last year. Displaying with pride the green tartan clover on a white field. It's Vararity United Ball Club."

"Clovers, Clovers, Clovers!' rang out from the crowd. "We're gonna knock ya over!"

"They do more than just grind our grain. They do it in style. Sporting a white grinding wheel on a purple field, it is the Union Miller BC."

"Fight, fight, fight! Grinders! FIGHT!"

"This ale-loving team put up more than a fight last year. These black and golden bears from Freeside want the honey of a championship. It is the Freeside Fight Squad."

"F-R-E-E. Free, Free, Free!"

"Mining for more wins this year is the toughest team in the league. With their yellow pickax and blue hammer, this team is poised to move up the rankings. It is the Real Miners Battle Club."

"Bam! Bam! Slam! Slam! We're coming for you!"

"Last year's rookie team and ranked third in the league tournament from Cutoff University. In their black and maroon uniforms, this group is angling to be the champs. It is the CU Battle Crew."

"CU! CU! CU! Battlecrew! Battlecrew! CU! CU! CU! BATTLECREW!"

"Our runner-up and highest-scoring team in the league is from Banker. These bankers have raised the capital to be number one. Let's hear it for the green and gold, Bankers BC."

"Olé, olé, olé, olé! OLÉ! OLÉ!"

"Last and certainly not least, these soldiers have won the war with a crimson sword on a white field. The four-time champions and the MVP of the league three years in a row are from Arms. IT IS THE ARMS ARSENAL!"

"Arms, Arms, Arms, Arms! Arms, Arms, Arms! Arms, Arms, Arms, ARMS!" The largest and loudest Battleball fans were raising their hands and counting off the number of championships.

Mayor Kokinkus revved up the crowd. "Our honored guest of the evening is here to accept the championship banner for Arsenal. Your Battleball MVP, the captain of the Arms Arsenal, the leader of the Tween Legion, the man of the hour, and a tower of power, the captain of your hearts and your city! It is Captain! Jak! Chico!"

The extra-large battleball banner was raised high above the stage with the Arsenal logo emblazoned in the center. The crowd erupted in repeated chants, "Chico! Chico! Chico!"

Chico raised his hand and moved toward the stage as the fans became fever pitched. He waved, winked, hip-bumped, high-fived, fist-pumped, and finger-pointed all the way to the podium. He stood there for a minute, soaking it all in. He gave a big smile. Then, unexpectedly, he bowed his head and closed his eyes. The crowd eerily hushed. The mayor and the leaders began looking around. Everyone seemed to be anxious. Tood took a step toward the stage.

When the silence was nearly unbearable, Chico shot his hands in the air. "Just kidding! Keep going!"

The crowd responded with a deafening noise which shook the walls.

Chico put up his left hand. "Thank you. Thank you all so much. I really appreciate all the cheers and all the fans. Even you, loud guy." Chico pointed him out.

"I love you, Captain Chico!"

"Thanks." Chico rolled his eyes. "Anyway, I did not realize you all liked me that much. I mean, I made the winning field goal last season against the heavily favored Bankers." The crowd laughed, but not the Bankers or their fans.

"I just have one question for you. Are you ready for Battleball 300!" At his comment, another large banner rose next to the Arsenal banner entitled BATTLEBALL 300. The crowd went wild and then awed at the new mega flag.

"I know who I will be rooting for during this historic season, but..."

The Arsenal fans shouted, "A. R. M. S! Arms, Arms, Arms!"

Chico controlled his fans with a single finger. "But we do have a new team this year. The Waydownz Undivided! Their team captain is Tood Doorf." The crowd cheered at the team name, but as soon as Doorf was mentioned, the applause died.

"This new squad will provide some fierce competition for the whole league. Come on, folks," Chico scolded. "Let's hear it for the junkman. Let's hear it for Tood!" The fans clapped only because their captain ordered it.

Chico continued, "Now our junkman here, Tood, stand up!" Tood awkwardly stood up and waved. "He has provided a gift for the whole town. At the conclusion of these festivities, we will all gather at the City Sphere. Believe me, folks, you are in for a marvelous surprise. Let's give Tood a hand." The people were slowly warming up to the junkman, and some even waved the castle flags.

"I also would like to thank Mayor Kokinkus, Lord Banker, Colonel Miller, and Lord Miner for all their hard work in this celebration and championship tournament prepared for the upcoming season." The crowd cheered. "I would also like to thank the people behind these great men. These wonderful ladies make the city come alive with their love, hard work, and compassion throughout the community. "Lady Miller, Ms. Mayor, Lady Banker, Ms. Miner, please come to the stage. Come on, folks! Don't these ladies deserve this honor too?" The people loved it and cheered the surprised women forward.

The beautifully attired and stunning ladies each reluctantly came to the stage. Captain Chico helped each one up with a wink and a sweet kiss on their right hands. The male leaders stood up and looked uncomfortable as their smiling beauties joined them. Chico smiled at each of them in turn and then spoke to the crowd. "These are the great pillars of our society!" The people gave a standing ovation. Chico scanned the crowd and encouraged them to cheer louder.

"On a personal note," Chico started, and the people hushed. "Ladies, I am officially off the market. Would Ms. Mayor, Jennifer Kokinkus, join me at the microphone?"

Ms. Mayor reluctantly stepped away from her father and stood next to Captain Chico.

He gently held her hand and took a deep breath. "Jenny, when I first saw you, it was on that corner over there. Your beautiful silken chocolate hair was flowing in the spring breeze." Chico grabbed both hands and stared at her. "Your green eyes sparkled as you stepped out into the street."

Silent smiles covered the people.

"Then you stepped into a puddle, slipped, and fell with a splash."

Jenny laughed with the crowd.

"But you didn't stay down. You laughed with the soul of a thousand angels. You brushed yourself off and kept moving, avoiding the next puddle. Right then, Jenny, I knew. Before I even knew your name…I knew." Chico got down on one knee.

Jenny moved one hand to her mouth. The pillars of society gasped, and the people held their breaths.

Chico submerged into the pool of her emerald eyes. "Jennifer Ann Kokinkus, my Jenny, will you marry me?"

Everyone held their breath.

She dropped to her knees and sweetly kissed him on the lips. She whispered in his ear and nibbled, "Yes. My father is going to kill you."

Chico smirked and soothed, "I know."

The loud man yelled, "What did she say, Chico?"

"Yes! She said yes!" he announced and stood up with his fiancé. They embraced and kissed passionately.

Explosive cheers of laughter and crying radiated from the people.

Chico raised his hand again to quiet the fans. He held on tight to Jenny's hand. He gave an almost-imperceptible side-glance to Tood. The captain opened his mouth for his next grand speech.

Before he could utter a word, a bizarre trumpet sound blared from the center of town. The strange tune blasted again as all the people muttered in confusion and fear. Tood immediately recognized the obnoxious car horn. He bolted from Sembly and sprinted alone down the shadowy streets.

Chico was the first to recover. "Don't worry, folks. This is all part of Tood's surprise. The junkman is on the case!" The people relaxed and laughed. "Once he gives the signal, we will head to City Sphere."

Tood discovered the revving hot rod with flames spitting from the hood. It was parked next to the statue. Inside the vehicle, Woof and Emmy screamed for help. He ran to the fountain and pulled the chain. He slid over the trunk and snapped open the driver door. He slammed it shut. The hot rod peeled out down the road. The melodious trumpet blast echoed once again as the flaming vehicle zoomed down the street.

Chico announced to the city, "That is the signal! Let us go to the City Sphere!"

The whole crowd slowly moved together and waved their various banners toward the newly illuminated spherical fountain.

CHAPTER 6

Open Rebuke Is Better than Love Carefully Concealed

"Are we *so* glad to…," Emmy started with a smile, but it quickly faded.

Tood jumped in the Chevy and shoved Emmy and Woof over to the passenger side. "I told you to stay in the house!" he barked.

He shut off the radio and angrily shifted the car into drive and slammed his foot on the accelerator. He pushed the car horn, and the bugle charge reverberated down the empty street.

"I am so…," Emmy tried.

"Woof! How could you let this happen? There is no excuse. I told *you* to keep her safe. You know how dangerous this car is!" Tood bellowed.

Woof whimpered and put his sad head on Emmy's lap. Tood swerved the car to the right and then back to left, barely avoiding an apple cart in the street.

"It wasn't all his fault," Emmy explained. "I went into the garage, I opened the car door, and I coaxed—"

"Put your seat belt on. This is going to be a bumpy ride!" Emmy grabbed the seat belt and strapped herself and Woof. Tood intensely looked at his pocket watch and pushed a button on the right side. Tood reached down to a different gearshift on the floor and abruptly changed gears. The engine roared, and the hot rod lurched forward at a subsonic speed.

Emmy said, "Hey, that shifter thing wasn't there before."

"Emmy, this is a delicate situation. I'm sorry that I don't have time to explain the intricate details of magical time-warping in a car moving at over 300 mph," Tood grumbled. "I have to get this just right, or we could end up in the wrong world or wrong time in history or both."

Emmy sassed back, "I think *that* is a bit extreme."

"So you have become an expert in interdimensional travel and time-warping after watching *Back to the Future*!" Tood seethed.

"How did you know we—"

Tood snapped, "It's Woof's favorite movie."

Woof gave a low growl and then another sad whimper.

"Oh, technically, you never left the house!" Tood's voice cracked. "Give a break to me! You both have endangered this whole world's existence."

"I'm sorry. It's all my fault," Emmy cried out.

Tood seemed to be calming down. "Emmy, what would have happened in your history if a caveman found fire too early or not at all or—"

"Technically, cave persons were just people who lived in caves."

Tood stared at her in uncomfortable silence.

Emmy whispered, "Maybe I should be quiet now."

Tood shifted down and then swerved left and the right. He shifted down again as the car's speed lowered to 176 mph. They were slowing down, but Tood's face was highly concentrating on the road. Emmy decided to keep quiet and pet Woof as the vehicle slowed to 88 mph. Tood looked at his watch again, counted to three, and hit the watch's left button. Abruptly, the Chevy slowed to 45 mph.

Mount Doorf suddenly appeared on their left. In silence, Tood carefully drove to his house. He pulled up to the front porch and stopped.

Tood sighed and broke the quiet. "Please get out now and go inside the house. Please meet me in the living room. We have a lot to discuss."

Emmy opened her mouth to apologize but quickly shut it. She opened the shiny car door and stepped out. Woof joined her. She pushed the steaming handle closed. She and the canine lumbered up the stairs and into the dark home. The red taillights glistened as Tood drove the vehicle around the corner. The garage door automatically opened, and he reversed it into the garage.

The living room lights turned on as Woof and Emmy entered, and they plopped down on the couch. She stroked the canine's fine fur. He placed his head away from her. He gave a small bark.

"I understand, and I'm sorry I got you in trouble." She rubbed between his ears. "Will my mighty hunter forgive me?" She wanted to run away, but she knew she had nowhere to go in this bizarre place.

Woof looked at her and stuck out his tongue.

"Thanks." She sighed. "I hope Tood will forgive me. He was so angry."

They sat in a deafening silence for several minutes. The endless wait outside the principal's office. The moment when blue lights flashed behind you. The doctor's return to the waiting room. Suddenly, she could feel the walls shrinking around her. Her breathing became erratic and labored. When she closed her eyes to control the fear, she could not breath or speak. Unforgiving ocean waves battered, smashed, and dragged her deeper and deeper. Deeper. She jumped up from the couch in panic.

Tood entered as she launched herself up. Emmy noticed him carrying a tea tray with Danish cookies, a teapot, a honey bear, sugar cubes, and two fancy saucers and cups.

"Please sit down," Tood soothed. Emmy took a deep breath and sat down. "Would you like a cookie or some tea?" he calmly asked.

Emmy snatched a cookie and defensively crossed her legs. She nibbled on the treat while Tood poured steaming tea into his cup. He drizzled honey into the tea and stirred it in. The soft clinking spoon erupted in her ears like bass drums. He poured some tea into Emmy's cup.

"Would you like honey or sugar?"

Emmy whispered, "Sugar, please."

Tood scooped up two cubes and gently delivered them into her teacup. He handed the saucer and warm drink to Emmy. She put the cookie in her mouth and received the peace offering.

"Thank you," she mumbled.

Tood nodded and grabbed a sweet snack. He dipped it in his tea. He ate the cookie whole and then loudly slurped his drink. Emmy slightly grinned and finished her cookie. She politely sipped the tea twice and placed it back on the tray. She quietly grabbed two more cookies.

Tood slurped again. "My mother," he started, "would always give me tea and cookies before we would discuss…anything important."

Emmy bit into another snack and nodded. Woof had flipped around and put his head back in her lap. She looked at Woof and gently rubbed his furry head.

"Emmy, I want to apologize to you for how I acted and spoke to you in the car. Will you forgive me?" He placed his cup down on the tray.

She scanned the room and noticed the television was still on. She looked down. "Yes. Will you forgive—"

Tood interrupted, "Thank you. Yes, of course. I'm sorry I left you waiting in here for like forty minutes, but I had to figure out some things about you and the car."

"Forty minutes? It was only about five minutes." In confusion, Emmy looked at Woof and Tood. The mighty hunter whimpered and snuggled close to her. "Does it have to do with the car?"

"It is probably the lingering effects of the warping," Todd explained.

"Why did the car do that? Come alive and move so fast?"

"The car had been modified by the owner to recognize and only operate for anyone with…" Tood hesitated.

"With what?" Emmy asked.

"Magic," Tood explained. "It is attracted to anyone with magic."

"So I have magical powers?" she said in disbelief. "So I caused it to take off?"

"Yes, you may have magic. You and Woof should have only been able to start the Chevy. I don't know why it time-warped and went precisely to the fountain." Tood scratched his head. "I have figured out a few things."

"Well, what did you figure out?" Emmy asked and put her hand to her chin.

Tood stood and started pacing. "I don't know how to say it exactly, but your arrival here was not an accident. May I ask you a few questions?"

Emmy reclined into the couch. "Sure. Ask away."

"What is the last thing you remember before waking up in Between?"

Emmy closed her eyes. "I remember I was walking. I could hear waves crashing. No, I was running…on a dark ocean pier…alone."

"Where? What city?" Tood inquired.

"Near Wilmington, North Carolina. I was investigating… something about my family…about my grandfather!"

"What about him? What had happened to him?"

"He died mysteriously…years before, and I was looking…," Emmy recalled.

"He's dead? How?"

"I don't know. I was looking for his killer. I'm an investigative reporter for…Channel 3 News. I received an anonymous tip to check out Jolly Roger, a rough dive bar…on a pier…by the ocean."

"Do you remember anything or anyone at the bar?" Tood sat down in a chair.

Emmy continued, "A man bumped into me as I entered. I walked up to the bartender. I asked for…what was the name? Someone. The bartender muttered. Then he pointed to the back door. I walked out the back door." Emmy opened her eyes.

"Anything else?"

Emmy wrinkled her brow. "Nothing else. Wait…ocean waves. Wait, I remember barking. The barking became louder and louder.

A man's voice. He was yelling at the dog. Then I woke up on your couch."

Tood sat silently as Emmy devoured another cookie. "Emmy, you…" He stopped.

"What? Please explain," she begged.

"Every fifty years or so, Between had visitors from other worlds."

"Worlds? I thought you said…"

He reached under the living room table and pushed a button. The picture above the couch flipped over and revealed a large map of Between with several red tacks randomly placed.

"Most of the junk comes from your world, but I know of at least three other worlds that send stuff and people here." Tood pointed to the map. "You are from Westard, but there is also Eastard, Northerd, and Southerd. Humans dominate the west, elves in the east, dwarfs the north, and Oogers in the south."

"Ogres?"

"That's what I said. Oogers."

"Say *o*," Emmy tried to correct. "Now say *ger*."

Tood repeated her words correctly. "O and ger."

"Now say it altogether. Ogre."

"Ooger."

"Bless your heart." Emmy asked, "Have you ever had visitors from other places?"

"Yes. Twenty-five years ago, from Eastard, a large migration seventy-five years ago from Westard, 125 years ago from Northerd, and two hundred years ago from Southerd. When someone comes through to Between, it is a big deal. It usually means an end-of-the-world event could be occurring soon." Tood turned around and perceived Emmy's widened eyes. "But…but sometimes it is positive…sometimes." Tood tried to give a reassuring smile.

Woof barked and buried his head.

"So you are telling me," Emmy responded, "I have magic, and I was brought here on purpose. And I am a harbinger of death for Between!"

"No, not exactly. It could be the destruction of your world or both worlds. But that is the worst-case scenario. I don't know much about the other visitors, but I knew the one from twenty-five years ago. He was from Eastard. He did so much good here and helped me keep Tween safe."

"That sounds nice. Wait, did you say twenty-five years? You don't look more than twenty-five. How old are you?"

Tood paused and then replied, "I'm actually fifty years old. Time-warping has strange effects on me and how I speak sometimes."

"Seriously? Wow. Okay, we will come back to that," Emmy countered. "What happened when this visitor was here?"

"Well, you see, that is one of the problems." Tood looked up to the ceiling and sighed.

Emmy questioned, "One of the problems?"

"There is no easy way to say this."

"Say what?" Emmy was going to explode.

"Emmy, the man who came from Eastard twenty-five years ago was your grandfather. David Rebus Castillo."

"My grandfather? *My* grandpa is from another world?"

"Yes." Tood tried to encourage her. "He came here to escape from a tyrannical elf ruler. He had an arrow stuck in his stomach and one in his right leg."

"He always favored his right leg," she remembered and touched her side. "He said it was an appendectomy."

Tood continued, "After he healed, he lived here for almost three years. He became my best friend. He loved it here and even fell in love with a girl from Waydownz, Jocelyn. He could not stay here because he was attracting…things from the other worlds. He could not go back, so…"

Emmy inquired, "Wait, my mom is from Between? You know her?"

"Yes. Josie was a friend."

"So you decided to help them to escape."

"Yes. I decided to send him to Westard, along with his wife. Westward is relatively peaceful but has no magic. It was the best option. Magical beings normally do not travel there. It took some time, but with your grandfather's help, we did it. I sent them to the year 1999."

"Interesting," she pondered, trying to grasp it all. "I was born in 2000."

"Here is the other problem." Tood paused and rubbed his chin. "The elf from Eastard is not your grandfather."

"You just said...the what from Eastard? Who is..." The room started to spin for Emmy.

Tood paused and then let it out. "He is your father."

She jumped to her feet and muttered, "My. My...oh my..."

Emmy stumbled forward, slapped Tood in the face, knocked over the tea, and passed out on the floor.

CHAPTER 7

For They Eat the Bread of Wickedness and Drink the Wine of Violence

Captain Chico carried a large tray of food in one hand and two half-gallon ale mugs with frothing liquid in the other. He had returned to Arms as promised, but there was no guard outside. It had taken him longer than he thought to return. The people loved his proposal to Ms. Mayor. The Tweeners loved the City Sphere fountain and praised him for it. He deflected to Tood, but the people and leaders would not hear of it. They heaped kisses, gifts, food, and drinks on him. Ah! The drinks! This land made fine drinks. He had almost forgotten about Popson and Chang. He remembered his real prize was in the Arms cell.

THE DOORS BETWEEN

He knocked on the Arms door with the mugs and splashed a little on the handle. "Popson! Chang! I brought some food and drink for you."

The door popped open, and Chang stuck out his head.

"Sir? We have a situation. Get in quick." Chang hushed, looked around, and dragged the captain inside.

Chico carefully placed the tray and mugs on the desk. He saw Popson in the cell punching and kicking the elf.

"Popson! Get out of there! What did I tell you, rookies?"

"Stay out of the cell, but…," Chang sheepishly replied.

"Then why would you…" Chico observed the elf's eyes were open and had a sock in her mouth.

Popson explained, "Well, Captain, sir, she started squawking all this nonsense about switching bodies with you, Captain. Anyway, I warned her to shut her mouth. Then she started using cusswords my own Grannie Popson, rest her soul, never used. She was mocking me and Chang, the Legion, and even Tween. When she said something, which I shall never repeat, about my mum, I punched her in the guts and stuffed a sock in her."

Captain Chico went to the cell. "This is not possible," he muttered to himself. "How long ago did he…she start talking?"

Chang and Popson looked at each other and agreed, "When we heard the strange horn."

Chang asked, "What was that?"

"Nothing. Just some new fireworks." Chico studied the elf and was glad it was socked. "You did good, men. Now grab some food and head to the celebration. Leave the drinks."

"Yes, sir!" the guards replied and went to the tray. "Thanks, Cap." They stuffed some sweet cakes in their mouths. They picked up the tray and carried the heavy load to the door. Chico stopped them.

Chico entranced the guards. "You will have an amazing time at the celebration."

The guards repeated, "We will have an amazing time at the celebration."

"You will never remember picking up any junk."

"We never picked up any junk."

"Elves do not exist."

"Elves do not exist." sounded the hypnotized guards.

"Every time you hear the name Chico, you will squawk like a chicken."

"What is a chick-hen?" Chang and Popson muttered.

Chico slapped his forehead. "You will squawk like any bird."

"Yes, Master," they mindlessly replied.

"When you get excited, you will speak in a foreign language."

"Yes, Master."

"As soon as the door closes, you will not remember why you were on guard duty. You will be relieved to finally be going to the party. Now leave."

Chang and Popson opened the door and went outside with the food. The door snapped shut. The guards walked down the street, nibbling on the food.

"I am so relieved to finally be going to the party," Popson called out.

"Me too. Why were we on guard duty?" Chang asked.

"I don't know. Maybe it's...I really can't remember. I'll have to ask Chico."

Chang screeched like a hawk.

"That was funny." Popson laughed. "Why did you do that?"

Chang giggled. "I don't know. I think I did it after you said Chico."

Popson unexpectedly hooted like a barn owl.

Chang gave him a mischievous smile. "Chico, Chico, Chico."

Popson sounded off as an eagle, blue jay, and a crow. "Now stop that!"

Chang apologized. "Sorry."

"Now let's forget all this and have some fun without Ch...El Capitan," Popson encouraged.

"Vamanos, amigo, a la fiesta!" Chang yiped.

"Si! Si! Si! ¡Yo quiero comer muchos pingüinos ahora!" Popson yelled.

They threw the tray down and sprinted to the celebration.

THE DOORS BETWEEN

Captain Chico closed the Arms door and locked it. He glided to the cell. He unlocked the iron gate and sat next to the elf's head. The visitor glared at Chico.

"So you think you are so clever in breaking my trance. What's that? I can't hear you. You have a smelly old sock in your mouth." Chico patted the face of the annoyed prisoner. "I know what you're thinking. Why are you doing this? You'll never get away with it. Please stop. Let me go. Why is it so hard to find true love? Would my mom be proud of me? Will I be ready for my battleball match? Never mind the reasons. We will have a visitor in the morning. I have to doll you up for him." He slapped her in the face. Blood dripped from her puffing lips.

"After I finish with you, I will consume that delicious ale. I must write up some promotions. Deliver a few breakup love letters. Spend a few gems. Of course, I will attend my own party. You didn't know about the party? The whole town was invited. Don't worry. I will take incredible care of the new house and your sweet fiancé, Jenny."

The prisoner's eyes widened in disbelief, and angry muffles came from the sock.

"Your fiancé? You will find out soon enough. You really should not struggle so much. It is not good for your health." Chico grinned at the elf. "When we switch back in the morning, you will not remember anything. Enough talk. I have so much to do. Thanks again for this body. Very helpful. I did have some fun today, and the night is young." Chico stepped out of the cell, snatched his wooden military baton, and returned to the prisoner.

"Don't worry. You will be ready for battleball on Friday. At least, I hope so."

As Chico raised the baton, the elf's eyes widened in fear. With the first strike, the junk faded to black.

CHAPTER 8

The Silver-Haired Head Is a Crown of Glory

"Mom. Mom, is that you?" Emmy's voice strained. She was wrapped up in a cozy quilt and lying on a queen-size bed. A silhouette rocked back and forth in the corner. "I had the weirdest dream."

"There, there now. You are safe and sound," the silhouette softly replied.

"It felt so real. There was a humongous dog, a strange man in uniform, and the coolest 1957 Chevy." Emmy stretched her arms in the dark room.

"Everything is all right now that you are back in Tood's house. The House of Doorf keeps all visitors safe," the voice reassured her.

"Yeah. Tood was so nice yet strange." Emmy quickly sat up in surprise. "Who are you? Where am I? What am I wearing?"

As she became upright, the bedroom lights turned on, revealing a diminutive older woman with white hair sitting in a creaky rocking chair. "Just calm down, dear. My name is Mrs. Hemingway. You are in Between. In the house of Doorf. You are in the third bedroom on the second floor to be precise."

"How did I get up here? Why are you here? Where is Tood?" Emmy flooded questions to the older woman.

Ms. Hemingway slid out of the chair and placed her wide bare feet on the floor.

"My, oh my, you do ask a lot of questions." Her white hair was in a messy bun. She was wearing a pascal-colored apron over a plain blue country dress. "Where to start? Okay, dearie, I am the caretaker of the Doorf Estate. Tood asked me to take care of you until he returns in the morning. I removed the robe from you and dressed you in that nightgown. Oh, Tood carried you up here."

Emmy opened her mouth, shut it, then responded, "I thought Tood and Woof lived here alone."

Ms. Hemingway smiled. "I have been the caretaker here for many, many years. Before Tood was born. I helped raise him and his brother after his parents died. Do you think Tood and Woof would clean up this whole house by themselves?"

"No, I don't think so. I actually do not know them that well. I just arrived here yesterday. It is nice to meet you. I am Esmeralda Castillo. My friends call me Emmy."

"Well, you do have a lovely name. I am certainly your friend, so I shall call you Emmy." They politely shook hands.

"How are you feeling, honey? Tood mentioned you've had quite an experience so far."

Emmy rubbed her hair. "Okay. I guess my head hurts a little."

"You did hit your head when you fainted," the caretaker explained. "That car is beastly."

"Where is Woof?"

"That rascal went with Tood. He growled about going on a hunt."

She remembered the shocking news about her grandfather/father.

"I must speak to Tood. Where is he?" Emmy removed the covers and put her feet on the floor. She stumbled forward, and Ms. Hemingway caught her.

"No reason to get yourself upset, dear. Tood had to do some research and will be back in a few hours. He left me instructions to help you be comfortable in any way possible, including answering all your questions. That is what I am going to do." Ms. Hemingway patted Emmy's back and escorted her back to bed. She held her hand.

"In the top drawer of the dresser are shirts. The second one has shorts, pants, skirts, and dresses. The third has all types of undergarments. The last has a great assortment of socks." Ms. Hemingway pointed out. "Take whatever you like. What doesn't fit, I can fix it." She grinned. "I am an excellent seamstress."

"I have no doubt," Emmy complimented.

Ms. Hemingway proudly announced, "I even designed the new Battleball uniforms for the Waydownz Undivided."

"I can't wait to see them."

"Don't worry. you will. Anyway, there is a washroom down the hall. Soap, tooth soap, toothcombs, hairbrushes, shampoo-poo, and all the towels are in the shower cabinet. I believe a good cleanup and shower would do you a world of good."

Emmy relaxed. "Thank you so much."

"No problem, Emmy. Remember to thank Tood as well. Oh, by and by, the sun will be up in a few hours. What would you like for breakfast?"

"I'm not really hungry. Maybe some juice?" Emmy claimed, but her stomach made a different statement. She grabbed her midsection and grinned.

"We will see." Ms. Hemingway smirked. "Now go get yourself cleaned up and then come to the kitchen." She left the room and waved goodbye.

"Thanks again," Emmy said as the door shut.

She stepped lightly to the dresser and opened the top drawer. She found the shirts rolled up and color coordinated. She picked a long-sleeved green shirt with a small sport logo on the front. She found baggy jeans in the next drawer, just a bit too big. Emmy went to the third drawer. "What do we have here?" She lifted up an extra-large men's underwear. "You are in the wrong place." She placed it on the bed. As she searched, she found the appropriate size bra and underwear. Finally, she opened the last drawer and grabbed a cozy pair of pink socks. She bundled her ensemble under her arms and left the bedroom.

Ms. Castillo discovered the washroom just as Mrs. Hemingway described. She turned on the shower, and hot steam soon cascaded over the curtains. She found the washcloth and towels along with the soap and shampoo.

"She said *shampoo-poo*." Emmy laughed. She removed the old lady gown and stepped into the hot shower. The warm streams of water made her relax. The soap had a flowery odor, and the hair cleanser was light lavender. She could have remained in this steam bath for hours, but a loud stomach growl moved her to finish rinsing off. She turned off the shower and reached for the towels.

She felt like a new woman as she wrapped one towel around her chest and the other wrapped up her hair. Her midsection growled louder. "Now be quiet. I must get dressed first." She wiped the condensation from the mirror and peered at the reflection. "My eyes look really blue." She removed the towels and quickly dressed in all her items, except the socks. She found a large hairbrush under the sink and brushed out her damp hair. Within a few strokes, she realized her usually knotted dark hair was silky smooth. She felt like an alluring model from a TV shampoo commercial. Her fingers slipped through her mane like a summer breeze.

The steam had dissipated from the washroom, and she wiped the condensation from the mirror to clearly see her reflection. Her newfound velvety hair shimmered azure in the light. "Wow. I like this. What is in that shampoo?" She found the toothpaste and toothcombs, as Ms. Hemingway called it.

"Better than nothing." She brushed her teeth and looked deeply into the mirror. Emmy spit out and rinsed her mouth out. "What is this?" A small teardrop beauty mark appeared on the corner of her right eye. "Cool."

Emmy stepped back from the sink and turned left to the full-length mirror.

"Not bad," she commented and smiled. "With no makeup and in a strange world."

She gathered some loose strands of hair and arranged them behind her left ear.

Her ear felt different. She shrugged her shoulders and grabbed the brush. She hummed a few bars of her favorite Big Band song as she groomed her smooth coif. Her eyes widened in shock. She dropped the hairbrush and rushed to the mirror.

She shrieked, "AHHHHHH! I'M AN ELF! I AM AN ELF!"

Ms. Hemingway burst into the bathroom with a frying pan in one hand and an onion in the other. "Emmy, honey, what happened? I heard screaming."

Emmy trembled as she traced the outline of her pointy ears. "I am an elf." She cried and touched her new face tattoo. "I'm just fine and dandy. Great. Freaking fine and flipping dandy. Did my eyes always look this blue?"

"I don't know, honey. I just met you. They do seem quite brilliant," the caretaker encouraged her.

"Thanks. This is sorta cool, right? Am I going to get superpowers and stuff like that?" Emmy stammered.

Mrs. Hemingway explained, "Oh, honey, I don't know about that stuff. Let's go downstairs, and I will explain all I know."

"Okay. That sounds good. Yeah, some good food, talk, and a beer. Yeah, that sounds good. No, it's too early for a beer." Mrs. Hemingway was leading her to the stairs. "Let me grab my socks."

"I will get them in a moment. I'm sorry, honey. We don't have beer. We have some nice ale."

"Ale." Emmy laughed. "Of course, you have ale. Is the room spinning, or is it just me? Are my feet bigger? Where are my pretty pink socks?"

"It's just you, honey. Your feet are just fine."

"Are you an elf too?" questioned Emmy.

"Heavens, no!" exclaimed the older woman. "I'm Mrs. Hemingway, the caretaker."

Emmy nervously giggled. "Silly me. You are so little, I thought you were an elf."

"What a thing to say. Everyone knows elves are tall and dwarfs are short."

"Everyone does." Emmy comically stared at the caretaker. "Are you a fairy?"

"Honey, fairies are not real," the caretaker proudly proclaimed. "I am a dwarf."

Emmy's eyes rolled, and she fainted into the strong arms of the elderly maid.

"My, oh, my." Mrs. Hemingway sighed. She carried the elf back to the soft bed and covered her sweetly with the hand-stitched quilt. She stared at the unconscious young lady. She wiped away the tears. "The spitting image." She smiled and kissed her softly on the forehead.

CHAPTER 9

Where There Is No Wood, the Fire Goes Out; Where There Is No Talebearer, Strife Ceases

"Goooood! Morning! Beetweeeen! Welcome to the first ever radio sports broadcast in our beautiful land. I am your host, Tom Hobbs, play-by-play announcer here at the Battlegrond Stadium for twenty years. If you are hearing a voice coming from a little square box, you are not going crazy. These little boxes have been placed all over the land so our citizens can listen to the greatest game, battleball. I have been announcing from megaphones for years, but now, thanks to our friends from Cutoff University, we can broadcast the games all over Between.

THE DOORS BETWEEN

"This new technology called radio will carry our voices from microphones through the air to the speakers attached to those square boxes. Amazing. We are live in the announcers' booth, high atop the Battlegrond. Another amazing part of this broadcast is my esteemed colleague, former three-time battleball champ, and your color commentator, John 'Madman' Higgins."

"Hello, folks. Great day for battleball!" said the Madman.

"Indeed, it is, my friend. Indeed. What do you think about this new technology?"

"Flipping incredible. Our voices here. Boom! The speakers there. Bang! The radio waves fly everywhere. Pow! Touchdown for everyone! I can't explain it any better."

"Madman, I must say, your war paint this morning is tremendous. It is yellow on exactly half his face and head."

"Well, Hobbs, I am not just a commentator and former player, but I am also a battleball fan. Touchdown!" He raised his hands in the air.

"Speaking of touchdowns, we have both been itching to watch some incredible battleball action. We have been to all the practice fields of our ten teams. Yes, I said ten. The squads look eager to get back on the field, especially our champions, Arms Arsenal."

The Madman interrupted, "They want to destroy the competition and leave no doubt they are the real champs."

Hobbs clarified, "If you fans don't remember, Arsenal won on a controversial last second field goal over the Bankers."

"Controversial! Nonsense. Captain Chico made the amazing kick in bounds and before time expired."

"Some say the MVP was out of bounds as time expired. We may never know. However, during this broadcast before each match, we will be discussing the teams, the players, the history, the strategy, and of course the games. We are calling this show Between the Battle Lines," Hobbs explained.

"Love the name!" Higgins exclaimed. "Did you think of it?"

"Not this time, but our generous sponsors, the *Daily Muck*, penned it. For all your local news, weather, gossip, and awesome pinguino recipes, get a copy of the best newspaper in town, the

Daily Muck. Speaking of gossip, Madman, did you hear the latest on Captain Chico and Ms. Mayor?"

"Yes, I did, old friend, right here in the *Daily Muck*. Boom! Get your copy today! Boom!"

Hobbs transitioned, "A big boom was recently announced that a tenth team had joined the league this year from Waydownz, the Waydownz Undivided. This new squad will be sporting black and green uniforms with a castle emblem. Their flag is a green field surrounding a black castle. The Wandering Knights are sponsored and led by Tood Doorf."

"You mean the junkman from the Ruins! Are you kidding me? Has he even played the game? This will be a disaster. The Knights? Ha! More like the junks this season!"

"With all new players, no experience, no veterans, and a questionable leader, the Undivided will have their hands full on Saturday with their opponent, the Freeside Fight Squad."

"F-R-E-E. Now that's a team with some spirit and fire!" the Madman spouted. "Win or lose, those bears can put down some ale."

"Indeed. They were a tough squad all season and almost beat the Arsenal in the semifinal matchup. We spoke with the Freeside captain, Robbie Ronk, about his upcoming opponent. He was not complimentary of the new team from Waydownz."

Madman laughed. "Ole Ronk ripped them a new one!"

Hobbs continued, "I was going to give his quote, but Ronk is in the studio. Ronk, welcome to Between the Battle Lines."

"Thanks, Hobbs. Always an honor to talk to legends, Madman," Ronk greeted the hosts. "I have to get back to practice, but I have something to say."

Madman returned, "Tell Tween and all the Battleball fans what you told us earlier."

Ronk growled, "Those farmers don't stand a chance. We will rip them to shreds and send them crying home to their mommas. The beatdown, no, we will inflict crushing pain like a giant boulder dropped on a tiny, little bug. Tood, I'm calling you out! You think you can buy your way into the league with your family's money? You have no respect for the tradition of the game or Tween. It will be my personal pleasure to destroy this team and cause them to forfeit the rest of the reason. The castle lies in ruins for a reason, and I'm going to keep it that way."

He grabbed the macrophone with his club for hands. "Tood, what you said to my sister about my season last year will not be forgiven. Overrated! I will show you what overrated really means! She told me you are a bad kisser. What do you think about that, Tood! I will bring the pain. I will have revenge. I am coming for you, junkman!" He dropped the studio equipment, and a high-pitched squeal emitted from the radio.

"I am so pumped for battleball!" Madman hollered.

Hobbs said, "There you have it, folks. This Saturday will be a grudge match between Freeside Fight Squad and the newcomers, the Waydownz Undivided. Buy your tickers now at your local Vararity Tickermaster. Two new ticker stands have now opened in Sembly and Freeside for this new season."

"Vararity Tickermaster, boom!"

"Well, we do have some battleball business to attend to. The new rules, new equipment, and other changes to enhance the game."

"You know, Hobbs, I didn't like these changes at first, but I believe they can protect the players, keep the game clean, and increase the enjoyment of the whole stadium experience," Madman commented.

"Wow, that was insightful, Higgins. I could not have said it better. The first team rule change is about the number of female players allowed on the field. In the past, it has been a maximum of two, but with the emergence of several women star athletes, the Battleball Rules Commission has changed the rules and allowed an unlimited number of female athletes to be a part of a team."

"During my years on the field," Madman started, "I had wonderful women teammates who were amazing on the field. So amazing, in fact, I married one, my wife, Marinna. She would tackle me so hard in practice, I knew I couldn't let this one get away."

"Great story, Higgins. This could lead to a whole team of women players."

"About time, I say. More women! Boom!"

"Players could now have up to five fouls or schlapps during the game. At the fifth schlapp, the player will be ejected from the game."

"More fouls could mean more rough play, Hobbs."

"The Rules Commission has also added more penalty shots for aggressive fouls and more time in the penalty box for fouls 3, 4, 5."

"Which probably means more of those stripped officials," Madman said.

"That's correct. Four battleball referees will be patrolling the field. We also have some new equipment for the players. Shin pads for the legs and a leather helmet to protect the athletes' heads."

"More protection. Boom! Less injuries. Bang!"

"Let's not forget about our new Battlegrond scoreboard. This huge addition to the stadium is another marvel provided by Cutoff University, Mayor Kokinkus, and the Banker."

Madman interrupted, "Hobbs, can we finally get to my favorite change this year?"

"I know you love this one."

"It's the leaders of cheer! Zoom, zap, boom!"

"Each club this year can have its own leaders of cheer. In the past, the Battlegrond Stadium would provide individuals to lead the fans in shouts of approval or disapproval during the action on the field."

"I wish they had these leaders when I was playing. Well, maybe not. I would have been too distracted. Zow!" Madman grinned.

"Each team can have a total of five cheerleaders, both female and male. They can rile up on the crowds on the sidelines, during time-outs, between quarters, and of course, halftime."

"This is really going to spice up the matches. Hot! Hot! Hot! Bam!"

"Well, if you are looking for a hot and spicy meal, get on over to Pepe's Grill. Now serving your favorites before, during, and after all the battleball matches."

"You know, Hobbs, Pepe is a personal friend of mine, and he guarantees you will love his food, or you get your gems back. That is the Pepe Promise."

"Well, Madman, I promise never to go to another Captain Chico party. Ever."

"Hobbs, that man is crazy. His house will never be the same. BOOM! That party was historical!"

"Indeed, Madman, indeed. In just two days, on Friday, we will have our first three games of the season—Arms Arsenal versus Bankers BC, Vararity United versus Real Miners, and the Federales versus CU Battlecrew."

"What! The rematch of the championship contest. The Bankers will be out for blood!"

"The last two games will be on Saturday—Tween City BC versus Union Miller and Freeside Fight Squad versus Waydownz Undivided."

"The grudge match between Ronk and the junkman! Boom!" Madman proclaimed.

"When we come back from this musical break, we will break down all the matchups and give our predictions for the upcoming battleball season. Any last comments before the break, Madman?"

"I can see the leaders of cheer on the field. Oh my, penguins! Those outfits are incredible. I can see their calves. Oh, baby! Come to Papa!"

"Easy, big guy. They are for the crowd to enjoy, not us, old-timer. Please enjoy this musical interlude. Another wonder supplied by the magicians at Cutoff University and our sponsor, the Markets on Vararity. From apples to zucchini, from fresh bread to fresh fish, we have it all at the Markets on Vararity! I'm Hobbs, and he is the Madman. Keep listening…"

"Or you just might miss out! Bama Lama!" Higgins finished.

CHAPTER 10

A Little Sleep, a Little Slumber...So Shall Your Poverty Come Like a Prowler

Captain Chico abruptly opened his eyes. He was awakened by a scarlet cardinal scratching on a windowsill. He shut them and rubbed his temples. The pounding in his head hurt almost as much as his throbbing arms, chest, torso, thighs, and knees. He felt like he had been in a brawl with three Wamp monsters. As his brain defogged, he observed his surroundings. He recognized his bed, pillows, blankets, desk, and dresser.

"How did I get here? What happened last night?" In a haze, he muttered out loud, "That was the weirdest dream."

"I hope I was in the dream, love," a sultry female voice whispered next to him.

Chico sat upright, gathered a bedsheet, and scurried with fright away from the voice. He banged his skull against the headboard. "How did you get in here? What do you want?"

"I'm not going to hurt you, love," the voice soothed the captain.

"Where are my clothes?" Chico just realized he wore only linens.

"I, unfortunately, cannot take credit for your lack of clothing. I understand you undressed yourself during your festivities last night. You paraded around your fine physique in only a loincloth. I missed all the fun." She pouted.

"Mrs. Banker?" Chico remembered the sensuous voice. "Irene? How?" He stared across the bed.

Lady Banker lay next to him fully dressed, but with her purple bodice loosened. The lovely brunette's hair cascaded around her piercing brown eyes and elegant face. She sat up on her right elbow and leaned on her hand.

"Well, my love, you sent me this sweet note to meet you here at midnight. I arrived a little late due to family obligations. When I got here, you were sound asleep on your bed." She sighed. "You looked so peaceful. I snuggled up next to you. I must have fallen asleep." She looked at her watch. "Oh my, it is already six thirty am. I must be off." She stood up and moved to the door. She seductively tightened up the bodice strings in front of him.

"I don't remember anything." Chico squinted and rubbed his scruffy face.

"After the announcement during your celebration speech, I thought I would not be able to see you again."

"What announcement?" Chico moaned and closed his eyes in sleepiness.

"Your engagement to Ms. Mayor. Jennifer Kokinkus, your fiancé."

Chico instantly sobered up. "My what to whom?"

Mrs. Banker playfully hit him with her gloves. She slowly moved to the exit.

"Jak, you are such a scoundrel. Stop that. What you said was so beautiful. Treat this lady right. It sounds like true love." She sighed deeply. "I knew this day would come. You would find an available cute young flower to be your bride. It was great while it lasted." She sighed again. "Great. See you around."

Chico sat in stunned silence as Mrs. Banker tenderly put on her gloves. She opened the door. She stepped outside, but only one step. The beauty peeked over her shoulder at the captain.

She smirked. "If you recall the concoction you were drinking last night, send me a bottle. By the way, there is a note on your desk." She blew him a sweet kiss. "I hope you will remember me fondly. I will always be thinking of you. I am your biggest fan. In secret." Her alluring smile was followed by a long wink. She wiggled her fingers goodbye as she sauntered away. The bedroom door slowly creaked closed.

"What just happened?" Chico pondered and rubbed his head. "I am engaged? To Jenny? Where are my boots?"

With his bedsheet gathered around him, he shuffled to the door and opened it. There was no one else in the hallway, and the other doors were closed. He closed the door and shuffled to his dresser. He dropped the linens and picked out his usual casual wear and socks. He scanned the room but did not see his knife or his boots. He must have left his boots and knife downstairs. He dressed quickly and remembered the note on his desk. He found the paper under his Arms keys. He placed the keys in his pocket. It was written in his own handwriting.

"Meet Tood at Pepe's Grill at nine a.m. for breakfast," Chico read and rubbed his chin. "Why would I be meeting the junkman this morning?"

The Legion leader walked out of his room and slowly clamored down the wood stairs. He spotted his favorite shoes on the last stair. His black leather midcalf boots were neatly arranged facing out in their customary spot. His first purchase as Legion captain were custom-made in Free Side. He sat on the bottom stair and slipped on his comfortable footwear. He brushed off a little dust from the left one. He closed his eyes and took a deep breath of relief.

His body felt better, but his head pounded like a miner's hammer. "I wonder if Chang brought his homemade spirits."

THE DOORS BETWEEN

The relief quickly turned to shock and horror. As Chico stood, he witnessed the complete devastation of his home which had occurred the night before. All the windows were shattered, debris lay scattered on the floor, and the front door was hanging on one hinge. At least a hundred people lay asleep everywhere. Empty bottles, dirty plates, and half-eaten fruits, cakes, and cooked meats littered most tables and chairs, which had not been destroyed by partygoers. A five-feet-high tightrope had been strung from one corner diagonally to the other.

Chico took one step away from the stairs, and several penguins squawked and waddled past, nibbling on the leftovers. Then he noticed several colorfully dressed circus performers were among the sleepers. Along with two goats, three monkeys, a donkey, there was a large bear wearing a tiny hat. Chico slowly made his way through the snoring crowd, attempting to get to the front door. He made it to the center of the living room and realized he could not progress any farther. He looked around and located a metal saucepan and a musical drumstick under some soaked pants. He reluctantly gathered the items. He stood up. He held the pan into the air. With blazing anger, he banged on it continuously louder.

"Out! Out! Out! Everybody out!" Chico screamed as he slammed the metal and marched around the destroyed house. "Out! Out! Out!" He kept banging and yelling for several minutes.

Some of the partiers stirred and yawned. One man with half his face painted yellow bolted awake and then jumped out the nearest window. Chico heard knocking coming from under a large rectangular box near the stairs. A large female circus clown slept on top of the box.

"Help. Please help us," whispered the box. "We can't breathe."

"Hold on," Chico encouraged the box. He struggled to push the circus clown off the box. The human boulder inched closer to the edge. She slammed on the floor with a solid thud but kept snoring.

The captain strained and lifted the wooden rectangle.

"Popson? Chang? How did you get in here?"

Chico dragged his guards one by one to the stairs away from the clown. He sat them up and found some glass bottles. He filled them with water and brought them back to his coughing soldiers. "Don't try to talk. Stay here." Chico scanned the room again, this time looking for anyone in distress. No one else was in danger. He walked to the center and grabbed his pan.

"All right, everyone! The party is OVER! Time to leave now! Let's go!"

Individuals and groups awakened and slowly stumbled out of his house. Chico tripped and accidentally kicked a large man. The man woke up cursing.

"Chico? Why did you do that, bro?"

The captain banged the pan louder. "Sorry, friend, but it is time to leave."

"Chico, it's me, Pepe!" grumbled Tween's famous chef.

"Pepe? I didn't know it was you."

"All forgiven, amigo. You are the man, bro. You threw the most slapping party EVER! Ever, bro!" Pepe raised up on one elbow.

"Thanks, I think."

"Don't be modest, bro. Best party ever. You had the band, the booze, animals, the dancing girls, and the circus performers. The fireworks were inside your house, bro! You ripped off your clothes and screamed, 'We are rocking all night!' It was epic. No! What is beyond epic?"

"Historical?" Chico answered and helped Pepe to his feet.

"Historical. Bro, it was historical." Pepe smiled and balanced himself. "Free food for the season, bro. You rock!" He squeezed through the sideways front door and meandered down the street. "Historical!" he screamed at no one.

"Thanks, bro. Maybe I will see you in a few hours," Chico replied.

He returned to Popson and Chang. They had managed to stand up and headed to the open window.

"Thanks, Cap. You saved us. We owe you big-time," Popson muttered, and Chang nodded in agreement.

"Just get out of here. Go to the barracks and sleep this off."

"Yes, sir."

"Chang, did you bring your stuff to the party? You know, the hooch you've been cooking in the Arms basement?" Chico inquired.

Chang replied, "No, sir. That went bad a month ago."

Chico scratched his head and waved goodbye as the guards left the ruins. He had a lot more Tweeners and animals to wake up. He wondered which would be worse, waking up the drunk bear or the capsized snoring clown.

CHAPTER 11

The Tongue of the Righteous Is Choice Silver

Clippety-clop, clippety-clop, clippety-clop, clippety-clop. Emmy heard the steady rhythm of a horse-drawn wagon. She swayed to the motion and heard the carriage boards creaking and grinding wheels. She breathed in the fresh hay and pungent odors of farm animals.

She opened her eyes to see hay drifting from the back of a wagon on to a cobblestone road. She noticed well-worn tan boots, perfectly tied, covering her pink socks. The Carolina blue sky with white puffy wisps reminded her of home. She was far from home. She sat up on the scratchy burlap sack and stretched her arms. As she turned forward, she witnessed silvery white hair in a bun bopping to the motion of the wagon. She lay back down, extended, and then contracted her long denim-covered legs.

"Emmy, how are you doing back there?" the silver bun spoke.

"I am feeling fine. It is such a beautiful day," Emmy sleepily replied.

"Yes, dear, it is quite lovely."

"Ms. Hemingway? Why am I on a wagon?"

"Mrs.," the elderly woman corrected. "I am taking you to the Markets on Celos."

"Oh, okay." She bit her bottom lip in thought. "Where are Tood and Woof?"

"Tood was not back yet. I left him a note. Woof is at the estate, keeping watch." She muttered incomprehensible phrases and finished with "I will skin that rascal."

Emmy sat up again. "That was thoughtful. May I join you on the bench?"

"Sure, dear, sure. Just be careful," Mrs. Hemingway warned. "I couldn't leave you cooped up in that old house. I decided to show you around and take you to the Market."

Emmy gingerly stood and made her way to the front bench as the wagon traveled onward. She felt like a giant sitting next to the diminutive driver. Emmy smiled, and the driver smiled back.

"Thanks for putting my socks on and finding these comfortable boots for me."

"Freeside makes the best boots in Tween, but I found those in Tood's shoe collection."

"I lost a pair just like this three years ago. Back home."

"You don't say, dear. Look under the bench. I have something for you."

Emmy reached under and pulled a wicker basket with a latched top. She opened the basket and removed a white napkin covering the contents—mini loaves of bread, apples, fried poultry, hard-boiled eggs, Danish cookies, and RC Cola bottles.

"I thought you might be hungry, so I prepared some breakfast and lunch."

"Thank you so much. I'm starving." She reached into the basket and pulled out a warm breaded drumstick. She breathed in the savory aroma. Her teeth ripped it apart in seconds. She swallowed and sighed in instant relief. "Wow. That was delicious. It's better than KFC, Bojangles, and Popeye's combined." She reached down for another piece of poultry. She found another leg and a bottle. She bit into the juicy meat. "You want a drink?"

"You're welcome. And thank you, dear. It's my special recipe. No, I ate before we left. That soda pop is too fizzy for me," Mrs. Hemingway commented.

Emmy spoke with her mouth full. "Thanks so much, Mrs. H. You are so sweet."

"Mrs. H. I like it, dear. No problem at all. When you are finished eating, I have a few items to give you."

"Great," Emmy mumbled as she devoured more meat, crusty bread, an apple, and two cookies. She washed it down with the RC Cola and then erupted with a loud burp. "Excuse me."

"You are excused." Mrs. H smiled. "Almost as loud as Woof's. Look in the back and you will find two sacks, one light and one heavy."

Emmy twisted around and spotted the sacks. She reached back with her left arm and snatched them.

"Open the light one first," the petite driver announced. "Choose whatever color you like, dear."

Emmy looked into the bag and found three knit hats—white, black, and green. She chose the green. It matched her shirt. She unfolded it to reveal a knitted black castle. She wiggled it on.

"How do I look? Pretty cute?" She moved her head side to side. "I love the chess rook."

"That one is my favorite too," Mrs. Hemingway cheered. "You love what?"

"Chess. It's a board game. One of the pieces is a black castle or rook."

"Oh, I never made the connection. We call it the king's game or just kings," the dwarf explained. "It is also the new emblem of the Waydownz Undivided. Tood is the captain. It's a battleball team." They rode in silence for a few moments.

"I love sports. I have never heard of battleball," Emmy questioned.

"I love sports too! You don't have battleball from where you are from?"

"No. I don't think so. Unless it's from Australia. Is it like rugby or soccer?"

"Yes, for both." Ms. Hemingway had a fanatical grin on her face. "You see, it is an awesome combination of many of your sports into one. The Tweeners do not realize they are separate sports. For them, it has always been one game."

"All of the west's sports?" Emmy challenged "Football? Basketball? Hockey?, Golf?"

"Yes, yes, yes, no," the short sports fan cheered.

"Baseball, volleyball, oh, what's the odd one from England?"

"Cricket," Ms. Hemingway chirped. "Yes to all of those. You have to see it. It is incredible."

"How do you know about all these sports? You are from…from dwarf land?"

"Northard, honey. Tood has books and videos all about those sports. I love watching them. We can talk about it later and maybe even buy some tickers to an upcoming match."

"I would love to go," Emmy responded.

"I am so excited to have someone to talk to about the games, but first we have more important matters to discuss."

"Sure. What's up?"

"The sky, of course, dear. When we get closer to the Market, you will need to keep your hat covering those fine new ears. The locals have not seen an elf in a few centuries. We don't want to cause a stir."

Emmy secured her hat, which was already covering the ears. "Got it. Cover my Spocks. No pitchforks."

"Sure, dear, sure." Mrs. H looked confused but continued, "You have experienced a lot recently with so many changes at once. It can feel overwhelming. I know how you feel. I arrived here from a war-torn land with no peace, no future, and no hope of it changing. Tween is all about peace, hope, love, and a chance for a future. It took me a while to adjust. It is not perfect or heaven, but it is all we got. This place is important because it keeps all four worlds in balance until the End of Days. Tood is the keeper of the balance and protects Tween and all the lands, whether they realize it or not. I know you have a multitude of questions, which will only lead to more questions. I will do my best to clarify all I can." The caretaker smiled and rubbed Emmy's arm.

Emmy smiled sadly. She wiped away a tear. "Thank you. I just don't know where to begin." She looked at her feet. "Oh, I know. Where does the electricity come from which powers the house?"

"Elect-tri-city?" Mrs. Hemingway asked. "Oh, you mean the magic which comes from the sun, wind, and water?"

Emmy scoffed. "Okay, magic. I will just ask Tood later."

"Now before I start answering all your inquiries, I need to tell you something vital and necessary. I knew your parents quite well when they lived here, before they traveled away. I know you have probably heard this all your life, but you look precisely like your mother."

"Once or a million." Emmy grinned. "How well did you know them?"

The diminutive driver smiled and peered in the visitor's blue eyes. "Extremely well, dear."

Emmy laughed and then stopped. "We aren't cousins or something, are we?"

"Oh, heavens no, dear!"

"Great!" Emmy sighed in relief. "For a second, I thought you were my grand—"

"I am your great-great-grandmother." Only the twittering birds could be heard. "Please don't faint. I won't be able to catch you from here. Emmy?"

The visitor put her head to her chest. "I am not going to faint. Two times is more than enough." Emmy lifted her head and put her hands on Mrs. Hemingway's hands. "I have never had a lot of family when I was growing up. Now I learn I have a great-great-grandmother. I always wanted a granny." She hugged her granny and kissed her on the cheek. "How old are you?"

Granny thought for a second. "I stopped counting after 150. That was about sixty years ago. You are taking this much better than I thought."

"I think I am getting used to the shock and awe. You don't look a day older than seventy-five." Emmy embraced her again. "How did my parents meet?"

"You're sweet, dear. Wrong, but sweet. Well, I was planning on retiring from being the caretaker. Your grandmother at the time still had young ones, so she did not want to do it."

"Are you saying I have a grandmother, aunts, and uncles? And… and maybe some cousins?"

"Of course, dear. You are part of a big family in Waydownz."

Emmy's blue eyes glistened, and she whispered, "Do you think…I could meet them?"

"We will see. We have to ask Tood."

"Great." Emmy smiled. "Please continue."

"Where was I?" Granny pondered. "Josie, your mother, volunteered to be my replacement. I was teaching her all the things to do on the estate."

"Joselyn." Emmy closed her eyes in thought. "Only Grandpa would call her Josie."

"When your grandpa…father arrived in Tween, he had grievous injuries from two arrow wounds—one in the knee and the other in the stomach. He almost died several times through the first night. If Tood had not known medical practices from your world, he would have died of infection and poison. Josie and I cared for your father for weeks as he lay unconscious. Because I had to return to my responsibilities, Josie would primarily care for his wounds, cool his fever, feed him, read to him, and talk to him."

"Poison? How was he poisoned?"

"Through the arrows," Mrs. Hemingway explained. "The arrow wounds were fatal precise shots, but that poison on the tips was vicious."

"Oh, I see."

"Tood and I got most of the poison out, but your father had to battle the rest. After three months, he had won the fight and finally woke up. Your mother helped him recover in body, mind, and soul. Josie was smitten, and your father returned the affection. A year later, your father changed his name to David Rebus Castillo, from his elf name. They wed in a ceremony under the Big Tree. I was so proud of them."

"I always wondered about the *R* in his name. That is beautiful. Were they really in love?" Emmy muttered. Then she asked, "What happened next?"

"Yes, I think so. Well, they moved in here at first and then built a house near the Junks. Tood and your father worked together gathering junk, helping Tweeners, building all sorts of stuff, and finding stones for the magic doors. Then one day, it happened."

"What happened?" Emmy asked.

"Creatures from other realms started appearing all over Between. Some friendly and docile, but many others dangerous and destructive. Woof actually came here during that time. I am still not sure which one he is, that brute." Granny snorted. Emmy listened intently. "So Tood and David had to fight the beasts secretly. They befriended some, captured a few, relocated one or two. They destroyed all the wicked ones. However, the more they removed…"

"More kept coming." Emmy understood.

"Tood had collected enough stones to build a door. He transported your parents to the west. The monsters stopped arriving, and Tood and Woof dispatched the rest."

"I don't know what to say." Emmy sat, baffled. They rode in silence for a time.

"One more thing. I have to explain about the Market. We are getting close." Mrs. H pointed to the right. "Those are the Celos. Apartments and housing near the Market."

Emmy looked and observed giant corn silos at least a hundred feet high and fifty feet wide peeking over the horizon like mountain peaks.

"If anyone asks about you, you are my granddaughter from Waydownz. Your name is Emmy Zinger."

"Zinger?" Emmy mocked. "That sounds like a chocolate pastry."

"Well, technically, it is your family name. I am a Hemingway-Zinger."

"Oh, sorry. Why not Smith or Jones or Castle?"

"All the Jones live on the west side of Tween. The Smiths are on the east side, and the Castles live around Sembly."

"Good to know," Emmy remarked.

"Everyone from Waydownz has last names which all start with a Z. Some first names too."

"Okay?" Emmy said.

"You see, dear, no one up here in Celos is going to check who you are related to in Waydownz. They don't know and don't care. But if you mention Jones, Smith, Castle, Miller, etc., they will be asking all sorts of questions about family, cousins, and all the families they do know."

"I see." Emmy had another question. "What if I meet someone from Waydownz?"

"You will tell them—"

"I am the granddaughter of Granny Zinger. Emmy Zinger." The new Zinger grinned. "I must remain incognito to avoid any unnecessary questions."

"Incognito," Granny pondered out loud. "I like it. May I use it?"

"Of course, dear," Emmy imitated Mrs. Hemingway.

"Funny. Very funny, you rascal." She playfully pinched Emmy's arm.

"Ouch." Emmy laughed but gave a mean look. "So, Granny, what are we getting at the Market?"

"I thought you would never ask. How good are you at picking nice juicy fruits, vegetables, and pinguinos?

Emmy was about to answer and stopped. "Did you say pinguinos? Like penguins?"

"Yes, of course, dear. You have been eating them since you arrived."

She had just picked up another drumstick but dropped it back down. "I thought it was chicken."

"Chick-hens? We have not seen a chick-hen in Tween in over two hundred years. They are extinct. Creatures with no magic do not last long here."

"Extinct?"

"We have an old Between expression. 'Gone the way of the chick-hens.'"

"Dodos," Emmy corrected.

"Dodos? Dodos can be found in the Firrest. Tough little bird. Hard to catch."

"What? I have so much to learn." Emmy scratched her hat. "So you all eat pinguinos on a regular basis?"

"All over Between. There is a farm by Little Smackover Falls. They love the water and act so strangely in the snow. They slide on their bellies," Granny confessed.

"You don't say." Emmy smirked at her caretaker.

"Are you teasing me? You should not tease your granny."

"I know my Granny Zinger will teach me all I need to know."

"Now that is the most sensible comment you have made all day." Granny tapped her knee. "You'll be fine, young one. Just fine." Mrs. Hemingway looked up and saw a wagon coming toward them.

An older gentleman with a white beard wore a straw hat and had his team of oxen slowly moving down the road. He had a wagonful of vegetables and a four-year-old boy sitting in the back on some hay. He held a miniature green flag with a black castle.

Granny started the greeting. "The Good be with you."

"The Good bless you," the gentleman responded.

As the carts passed, Emmy and the little boy locked eyes and gave each other friendly smiles.

"I'm Jonny Zenith. This is my Pop-Pop."

"I'm Emmy Zinger. This is my Granny."

"We are going to battleball on Saturday. We just got tickers," Jonny proudly announced.

"We are going to Market to get pinguinos. Maybe we will see you at the game. Bye." Emmy waved farewell. "The Good bless you."

Jonny cheered, "Yeah! Go Waydownz Undivided!" He waved his flag and goodbye excitedly.

The Grandfather nudged Jonny. "The Good be with you!" the little boy shouted.

Emmy turned back around. "How did I do, Granny?"

THE DOORS BETWEEN

Granny grinned. "You are a natural. Hold on." She made a strange noise with her mouth, and the horse bolted into a gallop. Emmy barely held on to the wagon as it sped down the cobblestones. Ms. Hemingway explained, "We have to get some tickers to battleball."

CHAPTER 12

A Man Who Has Friends Must Himself Be Friendly

Tood made it to Pepe's Grill exactly at 9:00 a.m. A tall man with long dirty-blond hair stumbled to the front door and dropped his keys. As he bent down, his hair covered his eyes, and he hit his head against the solid oak door.

"Flipping dodo!" he muttered under his breath.

"Excuse me, Pepe. Have you seen—" Tood started.

"Bro, why are you yelling at me?" Pepe responded.

"Sorry. This is my normal volume."

"Well, bro, it's killing my vibe. Turn it way down."

Tood whispered, "Okay. Have you seen—"

"Much better, bro. Thanks." He looked up through his hair strands. "Tood, it's you, bro. I'll be open in un momento, hermano." He opened the door and walked through with Tood right behind. "You missed the best party ever last night at Chico's house. He had the circus, fireworks, dancing animals, drinks from all the—"

Tood interrupted, "You were at Captain Chico's house last night?"

Pepe proudly announced, "Bro, I just left there a few hours ago. What did he call the party?"

"Is he still there?"

"Most likely, bro. He kicked me out, along with the rest. His house was literally trashed. I think he is cleaning up. He was holding a pan and banging it. Not cool, bro. The circus was there, but now they are history." Pepe took down several upside-down chairs and pushed them under the tables.

"We were supposed to meet here at nine."

"You are welcome to wait, bro. I'll have the java ready in a few minutes." Pepe stepped behind his food counter and ignited the stove and turned on a fancy espresso machine.

"Thanks, Pepe. I'll take two java juices and—" Tood pulled out a chair and sat down at a table.

The cook shouted, "That's it!"

"What? What's the matter?" The junkman had jumped to his feet.

"What did Chico call the party, bro?"

"Monumental?" Tood asked.

"No, but a good one. Historical, bro. Historical."

"I think I will wait outside for the captain."

"No problem, bro. Be up in a minute."

Tood stepped outside the cafe. He went to the nearest outdoor table and flipped the chairs over. He sat down and crossed his legs. Tweeners appeared to be in slow motion this morning.

Pepe found Tood a few minutes later with his eyes closed. He watched the junkman. Tood realized someone was watching and opened his eyes.

"Sorry, bro. I did not want to interrupt your meditation. Here is the java."

"I was sleeping. I had a long night too. Thanks." He reached for his money pouch.

"On the house. So, bro, how is your bro, Dood, doing?"

"Fine." He drank the warm beverage. "He lives down in Flat Gap near Foot Lake. Beautiful place. Ever been?"

"No. Bro, I get lost crossing the Bridge. You remind me of him, bro, before the whole Junk Incident. Dood was always a bro to me. You tell him, Pepe still remembers the good stuff, bro."

"I will. Thanks, Pepe." Tood sipped his java.

"You know, bro. When you have a bro, then you know, bro," Pepe pondered.

Tood agreed. "Exactly."

"Good be with you, bro. I gotta get the kitchen ready." Pepe patted Tood's back and headed back to the cafe.

"Good bless you, Pepe." Tood swallowed more morning juice. "And you too, bro."

The junkman waited until 9:30 a.m. and decided to head to Chico's house. He was going to ask Pepe for directions, but more customers were arriving every minute. He picked up his cups and walked in the direction of the pounding pan. Groups of two and three Tweeners staggered past him. He observed a large female clown stumbling down the street holding the leash of a massive bear. He wondered how the little hat remained on the giant bear's head. He found Captain Chico standing in a window, directing the last of the vagabonds out the front door.

"Yes. Yes, please take the goat and the pinguinos. Yes, it was a great party. Thank you," Chico said to the final partygoers. He turned and noticed the junkman. "Tood? What are you doing here? I thought we were meeting at Pepe's at nine."

"Well, Captain, I waited until nine thirty. Pepe told me about the party, so I decided to check it out. He said the party was—"

Chico stopped him. "Don't say it, please. I've heard it all morning. I never want to hear that word again."

"No problem." Tood laughed. "I brought you java juice." He lifted it up.

"Seriously?" He reached for the beverage. "Thanks. It is just what I needed." He slurped it gratefully.

"So do you need a hand cleaning up?" Tood asked.

"If anything can be done." Chico snorted and scanned the mess. "Why not? Where do you want to start?"

"Why don't we fix the front door first? Then we can clean up the other messes," Tood suggested.

"Sounds good. I'll get some boards, nails, and a hammer from the back."

"Is that animal or human dung on the dining room table?" Tood asked.

"I don't want to know." Chico shook his head and headed to the back room. "I just don't want to know."

Chico returned with the tools, the wood, and two brooms. The front door was heavier than they imagined, but with a little ingenuity and power, they lifted the entry door back in place. Tood found the door pins under shattered glass. Chico held the door in place while Tood slid in the pins. Chico gave it a test push. The oak door creaked on its hinges but closed on the first try.

"One down," Tood announced cheerfully.

"A million to go," Chico sarcastically proclaimed. "You better with the hammer or the broom?"

"The broom." Tood reached for it. "I'll start at the stairs. You have any trash cans?"

"I'll check near the back door." The captain jogged to the back and called back, "I found the trash cans. Tood, could you come here? I may need your help with something."

Tood walked toward the back and heard various animal calls and noises. In the small backyard, at least twenty people lay unconscious, along with two white horses, long-horned cattle, several monkeys, a peacock, and two dogs wearing pink tutus. Tood put his hand to his chin.

"What exactly happened here last night?" asked the junkman.

"I don't know. I just don't want to know," Chico said in disgust.

It took another hour to remove the remaining guests and the animals from the backyard. The remaining cleanup was uneventful. Chico boarded up the windows while Tood picked up the trash and glass. He filled up both trash cans, so Chico had to borrow more from his unhappy neighbors. Chico apologized and promised them battleball tickers. They worked together for another hour and placed all the broken furniture, trash, and animal dung in the receptacles by the street.

Chico was sweeping the stairs and examined the main room. "Tood, this looks great. By the way, did you find a hunting knife with my initials on it?"

"No, sorry. Maybe it's in your bedroom or Arms office?"

Chico replied, scanning the floor, "Maybe. How about some lunch at Pepe's? You earned it. I'm starved."

"Thanks. I am getting hungry, and I could use another java juice," Tood said.

"Let me grab my coat." Chico put the broom down and ran up the stairs.

"Hey, Captain," Tood called out. "At Sembly, you mentioned you collected some junk. Where would you put it?"

Chico came downstairs while putting on his jacket. "I vaguely remember picking up something. Popson and Chang helped me, I think. Standard procedure is to lock it up at Arms. Is it important?"

Tood said, "Might be. What did it look like?"

Chico and Tood opened the front door and walked to the street. Tood closed the front door with no problems.

"I think," Chico started. "I think it was white, covered in linens."

"I find those all the time," Tood replied nonchalantly as they walked toward Pepe's.

"Straps," Chico recalled. "Three leather straps."

"Interesting," the junkman said without any emotion. "It might be a compooter."

"Oh, okay. What do you want at Pepe's? I could eat a giant pinguino."

"Captain, you mind if I skip lunch? I should take the junk away."

"Duty calls. I get it." Chico reached into his coat pocket. "No problem. Here is the key to the cell. Just leave it with the guard on duty."

"Thanks. Maybe lunch another time?"

"Definitely. I could not have cleaned up that mess without you. Thanks."

Tood nodded and ran off in the direction of Arms. He called back, "See you soon. Watch out for that clown and bear."

Chico yelled back, "I will!" He chuckled.

As the captain turned around, he smacked directly into the colorful female jester holding the leash of the grizzly. The strong woman gave him a crushing hug and lifted him into the air. He struggled to get out but could not move.

She whispered in his ear, "Last night, you were historical."

Confusion and fear filled Chico as the bear snuggled up close to them.

Tood reached the Arms barracks within a few minutes. Popson and Chang were leaving as he walked up the stairs.

"It's the junkman," Chang teased.

"What are you doing here?" Popson barked.

"Captain Ch—"

Chang roughly put his finger on Tood's mouth. "Don't say Cap's name. Get it?"

Tood nodded in agreement. He mumbled, "Got it."

Popson said, "Good."

Chang removed his finger.

Tood started slowly, "The captain sent me here to collect the junk."

"It's in the cell, whatever it is," Popson snapped and pushed past Tood.

Chang bumped shoulders with the junkman. "Just get your precious junk and don't come back. No one wants you here."

Tood moved past Chang and opened the door. He looked back and asked, "By the way, how was the box at Captain Chico's party?" He did not wait for a response and closed the door.

Popson squawked like a penguin, and Chang gobbled.

Tood saw the package in the cell. No one was at the desk. He removed the key from his left pocket and opened the iron door. He left the door open and placed the key on the desk. He pulled out his chain watch from his right pocket. He lifted it to his eyes and scanned it around the whole area. A green diamond materialized on a cornerstone by the captain's office and then disappeared.

He walked back to the cell and picked up the junk. He wrangled it over his left shoulder. Slowly, he struggled to the captain's office and touched the cornerstone with his right foot. The floor near the office shimmered. Brick by brick, the stone flooring rearranged noiselessly into a descending spiral staircase. He looked around and then marched down the stairs with his package. Green lights illuminated the junkman as he disappeared into the transformed floor. When the illumination vanished, the floor resumed its original shape.

CHAPTER 13

Buy the Truth and Do Not Sell It

"Here we are, dear," Mrs. Hemingway started. "Market at Celos, where we can buy, sell, trade, and barter just about anything in Between." Their horse and cart passed through two large Roman-style columns connected by a metallic banner reading Market at Celos. On each column was a smaller sign with fine print.

"What are the small signs? Rules for the market?" Emmy scoffed.

"That's right. Basic stuff. Do not steal. Do not lie. Do not bear false witness. Do not make false scales. Do not covet. Do not touch livestock unless the owner agrees. Do not feed the livestock. Do not get angry. Do not murder. Do not commit adultery. Do not taste the food unless it is a sample. Do not waste time. Only stop at the vendors you want to buy from. Love and honor the Good. Good is watching. Be kind to others. Be fair and understanding. Be honest and truthful. Honor your mother, father, brother, sister. Enjoy the view. Take a rest. Closed on Sundays."

"You have that memorized? There are a lot of rules."

"Not really, dear. It's about ten. Some are repeats and others more specific rules for the market. It comes from the Book of Good. Almost everyone here has those memorized. No one usually violates them."

"Ah, the good book. What a joke," Emmy muttered. "We have something similar called the Ten Commandments. At our markets, we don't post them anywhere. Not anymore."

"Do you have any problems with stealing or lying or cheating?"

"Of course, we do. Billions of dollars of goods and services are stolen each year."

"You don't say," Granny pondered.

"Do you believe posting those stupid signs deters any those actions?" Emmy scoffed.

Granny explained, "From my experience, we all need reminders of how to act properly with others. Accountability, dear."

Emmy challenged, "People can live how they want. They don't need signs on how to treat others. Their conscience is their guide. Forcing rules on them only breeds rebellion and resentment."

"What if their conscience is wrong? So people in your world live how they want with no rules and no consequences?" Mrs. H asked.

"Yes, they will live how they choose to live. Of course, there are rules and consequences for doing wrong."

"Who determines who is right and wrong? You? Your friends? What are the consequences?"

"I follow my own standards, and I don't let narrow-minded people dictate to me how I live. I am my own judge. The court system, judges and lawyers, politicians, themselves. People are punished with monetary penalties, prison, death, ruined reputation, loss of property, murder, theft," Emmy recalled.

"Your own standards. What happens when your standards are violated? That sounds selfish, unjust, and unfair. Everyone makes up their own rules, and they don't care about the ramifications. Seems like a lot of people are selfishly hurting each other for no reason."

"At least, they are free to make those decisions instead of being imprisoned with obsolete and archaic laws enforced by religious superstition and fanatics," Emmy sneered at her elder.

"Free? You call that freedom? They are imprisoned by their own selfishness. Look around you, Emmy. Do you see anyone imprisoned or rebelling against the archaic laws? We don't have a prison in Between, and commerce thrives here for everyone. Everyone here has a chance to be whatever they want. The last actual murder, not accidental manslaughter, occurred here twenty years ago, and thirty years before that. People treat others with respect and kindness for the most part. People here die of old age and in honor, surrounded by family and friends. Obsolete? We live by these laws every day in peace and harmony. Can you say the same for your world? Believing in Good is not superstition but faith in a person greater and better than mankind. It inspires me not to fanaticism but to love and help my fellow man," Granny gently rebuked.

Emmy remained silent and observed the market. She saw mostly happy people buying and selling their goods, living their lives in peace and freedom. She did not see any police. She really had never seen a society that followed those biblical rules, and it worked successfully. Granny moved the wagon to the parking area. She stopped the wagon in front of a green post. She jumped down and tied off the horse and cart to the post.

"Emmy, please grab the food basket and your second sack," Granny requested.

The visitor climbed down and reached up for the items. "Granny?"

"Yes, dear?"

"I'm sorry if I offended you."

"No offense taken, dear. I know this world is so much different, but the differences can be good if you learn to understand them."

"Yes, ma'am. I will try to keep an open mind."

"Great, dear." Granny gave her a hug. "I will too. Now open the second sack."

Emmy pried the laces apart and looked in. "Are those diamonds, rubies, and emeralds?" she shouted. She shoved her hand in the sack and pulled out a fist-sized diamond. "Are you kidding me?" she yelled with glee.

Most of the market goers turned and stared at her and Granny. Granny hushed her and smiled at the crowd. "It's her birthday." She turned to Emmy. 'This is our currency."

"What? You don't use coins, bills, or gold?"

"We don't use coins of any kind. What are bills? Bill's what?" said the confused elderly woman as she walked Emmy through the market.

"Not a person's name," Emmy explained. "Paper money. In different amounts like ones, fives, tens, twenties, hundreds."

"No." Mrs. Hemingway wriggled her nose. "Why would you use paper to buy and sell? It is too easy to destroy and counterfeit."

Emmy wriggled her nose. "I never thought of that."

"This bag is yours per Tood's instructions, and you have more at the house."

Emmy reached back into the sack and brought forth precious stones of various sizes and weight. "I would be a millionaire back home with just this handful. By the way, my birthday is December 12."

"Good to know, dear. We will have a nice shopping spree today." Mrs. H smiled and examined the stones. "Definitely pay for all the food, a new outfit for you, a trinket or two, a treat for Woof, and battleball tickers. How did that get in there?" She picked out a fist-size pure gold nugget and threw it on the ground.

"That was gold!" Emmy picked it up and examined the shiny element.

"You don't say. It is the most useless stuff on the planet. We use it to fill in potholes on the roads and walkways."

Emmy's mouth hung open, and then she smugly grinned. "So your streets are paved with gold?"

"I just said that, dear. Are you having another moment?" Granny looked concerned.

"No, it's an expression from my world. Never mind." Emmy huffed.

"You will be all right, dear," Granny consoled her. "Put those back in your sack. Even the gold, if you want it. It will become easier as we start shopping. I'll pay for everything. You just pay attention." She giggled at the wordplay.

"You got it, Granny. Maybe one day I will pay you back." Emmy smiled.

"On payday!" Granny snapped back.

"You're on fire, Granny!" Emmy cheered.

"I am. Where? Put it out!" she cried out in fear and looked around for fire.

Emmy doubled over in laughter. "I can't. You are killing me!"

"I am not killing you," Granny sassed. "Now stop that laughing! Help me put out the fire."

The great-great-granddaughter chuckled even harder and fell to the ground in tears as Granny frantically spun in circles.

CHAPTER 14

For Wisdom Is Better than Rubies and All the Things One May Desire

Tood lay the linen junk on the living room couch. It had taken him only a few minutes to transport it from Arms to the Bridge and then from the Bridge to his house.

He sat across from it and inwardly debated whether to open it now or wait for Mrs. Hemingway. He stood and removed the first layer of linens. He carefully unbuckled the three straps. He stood back and took a deep breath. The linens morphed into an obvious shapely female silhouette.

"I should have waited," he mumbled under his breath. "Two visitors at one time. What am I going to do? Woof, come here, please."

The massive canine lumbered into the room, stretching his hind legs.

"I need you to send a message to Mrs. Hemingway."

He turned around and moved back to his spiral rug. He growled.

"Emmy will be with her."

Woof stopped in his tracks and stared at Tood. He barked.

"I'm not teasing you. It is important."

He sat down on his hind legs and tilted his head.

"Please ask Mrs. Hemingway and Emmy to return to the house as soon as possible. Tell them we have another visitor."

Woof sniffed the air and then barked. He bounded out the back door.

"This one is injured and needs help," Tood interpreted. "Thanks."

Tood removed the remaining six layers of linens, especially around the face of the guest. He noticed her bruised cheeks, blackened eyes, swollen lips, pointy ears, and blood streaks in wavy blond hair. A gold chain necklace with an emerald dangled from her neck just like Emmy's. He put his ear to her bloody nose and heard slow rasping sounds. He ran to the kitchen and grabbed his medical kit. He opened it and grabbed a stethoscope. He placed on the earplugs. He breathed on the chest piece before placing it on the elf's upper chest. He listened for a moment. He moved it to the elf's stomach and listened.

He spoke softly to himself. "Lungs sound clear, but she may have a bruised or broken rib." He removed the device and put it back in the bag. He went back to the kitchen and opened the frigger. He moved several items and found a medicine bottle with a clear liquid. He closed the frigger door and moved back to his guest. He opened the bottle. He removed an eyedropper from his medical bag. He suctioned the liquid into the dropper. He gently lifted the elf's head and brought it to her lips.

Tood cautiously poured a few drops into her mouth. When he heard a faint swallow, he released two drops and then emptied it. He refilled the dropper and then emptied it into her mouth again. Three more times he administered the liquid and laid her head back down. He put away his medical bag and returned the medicine to the ice box. He sat across from the visitor and waited.

After several minutes, green eyes fluttered open. Tood had noticed how quickly the medicine had worked to reduce the facial bruising and swelling. She tried to speak, but only whispers came out. He grabbed his bottle of water from his hip. He gently placed his hand under her long neck and maneuvered the bottle to her lips.

She drank slowly and cautiously until some dribbled from the corner of her mouth. She wiggled, and he sat her up and placed a throw pillow behind her back. She tried to speak, but nothing came out. She pointed to him.

Tood started, "My name is Tood. You are in my house. You are safe. You were injured on your journey here. I will take care of you. Bumpy ride?"

The she-elf shook her head.

"You have bruises all over your face and body. You may have a broken rib or two. I gave you a special potion which should help in the healing process."

She acknowledged him and strained her vocal cords. "Thank… you…Tood."

He gave her more water. "You're welcome. What is your name?"

She cleared her throat. "Ser…Sera…"

"Sarah, you have a lovely name. It is nice to—"

The elf shook her head negatively. She cleared her throat again. "I am Sera…vina Re…bus…Diva…dus."

Tood recognized her surnames. He stared into her green eyes. "It is an honor to have the royal princess and first consort to the ninth Elven Dynasty in my humble home."

Seravina nodded and strained, "Thank you for rescuing me. You have good manners. Where is your home? Why am I here?"

"This is the Land of Between. I do not know how or why you are here. I can assure you, I will do all in my power to provide assistance to my Lady Seravina." Tood pledged with his right fist over his heart.

The princess's eyes closed and then barely opened.

"My lady, the medicine I gave you will induce sleep, which you need to recover. I am going to pick you up and carry you to a secure bedroom."

THE DOORS BETWEEN

"Thank...," she whispered and closed her eyes. Soft snores drifted from the princess. Tood paused and stared at her beautiful face. He lifted her up and carefully carried her from the living room to the stairs. She mildly sighed and placed her head against his chest. He climbed the stairs without a sound and placed her in the second bedroom. He pulled back the quilt with one hand. He softly laid her on the mattress. He wiggled a pillow under her luminous hair. He kindly covered the princess with the comforter and tucked her in. He tiptoed to the door and noiselessly closed it.

Sunshine peeked through dark curtains. One shaft of light illuminated the peaceful face of the elf princess. She inhaled the sweet aroma of the clean room but did not open her eyes. She heard a faint bark of a hound. She stretched her long legs and sleek arms under the soft and warm covers. She thought, *What do they call dogs here? Not hounds, wolves, no. I remember now. Woofs.* She smiled remembering her own pet hound. She drifted back to sleep and dreamed:

"Father had told me not to get attached to the hounds, for they were only tools for the Hunt, easily discarded and replaced. He would say, 'Do not name the creatures, Vina.' I tried to obey his commands and not give attention or affection to my hound. I gave him scraps only twice, and he followed me everywhere. I did not name him until after the rescue.

"I had been tracking a black ursa for weeks. This ursa majoris had been harassing local villages near the borders of Ponn. My hound and I had followed his tracks to an abandoned cabin deep in the woods. As I stood in the cabin doorway, the ursa surprised me and smashed me into some rocks. I screamed in anger and pain, for I knew my right leg was broken. The ursa roared at me and surged forward to finish me off.

"My brave, stupid hound stood between me and the beast. He snarled and barked at the monster. The ursa hesitated for a moment and then attacked the hound. The dog dodged every bite and swipe from the massive beast, leading it away from me. The ursa roared in frustration and made a furious combination of slashes. These were too quick for my hound, and he was sent flying into the air. He landed with a thud and a welp. The ursa majoris roared and then charged my friend. I leaped from my position, wielding my great sword. I screamed as I slashed and beheaded the great beast. I collapsed to the ground.

"When I awoke, I was leaning against a cedar tree. A blanket had been placed around me. My rescuer was sleeping at my side. I named him Tiac, after the brave king of Ponn. I tended to his wounds, and I made a brace for my leg with branches from the cedar. Tiac hunted for us and would bring back conies and birds. I built a fire to cook them and keep us warm at night. After three days, I was able to stand. I stumbled to where the mighty ursa lay in a heap. I removed all its claws and retrieved the severed head. It was our conquest.

"I hobbled for two more days until we met a hunting party. Upon our return to the capital city, I made an ursa claw collar for Tiac and a necklace for myself. Tiac remained with me, and we never parted until..."

There came a small knock on the door. "Who is it?" Seravina called quietly.

"It is Tood, my lady."

"One moment." She quickly sat up in her bed and realized she was wearing a peasant's short nightgown under the covers. "This will never do," she said with disgust. "Please, enter."

He slowly opened the door. He was carrying a tray of various foods and bottles.

Tood took one step and stopped. The sun's ray showered upon the princess, casting an ethereal glow upon her face and upper body. Tood cleared his throat. "I heard some mumbling, so I thought you might be awake," Tood explained.

"Thank you for your concern. I have just awakened from my slumber."

"How are you feeling? I have brought you some food and drink." He placed the tray down on a small desk. "Are you hungry, my lady?"

"I am feeling much better. Thanks again for your care and hospitality. I am not hungry currently. How long have I been asleep?" She stretched her arms.

"About fifteen hours."

"I must be off. I am here to find a powerful mage."

"All in good time, my lady. The effects of the potion are still working. In a few hours—"

Seravina protested and tried to stand. "It is a matter of life and death. I must find this man. He is the key to finding my brother." She fell back on the bed.

"I promised you last night, my lady, I would do all I can to help you. What is his name? I will search him out."

"Doorf. All I have is a surname. Have you heard of him?"

"Yes, I have. He is more powerful than many think. This person will be easy to find, my lady."

"Wonderful." She clapped her hands. "When can you bring him to me?"

"Right now, if you like."

"Amazing! Please do."

"Be right back." Tood walked to the door, closed it, and then reentered.

"My name is Tood the Doorf. The only Doorf in the land." He bowed before her.

"Sir, you jest." She laughed out loud. "You jest with me. For you cannot be the Doorf. I was told he was powerful, ancient, and wise. You are young and fair of countenance." She slightly blushed and looked down.

"I assure you, my lady," Tood started. "My knowledge is as deep as the sea. I am stronger and older than I appear. As for my countenance, you can thank my mother and father."

"You are witty and charming. I see you wear a gold ring. Are you betrothed, Lord Tood?"

Tood lifted his right hand. "No, my lady. I haven't had the pleasure. It was a gift from a friend."

"She must hold you in the highest regard," Seravina commented with a smirk.

"I never mentioned who gave me this gift," Tood carefully replied.

"A wise answer, Lord Tood. But do you possess both knowledge and wisdom?" Seravina placed a finger to her chin in thought. "Answer my questions of my world, Lord Doorf, and I shall believe you and follow you to the ends of the earth. Do you accept my terms?"

"Yes. Proceed with your inquiry. It is just Tood, my lady."

She nodded. She scanned the room and discovered a picture of a spider on her nightgown. She knew what she would ask and grinned. "Tood, what are the two ways to destroy the tarachtans? And how do you cure a tarachtan's bite?"

"I have been to the Blasted Lands and encountered these beasts," Tood thought out loud. "Fire frightens them and damages but does not destroy. Water only enrages them. Rocks and crystals also only injure." Tood sat down at the desk chair and closed his eyes.

"Do you wish a hint, Lord Tood?" she teased.

"No, thank you, my lady." He opened his eyes. "The easy way is to decapitate the tarachtans. The clever way is sunlight. For the monsters turn into pillars of salt in the light of day."

"It is never easy to behead this beast," the princess acknowledged. "You are correct, sir. Please proceed."

"For the second, it cannot be answered. You have provided me with a trick question."

Seravina smiled. "Really? Explain."

"It is how the question is worded. First, the tarachtans do not bite their victims. They spit at them. Second, direct skin contact with the creature's saliva turns a body immediately into a tarachtan. Third, the beast has no teeth but rather injects its stinger into the prey and suctions out all the bodily fluids. Lastly, there is no cure for the beast's mucus. Unless you consider death a cure."

"Excellent!" She clapped and then pushed off her covers. "Lord Tood, excellent." She moved herself off the bed and stood before him. "Many charlatans have been vexed by my questions to their demise. You have answered with knowledge and wisdom. I do believe you are the Doorf." She made a fist with her right hand and placed it over her heart. She bowed her head. "I will trust and follow you to the ends of the earth."

Tood placed his fist over his heart. "Thank you, my lady."

Her knees buckled, and Tood graciously caught her. Their eyes locked for an instant. He helped her back to bed and covered her up.

"I think you need more time to recover, princess," Tood cooed.

"I believe you are right again," Seravina whispered and snuggled up with her quilt. She closed her eyes. "You may call me Vina, if you wish."

"Sleep well, Vina."

"Thank you, Tood."

He turned to leave and reached the door. He curiously spotted a balled-up sock in the corner by the window. "By the way, what is your brother's name? I may know him," he called back.

"David," she muttered and yawned. "Rebus…Castillo."

She drifted off to peaceful slumber while Tood stood in disbelief in the doorway and miniscule sweat beads formed on his forehead, upper lip, and ear.

CHAPTER 15

A Man's Heart Plans His Way, but the Lord Directs His Steps

Emmy decided on a new outfit and held two summer dresses in the air. One had purple flowers embroidered on a cream fabric, and the other one was a Caribbean blue fabric with tiny red flowers. They were long dresses all the way to the ankles. *When in Rome*, she thought. The dress shop owner helped her at first but now seemed annoyed. Emmy smiled at her.

"Do you have any a little shorter? Perhaps to the knee?" she asked politely.

"To the knee?" the shop owner questioned. "Why would you be showing off that much leg? To your husband, mayhaps?"

"No, I'm not married, but I can show my legs to anyone I want."

"Oh, I see. I just saw your ring and thought a pretty girl like her must be married or engaged, especially at her age, but you are one of those girls." The shop owner frowned.

THE DOORS BETWEEN

Emmy looked at her ring. "Married? My age? I am not one of those girls. Whatever *those* you are implying."

"No offense, miss. I just mean the new fashion types. Those who like to push the boundaries of clothes and jewelry."

"Oh, I understand." Emmy eyed her dubiously.

"So which one will it be, miss?"

She wrinkled her nose and smiled. "I will take both." She handed over the gems. The shop owner gave a surprised look but accepted the payment. "Would you like it wrapped, miss?"

"Yes, please. Thank you." The shopkeeper was busy wrapping her purchase when she spotted Mrs. Hemingway coming toward, her holding a scroll.

"There you go, miss. Thanks again for your business." The shop owner handed over the package.

"Thank you. Goodbye," Emmy said. She bounced away toward Granny.

"Good buy? What did the Good buy?" the puzzled shopkeeper muttered. "To the knee? Wait until Myrtle hears of it." She snickered. "Though, that was a pretty gold ring. I wonder if Jethro could make me one. Jethro!"

"Hey, Granny, I got two dresses for the price of one. What a deal, right?"

"Pretty good, dear. You see that dress shop over there?" Granny pointed.

"Yes."

"They sell the same dresses, but you could have three dresses for the price of one."

"What? Are you kidding me?" Emmy fumed.

"Don't worry, honey. You will get better. This is your first trip to the Market."

"Thanks. So how did you do, Market master?"

"Exceptional. I bought all the food and a few sweet treats for half price. And these!" Mrs. H waved the scrolls around in circles. She could barely contain her excitement.

"Battleball tickets?"

"Tickers, Emmy. Front-row seats on the centerline! It is going to be so great. You are going to love it!"

"When do we go?"

"This Friday for the match between the two best teams last year: Arms Arsenal and Bankers BC. Arsenal won the championship game by a field goal in the last second. It was an impressive shot, but he was out of bounds. I was there. I saw the whole sequence." Mrs. Hemingway stopped for some air.

"You all right, Granny? You are out of breath."

"I'm fine, dear. Let's walk to the wagon. I am a little tired. I had to run all the way to the Tickermaster."

They walked to the wagon arm in arm. Emmy gratefully smiled to have her first ever outing with a real grandparent. She frowned, remembering the truth about her father. Then she realized Granny had been talking for several minutes, and she had not heard a word. "Really?"

"There are so many ways to score at Battleball. Aces, duces, trey or field goals, sixers or touchdowns, and home runs, which is a combination score, but it is fun to watch."

Emmy tried to figure out the scoring. "Ace is one point. Duce is two points. Trey is three points. Obviously, a touchdown is six points, but what is home run?"

"A home run is nine points. You throw the battleball through the field goal, and a teammate catches it in the endzone."

"Oh, I see." Emmy looked perplexed.

"I have started from the middle instead of the beginning. Sorry."

"I really do want to understand," said Emmy.

"So the field is roughly the size of a professional soccer field, except it has an endzone of twenty yards. Each end has football field goals, with a basketball hoop and net in the middle of the crossbar. Under the crossbar is a soccer net. Scoring can occur anywhere on the field. Got it so far?" Coach Hemingway explained.

"Yes."

"There are six distinct lines on the fields—goal lines, strike zones or schlapp lines, center line, sidelines, batter's box, and in the center, the battle circle.

"What is the schlapp line?" Emmy asked.

"And strike zone," Granny corrected., "It is the penalty line named after Vicente Schlappinski, the most penalized man in the game. It is also the designated line, when crossed by the offense, where they must decide how they will strike or score."

"They must decide?" Emmy asked as they made it to the wagon and secured their purchases.

Granny stooped to the ground and drew a rudimentary battle-ball field. "If the offense advances the ball past the strike zone, then they have four chances to score in various ways. If they line up like football or rugby, they are trying to score a touchdown or home run or field goal. If they line up like basketball or volleyball or soccer, they are trying to get a basket, goal, or spike. They must try to score. Each chance can be a different lineup. If they don't score on the fourth try, the offense turns the ball over to the defense. The defense scores one point for their team. The defense can steal the ball, recover a fumble, and overall stop the offense."

"The pictures help, Granny. Thanks."

She stood upright. "I know I get excited, but I love it so much."

Emmy teased, "You don't say." They climbed into the wagon.

Granny whistled, and the horse meandered from the Market. "It will make more sense when I explain the positions."

"Okay." Emmy rolled her eyes.

"Twelve players on the field for each team. You have six players on offense and six on defense. The play is continuous until an offense reaches the strike line. On offense, the strikers and spiker stay on offense during the whole game. The flashers or forwards and point guards play offense and defense. On defense, the fullbacks and rover play defense and offense. The cornerbacks and batter remain on defense the entire game. The batter has a bat, like a hockey goalie stick, he or she must remain behind the schlapp line. The batter can only use the bat in the batter's box. Unless it is the start of the game or quarter, during the faceoff in the battle circle."

"Clear as mud." Emmy crossed her eyes.

Granny did not notice. "I knew you would get it," Granny encouraged. "Let me tell you about the teams."

They had moved past the entryway. Emmy spotted a familiar canine strolling down the cobblestones. "He really is a beautiful creature, friendly and fierce at the same time, and so cuddly," Emmy pondered silently. She was glad to see him. She waved enthusiastically.

"Dear, what are you doing?" Granny commented and noticed her strange movements.

"I'm waving to Woof. He is walking down the road. He is right there." She pointed.

Mrs. Hemingway looked down the road and squinted. "I don't see anything."

"What? He is like a hundred feet away." She looked again, and Woof had vanished. "Where did he go? I swear he was right there."

"Interesting," Granny surmised. "I believe your eyesight has been upgraded. If he is on the way here, Tood must have sent that rascal to fetch us. Call out to him and see if he comes."

"Woof!" Emmy called out. "Woof! Come here, mighty hunter!"

The giant canine materialized, walking next to the wagon. His tongue was sticking out, his tail wagging. He barked a greeting.

"Wow, that was fast. It is good to see you too, my friend. How did you do that?" responded Emmy.

Granny explained, "He can...what did Tood call it? Tele...telephone. Telemarket...television?"

"Teleportation. Awesome! Woof, jump up here."

Granny interrupted, "No, no, no! He cannot come up here. He is too big, and he can't go in the back. It is full of our food."

Woof growled and barked at Mrs. Hemingway.

Emmy put her hand to her mouth in shock. "That was not nice, Woof!"

"What did he say?" Granny inquired.

"Never going to tell you that." She wagged a finger at the beast. "But he did say Tood needs us back right away. We have another visitor."

Mrs. Hemingway's eyes widened in shock. "Hold on, dear. We have to hurry." She gave a shrill whistle. The horse whined and then bolted forward into a gallop.

"A visitor? You mean another visitor like me?" Emmy asked into a gust of wind.

"Possibly." Granny was concentrating on the road.

Woof howled and easily kept pace with the horse.

Emmy asked Granny, "Elf? What does he mean elf?"

"This is worse than I thought," Granny muttered.

She whistled again, and the horse surged again into a breakneck sprint. Woof was left behind in a cloud of dust.

"See you at the house!" Emmy called back to the coughing savage.

CHAPTER 16

Whoever Digs a Pit Will Fall into It; He Who Rolls a Stone Will Have It Roll Back on Him

Captain Chico had finished his second meal at Pepe's Grill when a skinny messenger arrived. He recognized the courier from the mayor's office. The teenage messenger just stood there with three scrolls in his hands, staring at Chico.

"May I help you, messenger?"

"Yes, sir. I'm sorry, sir. I was told not to rush you if you were eating or drinking," jittered the nervous errand boy.

"Thank you for the courtesy," Chico responded. "What's your name?"

"Kevin…Kevin Roundtree, sir."

Chico grabbed his java, slurped, and then sat back in the chair. "Well, Mr. Roundtree, what do you have for me?"

"I have four urgent messages, sir."

The captain cleared his throat. "From whom?"

Kevin handed over the scrolls, but Chico pointed to the table. The courier placed them on the table. "One is from the *Daily Muck*, one is from the mayor, and one is from Colonel Miller."

"That is three, Kevin. Where is the fourth?"

He quickly reached into his worn messenger bag and pulled out an envelope tied up with a lavender-colored silky ribbon. A slight wildflower aroma wafted from the note. Chico snatched it from his hands, sat back, and reclined on two chair legs.

"Tell me, Kevin. Have you ever read the mail given to you?" Chico eyed him suspiciously and sipped his cup.

"Never. Never, sir. It would be against my oath as a courier," Kevin proclaimed.

Captain Chico stared at him in awkward silence. Kevin stood firm. Chico saw a single sweat drop waxing near his left ear.

"You know, Kevin of Freeside, is it?" the captain started.

Kevin nodded.

"I would hate to have to tell your brother, Pablo, who is in the Legion, about any problems you are having at the postal office. Would I?"

Kevin gulped. "No, sir."

Chico continued, "Or tell that sweet sister of yours, Tiffany. What is she, twenty years old and a baker now, right? She makes some amazing cookies. I would hate to have to tell her about the little fire in the mailroom?"

Kevin's eyes darted, and he whispered, "How did you know about that?"

The Legion leader sat upright in his chair and motioned the mail boy to move in closer. He whispered, "I have my ways." He paused. "If I hear of any of this information"—he pointed to the messages—"from any other source." He pointed to the messenger. "Then Kevin Roundtree of Freeside, you better pray to all that is Good that I don't find you. For when I find you—"

"I understand, sir," Kevin stammered.

"Great, Kevin. Great. We have come to a mutual understanding. Have a wonderful day." The captain tapped the courier twice on the cheek and smiled without a care in the world. The courier turned around and marched dejected from the restaurant.

Chico called to him and threw him a red gem. "Hey. Say hello to your sister for me. Would you? Thanks, bub."

Kevin angrily caught the gem in the air.

Chico picked up the least important note from the *Daily Muck*. He smiled. "They want to interview me about the upcoming season on Wednesday at the stadium." He stuck it in his pants pocket. The mayor's scroll was next. He read, "Captain Jak Chico, please come to my office for an unscheduled meeting with the Pillars of the Community at 6:00 p.m. tonight. Sincerely, Mayor Kokinkus."

"There go my dinner plans," Chico remarked and opened the third message from his commander. He looked at his watch—3:30 p.m.

He read, "Captain Chico, I have granted all your recent promotions. I have some concerns about one. I would like to discuss it in person. I will bring the certificates of rank and appropriate bars for the promoted guards. We can meet in your office at 3:00 p.m. With all honor and duty, Colonel Miller."

Chico grabbed the fourth message and placed it carefully inside the left pocket of his jacket. He dashed from Pepe's and headed to Arms. As he got closer to his office, he observed two of the colonel's personal guards standing alertly at the front door.

"Guard Baron."

"Captain Chico." A female guard saluted and held out her hand to stop him. Chico stopped. "One moment, sir." The other guard went inside to notify his superior. A minute later, he returned and escorted the captain to the closed office door.

"Wait here, sir." The guard turned and exited to the rear door.

When the door clicked shut, the colonel's voice boomed out, "Jak! Please come in."

Chico opened the door reluctantly. He stood before Colonel Miller, sitting at his desk. The colonel wore the uniform well for a balding middle-aged man and still physically fit. He was a friendly and competent leader but gullible. He had multiple commendations pinned on his right chest.

Chico saluted and was surprised to see the colonel's wife, Lady Miller, looking out the small corner window. She turned around and gave him a radiant smile. She was thirty-something and lovely. She had fiery red hair in two long braids connected at their ends. She wore a canary yellow dress with white and pastel green corset-style top trimmed in an elegant white lace.

"Jak." Mrs. Miller walked up to him and gave him a polite hug. Seemingly without detection, she slipped a note into his right jacket pocket. "It has been far too long since we had you at the house for dinner." She stepped back from the captain and stepped over to the colonel. "Do you think we could have him over, Marvin? Him and his fiancé? Please, we will have so much fun."

"I would love it. What do you say, Jak?"

"It's always a great honor. However, I need to coordinate with Jenny first."

"Look at that Marvin. Not even married and so thoughtful of her wishes." Mrs. Miller winked at Chico.

"Starting out right, my boy. Starting out right." He glanced at his wife.

"Thank you, sir. I mean, no offense, sir, but why are both of you here?" Chico asked.

"Well, Jak, when we first learned of your engagement, we were all a bit shocked."

"Shocked to tears," Mrs. Miller corrected. "Tears of joy. For you and your sweet fiancé."

"You know Lady Miller loves weddings and coordinates all the big weddings in Tween."

"Yes. She is the best."

"Thank you, Jak," Mrs. Miller cooed. "Well, I would love to plan your wedding."

"I don't know anything about...," Jak stammered.

"I have already asked Jenny, but she wanted me to ask you. She is too sweet." She walked over to Chico and put her hands on his shoulders and looked into his eyes. Her chocolate eyes blazed with fire, but her voice dripped honey. "Please let me do this last thing for you. Please, Jak?" She slightly rubbed his strong shoulders.

"Sure. Sounds wonderful," Chico announced.

She quickly hugged him and moved to the office door. "Thank you so much. You won't regret it. I will let you know about the dinner party at our house with Jenny. I must be off." She blew a kiss to her husband, waved goodbye to Jak, and closed the office door.

The colonel stood up and moved to the other side of the desk. "She is the best, isn't she?" He smacked Chico on the back. He quickly sat down. "I owe you big-time for that one, Jak."

"No problem, sir." He grinned. "Anytime."

"Now down to business. Sit down, please."

Chico did as he was ordered.

"Now, Jak, here are the certificates of promotion and the bars for the men's uniform." He handed them over to the captain. "I was not at all concerned about the first two. Popson and Chang are fine guards and will be a fine sergeant and corporal, respectively."

"Yes, sir. Those two have put in the time, work, and put up with me for years. They deserve it," Chico proudly announced.

"But the last guard? He has only been with your Legion a short time and he has a bad reputation. However, when I read your glowing review of his training, deeds, and character, it flooded my brain with so many memories of my time as a guard. I nearly teared up. You really have a gift with words." The colonel's voice broke with emotion.

"Thank you, sir," Chico ad-libbed. "The man is all that and so much more."

"Great to hear, Captain. Then I am honored to grant the rank of lieutenant to Tood Doorf."

Chico's eyes widened. He choked up and began coughing intensely.

Colonel Miller said, "Jak, are you okay? Sounds like you swallowed a horse."

Chico hoarsely responded between coughs, "I think it…was a…junk fly."

THE DOORS BETWEEN

The colonel continued, "It has been quite some time since we had a lieutenant in the Legion. I believe you were the last lieutenant. So make sure you brush up on your protocols for the troops. I also order you to do some of your suggestions for the announcement of Lieutenant Doorf. They were wonderful ideas. I especially like marching the legion around town with you and your new ranks in the lead. I could join you."

"Like a parade, sir? It would be an honor."

"Exactly." The colonel beamed with pride.

Chico gasped for air. "May I see the suggestions, sir? Some have slipped my mind."

"I made a copy of it. Here it is. There is only one other idea I order you to do."

"Yes, sir?"

"I want you to personally deliver the certificate and bars to Lieutenant Doorf's home, like you suggested."

"All the way past the ruins? I mean, of course. I will get it done, sir."

"Good man, Captain. The sooner the better." Colonel Miller stood and walked past Chico. "I gratefully return your office to your capable hands." Chico stood at attention. "One last thing. Off record. I am considering retirement. I have been doing this for twenty years, and I have a wonderful young wife who wants a family. I need to be more available for her. So I have recommended you to be the next colonel when the time comes. Don't make any big plans, Jak. You might be running this town sooner than later." He patted Chico on the back. "Let me know the time of the parade. See you tonight at the mayor's office." The colonel closed the door.

Chico slid behind his desk. The chair squeaked. He looked in his bottom drawer, but his favorite hunting knife was not there. He leaned back in his chair and pondered where it could be. No squeak.

He placed his leather boots on his desk. "Well, well, well. I believe I have underestimated the junkman. He seems to be more cunning than his country boy facade. This round goes to you, Tood." He laughed. "So you want some power, Lieutenant Doorf? I will show you the real power in this town."

He put his feet on the floor. *Squeak.* He removed the note from Lady Miller.

He read, "Jak, meet me at our favorite rendezvous. I have a surprise for you. Tonight at ten. Always yours, Red."

He grabbed some wooden matches from his desk drawer and burned the note. It took only seconds for the note to disintegrate into a puff of smoke.

"My evening is looking much better," Chico smugly remarked.

The captain reached into his other jacket pocket and retrieved the ribboned note. He sniffed it, and the wildflower scent sparked wonderful memories of his favorite paramour, Andrea. He gently untied the ribbon and opened the folded paper. He read the message silently. "Oh no. Oh no. Oh. No. This is going to be a big problem." Chico slapped his forehead.

There was a tender knock on the door. He opened the middle drawer and dropped the note and ribbon inside. "Who is it?"

"It's Jenny."

"Please come in." Chico quickly moved from behind the desk.

Jenny opened the door and walked inside. "I was hoping to find my—"

Chico had abruptly ended her sentence with a passionate kiss and embrace.

Jenny placed her arms around his neck and returned the passion.

Ms. Mayor regained her composure and pushed Chico slightly away, although they were still in each other's arms. "Hello, my sweet. That was quite a greeting. A girl could get used to—" Chico kissed her again, but Jenny pulled back. "We need to talk."

Chico kissed down her cheek on to her jawline and right below her right ear. He whispered, "We are talking." He nibbled her ear. "I love talking to you."

Jenny began to swoon, but once again, she gently pushed him away. "About the proposal, engagement, and wedding."

He stopped kissing but held her tight. "I meant everything I said. You and me forever. What do you say, Jenny, we run away right now and elope."

"Are you serious?" She eyed him with suspicion. "You want to elope now?" She pushed him away.

"What did I say? I'm sorry."

"You make this grand spectacle in front of the Good and the whole world, and now you want to run away with me. You think my father was angry about the proposal without speaking to him first. If I tell him now you want to elope, he will have you thrown into the pit." Jenny fumed and paced back and forth.

"Jenny, I'm sorry. I was just kidding." She did not smile. He grabbed her hand. "Really. I want to spend the rest of my life with you. I want to have the best wedding with the most beautiful, kind, and sweet woman in all of Tween. Stupid joke. Sorry. Will you forgive me, please?" He got down on one knee.

She lifted him up and kissed him lightly on the lips. "Of course, I will."

"How can I make it up to you, my love?"

She looked at her watch. "I have to go and get ready for the meeting tonight." She thought for a moment as she scampered to the door. She hushed. "We really do need to talk. Meet me at our secret place tonight at ten. To talk. See you there, fiancé."

Before Jak could respond, she had left him alone in the darkening room.

"Not good, Chico." He pondered the situation. "Not good at all."

He went to the door and opened it. He yelled, "Guard!"

A guard peeked around the corner of the barracks. "Chico? I mean, Captain Chico, sir!" He stood at full attention. "Sorry, sir. I did not know you were back."

"Roundtree, are you on duty?" Chico barked.

"Yes, sir."

"I need you to find Popson and Chang as soon as possible. When you find them, have them report to me here for a special assignment."

"Yes, sir."

"If they protest, just say fat clown."

"Sir?"

"They will know what it means. I'll watch your post until they return."

"Yes, sir. Sir, do you know where they are?"

"Roundtree, I'm going to pretend you didn't ask me that."

"I'm on my way, sir. I will not fail, sir." Roundtree grabbed his Legion jacket and placed it on as he exited the front door.

Chico looked at his watch. It was 4:05 p.m. He went back to his desk. He removed three blank sheets of paper and three envelopes. He folded each paper in half. He wrote Lady Miner on one envelope, Lady Miller on the other, and Lady Mayor on the last. He scribbled the same message in each and signed his pseudonym. He placed each in their own envelope and sealed them with the Arms seal.

He heard the front door open. Roundtree, Popson, and Chang entered his office, breathing heavily.

Roundtree saluted. "I found them, sir, at the Freeside Pub."

"Thank you, Roundtree. Commendations to you. You may return to your duties. One last thing. Get my horse ready for me and leave it by the back door."

"Yes, sir. Thank you, sir." He saluted and left the office. Popson and Chang remained and were a little confused.

"First, I would like to congratulate you both on your recent promotions."

"Promotions?" Chang asked.

"Yes. You are now Corporal Chang." Chico stood and shook their hands. "You are now Sargent Popson."

They both beamed with proud smiles. "Thank you, sir," Popson cried out. "We won't let you down."

Chico sat back down at his desk. "I am counting on that. I have three messages which must be delivered as soon as possible to three persons precisely. I am sending you together to ensure they are delivered properly. Give them directly to the person named. I have an errand to run by the ruins. Meet me at the Vararity Pub at six p.m. to report and celebrate your new ranks." He handed the notes over to Popson.

Sargent Popson asked, "Why are you going to the ruins, sir?"

Chico smiled mischievously. "I have to deliver some junk mail."

Corporal Chang spoke up. "Don't worry, sir. We will take care of it without fail."

"Make sure you do." Chico gave them a threatening glare. "Dismissed."

The newly promoted guards saluted and exited Arms together. Popson handed two of the notes to Chang as they walked down the street.

"The captain told us to deliver these together," Chang protested.

"I am asserting my new authority and learning to delegate my responsibilities."

"You are doing what?" Chang scratched his head.

Popson huffed. "If we divide the work, we will finish quicker and meet back at the Freeside Pub even faster."

Chang said, "What if the captain finds out?"

"How will he find out?" Popson reassured his colleague. "I'm not going to tell him."

"Me neither. I guess I will see you at Freeside in a few minutes, Sergeant."

"See you there, Corporal."

CHAPTER 17

A Gift Given in Secret Pacifies Anger

"Emmy, stay outside when we arrive at the estate," Granny explained. "I don't know exactly what to expect. Woof will be here soon to keep you company. Just call him, and he will come."

"Sure, Granny. Whatever you need. I am here to help with anything," Emmy said and placed her head on Mrs. Hemingway's head.

"Thank you, dear. I'm sorry our time together got cut short. Hopefully, this will not change our battleball plans." She smiled and slowed the horse to a slow walk as they came up to the house. Mrs. H whistled the horse to stop. She pulled the brake and jumped from the cart. "Emmy, please tie up the reins to the post." She darted inside.

Emmy tied off the cart and gave a gentle rub to the sweating horse. "Thanks. You moved fast. You want some water?" The horse neighed softly and slightly flared its nostrils. Emmy found the bucket of water and lifted it up to the horse's mouth.

Ms. Castillo jumped when she noticed Woof sitting on the porch in front of her.

"You have to stop doing that," Emmy faux scolded her canine friend. She lowered the bucket to the ground and walked over to Woof. She sat on the porch and embraced him. He placed his paw around her back. "I am so glad to see you." She rubbed his head, and he licked her face. "So how is our new visitor doing?"

Woof sniffed the air and gave a quiet bark.

"She is sleeping. Tood is coming down to speak to me. She, huh?" Emmy pondered and walked toward the back of the wagon. She reached in and hid an item behind her back. "I have something for you," Emmy teased.

Woof stood to his feet and opened his mouth. His tail wagged furiously.

Emmy revealed the largest animal bone she had ever seen, wrapped in brown paper. She found it at Market near the butcher's shop. "I hope you like it. It's fresh, I think."

The massive canine jumped from the porch and sniffed the entire package. Emmy unwrapped one end and handed it over to her friend. He licked her from chin to forehead. Emmy laughed. He snagged the bone and easily carried it to the side of the house. Satisfying crunching and licking sounds resounded.

"You're welcome, my friend."

Tood had stepped silently to the porch and watched the moment. "You know, he will expect a treat every time you return from the Market."

Emmy grinned. "I have something for you too. Unless you will expect a treat every time I return?"

Tood gave a hearty natural laugh. "You know, I will. But it's not necessary."

"I slapped you hard in the face."

"I can still feel it." He rubbed his jaw and grinned.

She removed two small boxes from the wagon. "Open this one first."

He tore it open like a child at Christmas. "Chocolate fudge! Is this from the Sweet Shop? How did you know?"

"Mrs. H told me it was your favorite. I just wanted to thank you for all you've done for me so far."

"Thank you. This stuff will blow your mind." He opened the box and broke off a piece of the fudge. He popped it in his mouth. He smiled ear to ear. "Here. Try some. It is like nothing you ever tasted."

"No thanks. I've had fudge before. Not a big fan. It's for you."

"Emmy, imagine sweets made with raw unprocessed sugar, milk without any impurities, and cocoa plants that grow as tall as a house." He held out the chocolate. "I insist."

Emmy rolled her eyes. "Fine." He dropped the chocolate into her hands. "I don't know what the big—" She placed it in her mouth. Her eyes closed in complete satisfaction. Her taste buds exploded in confectionary pleasure beyond the finest treat she had ever experienced. She felt like she had been transported to another universe. She opened her eyes, and the sky was brighter, the air sweeter, and she felt like she was flying. She looked down, and her feet were a foot off the ground. She laughed and slowly descended. "Tood, is this normal? That was beyond incredible!"

"Only for those not from here," he said and popped another piece into his mouth. "So good."

Emmy tried to sneak another piece. Tood closed the box and placed it behind his back. "No more for you, rookie." He smiled. "Maybe later."

She bit her bottom lip. "Okay." She gave him the second box. "I hope you like it."

Tood removed the top of the box, and inside, he found an engraved gold ring.

"A ring." He slipped it on his right ring finger. It fit perfectly. "Thanks. I never received a ring before. It is so light and shiny. You know, we only use gold to fill potholes."

"Granny told me. I brought the nugget to the blacksmith, and he looked at me like I had three heads." She remembered, "When I gave him a few gems, he made several rings and even engraved them for me. He had them done in two hours. All our names are engraved."

Tood looked closely and observed the names around the gold jewelry.

"I am wearing mine." She proudly displayed her ring.

"This is so great. Thanks again." He surprised her with a hug and then released her. "No one wears gold in Between." He observed his shiny ring finger.

Emmy asked, "I'm surprised. It is in such abundance here. Gold is so easy to mold and craft."

He pondered, "This may have unknown consequences on our fashion and economy."

"Are you serious? It was one blacksmith. He gave me back the extra gold."

"Have you ever heard of the butterfly effect?"

"One small action can lead to a huge consequence," Emmy replied. "Why?"

"Hypothetically, this blacksmith makes his own gold rings, earrings, necklaces, or bracelets and gives them to his wife or daughter or girlfriend. His wife loves it and wears it around town. Her friends ask what she is wearing. They want some too. She has her husband make all sorts of things made of gold. She sells them to her friends. Her friends share with their family and friends and order more gold things. Then other blacksmiths use the gold to make their own gold things, and so on and so on."

Emmy responded with concern, "And so on? Do you think I just ruined Between?"

He looked at his ring. "No. No, I don't think so." He put his hand in his pocket and breathed deeply. "I'm sorry. I did not mean to spoil your wonderful gift. It is thoughtful and lovely. I really do love it. It's my responsibility to see cause and effect in Between. I am sure this will only be a light summer breeze and not a hurricane."

Emmy frowned. "Hurricane?"

"Don't worry, Emmy. We needed some new fashions here. Trust me, it will be just fine." Tood softly patted her back.

Mrs. Hemingway came out to the porch and sat down at the front step and sighed. "I removed the linens and cleaned her up. It looks like she had been beaten up."

Tood said, "I thought so too."

"I put her in the longest nightgown I could find. That Spiderman one. She has the longest legs. She is sleeping soundly now. She talks in her sleep. She kept moaning *Tiac* but did not wake up."

"Speaking of a hurricane," Tood said under his breath. "Thanks, Mrs. Hemingway."

"You're welcome, dear. She will probably sleep until morning with all the medicine you gave her."

"Did I hear Emmy call you Granny?" asked Tood. "So you two had a good talk and a great shopping trip?"

Emmy came up to her granny and gave her a hug. She sat next to her. "It has been quite enlightening. I do have more questions."

"I knew you would," Tood replied. "I think I will start—"

"No more talk right now," Granny remarked and stood up. "Time to get the groceries in the house and make dinner. After dinner, you two can talk."

"Yes, Granny," Emmy and Tood said together. They moved to the wagon and grabbed the food and items. The trio entered the house as intense crunching sounds echoed from Woof.

The dinner preparations proceeded quickly with three people working and laughing in harmony. Emmy worked on the salad and prepared the fresh massive vegetables. Tood peeled and prepared the potatoes and yams. He boiled them together and then mashed them. Mrs. Hemingway stocked the shelves and then prepared a succulent fish for dinner. It was a largemouth bass the size of a tuna fish. She wanted to show Emmy that Between offered more choices than just pinguinos. She did buy fresh poultry but kept it wrapped and hidden in the frigger. Emmy and Tood set the table with the most elegant China set she had ever seen. The hallway clock chimed five times as they sat down to eat.

"Where is Woof?" Emmy asked.

"He is asleep outside. He ate about half of the bone. He will come in when he is ready," Tood answered.

"He will only come in when I say that rascal can come in." Granny puffed.

"There has to be a story about Mr. Rascal," Emmy inquired.

"There is, dear. But first, Tood, will you say grace?"

Tood and Granny bowed their heads. Emmy lowered her head but kept her eyes open during the prayer.

"Dear Good, we thank you for your Good harvest, for Good friends and family, for giving us the strength to be Good to all people at all times. You are Good. Grant us your wisdom and power for the Good to show Good to our fellow man. In Good's son we pray. Amen."

"Amen," Granny and Emmy repeated reverently.

Granny served the fish while Tood passed the mashed potatoes. Emmy dished out the vegetables and salad. There was a satisfied silence as the hungry trio consumed the delicious meal. Granny gave an entertaining story of how she first met the rascal. Emmy and Tood's sides ached with laughter as she described the encounter with comical details.

Without warning, Woof's menacing bark and echoing growl shattered the joyful meal. A horse screeched a scared whiny. They immediately heard a loud thud of a fallen body. They heard a muffled voice pleading for help.

"Easy doggie. Nice doggie. You are a big one, aren't you? Can someone call off this pretty puppy? Nice puppy, I'm here to see Tood."

Woof pounced at the sound of his friend's name. He pinned down the mystery man in a second and sat upon his chest. He gave a friendly bark toward the house. Woof wagged his tail and whipped the stranger's shocked and breathless face.

CHAPTER 18

Faithful Are the Wounds of a Friend, but the Kisses of an Enemy Are Deceitful

Smack, smack, smack. "Would…" *Smack.* "Would you…" *Smack.* "Get this…" *Smack.* "Blasted…" *Smack.* "——!" *Smack, smack.* "Mongrel…" *Smack.* "Dog…" *Smack.* "Off me!" *Smack!* "This is…" *Smack, smack.* "Captain…Chico!" *Smack.*

Tood called out, "Woof, get off the captain now!"

Woof growled deeply and barked.

"I know he startled you," Emmy soothed. "But you kept us all safe from the trespasser."

Woof released Chico and moved toward Emmy, but not before he gave him one last smack with his tail.

Emmy rubbed his head. "Thank you, my mighty hunter."

THE DOORS BETWEEN

Tood moved quickly to help his captain off the ground. "Captain, what are you doing here? It's five thirty."

Chico dusted himself and spoke. "That is quite a security system. Is his bark worse than his bite?"

Tood answered, "No. I have the bite scars to prove it."

Chico straightened out his jacket and stood tall. "I'm here on official Arms business from Colonel Miller."

Tood said, "Oh." He stood at attention and saluted.

"At ease," Chico commanded. He removed a note from his pocket. "As a valuable member of the Tween Legion, you have shown yourself to be exemplary in word and deed as a guard and citizen of Between. Due to a lengthy and detailed report of your actions and recommendation from your superior officer, Captain Jak Chico, and approved by Colonel Marvin Miller, you, Tood Doorf, have been given a promotion in the Legion."

Tood looked in shock at Captain Chico and then Mrs. Hemingway. "Sir, you must be mistaken. I have only been with the Legion for a few months."

Chico continued despite the protest, "You have been commissioned to be third-in-command of the Tween Legion and designated with the rank lieutenant. Upon acceptance of this commission, you will fulfill all the duties assigned to your new designation, represent with honor the Legion throughout the city and the land, protect Between from all enemies foreign and domestic, and be held accountable for all words and actions to the captain, the colonel, the mayor, the city council, the House of Vote, and the Almighty Good."

Tood stammered, "Lieutenant? Sir, I am honored, but there are so many others more deserving."

Chico asked without faltering, "Do you accept this commission?"

"One moment, sir." Tood walked back to the porch and quietly spoke with Emmy and Granny. "This is unprecedented. No Doorf has ever been awarded a commission in the city. Should I accept it?"

Emmy shrugged her shoulders and raised an eyebrow at the dashing captain. She whispered, "Can he be trusted?"

Tood slightly shook his head in the negative.

Granny said, "It would be a great honor and a greater opportunity to influence Tween for Good."

Tood walked back to Captain Chico. "Sir, I accept this commission."

Chico responded, "Congratulations, Lieutenant Doorf. Welcome to the honored tradition of the Tween officers." They saluted each other and shook their forearms. Chico handed him a scroll. "This is the commission certificate and bars. Who are these lovely folks who will join you in celebration?"

Tood accepted the certificate. "This is Mrs. Hemingway, my adopted mother, caretaker of the estate. This Emmy Zinger, my cousin from the Waydownz," Tood announced. "You have already met Woof, my best friend."

Woof growled, but Emmy rubbed his head to pacify him.

Chico bowed to Woof and Granny but smoothly approached Emmy and reached out his right hand. "It is a pleasure to meet such a beautiful rose among the thorns."

She reached out her hand. The captain received it, turned her hand gently, and tenderly kissed it.

Emmy smirked. "So, Captain Chico, you are an officer, but are you a gentleman?"

Chico covered the kiss with his left hand. "Would you like to find out?" His black eyes sparkled at her, and she blushed.

Woof and Tood looked at each at the same time. The canine growled, and Tood cleared his throat. The captain tenderly released her hand and stepped back.

"Lieutenant Doorf, I have an assignment for you." He walked back to his horse. "You must attend and record the council meeting in my absence at six tonight. I have some urgent Arms business in Vararity. The meeting is at the mayor's house. Don't be late."

"Sir, it is five forty-five."

Chico smiled. "I know." He leaped onto the saddle. "You will also be on duty until ten p.m. I must be off. Until we meet again, Ms. Zinger." He gave her a wink and rode off.

"Well, that was very interesting," Tood said as he moved inside. "I have to get my uniform and helmet. Mrs. H, could you sew these bars on my jacket?"

"Certainly, dear." She rushed inside with the bars.

"Emmy? Hello, Emmy."

Emmy had watched Chico ride away and lingered in a daydream. She mumbled, "Huh? Yes, he was very interesting."

"What did you say?"

"I mean it was interesting meeting your captain." Emmy followed him inside. "Congratulations, by the way, Lieutenant Doorf. So what is he really like?"

"Thanks. Chico? He is likable, intelligent, charming, and trouble."

"Mama likes trouble." Emmy hoped she had not spoken that out loud. "What do you mean trouble?"

Tood dressed quickly and looked at his watch. "Granny, I need the jacket. Let me just say he breaks a lot of hearts and bank accounts."

Granny ran into the foyer with the Legion jacket ready to go.

"Thank you." He slipped on the jacket and headed to the door. "Come with me, Emmy, please." He grabbed his helmet and put it on.

Emmy followed him and walked toward the Ruins. She claimed, "Maybe he just hasn't met the right girl."

Tood looked at his watch as they marched up the hill. "That's the problem, Emmy. He has met tons of women. He views women as challenges or prizes to be won or a land to be conquered. He has no respect for the whole person. He only wants what he can't have. He cares only about himself. He will not care for you, only how he can use you."

"Wow, Tood! That was harsh and judgmental." Emmy scowled. "Doesn't your good book say, 'Judge not lest you be judged.' Who made you the judge? How do you know what he cares for and who he is?"

"That verse refers to having a righteous objective standard by which to judge behavior, not a hypocritical and subjective standard. We make judgments every day based on all sorts of personal criteria.

I am not his judge, but Good's Book is. 'A bad tree does not produce good fruit and a good tree does not bear bad fruit.' Just like a person's actions show the kind of person inside."

"People can't change? They will always be rotten trees?"

"Not unless you have the Good Gardener change you from the inside. He can make anyone into a new good tree."

"Tood, how can you—"

"Emmy, you must trust me. I have a lot of experience with him. Chico is a liar, thief, bully, two-faced, and a world-class manipulator. He is not the person you want as a friend. If you don't believe me, watch the tape."

"The tape?" Emmy questioned.

He called to Mrs. H, "Get her the Chico tape." Granny went inside.

"Emmy, you can make your own judgment about him. Watch the tape or not. You can see who you want. As your friend, I can only warn you. Chico is not a good person. He will hurt you and everyone you love."

"Tood, you make him sound like a mobster."

"Like Al Capone, Sam Giancana, John Gotti?" Tood pondered. "Those guys could learn a thing or two from Jak Chico."

"How do you know...he just seemed..." Emmy stammered.

"Emmy, I have to go. I'll be back in a few hours. Please be patient with me. Granny can answer any immediate questions. The Good be with you." Tood vanished right before her eyes.

"The Good bless you," Emmy grumbled and stomped back to the house.

CHAPTER 19

A Wicked Messenger Falls into Trouble, but a Faithful Ambassador Brings Health

Tood arrived at the mayor's house precisely at 6:00 p.m. A female guard stood at the bottom of the stairs. She saluted him, and Tood gave a quick salute back. Tood was unimpeded until he reached the ornate wooden front door. He rang the doorbell. A lanky well-dressed butler answered the door.

"Yes, sir. How may I help you, Lieutenant, is it?" The butler stood in the doorway.

"I am here for the council meeting. I am Captain Chico's representative. My name is—"

"Well, sir, the meeting has already started, sir." He removed his pocket watch. "You are late precisely one minute and thirty seconds. I cannot allow you entrance. It is against protocol, sir." He started to close the door, but Tood stopped it with his left boot.

"Please, would you inform the mayor that Tood Doorf is here for Captain Chico?"

"Sir, are you not the current junkman who lives by the Ruins?"

"I am," Tood proudly answered.

"If you let go of my door, sir, I shall see what I can do."

Tood released the door. The butler slammed the door shut, locked it, and shut off the lights.

"He is not coming back." He looked around the area. He heard a soft chuckle come from the bottom of the stairs.

He barked at the soldier on duty, "Guard."

"Yes, sir, Lieutenant Doorf." The chuckling stopped, and she stood at attention.

"What's your name?" Tood descended and stood before the nervous legionary.

"Baron, sir."

"When did the last council member arrive and enter?"

Baron removed her pocket watch. "Five fifty-four p.m., sir."

"Has there been anyone else that came to the door before me at six p.m.?"

"No one and nothing at all, sir."

"Anyone been in or out of that alley?"

"No, sir."

"Thank you, Baron. You have been very helpful. Good night." Tood walked away toward the empty alleyway.

"Good night, sir. Sir, aren't you going to the meeting?" Baron asked.

"I will be, in just a minute or two."

Tood smiled and strolled down the dark alley, adjusting his watch. His watch glimmered when he pressed the left button. He set the time back to 5:56 p.m. He erased the previous timeline as he pressed the right knob.

He strolled back down the isolated street to the mayor's office, whistling a blues tune. The guard saluted as he walked past. Tood stopped and saluted.

"Guard Baron, right?" Tood asked.

"Yes, sir, Lieutenant."

"I've heard good things about you. Keep up the good work."

"Thank you, sir. Yes, sir."

Tood climbed the stairs and rang the doorbell.

The same lanky butler answered the door. "Yes, sir. How may I help you, Lieutenant, is it?"

"I am Lieutenant Tood Doorf, and I am here for the council meeting at six p.m. I represent Captain Chico."

"Well, sir." He examined his pocket watch. "You arrived precisely at 5:58 p.m." He scratched his head. "Well, that is odd, Lieutenant. Please come in. I will show you the way to the meeting."

Tood entered and followed him down an ornate hallway. "What is odd?"

"Well, sir, I could have sworn the time was 6:01 p.m. Must be that déjà vu."

"Don't worry. I get those all the time. May I ask your name, sir?" Tood asked.

"Sir, it is Reginald Longbottom." He stopped in front of glass French doors.

Tood reached out his hand. "It is nice to meet you, Mr. Longbottom. Thank you for bringing me to the meeting."

The butler shook Tood's hand with vigor. "Sir, you are the first council member to ask my name in ten years. You can call me Reggie. You are the current junkman, sir?"

"Yes, Reggie, I am."

"Well, the Good be with you, sir. Have a pleasant meeting. Just a moment, sir. I have to announce you to the group." Reggie opened the left side of the French door and spoke up. "Mr. Mayor, Ms. Mayor, Colonel Miller, Ms. Miner, and Lord and Lady Banker, I present to you Lieutenant Tood Doorf of the Tween Legion representing Arms and Captain Jak Chico."

As Tood entered the well-furnished study and meeting room, the shock and horror on the regally dressed lady's face slapped him in the face. The mayor and banker frowned into their wineglasses. The colonel smiled and happily approached him.

"Lieutenant Doorf, I am so glad to meet you. I was not expecting you so soon."

"I am sorry for any intrusion. I was only just recently informed of this meeting," Tood apologized.

"That will be all, Reginald, until dinner," Mayor Kokinkus announced, and Reggie left the room. "Welcome, Lieutenant Doorf, to my home and office. I also was not expecting you. I was expecting my future son-in-law. Do you know where he is?"

"Sir, I was told he had urgent Arms business in Vararity."

"Father, please lighten up. This is not an inquiry," Ms. Kokinkus announced. "The Good be with you, Lieutenant."

"The Good bless you, Ms. Mayor. Congratulations on your engagement."

"Thank you, Lieutenant. At least someone here is happy for me. I know it was untraditional." Ms. Mayor sighed. "But it was spectacular, wasn't it?"

Tood did not hesitate. "It was historical, Ms. Mayor."

"It was. You can call me Jenny." She shook his hand. "Welcome."

Ms. Miner's gray eyes curiously studied him. She teased her dirty blond hair and gave a silent friendly wave. Tood waved back.

Lord Banker spoke to him next. "You have good manners for the junkman. I was half expecting you to haul some of your junk in here." He laughed and sipped his wine. "Have you found anything profound lately?"

Tood knew how to handle the condescension. "As a matter of fact, Lord Banker, I have. I left it in the hallway. Would you like to see it?" Tood walked to the French doors, opened them, and then stopped. All eyes were glued on him. He reached into his jacket pocket and looked over his shoulder. "It is…an elf!" He suddenly materialized a rare lovely purple elf lily only found near the Wamp.

Mr. Banker jumped and spilled his drink on his clothes while the other guests laughed at the joke. Lady Banker approached him giggling and took the flower. "Do you do card tricks too?" She inhaled the fragrant lily. "Lovely."

"Only during a blue moon."

"You are funny. I like you. Welcome to our unofficial meeting or dinner party, whichever you prefer." Mrs. Banker gently grazed his right shoulder with her right hand and then held out her left gloved hand. Tood took her hand and kissed it. "And a gentleman too. You can call me anytime," she whispered, laughed, and sauntered away.

"Lieutenant," the colonel called him over to the bar. "What is your drink of choice, my lad?"

"Ale, sir." Tood walked toward his commander. He whispered, "Sir, I thought this was a business meeting."

The colonel handed him a mug of ale. "It is a little bit. We talk a little business. We socialize. We relax, drink, eat a hearty meal, and devour some desert. The best pie in the land. If Banker is not too upset, then we play a game or two."

Tood approached the banker. "I am sorry about that, sir."

"No problem, Lieutenant. All in good fun," the banker replied and shook his hand. "I deserved it, really."

"You are a good sport, sir."

Tood sipped his ale as the mayor approached him again. "So, Lieutenant, what did you think of the festivities the other day?"

"I enjoyed it for only a little while. Unfortunately, I was only able to attend during your opening and Captain Chico's speech. I received an urgent message from my caretaker about a problem at the house."

"I hope nothing serious," Jenny inquired.

"Nothing I couldn't handle. Just an issue with a wagon."

"Were you able to see the activated fountain? It is lovely. I love the pulsing light at night," Ms. Miner spoke.

"Yes. It is beautiful. Is it still running?" Tood asked with concern.

"Yes, I think so. Is that a problem?"

"Yes, of course. Especially if you are trying to catch it."

The pillars of the community gave a snobby laugh at the pun.

Ms. Miner grinned. "A witty play on words, sir. He will fit right in. Don't you think so, Mr. Mayor?"

Mr. Mayor had been speaking to the colonel. "Yes, I believe he has exceeded expectations. Lieutenant, how is your new team looking? Will they be ready for the season opener?"

"Yes, sir. The Undivided has been practicing—"

"What about this business? This bad blood between you, Ronk, and the Freesiders?" the banker asked.

"It is just a misunderstanding, and I never—"

Mrs. Banker interjected, "Battleball, battleball. That's all we talk about lately."

Ms. Miner asked, "Could we please discuss anything else besides battleball?"

Jenny jumped in. "We heard it on the radio. You called him overrated, and his sister claimed you were a bad kisser. He threatened to personally destroy you."

Tood explained, "Actually, I told his sister that Ronk was a great player, but the Freeside squad was…"

Lady Banker suddenly became interested. "Really? Bad blood over his sister? Is it true, Lieutenant?"

"As I was trying to explain the situation—"

Mrs. Banker said, "Is it true? Are you a bad kisser, Mr. Doorf?" She smirked and puckered her perfect glistening lips.

Tood's eyes twinkled. "I have never had any complaints before."

Lady Banker and Jenny giggled.

Ms. Miner cleared her throat and commented, "Life is much more than sports."

"I agree," the visitor explained. "Life is about living a good and honorable life with those you love with the time Good has granted. However, our whole community and economy depends on battleball and the revenue and taxes it generates."

Mayor asked, "Son, can your team win?"

Tood did not hesitate. "Mayor, we will be ready to kick some schalpinski."

"Hear! Hear!" the colonel, the banker, and the mayor cheered.

Reggie entered the study. "Ladies and gentlemen, dinner is served. Please retire to the dining room."

The entire group eagerly moved to the dining room, passing the butler. Tood entered last.

Tood whispered, "Hey, Reggie."

"Hello again, Lieutenant. Sir, I hear you are swimming quite well with the piranha."

"I am wearing a suit of armor." Tood grinned.

"Be careful, sir, you don't drown," Reggie replied and walked Tood to the dinner table with his ale. "The current is stronger in here."

The mayor was at the head of the table, and the colonel was at the other end. Mr. Banker sat next to his wife, and Ms. Miner and Jenny sat across from them. The colonel waved Tood over to his side.

"Join me over here, Lieutenant Doorf. My wife could not join us tonight," the colonel explained. "She was not feeling well. She has been eating salted crackers for days."

"I hope she gets well soon," Tood replied. "Does Lord Miner attend the dinner parties?" Todd asked as he sat down with the others.

"My father does not get out much," Lady Miner replied. "He is still sharp as a whip mentally at ninety-five, but his body has been failing. He has placed me in charge of all operations. My brothers don't like it. I've worked those mines just like them. They respect his decision for now."

"I am sorry to hear about his health," Tood consoled. "I would love to meet him. Didn't he discover the tiger eye vein? His discovery changed how we evaluate all the gems."

"That's right. I did not know you had such knowledge of the miners. I'm impressed, Lieutenant." She smiled.

"I know it all too well, Lieutenant," Lord Banker interjected. "For it also changed the banking system."

"Honey, please, don't talk about the banking system. Blah, blah, blah," Lady Banker interrupted. "Let's talk about something fascinating. Lieutenant Doorf, did you hear about the dragon in the streets of Tween?"

Tood swallowed his drink too quickly and began to cough and hoarsely replied, "No."

"It is true, according to the people. It has become quite a mystery," Mrs. Banker continued. "The servants were talking about it all day. Several villagers witnessed it on the night of the celebration. A fantastic metallic beast roaming the streets with glowing yellow eyes and fire breathing out of its mouth. Screams of devoured victims echoed from the creature's belly. Flames blasted with each step as it galloped down the cobblestones of Tween. One man asleep in an apple cart actually saw this beast leap into the air and vanish without a trace."

"What? That is preposterous! No such creature exists, and this did not happen. The man had too much of Granny's Hooch," the mayor protested.

"Rumor has it, when the City Sphere Fountain was activated, it conjured the dragon here to destroy us and our land," Mrs. Banker added.

"I saw a dragon once in the Firrest," the colonel announced. All eyes turned to him. "I was visiting Cutoff University as a lad, and I saw it…saw it right there." He pointed to the wall. "Right there, just staring at me. I was frozen. I had never seen anything so frightful in all my life. So I did what any young man would do in the face of death and danger."

"What did you do?" Jenny begged.

"I did my duty. I turned…the page. This book had the scariest picture of a dragon I had ever seen." He gave a hearty laugh.

The civic leaders relaxed and laughed at the tall tale.

The colonel bragged, "I had you going, didn't I, Jenny? And you too, Lieutenant."

"Yes, sir. You were spinning quite a yarn. I do believe the mayor is right though. Fire-breathing dragons? Someone made this up. Probably to make sure their children don't go out after dark," Tood replied.

"But, Mr. Doorf," Mrs. Banker slyly said. "All the fun happens after dark." Underneath the table, she rubbed her foot against his right leg.

Tood grinned and announced, "You may all call me Tood, if you wish."

Reggie and the staff brought in the first course of potato soap and set it before the guests.

Jenny asked, "Is that a family name? I've never heard it before." She sipped her soup.

"It is a family nickname of my full name." Tood sipped the broth. "My parents were a bit eccentric when it came to their children. I had a hard time pronouncing certain words as a child. It is quite unique. My brother, on the other hand…"

Lady Banker clapped her hands and inquired, "Tood, may we try to guess it? Your full name? It would be great fun."

"During the soup?" The mayor sounded annoyed. "Let's wait until after dinner."

"Dad, please?" Jenny looked into her father's eyes.

"Very well. Shall we play this game, Lieutenant?"

Tood thought for a moment. "Yes, but some guidelines first. Each of you may have only two guesses for the rest of the evening. If one of you can cipher it, I will have you all at my house for a wonderful feast and ball. If you cannot figure it out by the end of the evening, then each of you must have me as a dinner guest in your home. Do you agree to the terms?" He finished his soup while he waited for a reply.

The pillars looked at each other. No one had ever challenged them with such a game and a wager. They were taken aback by his forwardness and friendliness. They were also curious to know more about this mystery man.

"I'm game," Jenny replied.

"Me too," Ms. Miner and Mrs. Banker said together.

"Fine," the mayor resigned.

Lord Banker said, "This is a fine game. I'm in."

"I want the feast." Colonel laughed. "This will be a challenge."

Todd answered, "Great! Let the name game begin. I will give you one clue. It is the name of a great king of an ancient river."

The rest of the group finished their soup in silent contemplation. Jenny opened her mouth once with an idea and then quickly closed it. The butler and staff entered and removed the soup bowls and replaced them with luscious green salads. Reggie quietly approached Mayor Kokinkus and whispered in his ear.

"Yes, I will ask him. Lieutenant, Reginald and the staff would like to know if they can join the game?"

"Sure," Tood replied. "The more the merrier. If the staff can get it before the guests, then I will bring only them to my house for the feast."

The civic pillars' mouths dropped, but they made no verbal protest. They did not like the competition but accepted it.

Reggie clapped and gushed, "Thank you, sir. Temecula was always an interesting name."

The guests and staff all gasped again at the first attempt coming from the butler.

Tood laughed. "Nice guess, Reggie, but it is not Temecula."

Mr. Banker wondered, "Wait. How will we know if we have the real name?"

"Reggie, may I have two papers and a pen?" Tood requested. "I will write the name down on the paper. I will put the paper inside my boot. If someone gauges correctly, I will pull out the paper and match it with their guess. If all the opinions are used up, I may reveal my name or not," he teased the crowd.

The butler returned with the papers and pen. Tood stealthily wrote the name down, folded the note several times, and stuffed it deep inside his right boot. "On the other paper, I will write everyone's name and then record their ideas." On the top of the paper, he titled it Name Game and proceeded to write the guest's names on the left side.

"Reginald, how many staff members are present?" the mayor asked.

"Nine, sir, including me," the butler replied.

The banker interjected, "Lieutenant, that would give them eighteen guesses. While the leaders would have only twelve. I suggest my colleagues and I get an additional guess in all equity."

"Eighteen for each group and thirty-six total? Sounds fair," Tood asked. "Does everyone agree?"

Everyone agreed.

Tood wrote down Reggie's guess and then handed the paper to him. "Would you mind collecting the staff's names for me?"

"Certainly, sir." He happily took the paper and went to the kitchen.

"Unprecedented, Lieutenant," the mayor protested. "Including the staff in the game."

"I apologize, Your Honor, if I have offended you," Tood replied.

"Father," Jenny soothed. "It may have been a little unorthodox. But our staff deserve a chance for a little fun and possible reward."

"I believe your father likes to win," the colonel announced, "and has been calculating that the odds are against us."

Lady Banker spoke up. "How? We have the same amount of tries."

"They have nine minds working on the solution," the mayor explained. "And the staff has been working together for years as a cohesive unit. When was the last time we agreed on anything?"

The pillars of the community frowned at the facts facing them. They picked at their salads in quiet despair. The staff returned and removed the salad plates and simultaneously served the mini loaves of bread.

When the kitchen door closed, Ms. Miner whispered to her friends, "We can do it. We are smart and capable. We can work together as a team."

"This bread is amazing," Tood commented. "It actually melts in your mouth."

"I know, it is delicious," Lord Banker commented. "If we think together and forget our petty squabbles, we cannot be beat."

"Yum, so moist. How do they do it?" the lieutenant asked.

Jenny replied, "They use fresh cream and butter. I have several volumes upstairs of ancient history and books of names. Should I go fetch them?"

"Yes," the mayor called, "before the staff gets up there."

"Come with me," Jenny asked Ms. Miner. They hiked up their skirts and ran from the room.

Reginald returned with the completed list and saw their hasty departure.

"Is everything all right, sir?" He handed the list to Tood.

"Thanks. They are fine. They ran upstairs to get some books. May I please get more bread? It is amazing."

"Oh, are they, sir?" Reggie grinned. "Certainly, sir. The main course will be out in two minutes." The butler returned to the kitchen. A male servant returned with the bread.

Jenny and Ms. Miner returned with two large volumes under each arm. The colonel and Mr. Banker helped with the books and set them in the corner.

"I could not find the books of names," Jenny whispered. "I think the staff has them."

"I think what you all are doing is wise," Tood commented as he bit into the bread. "Compile the best eighteen ideas before you present them. Do you think I could get the recipe for this bread? My caretaker, Mrs. Hemingway, would love it."

All but one of the city leaders huddled around in conference. Lady Banker smiled at Tood and walked over to him. "You're enjoying this, aren't you?"

"Of course." Tood smirked as he drank his ale. "This has been a great meal, and we haven't even had the main course."

"You are a tricky one, Lieutenant." Mrs. Banker sat next to him and sensuously removed her gloves while gazing into his eyes. "Here you sit, speaking of rolls and dinner, while we fuss about your name. But, Mr. Doorf, can you handle the best part of any meal?"

The junkman gulped. "And what is that, Mrs. Banker?"

She put her hand on his left knee and squeezed. "Why, Lieutenant, I thought you would know. It's dessert." She leaned in and placed her supple lips next to his ear. "If you tell me..." She nibbled his earlobe. "Your name...I will give you...endless desserts... and delights." She softly breathed into his ear and moved away from his face. The temptress locked eyes with her next victim.

Tood cleared his throat and gave a slight grin. He carefully moved closer to her far ear. He soothed, "I would be in denial...if I didn't say your delightful voice and sweet offer...wouldn't haunt me to the tomb." He paused and grabbed her hand reaching into his boot. "My name...will *not* be given to you." He released her hand.

THE DOORS BETWEEN

She backed away in surprise and whispered, "Who are you?"

Tood whispered back, "I'm the junkman, baby." He sat back and whistled a blues tune.

Mrs. Banker abruptly stood up, swiped up her gloves, and stormed back to her colleagues.

Jenny asked, "What did he say? Did he say anything?"

Lady Banker angrily placed her gloves back on. "No. He would not give me the name."

Reginald and the staff entered. "Ladies and gentlemen, the main course is served."

The community leaders returned to their seats for the main course of beef tips and steamed garden vegetables. The meal was delicious, but there was little to no conversation between the guests and staff. The tension in the room was like the seconds before the start of a playoff game, the moment right before an orchestra plays its first note, and the beat of an anxious heart before the first kiss.

Tood thoroughly enjoyed the dessert of apple pie à la mode. He and the colonel were the only ones to finish it while the others only picked at the house favorite.

When the dessert plates were removed, Mayor announced, "Reginald, we will retire to the library for the coffee and cocktails."

The butler responded, "Yes, sir. Will the lieutenant be joining you?"

The pillars looked at Tood. He shrugged his shoulders.

"Sir, perhaps the lieutenant would be more comfortable in the billiard room during the game."

"Reginald, that is a fine neutral location for our guest during the battle of the name," Jenny commented.

"Battle of the Name. I like it," Tood said. "I guess you will come to me to make your guess. Lead on, my good man." Tood followed the butler to the billiard room.

Reggie opened the twin doors to the brightly lit area with a large billiard table in the center, a dartboard in the corner, two lounging couches, and several small tables with burnished lamps.

"I hope you will be comfortable, sir. Would you like anything while you wait, sir?"

"Would you bring some more bread, water, and coffee? Please. Good luck to you and the staff."

"I will have those items brought right away, sir. Thank you, sir, for this opportunity." Reggie bowed, left the room, and closed the doors.

Tood locked the doors and reached deep into his Legion pocket. He walked to the opposite wall and pulled out a walkie-talkie.

"Mama Bear, come in, Mama Bear. This is Papa Bear. Over." Static echoed from the device. He repeated it. Still no response. He was about to repeat it when a sweet voice replied.

"Roger, Papa Bear." The voice paused. "This is Baby Bear. Over."

Tood replied, "Baby Bear? Over."

"This is your pal from the west. Over."

It was Emmy, thought Tood. "Roger that, Baby Bear. Where is Mama Bear? Over."

"Mama Bear is taking care of Goldilocks. Over."

"Roger. How are you? Over."

"Watching a movie with the Big Bad Wolf. Having some fun with this walkie-talkie, Papa Bear. Over."

"Roger that." He laughed. "I might be home a little later. Over."

"Roger. Any problems, Papa Bear? Over."

"Just an unexpected fancy dinner party, Baby Bear. Over."

"Roger that. They have some good porridge? Over."

"Roger. Yes, great porridge, but no broken chairs yet. Over."

Emmy giggled over the walkie. "Roger that, Papa Bear."

"Sorry about how I left, Baby Bear. Over."

"Roger. I watched the tape. It was enlightening. Over."

"Roger. Did you see what I meant? Over."

"Roger, roger. Thanks. Over."

"Baby Bear, try to get some sleep. Over."

"Thanks, Papa Bear. Sleep sounds good. I will let Mama Bear know about the time. Over."

"Roger. Baby Bear, I'm glad you're here. Over."

"Roger. I'm glad you are my friend. Over and out."

Tood turned off the walkie and put it back in his jacket. He looked at his watch. It was 7:45 p.m. There came a light knock on the door.

"Lieutenant," a female voice called. He went to the door, unlocked it, and opened it.

Ms. Miner held a tray of snacks, water, and coffee. "I heard voices. I thought the staff were getting the upper hand." She gave him a winning smile.

"Just talking to myself out loud. Helps me think. Please come in."

"Thank you." Ms. Miner entered and placed the tray down on the nearest table. She dusted off her hands. "I was elected to give our first guess."

"Thanks for bringing those. Let me get the paper." Tood went to the pool table.

"I have something to tell you first, Lieu…Tood."

"Yes?"

"I have been intrigued by you. You know so much about Between and all of us, but we know almost nothing about you. We know you are the head of the ancient family Doorf. I can tell you are well-educated and smart. You seem humble and simple, while at the same time you navigate a dinner party like a seasoned ambassador. Yet the Doorfs have been junkers for a long time and had no part in civil society."

Tood explained, "We have been a part, just on the outside looking in. I believe it is time for all Between to work together."

She took a deep breath. "Well said, sir. Whether we win or lose, I…" She paused. "I would like to get to know you better." She blushed. "My name is Andrea Miner Elfstone." She gave a small curtsy.

Tood smiled and bowed. "It is nice to meet you, Andrea Miner Elfstone. Why did you curtsy?"

"I don't know." She laughed and tried to exit.

"Andrea, aren't you forgetting something?"

She thought for a moment. "The guess. It will make you laugh."

"Give it a try."

"Toodles."

He did laugh out loud, and she giggled. "No, no, it is not Toodles."

"I didn't think so. I must be going. The others will worry if I'm too long."

"Andrea, how about java juice at Pepe's on Friday, nine a.m.?" Tood asked.

"Sounds like a date." She exited and closed the door.

"It sure does." Tood grabbed a cookie, tossed it in the air, and caught it in his mouth. "Hilarious. Toodles." He wrote it down.

For the next hour and a half, each team would bring their unsuccessful guesses to Tood. It was 9:30 p.m., and both groups had only one guess left. They were getting desperate and discouraged. Tood asked the staff and the guests to meet in the billiards room for the final guess. Reginald and the staff were in one corner, while the community leaders were by the dartboard. Tood gave them five minutes to give their final suggestion.

"We have nothing left," the colonel whispered in despair. "Did he give any clues we may have missed?"

Mr. Banker asked his wife, "What did he say to you when you were whispering together?"

Mrs. Banker stammered, "I-I-I…nothing of consequence. He just said no."

No one believed her.

Ms. Miner and Jenny said simultaneously, "Out with it."

Mrs. Banker closed her eyes and tried to remember. "He said, 'I would be in denial…if I did not say your sweet voice and delightful offer—"

"Offer?" Mr. Banker questioned.

"Go on," the mayor begged.

Mrs. Banker finished, "'Wouldn't haunt me to the tomb. But you will not get the name.' It was a lovely poetic rejection." The staff eavesdropped on the whole conversation.

"Denial?" Jenny pondered. "Denial. I have read it before." She ran to the study and, in a flash, came back with a worn history book.

She flipped several pages and then stopped on a map of Egypt. She yelled. "I found the ancient river."

The guests hushed her and crowded around the book. The staff were also talking it over.

Tood announced, "Two minutes."

The colonel whispered, "The Nile River?"

Jenny hushed. "He is so clever. Not denial, Da Nile, the Nile, the Nile!"

Mrs. Banker was confused. "Why do you keep repeating the same word?

Jenny explained, "Denial is *the* Nile. The great king is from the Nile River, Egypt."

"He also mentioned *tomb* and *haunt*," the mayor thought.

"Was there an Egyptian king who had a haunted tomb?" asked the colonel.

Jenny replied and opened the history book, "Not haunted but cursed." She displayed a page full of pictures of famous Egyptian golden crypts. "There! That is his name."

"To…tank…ham…on," the mayor read. "Jenny, are you sure? We only have one guess."

"One minute," the junkman called.

Jenny corrected the pronunciation in hushed tones. "Tu…tan…kham…un. He was also known as King Tut. I believe this is Tood's name. Look at this." She closed the book and went to the back cover. She showed them a faded sticker and read, "Donated by the Doorf Estate. His family had this old book and probably knew of this person."

Mrs. Banker softly objected, "Jenny, this king's nickname is Tut, not Tood."

Jenny closed her eyes. "Tood said he had problems pronouncing words as a child."

Ms. Miner wrote the name down. "We trust you, Jenny. Turn it in."

Jenny proudly walked to Tood and handed over their guess. A servant girl walked up and handed in the staff's guess. Tood read both notes and stuffed them in his pocket.

The lieutenant asked, "Reggie, how did you come up with your final guess?"

"Well, sir, to be honest, we were plum out of ideas. Then Lady Banker said something about delights, graves, and haunting," Reggie explained.

Mr. Banker whispered to the colonel, "I knew she was too loud."

The butler continued, "So I thought what story gave me great delight as a child but also had graves and haunting? So I remembered my mum telling me a story. It was about a boy king who always wanted to play with his golden toys. So he buried himself with all his golden trinkets in a tomb. The boy would never be able to play with his gold things because the gold was cursed. I finally recalled the boy king's name."

"Thanks, Reggie. The moral of the story: don't play with golden toys."

Everyone laughed.

"Jenny, would you like to explain your guess?"

"No, thank you," Ms. Mayor nervously replied. "Please tell us who is correct."

"Of course. I am proud of all for your hard work and fun we had tonight." He reached down into his boot, removed the note, and placed it on the billiards table. He placed their notes next to it. "I must confess, I did not think anyone would generate the correct answer. Reggie and staff, I am sorry—"

"Yes! I knew we—" the colonel prematurely cheered.

Tood continued, "Sorry you were at a disadvantage. I gave some clues to Mrs. Banker and not to you. However, your guess was correct." The staff cheered.

"The wonderful pillars of our community, it was great to see you all working together for a common goal. Ms. Mayor, your team was right to trust you. You also were correct." The leaders cheered.

"The staff guessed King Tut, and the leaders guessed Tutankhamun. I wrote down Tutankhamun or King Tut. See for yourselves." Tood walked away from the table and headed to the door. He picked up two loaves of bread and the recipe.

"Congratulations to all. You all have bested me. I get the great honor of hosting all of you at my estate. I will shortly send invitations to all of you. It is almost ten p.m., and I am off duty. Thank you for a wonderful evening. It has been a pleasure and honor to meet you all. Good be with you all." Tood turned and left the room. Reggie followed.

"Have a wonderful evening, sir." The butler opened the front door for him.

"Reggie, I have a question."

"Anything, sir."

"Did you invent that golden story to cover how you stole the answer from the leaders?"

Reggie smiled. "On my mum's honor, you will never know, sir. Good night, sir."

Tood whistled and walked to the bottom of the stairs.

Reggie thought for a moment, stepped outside, and called out to him, "Lieutenant?"

Tood turned around and looked up at the butler. "Yes."

"Tutankhamen. Is that your real name, sir?"

"On my mother's honor, you will never know, sir. Good night, Reggie." Tood whistled his favorite blues tune and happily strolled down the street to the Bridge Between.

CHAPTER 20

Even a Fool Is Counted Wise When He Holds His Peace

"Over and out," Emmy said in the walkie.

She returned to the living room to finish watching *Back to the Future 2*. Woof was sitting on the couch, staring at the screen. She plopped down next to him and slowly rubbed his back. She yawned very loudly, and Woof turned and looked at her.

"Sorry." She tried to watch for a few more minutes, but she kept nodding off. "Woof, I'm going to bed." She stood up and stretched. Emmy noticed the *History of Between* sitting on the coffee table. She picked it up and walked to the foyer. Woof barked at her.

"Good night to you too."

Mr. Hemingway lumbered down the stairs and met Emmy at the bottom. "Our guest has been restless. She had a fever, so I had to give her more of Tood's potion. She should sleep until morning." She breathed a sigh of relief. "She has been a handful, but the rest of her injuries are almost healed."

"Has she said anything else?"

"Lots of mumbo jumbo. She has repeated *uncle* and possibly *mother* or *brother*."

"You are so good to care for her." Emmy gave her a hug.

"I care for all Good's children from the eastard or westard." Granny hugged her back.

"Aw, shucks, Granny." She kissed her on the cheek. "I'm going to bed. See you in the morning. Good night."

"Good night, dear. Try to be quiet, please. She is finally sleeping soundly."

"Yes, Granny." She blew a kiss and tiptoed up the stairs holding the history book.

Emmy sneaked past the guest's room, opened her door in silence, and placed the book on her bed. She left the door open and tiptoed down the hall to the bathroom. Mrs. Hemingway had found her toothpaste at the Market. It was inside a glass jar. It looked like creamy baking soda but had a sweet minty flavor.

"It was better than nothing," she mumbled as she vigorously brushed her teeth and tongue. She hummed her favorite tune as she finished and spit. She grabbed the fragrant handmade soap and lathered it easily in her hands. She washed her face and forearms. She rinsed the bubbles away and dried her face and arms on a soft towel. Emmy grabbed a hairbrush and quickly flowed through her silky black hair. She gave a deep breath. Now she was ready for bed. She put the brush away and walked down the hall humming.

The door to the elf's room slowly opened. Emmy stopped when she saw blond hair and a green eye peeking around the door.

Emmy bent over and gave a friendly greeting and waved. "Hello. Hi, friend. Don't be scared. I'm Emmy…waaah!"

At her name, a blond blur grabbed Emmy and thrust her into the elf's bedroom. In a flash, she slammed the door and had Emmy easily pinned to the wall. She put her right hand over Emmy's mouth and threatened her with something in her strong left hand. The powerful six-foot-tall elf glared at the surprised greeter.

"If you don't scream," the elf warned, "I will remove my hand."

Emmy's eyes were bulging, but she agreed.

"Who are you? Why are you skulking around here?"

"My name is Emmy. I am a friend." Seravina tightened her grip. "I was not skulking. My room is next door. I am also a guest, Seravina."

"How do you know my name?"

"Tood told me."

"Who is this Tood?"

"The tall, muscular, handsome man. He found you and brought you here. This is his estate."

Seravina seemed to recall. "Who is the dwarf caring for my wounds?"

Emmy struggled to move. "Mrs. Hemingway. She is the caretaker."

"You have a strange accent. Are you a spy? Did my uncle send you?"

"If you let me go…" Emmy squirmed.

Seravina pushed her hard against the wall and lifted her off the floor. She moved Emmy's head from left to right. "Why do you have the look of the high elves and bear the teardrop? Who are you in truth?" She pushed the blunt object into her skin.

"Ow! Don't do that!" Emmy screamed. "Is that a pencil?" She looked down at the weapon.

"I found this stick in the drawer. Call it what you wish. Have you ever seen an eye scooped from its socket? You don't want to see all I can do with this. Answer my question!"

"I was sent by…your uncle…I am…I am your uncle's illegitimate daughter. I am Esmerelda. White."

"Why were you sent?" Seravina ordered.

"I was sent…I was sent to assist you…in finding the Doorf."

Seravina released her and walked backward to the bed and sat down. "You do look like one of my cousins. Apparently, my uncle is not as squeaky clean as he appears."

Emmy dropped like a brick and fell to her knees, catching her breath. She touched her neck and felt blood. "You cut me with a pencil! A blunt pencil!"

"Sorry, cousin. Just a small nick." Seravina gave her a wry smile. "I thought I knew all the royal secrets. How have I never heard of Esmeralda White?"

"Your uncle, my father, had an affair with a scullery maid, my mother."

"Your mother was a scullery maid." The elf stared at her blankly.

"Yes. She loved your uncle despite her lowly station."

"Interesting. May I see your hands, cousin?" She tapped the pencil in her hands.

Emmy was perplexed but showed the elf both sides of her hands.

Seravina observed, "Fascinating. You have pretty painted manicured hands, no dirt, no calluses, and a gold ring on your right hand. Do you maintain them yourself?"

Emmy proudly shared, staring at her nails, "Thank you. No, I go once a week to Madam DeNails, just down the street." She felt the elf's glare and realized it was not a compliment. It was an accusation.

"Cousin." Seravina examined her own nails and asked, "What does a scullery maid do?"

Emmy froze. She could not speak or move. She was a fuzzy unaware bunny just noticing a diving hungry hawk.

Seravina flipped the pencil in the air and caught it without looking. She pointed the instrument menacingly. "Cousin, I find it curious that you have delightful soft hands and know nothing of your mother's trade."

Emmy could only think of Cinderella. "She...uh...uh...she fed animals, cleaned dishes, washed clothes, washed floors, made meals, cleaned drapes and tapestries." Emmy thought, "Sang to birds, made little clothes for mice, had evil stepsisters, rode in a pumpkin."

The elf princess twirled the stick among her deft fingers and crossed her legs. "Continue."

Emmy explained, "I used to work as a servant with my mother in your uncle's household, until my teardrop began to show. He was scared for our lives if his wife and family found out. We fled to a secret cabin in the middle of the night, deep in the woods near the dwarves. At the cabin, three elderly sisters cared for us and trained me to be a royal. On the eve of my sixteenth birthday, my father met me and promised to claim me as his legal daughter. I was so happy. But he never came back for me. He only sent a note three days later, informing us of the tragedy at court and throne."

"What was the problem with the throne?" Seravina stopped tapping the pencil in her hands.

"We were not informed specifically," Emmy whispered. "All we heard was it was between the king and the prince."

"Would you say this happened about six or seven years ago?" questioned Seravina.

Emmy answered, "Closer to five years."

Seravina glared at her. "Proceed, cousin."

"About two months ago, we received another official notice from my father, along with a gold necklace and gemstone. I was to always wear the necklace. He sent instructions for me to travel to another land, help my cousin, and find a man named Doorf. My father's enemy discovered our secret cabin, and we had to flee again. They caught us on a bridge. My mother was gagged, bound, and taken away. The soldiers grabbed me and threw me over the side of the bridge. When I woke up, I was here. In this house. I was wearing nothing but linens and this necklace." Emmy displayed the gold necklace and gemstone.

Seravina touched her collarbone, stood up and embraced Emmy roughly. "I believe you. That is an incredible story, Cousin Emmy. I never knew you existed. I am so glad to meet you." She kissed her teardrop.

Emmy returned the hug and kiss. She breathed a sigh of relief. "You do? I am so glad. I know. It has been so hard."

Seravina looked into her eyes. "Come. Sit with me." They sat next to each other on the bed. "Rest assured, cousin, I will not rest until your mother is rescued and those brigands are brought to justice and executed. Family fights for family. I believe you completely." She reached into her nightgown and brought forth an identical necklace to Emmy's.

"What? This is impossible. Did your uncle give you this?" Emmy asked.

Seravina yawned. "No. This was given to me ten years ago by the prince, my brother. We are here to find him."

"I thought our mission was to find this Doorf person."

"The Doorf will help us." The princess's eyes fluttered, and she yawned bigger. "Find the prince. He disappeared five years ago. He is wanted for…"

"For what?"

"Murder." She yawned again.

"Who did he murder?"

"You were isolated, weren't you? My father, the king."

"Oh my. How did you know about the Doorf?"

Seravina placed her head on the pillow. "I interrogated…and investigated…I found…a scroll…" She fell asleep and lightly snored.

Emmy pulled the sheet and quilt over her new "cousin." Emmy tiptoed to the door and silently exited the room. She breathed deeply. She touched the necklace. Seravina had believed her outlandish story only after she showed the jewelry.

She entered her room and locked the door. She picked up the history book. *I have a lot to catch up on*, she thought. She was no longer sleepy. She looked inside the small desk and found a full-size notebook, two pens, an unsharpened pencil, and a pink highlighter. She snatched them up. She jumped on the bed. She began to carefully read, take notes, and study each page.

CHAPTER 21

Can a Man Take Fire to His Bosom and His Clothes Not Be Burned?

Captain Chico had celebrated with Popson and Chang in many Vararity pubs and nightclubs. Half the Legion joined them in revelries for their promotions. At 9:30 p.m., at the 5050 Club, Chico gathered his soldiers into one back room.

"Gentlemen and ladies, I appreciate you coming out to this celebration of Sergeant Popson and Corporal Chang. It has been a great night."

The soldiers whistled and hollered for their colleagues.

"Das goot yah!" Popson and Chang screamed, and everyone laughed.

Chico continued, "However, I do have some bad news. You remember Guard Doorf. Big guy, weird goggles, likes junk. Well, somehow, that jerk weaseled the city council and the colonel into giving him a promotion too."

Angry yells and boos cried out from the Legion.

"I know. I know. As your captain, I was shocked because the junkman will now be your new lieutenant. Third-in-command of the Legion."

Growls emanated from the soldiers, and some smashed their glasses to the ground.

"Somehow, he used his family name and money to buy this commission. You know where he is right now. He is having a dinner party with the mayor and all the leaders. Probably eating some fancy soup and an expensive meal. Celebrating his promotion with the high and mighty."

The soldiers grumbled louder, and one yelled, "I hate soup!" The crowd agreed.

Chico answered, "I hate it too. It should only be served when you are sick. Soup and salad make me sick." Chico mocked the butler. "Excuse me, sir, would you like some soup? *No!* Soup sucks."

The soldiers cheered, "Soup sucks! Soup sucks! Soup sucks!"

Chico calmed the Legion down. "Now let's not take our anger out on the soup. It is Tood Doorf we should be angry at. Excuse me, Lieutenant Junk." The men laughed. "This is my order to all you men and women here. Do not follow the orders of the lieutenant. Ignore him. Act like he doesn't even exist. Challenge him on everything. Make his life so miserable and hateful that he will resign and go running back home to the junks."

The Legion cheered and chanted, "Doorf sucks soup! Doorf sucks soup!"

"Now remember to pay your tabs. You are dismissed."

Legionnaires patted Chico on the back as they left the club. He called Popson and Chang over. "Hello, Sergeant and Corporal. Did you complete the mission I sent you?"

Popson answered, "Yes, sir. To the letter."

Chang replied, "Yes, sir."

"Great." Chico clapped and rubbed his hands together. "I am going on duty at ten p.m. Are you sleeping in the barracks tonight?"

Chang replied, "I am, sir."

"Would you inform the guard on duty that I will be in my office and I am not to be disturbed?" Chico explained. "I am going for a walk."

"Yes, sir. I will go right now." Chang opened the door.

"Let me head out first. Good night, boys." Chico walked out the door.

Chang closed it behind him. He looked at Popson and pulled out Chico's letters.

"No one was home," Chang whispered.

Popson laughed. He pulled out the other letter. "Me too." Chang laughed.

Popson grabbed all the letters and burned them in the fireplace. "He'll never know."

Chico left the club and walked to the City Sphere Fountain. He was headed to Arms. He stopped to admire the pulsating lights and water streams jetting from the fountain. The city clock bells chimed ten times. He breathed in the refreshing night air. He turned to leave but saw a beautiful friendly face walking toward the sculpture.

"Hello, Jak," Ms. Miner said as she walked to the fountain.

"Andrea. What a lovely surprise. How are you, my love? I thought we were…"

She went to the edge of the structure and placed her hands on the railing. "I decided to seek you out."

Jak moved closer to embrace her, but she put up her left hand. "Jak. Stop." She turned to face him. "It's over, Jak. I never want to see you again."

"Andy, this is just—" Chico started.

"You made your choice publicly. Now I make mine. Jenny is a wonderful person, and I hope for all the happiness in the world for you both."

Chico moved closer and touched her hand gently. "I don't want her. I want you. It has always been you." He held her hand and kissed it. "I love you."

Andrea snatched her hand away. "You have a funny way of showing love, Jak."

Jak stepped closer to her. "I said it, and I mean it. I love you, Andy."

"Don't call me that," she whispered. "You love me, Jak? Then why keep our relationship a secret? Why all the secret rendezvous? Why when we plan to run off together, you choose her in public?" Tears formed in her gray eyes. "When you spoke about your love for her…"

"To fire and the pit, my words that day!" Chico cursed. "It meant nothing. Just a show for the crowd. You are my world. You are every—"

Andrea stepped away. "Just more words, Jak."

"Andy…Andrea," Chico begged. "Please, don't do this. Don't do this to me…to us."

She turned to him with fire in her eyes. "There is the truth. It is all about you. My eyes are open to the way your love blinded me to the real you. Does Jenny know about us?" He looked away. "She doesn't know. How many other women have indulged the dashing Captain Chico? How could I be so blind? You probably use the same secret getaway."

Chico tried once more. "Andrea, I love you. Run away with me now. I promise—"

Andrea turned her back and looked away. "I thought I loved you once. But it is over. Do not try to contact me. Please only refer to me as my formal title. Don't worry, Captain Chico. Ms. Mayor will never know about us." She walked away into the cool night air. She paused and called back, "Good be with you, Captain."

Chico sighed. "Good bless you, my love, Lady Miner." He watched her disappear into the dark. He wiped a tear from his right eye. He breathed in deeply and looked down at the cobblestones. "Well, it was fun while it lasted."

He picked up his head and strolled toward Arms. He cackled. "She actually thought I was going to run away with her." He shook his head. "Dodged another one, Jakie boy." He did a battleball spin move and smiled. "Can't touch Chico."

He finally made it to Arms and slipped into his office. He removed his jacket and sat behind his large desk. He put his feet on the desk and leaned back in his chair. He placed his hands behind his curly hair and closed his eyes.

After what felt like only seconds, a guard burst into his office. "Captain Chico!"

Chico did not move or even open his eyes. "That is the name on the door."

"Yes, sir. Sorry to disturb you, sir. We have an escalating problem in Sembly, sir!"

Chico opened one eye and closed it. "Baron, right? What is the problem?"

"Well, sir, I first noticed two female citizens gathering outside of Sembly, just after ten p.m. Minute by minute, one by one, women kept arriving. It was peaceable until the women started to talk to each other."

"Did you get some guards and try to disperse the crowd?" Chico opened his eyes.

"Yes, sir. But more women arrived. There were some circus folks there and a large bear. They all got loud, violent, and angry."

"Why were they so angry, guard?"

"That is why I ran all the way here, sir."

"What are you talking about? To get reinforcements?"

"No, sir. They were angry. Angry at you, sir. They are coming to Arms to find you!"

Chico stood up and put on his jacket. "How many women did you count?"

Baron replied, "I lost count after the bear arrived. Sixty? Seventy?"

Popson burst into Arms. "Captain! There is an angry mob of at least a hundred women marching down the streets. They seem to be on a seek and destroy mission."

A smiling Chang ran in from the barracks. "What's all the noise? Is this the after-party?"

Popson ignored the corporal. "Who are they seeking?"

"Apparently, me!" Chico pounded his desk. "Options, Sergeant? Guard? Chang?"

THE DOORS BETWEEN

"You could face them, sir," Baron proposed. "You are a fine public speaker and could calm them down."

"Play some hype music," Chang offered and raised his arms in the air.

"*Or?*" Chico looked at Popson.

"Or you could sneak out the back door and hide out at the stadium while we delay and send them in a different direction."

Chico came up with a plan. "Baron, when the mob gets here, you will speak to the crowd. Try to calm them down. Popson, you will stand with her. Tell them something about how I will personally speak to them one at a time. Tell them whatever you want. Chang, you will run to the stadium and make sure it is clear." Chang ran out the back door.

"Delay them and try to disperse them. Keep them busy while I head to the stadium. I am leaving now. Thanks. Commendations to all of you." Chico placed his bag over his shoulder and quietly headed out the back door.

"Yes, sir." They saluted.

Within minutes, the angry mob arrived holding torches and yelling, "Down with Chico! Down with Chico!"

Baron and Popson exited Arms and put up their hands. The crowd calmed down.

"Fair citizens of Tween," Baron started. "The captain is here but has asked us to have you form a line. He wants to personally speak to each and every one about this upsetting situation."

Ms. Mayor led the crowd and held a torch. Lady Banker and Lady Miller were also in the crowd. Jenny raised her voice. "Guard, do you know why we are upset? Hey, ladies! Why are we upset?"

The mob screamed, "Chico, Chico, Chico!" Popson made several bird noises.

Jenny raised her hand and calmed everyone. "Do you know why we are upset at Captain Chico?"

The guard looked at Jenny. "No, Ms. Mayor. I really don't."

Jenny walked up the stairs and whispered in her ear. Baron's eyes bulged. Popson scrambled inside Arms and then ran out the rear exit to the stadium.

"All of you?" She pointed to the crowd.

The angry women nodded in unison.

"You too, Ms. Mayor?" the guard asked and put her hand to her mouth.

Guard Baron gave Jenny a hug. The crowd awed. She confessed, "He's not here. He is hiding out at the stadium."

Jenny roared, "To the stadium!" The Chico mob cheered and moved off to the arena. Baron joined the throng and lit a torch. Lady Miller made an unnoticed departure from the mob.

Captain Chico did not head to the stadium. This mob would have found him there. He had a feeling Baron would give up his location. Instead, he went to the Arms stable and got his horse ready. He quickly saddled and bridled his spotted mustang, Spitfire.

"Sorry to wake you, old friend. But we must get out of town for a few days. Time to visit Gramp's place."

Spitfire gave him a grunt and a nuzzle.

Chico pulled out an apple from his jacket. "Here you go, pal. I didn't forget."

Spitfire eagerly snacked on the treat. He led the mustang out of the stable doors.

The colonel's wife waited for him just outside the stables. "Hey, Jak. Where are you going?"

"None of your business, Lady Miller." He mounted Spitfire. "If you care for your safety, you will step out of the way."

"I'm not stopping you. I want to go with you."

"Please move. You can't come with me."

"If you care for your unborn child, you will wait."

Chico stared at her in disbelief. He snarled, "So that's the surprise. Or is it a trick to delay me so your mob friends can find me?"

"No trick. It's the truth. I was not part of the mob. I arrived late and saw the crowd. I snuck away before anyone noticed. Jak, I am not angry with you. I have known about the others for a long time. I knew one woman could never satisfy you. I came to find you to give you this joyous news."

"Joyous for who?" Chico snapped as he scanned the area for trouble. "So it's true?"

Mrs. Miller approached the side of the horse and touched Chico's leg. "Yes, it is true. I'm at least two months, I think." She softly placed her hand on her stomach and smiled. "I want to thank you for giving me the one thing the colonel could not."

Chico stared at her blankly. "You're welcome. Now please move away. I have to go. If the mob catches me, I will be dead."

"That's all you have to say? I am having your baby!"

"Good luck," Jak snidely replied. "I cannot claim him or her or the colonel would kill me." He reached into his bag and pulled out a small bag of tiger eye gems and handed it to her. "For the baby." He put his hands back on the reins.

She received the gems and stepped away from the horse. "You are headed to your secret place near Bee Cave, aren't you? I won't tell. I promise."

Chico stopped. "You promise? Is that a threat? How did you know about that?" He became angry. "What do you want from me, woman?"

Lady Miller begged and cried, "Take me with you. I want to be with you. I can't stay here, or I will be disgraced. Please, Jak! Please."

"No," he said coldly. "Go back to your husband. Spend some time with him. You have kept him in the dark for years. The old fool may believe the rugrat is his own." He laughed. She began to sob.

"Farewell, Lady Miller. Good luck with everything." He galloped away, leaving her weeping at the stable gates.

She heard a noise behind her in the stables. She turned around. "Who's there?"

A shadow emerged from a stall.

Mrs. Miller recognized the person and spoke harshly. "You. What do you want? Did you follow me here? You are so pathetic. Go away. I want to be alone." She turned her back to the shadow.

Before her next step, the shadow struck Lady Miller on the head and knocked her out. The shadow caught her before she hit the ground and dragged her into the stables.

Chico rode north for a quarter of a mile then stopped. He could no longer go to Bee Cave. He changed directions to the west. "There is only one place in Between that no one would go looking for me," he commented to Spitfire.

"Sorry, friend. We have to go the long way around to Cutoff. Just to be safe." He patted the smooth neck of his equestrian friend. He sat upright and gently kicked his heels.

Captain Chico rode west, hovering the tree line and avoiding using the West Driveaway. He trotted for about two hours until he saw the dim lights of Cutoff University. He had not been here for five or six years, but he knew the way back to his first home in Between. He knew every twist and turn through his second hometown. In a few moments, he halted in front of a quaint cottage with a white picket fence and flower boxes. He quietly slid down his mount. He tied Spitfire to the hitching post. He skillfully opened the yard gate without a sound. He stepped to the front door. He reached into the bushes by the front window.

Odd, Jak thought. *The key box isn't there.*

Suddenly, the porch light turned on. Its brightness temporarily blinded Chico.

An unfriendly deep voice called from the open front door. "Can I help you, friend?"

Chico stood up. "I hate what you have done with the place. But it is good to see you, brother."

CHAPTER 22

Anxiety in the Heart of Man Causes Depression, but a Good Word Makes It Glad

Emmy jumped awake with the sound of Woof barking. A piece of notebook paper was stuck to her cheek. She removed the paper and stretched her arms with a loud yawn. She stretched her lower back and stood up. The sunshine broke through the curtains, illuminating her room. She walked to the window and peeked out. Emmy smiled when she saw Woof harassing the penguins. She heard voices coming from Seravina's room. She looked around and found a glass half full of water. She chugged the water and then moved to the adjoining wall.

She put the glass up to the wall and her ear to the glass. She couldn't make out anything at first. She thought it was Tood and Seravina. Emmy lifted the glass and emptied the remaining water on the floor. She put the glass back on the wall and listened carefully. She closed her eyes as she began to make out an odd accent coming from Tood.

Tood said, "I assure you, my lady. My knowledge is as deep as the sea. I am not as young as I appear. As for my countenance, you can thank…"

Emmy whispered, "My lady?" Their speech became muffled. She moved the glass.

Seravina continued the conversation. "Answer my questions of my world, Lord Doorf, and I shall believe you and follow you to the ends of the earth."

"Lord Doorf? Is this a Renaissance festival?" Emmy commented.

Seravina said, "The two ways to destroy tarachtans? And how do you cure a tarachtan's bite?"

Emmy repeated, "Tarachtans? Blasted Lands. I read about that place."

She could not hear anything. So she moved the glass to the left and picked up Tood's voice.

"The monsters turn into pillars of salt in the light of day."

Seravina replied, "It is never easy to behead the beast. You are correct, sir. Please continue."

Tood said, "For the second, it cannot be answered. You have provided me with a trick question."

Emmy mumbled, "Oh no! She set a trap." Tood's voice became garbled, then she moved the glass again.

"There is no cure for the beast's mucus. Unless you consider death a cure."

"Excellent!" Seravina cheered and clapped.

At the clap, a severe high-pitched noise screeched inside Emmy's ear and knocked her across the room. She nearly dropped the glass and rubbed her right ear.

"What the flip was that?" Emmy said angrily. She put the glass on the desk and stood up. Her ears were ringing. "How did she do that? I am going to have a little talk with my cousin."

THE DOORS BETWEEN

Emmy heard the door close and Tood move down the stairs. She counted to ten and opened her door. She went to Seravina's door and silently turned the doorknob. She stuck her head in the door.

A threatening voice came from the bed. "You breathe so heavy I could have heard you a mile away. You should not have listened."

"But...," Emmy started.

Seravina slightly lifted her head from the pillow. "Eavesdropping on a royal's private conversation is punishable by death. Consider it a gentle warning, cousin." She yawned. "If there is nothing else, I need some slumber."

Emmy's mouth dropped open. She whispered, "Sorry." She closed the door.

She went back to her room and quickly got dressed in her jeans and a clean long-sleeved red thermal shirt. She grabbed socks and placed them in her boots. She picked up the boots and left her room. She remembered her notebook and snatched it from her bed. She headed down the stairs and spotted a shadow entering the dining room.

When she entered the dining room, she recognized the battle scene murals from the history book. As she stared at the largest battle, the images on the wall began to move. The armies, soldiers, generals, horses, and the scenes moved in sequential order to the battle displayed. The artwork came to life. The painting became more detailed and animated as she contemplated the picture.

The face of the dark shaded general attacking Between felt oddly familiar as facial details appeared. The completed face was about to be revealed when she faintly heard her name. She turned toward the voice. It was the light shaded general defending the land. The mystery face seemed blurred as it reached toward her.

"Esmeralda," the voice breathed.

"Emmy. Hey, Emmy," Tood called.

She snapped out of it. "Huh? Tood? Tood!" She gave him a hug.

He hugged her back. "Emmy. It's good to see you too. Good morning."

Emmy did not know what to say. She hugged him harder.

"What's the matter? Did you see a ghost?" Tood asked. "You did, didn't you?"

Emmy pulled away and stared at the floor. She did not want to look at the paintings. "Don't think I'm crazy. But...but the pictures in the paintings were moving."

Tood took her by the hands and sat down at the table. "Tell me what you saw."

Emmy peeked at the artwork. It was back to normal. Her blue eyes glistened as she stared at Tood. "You believe me?"

Tood moved in close and gently squeezed her hands. "Of—"

Emmy impulsively leaned forward and kissed him with passion. Tood was completely surprised but did not turn away. She pulled back. "I'm sorry, Tood...I..."

"You have nothing to apologize for. It was a lot better than a slap." Tood grinned.

"You have been so amazing. I am so grateful for all you've done. You smelled so sweet. I am impulsive, and when you said you believed me, I was like—"

Tood surprised her and leaned in close and kissed her back. Emmy closed her eyes and gave into the moment.

Tood pulled away and gently placed his forehead on hers. "Now we are even."

Emmy blushed and moved away slightly.

Woof materialized in the doorway, growling. Tood rolled his eyes. "Nothing is going on, Woof. Just a friendly kiss."

Woof walked up to Emmy. He snarled at Tood.

She rubbed the giant dog's head. "Does he kiss the dwarf like that? I hope he doesn't kiss Mrs. Hemingway like that." She teased and giggled. Woof heckled his friend.

"What? No. That's not what I meant. Ah, nuts."

Granny poked her head around the kitchen corner. "Did someone say they were going to kiss me?"

Emmy and Woof laughed out loud. Tood stood up and exited the room without making another comment.

"Oh, dear, did I say something to offend him?" Mrs. H asked.

"No, we were just teasing him. I'll give you a kiss, Granny." Emmy ran over to her and gave a big wet kiss on her cheek. "I will check on Tood."

"Thank you, dear. Breakfast will be ready in ten minutes!" the caretaker yelled after her.

Emmy went to the stairs. Tood was sitting on the third step, gazing at the morning sun.

"I am sorry for teasing you." Emmy walked over to him. "Tood, is everything okay?"

Tood looked at her and smiled. "Sit with me for a second."

Emmy sat next to him. He dove into the ocean of her eyes.

"We had a very nice moment there. You are a great kisser."

"Thanks. You are not bad yourself," Emmy joked.

"Thanks. Emmy, I have never met anyone like you. You are smart, sweet, intelligent, witty, beautiful inside and…I would love…" He paused, trying to get the right words. "If circumstances were different…how do I say this? Emmy, there is so much at stake for all of us right now. I don't want to jeopardize you or Seravina not getting back home by being distracted. There is so much changing for you, and I don't want to take advantage of the situation. I would love to offer more than friendship, but right now, that's all I can offer."

Emmy sat in sweet silence.

"See? I said too much already. Are you angry?"

"No. I honor and treasure our friendship. Tood, it was just an impulsive kiss. No big deal."

"Really?" He was perplexed. "I thought…"

Emmy answered, "Really. It meant nothing. I kiss guys all the time. No problem."

Tood sighed. "What a relief. Sorry. I just thought…you know…"

"Thought I was falling for you!" Emmy scoffed and stood up.

"No. I didn't want you to think"—he pointed to her and then back to himself—"that I was falling for you," Tood tried to correct.

"After one kiss! Please. It wasn't that good."

"Technically. It was two kisses." Tood grinned and held up two fingers.

"Well then, Mr. Kissy Face, let's make it three and remove all doubt."

"What?" Tood protested, stood up, and backed away from her. "No."

"So the kisses did mean something to you!"

"No. It meant nothing to me as well," Tood confessed, retreating toward the front door.

"Good. Prove it," Emmy goaded him and advanced toward him. "Kiss me."

"No." The junkman cautiously moved backward.

"Kiss me now. Kiss me gently. Kiss me strong."

"No. Emmy, you are being childish."

"Kiss me, Tood. Kiss me passionately."

"No! Emmy, stop advancing." His back pressed against the wooden door.

She took one step farther and whispered, "Kiss me. Kiss me like you've wanted since—"

Tood quickly stepped toward Emmy. He gently placed his hands on her flushed cheeks and moved in slowly. She placed her hands on his strong chest. She closed her eyes and pursed her round delectable lips. He closed his eyes and lightly touched his nose to hers and stopped millimeters from her lips.

His soft voice brushed her lips. "It. Meant. Nothing."

Emmy breathlessly replied, "Me. Too."

"Breakfast!" Mrs. Hemingway called from the kitchen.

Emmy and Tood opened their eyes and slowly released their embrace. They stepped back from each other and straightened out their clothes.

Emmy started, "Well, we had better get to breakfast."

"Breakfast sounds great. I'm starving," Tood replied.

"Race you there?" Emmy challenged.

"Only if you tell me about the pictures. Without kissing me."

"I promise." Emmy put up her right hand. "To beat you to the kitchen!" She sprinted toward the dining room.

"Hey!" Tood chased after her. "You didn't say go!"

CHAPTER 23

The Rich and the Poor Have This in Common; the Lord Is Maker of Them All

They devoured the delightful breakfast Mrs. Hemingway prepared. Emmy and Tood talked all through the meal about what she had seen in the dining room and her conversations with Seravina. Tood listened intently to the details but gave no insight. Emmy enjoyed his story about the dinner party and the name game. They went to the living room and continued the conversation for several hours. Emmy found her notebook and asked him numerous questions about Between, the Castle, the Junks, Tween, and the Doors.

Woof had lingered around during the conversation until the grandfather clock struck 10:00 a.m. He informed Emmy and Tood that he was going on patrol. He strolled out the back porch and vanished.

"Patrol?" Emmy asked. "He goes on a patrol of Between?"

Tood replied, "He travels to all the major points in Between at ten a.m. and then again at ten p.m. He usually completes his rounds in three to four hours."

"Why does he do it? What is he looking for?" questioned Emmy.

"You'll have to ask him all his reasons, but he wants to keep Between safe from any possible invading creatures. He reports and alerts me of any possible trouble. He also helps me find junk and doorstones. He collects the stones in a pile until I can retrieve them. He loves Between and would do anything to protect it."

"What is his story?" Emmy pondered.

"He doesn't like to talk about his past. I found him near the Wamp when he first arrived. I saved his life from the Wamp monster. It's a gigantic prehistoric-size sentient alligator. I think he wants to pay me back. You will have to ask him yourself," Tood explained. "You can go with him when he teleports. It is a great way to see all the land. I would not recommend eating before you try it. Hard on the stomach at first."

Emmy laughed. "Thanks for the advice, King Tut. I will try to remember. I do have another question."

"You? A question? That is hard to believe," Tood teased her.

"Okay, I sorta deserved that. Doorstones. How do you find them?"

Granny poked her head into the living room. "I am going to check on our newest visitor and bring her some more food and drink."

Tood responded, "Thank you. Let me know if you or she needs anything."

"Dear, I could always use some help cleaning up the kitchen," Granny commented and left the room.

"I guess that's our cue to help with the chores." Emmy smiled. "I guess we did get a bit carried away talking."

Tood stood up and went toward the back door. "Nonsense. We'll get to those dishes in a few minutes. Come with me and I'll show you about the doorstones."

"Okay." Emmy followed him out the door.

THE DOORS BETWEEN

Tood walked north about a quarter of a mile. He led her to the base of the Ruins. He reached his left hand down and pulled her up. She felt the calluses of his strong hand. He became aware of her smooth refined fingers. Seravina witnessed from her window the lingering handhold. Tood walked ten feet, stopped, and scanned the area for any unexpected visitors.

"When this castle was destroyed, the rocks and stones were blasted throughout all of Between, and some were cast into the other worlds. Here, near the base, you can still feel the power of the doors. Put one of your hands out. Now close your eyes." He gently touched her elbow and walked several feet away and watched.

Emmy put her left hand out and closed her eyes. She could hear the birds singing, the slight wind blowing, the heat of the sun, the sound of raised voices coming from the house, a heart beating, but not hers. She heard Tood's heart. She felt a tingle in her pinky finger. She ignored it. It probably fell asleep. She shook her hand and held it out. Emmy's thumb also tingled. It felt like static electricity bouncing between her pinky and thumb and then all her fingers. When she peeked, she had a ball of electricity floating between her fingers. She opened both eyes in amazement, but the electric ball fell out of her hand and absorbed into the ground.

"Tood, did you see that? I did magic! Flipping sauce! Where did the ball go?"

"I know! Great job on the first try. Just wait and you'll see," Tood encouraged.

Emmy stared at the ashen spot where the electric ball vanished. The spot twisted and turned and became a hole. Up from a hole, a green gray stone slowly emerged to the surface. Emmy reached down and picked up the engraved stone. She heard a door slam and turned to face the house.

A blond tornado stomped from the back door, heading straight to Tood. Mrs. Hemingway was in hot pursuit, but she was no match for the gazelle strides of the elf.

Granny called after her, "Miss, you are indecent! A princess should not be wearing her nightgown outside of the bedroom. Especially not that one. Please come back inside to change!"

Seravina called back as she strode past Emmy, "If you wish me to remove it completely, keep speaking, dwarf! Salutations, cousin."

"Salutations," Emmy replied casually with a smile.

She stopped in front of Tood and did a quick curtsy. He bowed his head.

Her indecency was a sleeveless white nightgown. It had tiny black, red, and blue Spider-Man symbols covering the garment. It fit tightly across her chest and only flowed down to her midthigh. She looked like a supermodel showcasing the latest Spider-Man fashion.

"Greetings, Lord Doorf."

"Good morning. How may I help you, my lady? You seem to have upset my caretaker."

Mrs. Hemingway finally made it to their location. She was huffing and puffing and stood next to Emmy. She said breathlessly, "She saw you and Emmy up here and ran out the door. Oh, dear, I'm getting too old for this schlapp."

Seravina turned to Mrs. Hemingway. "My apologies to you, mistress."

Granny nodded and sat on the ground.

"Lord Tood…"

"Just Tood, my lady."

"Thank you. Tood, your caretaker tried to prevent me from leaving the room after I felt magic in the vicinity. She brought me peasant clothes, which were out of the question." She looked at Tood and Emmy's clothes. "No offense, friends. However, I require suitable attire for my station and rank. I left the room in search of you when I felt magic."

"My lady. Seravina, thank you for explaining the situation. I am sure Mrs. Hemingway would agree with that assessment."

Granny nodded and whispered to Emmy, "Along with a few choice curse words."

Tood continued, "Seravina, your mission here is one of stealth and speed. To accomplish this, we all must blend in with the locals. If you were to wear any type of royal garments, it would only attract undue attention." Tood paused. "We have multiple selections of clothes of all styles and sizes. Mrs. H is an excellent seamstress, and your cousin, Emmy, could help you pick out something suitable and appropriate."

Seravina looked at Emmy. "It would be much appreciated, cousin and Mrs. Hemingway."

Emmy gave her the thumbs-up, which only perplexed Seravina. She turned back to the junkman.

"Tood, what were you and Emmy doing over here?" the princess asked.

Emmy proudly spoke up. "I used magic for the first time and collected a doorstone." She handed it to Seravina.

"A runestone?" The elf looked at Emmy and handed back the stone. "How quaint." She held both hands out, and ten electric balls appeared. She dropped nine into the ground and juggled the tenth in her hands. She made the last ball bigger and released it. Within seconds, nine small doorstones burst from the ground, and then a large runestone jettison from the soil.

Emmy said under her breath, "Show-off."

"What was that, cousin?" Seravina asked.

"Wow! That was great."

Tood spoke. "Vina, thank you for getting these for us. However, let's not attract any more attention. I do have neighbors who watch me constantly." He walked over to her, and she placed her hand on his arm. "Let's go back to the house so you can cover your long legs and strong arms with something suitable." They walked together back to the house. "Emmy, would you mind grabbing the stones?"

Emmy watched them walk together, and Seravina placed her head on his shoulder. The elf laughed at something Tood said, glanced back at her cousin, and grinned.

"Emmy, would you grab the stones?" Emmy muttered and mocked. She scratched her head. "What just happened?"

Granny sighed. "Dear, you were just upstaged. That girl has the tools to make men into fools. Tood doesn't have a clue. Let me help you with those stones." They gathered the stones and headed back to the house. They placed them on the porch and headed inside.

Tood had given Seravina his red bedtime robe to cover up. Emmy could hear them in the kitchen eating and talking. Was that a giggle from Tood?

Emmy could feel her temper rising. She took a deep breath and slowly let it out.

"He is just a friend. No big deal. He is just flirting and talking with her. We are just friends," she whispered to herself. More laughter bellowed from the kitchen. She took a deep breath again and slowly let it out before entering the kitchen.

Seravina sat on the kitchen island eating a pastry and wearing a red robe.

"Cousin Emmy! You must try a Torus cake. They are divine." She finished a bite and extended a platterful of round frosting-covered pastries.

Emmy looked at the plateful of colorful doughnuts. "Torus cakes?" She picked a chocolate-covered one. She took a small bite. "Delicious."

"Mrs. Hemingway made these for us," Tood explained. "Torus is the geometric shape."

"Don't you remember? It was a new delicacy at the Great Fair of Ponn." Seravina smiled and chose one with pink frosting. She sensually nibbled it.

"I never attended it. I was in hiding with my mother." She took another bite. Emmy realized the elf had tested her story.

"Of course. It must have slipped my mind." She passed the plate to Tood. "Try this pink one. It is like biting into a strawberry." She pushed the pink one into his mouth.

The junkman laughed with a full mouth. "Thanks. No more. I'm stuffed."

The elf finished the cake and licked her fingers. "So good."

Emmy angrily finished her pastry but asked with a smile, "Nice robe. Comfy?"

"Do you mean comfortable, cousin? It is," Seravina replied and hugged herself. "Tood has lent me his comfy robe until I acquire my own wardrobe."

"It's no big deal," Tood blushed and interjected. "I grabbed it from my boudoir."

"Boudoir. I love how that sounds. Boudoir," Seravina teased. "It means—"

"Bedroom," Emmy replied and went to the frigger. "What was so funny?" She grabbed the last RC Cola and opened it.

"Cousin, what is that?" Seravina jumped off the island.

"It is a soda or soda pop. It's a refreshing carbonated beverage," Emmy answered and was about to drink it.

"May I try a sip, please?"

"Sure." Emmy handed over the bottle.

"It smells sweet," Seravina commented and sipped a tiny bit. "It is bubbly. I can feel them in my nose. May I try a bit more, cousin?"

Tood grinned.

"Yes, of course." Emmy tried to remain polite.

Seravina drank nearly half the bottle and stopped with a refreshing "Ahhh." Seconds later, she erupted in a massive belch, which rattled the windows. Tood and Seravina laughed out loud while Emmy gave a wry smile.

"Excuse me."

"Enjoy the rest," Emmy announced. "I'll grab some water."

"Thank you," the princess replied.

"Emmy," Tood started. "Vina and I were talking about all of us going to town. If everyone is up for it, I could take you all to my favorite places in Tween. Tonight."

"Tonight? All of us? That would be great. Even Woof?" she asked.

"Yes. Woof loves it in town. After dinner, we can go into town and check out a pub and a few music and dance clubs," Tood explained.

"Doesn't it sound extraordinary, cousin?"

"You have clubs?"

"Yes. Vina claimed she was a fine dancer."

"Of course, she is. What would I wear? When would we…wait, did you just call her Vina?" Emmy asked.

Tood agreed.

Seravina put her arms around Emmy and squeezed. "All my friends call me Vina, remember?"

"Yes. All your friends. Yes, they do. Vina the Vivacious. But her enemies call her Vina the Viper."

Seravina seemed pleased with the titles. "They do? They do. How wonderful, these pet names." She laughed.

Emmy continued, "Don't forget Vina the Volcano or Vina the Vicious."

"That's enough, cousin. I believe our mutual friend gets the point."

"*My* personal favorites are Vina the Vengeful and Vina the Vix—"

Seravina grabbed Emmy's arm and pulled her into the dining room. "Be right back. I need to have a conversation with my relative," she called over her shoulder to Tood.

Emmy plopped down in the chair and hugged her legs. She muttered, "The Vixen."

"Cousin Emmy, do you have affections for Tood?"

Emmy refused to answer.

"You are clearly exhibiting jealousy toward me for talking with Tood. You are both wearing the same style of gold rings."

"Talking. Yeah, right."

"So you do have no issues with me speaking to him?"

"No. I don't want to fight over Tood. I don't want him to get hurt."

Seravina explained, "The only one who would get hurt is you, if you interfere with my courting rituals."

"Courting rituals? Excuse me!" Emmy yelled.

"You are excused."

"So you think you can win Tood's love through your looks, your laugh, and female manipulations?"

"Of course. I never lose."

"Tood will be able to see through your facade of beauty."

"Facade? It is not I who is playacting, cousin."

"Quit all the medieval talk. It is so annoying."

"Are you challenging me for Tood?" Seravina laughed.

"What? No. He is my friend. I…I don't love him in that way."

"Of course, but you do have affection for him." Seravina spoke fondly of Tood. "He has a fair countenance. He is strong, wise, kind, humorous…"

"I…I…"

"Loyal, wealthy, considerate, and a warrior," Seravina finished. "What else do you desire?"

"I do challenge you for Tood."

"Just give up now," Seravina proclaimed. "You are no match for me."

"If we are competing to win his love, then let us set up some ground rules."

"What do you propose, cousin?" Seravina sat at the table.

"First, we cannot kill or physically hurt each other. Second, Tood will make the final choice between us. Third, the loser will leave Between forever and will never return," Emmy explained.

"Anything else?" Seravina asked.

"Fourth, we can use all our female wiles to influence Tood except for…"

"Except for what?"

"Hanky-panky."

"What is hanky-panky?"

Emmy pointed to Tood's bedroom.

"Pointing?"

"No. When a man and woman get together…"

"Oh. You mean procreation."

"Yes. That is off-limits. One last thing. No magic. Agreed?" Emmy stuck out her hand.

"I agree to your terms," Seravina acknowledged and shook her hand. "I will enjoy destroying you on the battlefield of love."

"I don't think so. I do have an advantage over you," Emmy bragged.

"Your hair?" Seravina scoffed.

"I have already kissed him," Emmy bragged. "And he kissed me back."

"Excellent. Then I shall have a turn. Kissing is my favorite. I shall enjoy winning."

Emmy cleared her throat. "We have an expression from where I come from—"

Seravina interrupted, "Will I understand it? Did you say it now and I missed it?"

Emmy replied, "I don't know. No."

"Proceed."

"It's not over until the fat lady sings."

"Who is the fat lady, and why is she singing?"

"Forget that. All is fair in love and war."

"I do understand that. Love is war."

Emmy stood up. "See you on the battlefield." She moved toward the kitchen.

Seravina put a finger to her chin and asked, "Cousin, are you the singing fat lady?"

Emmy stopped and grumbled, "No."

"Do you even sing?"

"No." Emmy ground her teeth.

"I would call you chunky, not fat."

"What? I'm not chunky! It's the clothes I'm wearing," Emmy protested.

Seravina stood and removed Tood's robe, revealing her perfectly sculpted body. She folded the robe in her arms. "I'm sure. It is your clothes." She reentered the kitchen.

Emmy looked at her body and frowned. Then she realized the battle had already begun. "Man, she is good."

CHAPTER 24

If Your Enemy Is Hungry, Give Him Bread to Eat; if He Is Thirsty, Give Him Water to Drink

Mrs. Hemingway decided she would not be going to the clubs. She did help Emmy and Seravina pick out proper dancing dresses for Between. Granny went to a special closet in Tood's room and brought forth to the living room several outfits. Emmy complained the dresses were too long. Seravina complained the dresses were too loose. Mrs. Hemingway explained the dancing attire for Tween women were different from everyday clothing and also different from formal or society clothes.

They either wore midlength pleated skirts and long-sleeved blouses or a long-sleeved dress with pleats from the waist down.

Seravina chose a sky blue dress with white pleats, and Emmy chose a white blouse and pink pleated skirt. Mrs. H took their measurements and made the alterations to the outfits. As Granny measured Seravina, Emmy was in the kitchen with Tood, preparing dinner. Seravina could not hear all their conversation, but it was a bit too friendly for her. When Granny called Emmy to be measured, she could feel the tension between the young ladies as they passed each other.

"Please stand on the table, dear. Hands straight out to the side and legs together. Back straight and look directly ahead," the seamstress ordered.

"Yes, ma'am," Emmy replied and obeyed. "Will this take long?"

"No. As long as you listen to me." Granny used her measuring tape deftly.

Emmy heard laughter coming from the kitchen. She turned her head.

"Look directly ahead, dear. Stop twisting."

"Yes, ma'am." She turned around but was listening to the kitchen noise.

"You know, dear, wars are not won in a day."

"What?"

"Wars are not won in a day against a superior force. They take patience, wisdom, cunning, and a strategy. A superior force could be defeated with a superior strategy."

"Granny, what are you talking about? Are my measurements almost done?"

The caretaker kept measuring. "Just a few more, dear. You see, when you have an opponent who is faster and stronger, you can't defeat them with power and speed. That is their strength and your weakness. You have to find their weakness and use your strengths to counter."

Emmy turned and listened to the kitchen banter. "Got it. Great advice. Fight fire with fire."

"Eyes front, please," Granny corrected. "Not what I said. Emmy, do you know what happens when you fight fire with fire?"

"Granny, I don't need your help. I appreciate what you are saying, but I got this."

"Answer the question, please."

"You win."

"No! You get burned and lose," Mrs. H explained. "That woman in there is a fire. She knows what she is doing. She is the superior force. You need a superior strategy. Do you have a plan to win Tood's heart?"

"Well, yeah…it's…I have…" Emmy looked at Granny. "I have…no idea what I'm doing. Help, please."

"Of course, dear. Just think before you answer this. How do you fight a fire?" Granny asked again.

Emmy pondered for a moment and then smiled. "You fight fire with water."

"Exactly," Granny replied. She helped Emmy down, and they hugged. "Now get back in the kitchen and be the beauty you know you are."

"Yes, ma'am." Emmy walked into the kitchen with a bit more confidence.

"Princess Seravina!" Granny called out. "Would you come to the living room, please?"

Seravina walked into the living room, still wearing her revealing nightgown. "Yes, how may I help you, caretaker?"

"If you would follow me upstairs to your bedroom, I have suitable day clothes for you."

"Just a moment."

Mrs. Hemingway stood on the coffee table and looked her in the eye. "I insist, princess."

"Very well. Lead the way." Seravina sighed and followed the dwarf.

They went up the stairs in silence. Mrs. H held the door open for the princess as she entered. Mrs. H closed the door and locked it.

"Why did you lock the door, dwarf? You and that door won't keep me imprisoned here," Seravina snapped but looked calmly at her nails.

"You are not a prisoner. I am not your enemy. I am here to help you."

"Really, dwarf? I hope my superior fire will not interfere with your help."

"What I said to Emmy was to encourage her, not to disparage you."

"I do not believe you."

"Mistress Seravina, you are beautiful, wise, cunning, brave, and relentless. But you lack knowledge of Between."

"I'm listening."

"I offer you my counsel and wisdom in how to navigate Between and Tood."

"You appeared to be on my cousin's side," Seravina interjected.

"I am not on her side or your side. I am on Tood's side. He is a prize beyond measure. He is my son in all but blood. To have two noble and amazing women desire to love and be with him is any mother's dream."

"He is a good man, and you raised him well."

"Thank you, dear. I hope you understand if he gets hurts in this love battle between you and Emmy." Mrs. Hemingway grabbed Seravina's nightgown and lowered the princess to her eye level. "You shall answer to me. There is not a place on earth you could run where I could not hunt you down. Do you understand?"

"Yes, ma'am," Seravina humbly replied.

Mrs. H released her and walked to the door and unlocked it.

"I have placed blue pants on your bed called jeans. There are also undergarments. The small pink one is called a panty. It goes over your rear end. The white undergarment is like a tight shift and covers your chest. There are three colored shirts on the dresser. Choose whichever you like. Please get dressed and join us in the dining room for lunch. I still have two beautiful young ladies to outfit."

"Yes, Mrs. Hemingway," Seravina answered. "Thank you."

"You're welcome, dear. See you soon." Mrs. H left the room.

Emmy helped Tood finish the food preparations and set up the dining room for lunch. Pinguino fritters, fruit salad, garden salad, and fluffy white rice. Tood called Mrs. Hemingway and Seravina to the dining room. Emmy sat next to Tood as they waited. She was about to ask him a question when Granny came in and sat across from Emmy.

"Looks great. Thanks for finishing up," Mrs. H started. "I believe Seravina will be down in a moment. She is changing into peasant clothes."

Emmy commented, "She will look amazing in anything. Put her in a burlap…"

Seravina entered the room, and time slowed down. Her golden mane flowed like a blond ocean. Her eyes sparkled with an emerald glow. Her burgandy shirt and jeans sculpted her physique flawlessly. She appeared to be floating in stride to her chair. Tood stood up as she entered the room and moved to get her chair. Her slight smile was radiant. Her words of "Thank you" were sweet music to all the listeners. As Tood returned to his seat, she glanced at Emmy and winked. Emmy realized Tood and Mrs. Hemingway were entranced, but she was not.

"Thank you for waiting for me. This is so delightful. Thank you for preparing lunch," said Seravina.

"You're welcome, dear," Granny replied. "How do the clothes feel?"

"I was skeptical at first, but they feel quite liberating. As if I could accomplish anything in this world. Almost magical." She looked at Tood and then Emmy.

"Emmy, would you say grace?" Tood asked.

"Sure," she grumbled and bowed her head. "God is good. God is great. Thank you, Lord, for the food on our plates. Amen."

"Amen," everyone repeated.

Tood and Granny talked Between politics throughout the meal, while Emmy and Seravina ate politely but were quiet.

When Emmy finished, she broke her silence. "Tood, did you have any heroes as a kid?"

Todd thought for a second. "My brother at first, but I really enjoyed comic book heroes."

"Comic books?" Vina softly inquired.

"Illustrated storybooks with fictional characters with outstanding powers," said Tood. The princess nodded and kept eating her salad.

"Who were your favorites?" asked Emmy.

"Superman. Batman. Wolverine. X-Men. The Fantastic Four. My favorite is Spider-Man."

The elf dropped her fork. "Your favorite hero was a man-spider. A tarachtan!"

Tood stammered, "He is a fictional character. He is a man with the abilities of a spider. Don't be frightened. He is not a tarachtan. The creatures were eradicated here."

"I fear nothing, Tood," Seravina calmly reported. "You mistake my surprise for fear." She picked up her fork and made a slashing motion. "I only wish to confront this menace and detach his vile head from his decrepit shoulders." She lowered her voice and spoke to the females. "The very touch of these abominations is venomous. They lurk in dark shadows, waiting to pounce. These beasts entangle you with their wicked tentacles." She suddenly jabbed her fork into her salad. "Like a viper, they jab one into your body! They slowly suckle and drain your life and soul from existence." She grabbed her water glass and slurped it. "The sordid tales, I could tell you, from the Blasted Lands, would haunt your children's children's nightmares."

Emmy and Granny gulped.

"I will bring you some comic books. You can judge for yourself," Tood replied, unfazed.

Mrs. Hemingway cleared her throat. "Tood, I will clean up lunch. You take the ladies on a tour of the house and grounds. You have several hours before you hit the town. I will finish up your dresses and place them in your rooms with shoes," the caretaker announced. "Now go before I change my mind."

"Thanks. How about it, ladies?"

They both agreed at the same time. "Yes."

"Great. We will go outside first and then tour the rest of the house," Tood commented. "I have to get my staff. I'll meet both of you on the back porch." Tood exited the room and could be heard

THE DOORS BETWEEN

bounding up the stairs. The ladies sat in silence. Seravina stared at the war murals.

Emmy again broke the awkward silence. "Those clothes look nice on you. Are the boots comfortable?"

Seravina politely replied, "Thank you, cousin. The boots are a bit tight, but I will manage."

"Oh, I have something for you." Emmy reached into her pocket. She pulled out a small gold ring.

Seravina reached out and took the ring. "Thank you, cousin. It is very sweet." She slid it on her left pinky finger. "Perfect."

Emmy said, "Vina?"

"Yes." She admired the gift.

"I have to ask. How did you…you know…how did you make an entrance like that?"

Seravina innocently looked at Emmy and blinked her eyes several times. "Whatever do you mean, cousin?"

Emmy's temper rose. "You know exactly what I mean, you—"

Tood poked his head back into the dining room. "I'm ready. Let's go."

Emmy and Seravina smiled at him and followed Tood out the back door into a slightly overcast day.

They were greeted by a ferocious crunching sound. Woof gnawed on the giant bone Emmy had given him on the porch.

"Woof." Emmy ran over to him and gave him a hug. "How is my mighty hunter? When did you get back?"

The giant canine stopped eating and hugged her back. He lightly licked her cheek and then yiped and barked. He sat on his hind legs and stared at Seravina.

"You just finished your patrol, and you wanted to meet the elf," Emmy interpreted. She saw Seravina get down on the ground. "What are you doing?"

Seravina had squatted down to the ground on her knees and hands, extended her right hand palm up, and bowed her head. "It an honor and pleasure to meet one of the Malocharee, kings of the North Firrest."

Woof bowed his head and licked her hand. He softly barked.

Seravina pulled back her hand and stood up. "Thank you, King Wolfgang. I am feeling much better." The elf then spoke to Woof in an unknown language.

Woof barked, growled, yiped his story for several minutes, but Emmy could not understand it.

Emmy muttered to herself, "Malocharee? King Wolfgang? Why can't I understand him now?"

Woof padded over to Seravina. "May I pet you, my liege?" He agreed, and the elf gently rubbed his head and neck.

Seravina explained, "The Malochareans have been a great ally to the elves for centuries. Many a battle were decided on the strength of our friends. I learned his native tongue as a child. A Malocharean ambassador would visit the palace every summer. Did you not know he is the great ruler of his people?"

Emmy seethed but remained silent.

Tood leaned on his staff and interrupted, "So, great king, did you find anything interesting on patrol?"

Woof growled at Tood and then strolled back to his bone.

"Nothing today. Thanks," Tood replied. "Oh, we are heading to town tonight. If you want to come, you have to take a bath."

Woof whimpered but acknowledged the request.

Emmy volunteered, "I would love to give you a bath, Wo… Wolfgang."

The king happily barked.

Tood directed them. "Let's head over to the barn."

He led them to a worn brick pathway which meandered toward the gate. On the left was an organized fruit and vegetable garden with bees buzzing all around. On the right was a small pond with lily pads, willow wisps, and tall cattails. Two families of ducks were swimming in the greenish-blue water. Tood opened the black iron gate which was attached to a brown-red brick wall. Almost all the bricks had a letter of the alphabet or a word written on it. The brick wall was a perfect rectangle surrounding the Doorf House.

Seravina asked, "Lor…Tood, do you have other servants besides Mrs. Hemingway?"

Tood corrected her, "Mrs. Hemingway is not a servant. She is my adopted mother. My parents died when I was young, and she raised my brother and me. The people who work here are employees, not servants. There are about thirty altogether. Many collect trash and junk from all over the land. The city people call them junkers. I pay them fairly for their services."

Seravina replied, "Interesting. Do you have any fighting men or guards?"

"Not exactly." Tood explained, "I personally train the junkers weekly and have taught them some self-defense moves with the quarterstaff."

Emmy asked, "So you run a waste disposal business?"

"Yes, in a manner of speaking," Tood said. "But Granny runs the day-to-day logistics. I am the figurehead, the junkman."

"Oh, I see," Seravina said. "I'm sorry to hear about your parents. Was it a tragic death?"

"Princess!" Emmy interjected. "That is not a proper question."

Tood opened the gate and then stopped. "I don't mind. I was not old enough to remember. Mrs. Hemingway and my brother, Dudley, told me what happened." The ladies went through the gate, and Tood followed. He closed the gate. "A rift, a giant doorway, randomly opened above them and dropped a three-story brick building on them. The rift then disappeared and was never seen again."

Emmy and Seravina both gasped and gave Tood a warm embrace.

"How awful. I am so sorry, Tood," Emmy consoled.

"Thank you, both." He stepped back and followed the path toward a large white brick gazebo. "I have come to terms with it. I have their memory and love all around me." He pointed to the brick wall. "You see, the walls surrounding and protecting the Doorf Estate are from that building. When the people of Between heard of my parents' demise, they were emotionally moved, honored them, and constructed the pathway, the walls, and the pool house. My brother and I used the brick to rebuild their gazebo." He sat down in the gazebo with Emmy and Seravina.

Tood pointed to a spot to the right. "They are buried over there. My brother told me my mom and dad would sit in a white wooden gazebo every night to watch the sunset. I come here sometimes to think about them. They had their first kiss in a gazebo."

Emmy and Seravina both sniffled and wiped tears from their eyes.

Tood heard the sniffle and turned around. "Hey. Are you guys all right? I didn't mean to make you cry."

"It is just so sweet," Emmy blubbered. "It just reminded me of my mom and grandfather."

Seravina wiped her eyes. "My father was also tragically murdered. He died in my arms. I have vowed vengeance upon the killer."

"Vina, I'm sorry for your loss. My parents were not murdered. It was an accident," Tood replied. "Let's follow the path to the barn."

The ladies followed him in silence for a few hundred feet.

Seravina caught up to Tood. "I do not mean to disagree with you, but you were a child when it occurred and have only heard stories from loved ones. Your parents were powerful mages. An enemy could have caused their demise. What did your brother think about their deaths?"

"Seravina!" Emmy protested. "We have dug up enough of his past. Let it be."

Tood answered, "My brother. My brother never told me his thoughts about the matter, since it was an accident. He did vow to close all the doors and rifts. He tried to close all of them at once so it could never happen again."

"Apparently, he was not successful because we are here," the princess replied.

Tood took a deep breath and then answered, "His attempt caused the Great Junk Incident about thirty years ago. Instead of closing the doors, he opened more. Junk from all four realms flooded the land and nearly destroyed Between. As a boy, I helped him close most of the rifts and doors before it was too late. When I became of age to be the Doorf at thirteen, he left, and I haven't heard from him since. He moved to Foot Lake, the farthest place from here, if he is still alive."

THE DOORS BETWEEN

The group could hear all the wild birds chirping as they approached the barn. Tood opened the barn doors wide open with an obnoxious creak. A small group of penguins burst through the doors and startled them. They laughed at themselves.

"So this is the barn. Any special memories here?" Emmy asked.

Tood chuckled. "No, not really. Just lots of chores—cleaning, feeding, haying, and milking. Ever been in a barn?"

"When I was a kid. I am more of a city girl. I rode a horse once," Emmy confessed.

"I could teach you how to ride. We have some gentle horses."

Seravina had wandered to the stables and saw five horses and three cows. She rubbed the horses' noses and fed them some oats. She noticed some letters carved into a center post. "Tood, are these your initials? TD, a heart, SM. Who is SM?"

Tood turned red and tried to cover the carving. "It's nothing. Just young love. SM was the first girl I kissed."

Emmy came over. "Tell us about it, lover boy."

Tood rolled his eyes. "I kissed her. End of story."

Seravina answered, "You don't engrave initials into a structure without some passion. Details, please."

"Okay, I will tell you," Tood replied. "If you tell me about your first kiss. Not a relative."

Emmy responded first, "I was twelve, and this boy, Tommy, in my neighborhood was always teasing me. I told my mother about it. She told me to confront him about why he always picked on me. After school at the playground, I walked up to him while he was with his friends. I said, 'Tommy, why do you keep picking on me?' He turned red as a tomato and ran away. I chased him all around the playground, and then I followed him home. All the time, I was yelling, 'Why are you picking on me?' He stopped at his front porch and turned to face me. He said, 'Stop yelling and I will tell you. You are the prettiest girl in school, and I think you are nice.' I walked up to him, put my arms around his neck, and kissed him for a whole minute. Tommy was my boyfriend from then until he moved away two years later."

Tood smiled and commented, "Interesting. You have not lost your persistence." Emmy blushed.

"I was fourteen," Seravina started. "His name was Jarvis. He was a young dashing knight and commanded to provide his princess with hand-to-hand combat instruction. I was stubborn and conceited. Every day he would instruct me, and I would refuse. After a month, he reported to my father, the king, my lack of effort. My father publicly rebuked me in court. I was humiliated. I wanted to kill Jarvis. At our next session, I was so angry I tried to strike Jarvis. Without ever putting his hands on me, he dodged and avoided every strike. I became furious and wild, but he was calm and patient.

"With a simple move, he dropped me to the floor. He then pinned me to the floor. He said smugly, 'Glad to see some fire in you, my lady.' I spit in his face. I yelled, 'How dare you touch your princess?' He leaned in and melted me with a long kiss on the lips. I put a knee to his bollocks. He rolled off me. I stood and then kicked him in the face. I left the training room. I could have reported his kiss to my father, and he would have been executed. However, all I could think about was his smooth lips pressed against mine." Seravina sighed.

"It was that good?" Emmy asked.

"Yes. I could not sleep all night. I returned the next day, and Jarvis was there. He had a bandage over his broken nose. We never mentioned the kiss or the broken nose again. He was the best instructor. He instructed me for another year, and then he was sent to fight in the east."

Tood responded, "Those are great stories. Mine is not so in comparison, but I promised. It was on my thirteenth birthday party, and her name was Sheila McNamara. She was in my class at Cutoff University. I invited my whole class to the party. I gave her a personal tour of the barn while everyone was swimming in the pool. At that post, I told her how I felt about her and kissed her. She felt the same way, so I carved our initials. We kissed several times and then returned to the party holding hands." Tood strolled back to the barn doors. "Time to continue the tour."

"Nice. What happened with…ouch!" Emmy started to inquire, but Seravina pinched her. The princess whispered in Emmy's ear. Emmy kept quiet. The ladies walked out of the barn and followed the path to the pool house. Tood closed the barn doors and caught up with them.

"At first, this house was the servants' quarters and an outside pool," Tood explained. "Then it was storage for a long time. I filled in the outside pool right there when it could not be repaired." Tood pointed to a large flower bed. "Then I created"—he opened the glass doors—"Between's first indoor pool and spa."

The twenty-five-meter-by-fifty-meter cement pool was clean and clear with a small rock waterfall on the far side. The tranquil waterfall provided the only noise in the serene environment. Two metallic ladders were on the deep end near the waterfall. On the near side was shallow water which gradually descended into the deeper waters.

"This is like a beach. Tood, this is incredible." She walked in and touched the water and smelled it. "It's saltwater. It reminds me of the outdoor pool at my YMCA."

Seravina had gone to the opposite side and found a white laundry bin and white fluffy towels. "What is a yimka? Is it a sacred pool of the divine like this one? I've never heard it called a yimka."

"Yes. It is what my mother called the sacred waters," Emmy answered.

Tood said, "There are changing rooms, a food and drink bar, a frigger, a kitchen, lounge chairs, and tables." He headed to the frigger and removed three cold bottles.

"Tood, what is this table with a small fishing net in the middle?" Seravina inquired and laughed. "Do you serve fish here?" She picked up a small round wooden paddle.

Emmy went to the opposite end of the table. "This is a game. Tood told me earlier about this. It is called Ping-Pong."

"Oh, I see. Ping-Pong. So you slap fish into the net."

Emmy looked down and found a small white ball. She picked it up. "No fish involved. You just hit this ball back and forth with the small paddle. If you don't hit it back, I score a point. If you miss my side, I score a point, and vice versa." Emmy hit the ball to Seravina.

The princess did not move, and the ball fell off the table. "Why?"

"It is fun," Emmy encouraged. "Hit the ball back to me."

Seravina picked up the ball and looked at it crossly. She looked at Emmy and then Tood. She winked at him, smiled, and served a perfect ace which struck Emmy between the eyes. "Oh, sorry, cousin. It must be beginner's luck."

Tood interjected and whispered to Emmy, "I thought you knew that the elves invented table tennis?"

Emmy rubbed forehead. "Thanks for the warning." She put the paddle down and stormed out the exit. She opened the French doors into a patio area with a firepit. She sat down in an empty lounge chair near the firepit.

Seravina called after her, "Just a jest, cousin."

Tood carried the three bottles to the empty firepit and sat down. "Seravina, would you join us?" He handed one to Emmy and then Seravina.

Seravina sauntered her way to them and sat in a chair next to Emmy.

Tood opened his drink and sipped. He put his hands to his chin. "My friends, there is something I need to tell you both. Seravina, Emmy is not your cousin. She is from the west world."

"I knew it all along. There is no such thing as a yimka in my world. My uncle cannot have children. Scullery maid. Indeed!" Seravina proclaimed.

"Emmy, Seravina does not have a hidden agenda to conquer Between and use its power to control time and the universe."

"Are you sure? She still seems suspicious to me," Emmy replied.

"I'm suspicious?" Seravina stood up and pointed a finger at Emmy. "You have lied and misled me since the moment you spoke, cousin!"

Emmy bolted up and knocked her finger away. "Don't call me that, you vixen. You would too if a bizarre elf pins you against a wall and cuts you with a pencil!"

Tood whispered, "Ladies, please sit down and calm down."

They sat down slowly, folded their arms across their chests, and turned away from each other.

"Unfortunately, there is more to tell you," Tood explained. "It is easier if I show you." The ladies turned toward Tood. He pulled a photograph from his jacket but did not show them. "I am going to show you a picture. As soon as you recognize the person, say what is his or her relationship to you. Do you understand?"

They looked at each other and then nodded in agreement.

Tood flipped the photograph around.

They peered at the picture, looked at each other, and responded simultaneously:

Emmy said, "Grandfather." Seravina said, "Brother." They stared at each in disbelief.

Tood responded, "Emmy, you already know the person you thought was your grandfather was your father. Seravina is your father's only sister. She is your aunt." He turned to the elf princess. "Seravina, your brother, the prince, came here and fled to the west world. According to Emmy, he died several years ago. She is his only daughter. She is your niece and the rightful heir to the elven throne."

"You said what now?" Emmy questioned. "I am..."

"Tood, how could this be?" Seravina asked. "It has only been five years since my brother disappeared."

"Time moves slowly in the east, but here in Between, it moves more rapidly. In Emmy's world, it is lightning fast. Five years in the east is twenty to twenty-five years here and forty-five to fifty years in the west. It is not exact, so traveling between times and worlds can be difficult and disastrous."

"You said I was the...," Emmy mumbled.

"So that would make Emmy fifty years old. She looks great for fifty. I would have guessed twenty-four," Seravina commented.

Emmy muttered, "Thank you. I'm twenty-three. You said I am..."

Tood further explained, "Your brother, Divad, went to the time 1999. But after a year, I desperately required his help back in Tween. He came with me but left his wife and newborn daughter in the west. When I sent him back, something went wrong, and I miscalculated the time. I sent him back almost fifty years in the past. I tried everything to get him, but I never found him."

"So how did Emmy know him as a grandfather?"

"Divad knew the exact time and place when he came to the west. He just had to wait and try not to disturb the timeline and his own existence. After he left to help me in 2000, he revealed himself to his wife and acted like a grandfather to Emmy."

Seravina scratched her head. "Remind me never to time travel."

"You and Emmy already have," Tood replied. "I believe those gold necklaces have helped you travel through time and space to Between. Right, Emmy? Emmy?"

Seravina and Tood turned around and found Emmy passed out on the lounge chair. They rushed over to her, but she would not awaken. Tood scooped her up and carried back to the house.

"This is such a princess move," Seravina sassed while patting her hand.

CHAPTER 25

As Iron Sharpens Iron, so a Man Sharpens the Countenance of His Friend

Mrs. Hemingway came down the stairs and found Tood and Seravina sitting together in the living room. "She is asleep for now. Woof will stay with her until she wakes up. Do you think she should go out tonight?"

"It is up to her," Tood replied. "I still think it would be good. She said she loves to dance. We'll wait until she wakes up."

Seravina said, "I have been groomed my entire life to assume the throne. My uncle and I have been sharing the responsibilities of the monarchy until I come of age and we bring the murderous fugitive to justice. I could have reacted just like Emmy when the burden of an entire kingdom was untimely cast upon me. She was without notice or training. She just needs a little time and wise counsel to navigate this predicament. She is stronger than she appears."

"Well said, dear. I am going to finish up the dresses," Mrs. H said. "If you need me, I will be in the wardrobe." She disappeared around the corner.

"My lady, when do you come of age for the throne?"

"Next year, when I turn twenty-five. Why do you ask this? You should know of my coronation time."

"Why not wait to find the murderer after you are crowned queen and then have all the power of the dynasty behind you?"

"You know so much of my world." Seravina stood up. "Yet are ignorant of the truth. The fugitive not only stole the king's life, but he also purloined the Blood Stone."

Tood scratched his head and asked, "What is the Blood Stone?"

"My brother, Divadus, was here for years, and he never mentioned it once? What about your knowledge of elfin history?"

"Your brother said lots of things about your kingdom, even described you, but I do not recall any Blood Stone."

"My arrival now, in part, is to retrieve the stone to unify the elves and stop a civil war. The ancient elders unified the elves with the Blood Stone. Each leader gave up some of their magical powers and placed it within the stone. When used for good, the stone has brought prosperity and peace, but for evil, destruction and war. The elders elected a humble elf farmer, my ancestor, to be the first king, and entrusted him with the Blood Stone. He and the stone represented all the people. As long as he and his family stewarded it, the elves would remain together, and his family would humbly rule."

"I have never heard this before. What does your brother have to do with this?" Tood asked. "I don't understand."

"Why can't you understand?" Seravina pondered out loud. She paced back and forth. She stopped and sat directly in front of Tood. "Tood, look at me." The piercing green eyes delved into the enigmatic face.

Tood returned the gaze. "Yes, my lady."

"My brother, your friend, murdered my father. I saw it with my own eyes. He stole the Blood Stone and escaped to Between."

Tood moved away from her and stood up. "No. It can't be. No, you are trying to confuse me and trick me. He was not a killer. He was my best friend. He was gentle and kind. No. You are lying. Get out of my head."

"I am not in your mind," she calmly spoke. "I have only spoken the truth since my arrival here. I am not lying. I can prove it."

"How? It happened over twenty-five years ago."

Seravina invited Tood to sit back down. "When Divadus arrived here, did he have injuries?"

"Yes." He sat down.

Seravina said, "One arrow in the right knee and one arrow just below the sternum. Both arrowpoints were laced with a toxic poison."

"How did you—"

"After he murdered our father, I hunted my brother down and launched those arrows. I never miss my mark. I stood over him and watched him bleed out. His body twitched and shuddered as the poison coursed through his blood. The arrows alone would have killed him, but I desired to see the wretch suffer in death. I sat in silence for an hour as he screamed in agony. Just as he took his excruciating last breath, the worm smiled at me. I removed my sword to plunge into his heart, but his lifeless corpse vanished. He just faded out of existence."

"Clever story, but it proves nothing. This is unbelievable. His own sister. He is not the killer. You probably deposed your father. You are in denial and just deflecting."

"Do you still have the arrowheads?"

"What? The arrowheads from his injuries?" Tood replied. "No. Why would I? He was unfairly, brutally attacked and escaped from a ruthless tyrant."

"Tood, in the east, are poison arrows used in warfare?"

"No. It was outlawed by…" Tood struggled to recall. "They are only used as capital punishment against—"

"Murderers," the princess finished. "Tood, do you have the poison points?"

"I don't think so...I don't know...maybe in my closet."

Seravina gently placed her hand on his arm. "Go fetch it, please."

Tood stood up. "I don't know what it will prove. But I'll look for it."

Seravina had to wait only a minute, and he returned with a metal box and sat down. He nonchalantly tossed it between them. He did not open the box.

"Is this made of lead?" she asked but did not touch it.

Tood casually nodded. "Of course. Almost all my storage containers are made of lead."

"Why would you place these arrowheads in the only material which magic cannot distort? Why did you pick out this box?"

"I...don't know. I was going to throw them away. I don't... know."

"When you are ready, I want you to open the box and read the letters imprinted on the side of the metal points."

Tood carelessly reached for the box and placed his left hand on the top. He closed his eyes, and vivid pictures of Divadus filled his mind. His eyes opened, but the princess before him had lost all color, and her eyes were closed. She had become a beautiful granite statue. He moved in slow motion as he pulled open the lid. His hand trembled as before a deadly viper. He pulled out the tip and raised it to eye level. He read the letters out loud: "A-N-I-V-A-R-E-S." As he spoke the last letter, a fog lifted from his memories. He remembered when Divadus arrived. He had removed the arrows and healed the elf. He remembered speaking to Mrs. Hemingway about his suspicions about the elf and the name on the points. He warned Jocelyn. Josie, my... He recalled placing the arrowheads in the lead and then confronting Divadus. He closed his eyes again. When he opened them, the princess's vibrant colors had returned.

"When you are ready, I want you to open the box and read the letters imprinted on the side of the metal points," said Seravina.

"I don't have to open the box, princess. I remember everything. It is your name on the heads."

THE DOORS BETWEEN

"Exactly." She sighed deeply. "My brother placed you under a powerful multilevel mind trap. I could not break it. I could only lead you to the escape routes."

"Thank you, my lady. Ahh! Oww!" Tood leaned back and rubbed his head with both hands. "My head is vibrating. Rusty nails are scraping my skull. The room is a kaleidoscope. Ohhh! Owww!"

"It will soon subside," Seravina encouraged. "Divadus's accomplice did not fare as well. His brain literally exploded. A very untidy mess."

Tood lifted his head briefly and stared at the princess. He lowered his exploding melon back on a cushion and moaned loudly.

"About two months ago, I finally tracked this wizard down, and he revealed to me all about Divadus's plan and how he departed to Between."

"Could you get me some water, please? Ehhh!" Tood mumbled from the couch.

"Of course." Seravina ran to the kitchen.

When she zoomed back to the living room, Tood had disappeared. She caught an ungodly noise erupting from the back porch. She discovered the junkman in the yard bent over and exercising the liberty to evacuate the contents of his stomach. He heaved at least three more times until he achieved complete freedom.

Seravina walked over to the freedom fighter. She held out the glass of water. "I should have warned you about the vomitus possibilities."

Tood straightened up, wiped his unclean mouth, and grabbed the water. He sipped a little, swished it around, and then spit. "At least I still have my head."

A sincere laughter broke loose from the serious princess. She tripled over in incontrollable mirth. "Still have my head." She gasped for air. She made an explosion noise and gestures. Tood smirked and then joined her laughter. "I am…glad. You still. Have. Your head!" Seravina cackled. Tears formed in her eyes. "I'm sorry." She giggled. "Are you feeling better?"

"Much. Thanks again." He stumbled, but Seravina caught him and walked him to the porch steps. He drank the water. "How did you know Divadus had me in a mind trap?"

She wiped the giggle tears away. "I didn't know for sure, but I know my brother. He would torture and manipulate the palace servants without mercy. I had to undo his playing all the time. I first suspected it when I first mentioned his name to you. You thought I was asleep, but I noticed you had paused at the door. You had a sweat bead drip from your left ear."

Tood said, "That is amazing. I had no idea I had been tricked all those years. Your honest bravery broke me free. Thank you from the bottom of my heart to the base of my skull. Ow. Oh!" He rubbed the back of his neck and moaned again.

"It may take some time before all your memories come back. Expect more head throbs. I may know something which could be beneficial," Seravina interjected.

"Ice, some aspirin, and sleep," Tood moaned. "Don't say laughing."

"No. Although, laughter is good medicine," she teased. "Some movement. Walking or running. Sparring, if you have a training room."

"Sparring? Really?"

"Yes, of course. It is good for your mind to work with your body to heal."

"If it can stop this head agony, I'm in. I have a finished basement. Did your old instructor inform you of this technique?"

"Yes. Let us go to the cellar, and I shall show you."

Seravina helped Tood off the steps and back into the house. They walked together down the hall to the door next to Tood's room. Tood removed his keys and unlocked the door. He opened the door, and lights automatically turned on, revealing a downward staircase.

"Follow me and watch your head on the turn," Tood advised.

Seravina followed and ducked to miss a massive beam just above the final set of stairs. She expected to step down into a dank, unfinished cellar, but the room was clean and well-lit. The entire far wall was a mirror. The room had a wooden plank vaulted ceiling and a black tiled floor. Tood removed his shoes and silently moved to the left and opened a cabinet removing two quarterstaffs. Seravina removed her shoes, stepped on the floor, hesitated, and then marveled.

"What is the substance of the floor? It feels cool, spongy, and smooth." She knelt and pushed her left hand into the black tile. "Did you get it from a marsh? It's like an indoor bog without water." She called to Tood, "Look, it makes me bounce." She leaped up and down.

"I discovered it in the Wamp," Tood explained. "But it is actually a substance called rubber. It is an invention of the west. It has many applications, but it is superb for training floors. It absorbs hits and cushions falls." He smacked a rod to the floor. "It is durable and easily repaired. It is water-repellent, a breeze to clean, and bouncy." Tood tossed the princess a quarterstaff.

She easily snatched it with her left hand, spun it, and twirled it around her back. "How quaint. A quarterstaff," she teased. "I believe I mastered this wooden toy at sixteen."

"I didn't want you to rough me up too much." He spun his staff around his waist and smoothly twirled it in his right hand. "I also mastered it, but at age fifteen."

"I believe you are feeling better, my lord. Care to spar with me?"

"I would love to." Tood smiled. "Shall we set a standard for victory?"

"Death." Seravina grinned. "Just a jest. Last to fall is the victor."

Tood agreed, and they placed the quarterstaffs by their sides. The warriors bowed to each other. Tood stepped back on his left foot and held the staff defensively. Vina stepped back with her right foot in an aggressive stance.

Tood quickly attacked Seravina's left, but she easily blocked it and countered with a right strike. He dodged it and sprung backward to block an overhead swing. He parried her numerous attacks and countered with left and right strikes, which she blocked. This went on for several minutes, with neither gaining an advantage or hit.

Tood lifted his hand for a break. Seravina halted. Tood was sweating profusely, but the princess remained dry and calm.

"You are taking it easy on me," Tood panted. "I admit, you are faster than me."

"It was more of a warm-up. You are better than I expected. I admit you are stronger than me, but I don't sweat like a hog." She grunted like a pig toward Tood. "Ready to go again, piggy?"

"Psychological warfare? Insulting me to cause a foolish reaction and mistake."

"Is it working?"

"Not yet. But I'd rather be a pig than a woman."

Seravina screamed and attacked with such fury and speed, Tood could not block them all. She landed a right thrust into his stomach. Oof! He flew and crashed into the right wall. He buckled to one knee but did not fall.

"So what do you think of a woman now, Lord Pig?"

Tood stood to his feet. "Impressive. Impressive for a princess warrior." He removed his outer shirt and tossed it in the air.

He attacked with lighting moves from every direction. Seravina defensively blocked every swipe, lunge, and strike but could not counter. Then she dodged when she should have parried and caught a strike on her back. *Smack!* She stumbled forward and nearly fell. She caught herself with one hand and performed a perfect one-handed cartwheel. She landed and turned to face her opponent. She removed her outer shirt, pulling it over her head. "Lord Pig is no longer wallowing in the mud! Come on!"

Two battle cries echoed in the enclosed basement as they charged each other at a full sprint. They raised their quarterstaffs and leaped into the air. While in midflight, the combatants simultaneously noticed and turned their attention to a quiet spectator on the stairs, smiling and waving vigorously.

"Emmy," the distracted warriors said right before an airborne head-on collision. *Smash! Ahhh! Thud!* They smacked the ground at the same time.

Emmy ran over to them. "Are you guys okay?"

Tood and Seravina moaned and rubbed their skulls.

"You guys were fabulous. All those moves, spins, the banter, and the cartwheel. It was like watching a Bruce Lee movie, but for real. I really thought you were going to kill…" She kept speaking, but the wounded ignored her.

Seravina rubbed her forehead. "Who is Bruce Lee? Does she always prattle on when she is excited?"

"He is a mighty warrior from her world. Yes, it is difficult for her to stop."

"Vina, that thing you did when you got him in the stomach. Wow. Tood, you zipped…"

"In about three seconds, she will realize we have not been listening," Tood remarked.

"Around so fast. It was like a blur. When he smacked your back, I cringed, but the cartwheel was so cool. I wish I had learned…"

Seravina held up three fingers. Three, two, one.

"Have you guys been listening to me?"

"What are you doing down here? I thought you were resting," Seravina asked.

"Well, I woke up about an hour ago, feeling incredible. So good in fact—"

"I feel a little bad for not listening, but this could go on a long time," Tood said.

"And he was so filthy I had to drain the bathtub twice before the water…"

"She is adorable when she uses her hands to describe everything," Seravina commented.

"He is all cleaned and dried. The bathroom was a disaster, and I couldn't just…"

Tood held up three fingers. Three, two, one.

"Why do you all keep putting up three fingers?" Emmy replied.

"Just making sure we don't have concussions." Tood grinned. "We don't."

Seravina whispered to Tood, "Not yet."

"I'm so glad. When I came downstairs, I heard this banging and grunting. I followed the sound and watched the battle. I didn't disturb you, did I, Xena and Lord Pig?"

"Who is Xena?" Seravina inquired.

Before Emmy could provide another lengthy explanation, Tood stood up and politely interrupted. "She was also another warrior from Emmy's world. I'm so grateful you washed up Woof. Is it time to get ready for tonight?"

"Yes. Granny sent me. Wait a minute. Is there something going on here?"

"Just a little sparring practice," Seravina replied.

"Sparring. Nothing else. Lead the way, Emmy," Tood said.

She smiled and hugged them and then started up the stairs. "Okay. You know I would love to get some lessons from either one of you. I took one karate lesson, and I didn't like it. I was more into soccer and softball, number 12. Wow, I just realized I had the same uniform number…"

"Thank you, Lord Pig. I had a lovely time." Seravina bowed and walked up the stairs.

"As did I, Lady Xena." Tood bowed and followed.

"Don't ever call me that," Seravina playfully sneered and held up three fingers.

Three, two, one.

"Are you guys listening to me?"

CHAPTER 26

A Merry Heart Makes a Cheerful Countenance

After eating an early dinner at 4:00 p.m., Emmy and Seravina got ready for the outing. Mrs. Hemingway had finished the dancing outfits and assisted the young ladies. Tood took two aspirin and laid down for a nap to recover from his mental and physical sparring before he dressed. Woof waited on the couch in the living room.

Emmy came down the stairs first. She was glad Granny had shortened her skirt to just above knee length. Her black hair was slicked back into a tight ponytail. She spun herself in the foyer, and the pleats wonderfully encircled her. She walked into the living room.

She spotted her canine friend. "There you are. I have something for you."

Woof sat upright and stuck out his tongue. He barked.

"No." She rubbed his head. "It is not a bone. It's a ring. I had it made for you. I attached it to this leather strap."

Woof bowed his head and gave a low howl.

"It would be an honor. You've never worn a collar in Between." She placed it around his neck and fastened it. "I am honored. You look dignified, mighty hunter." He licked her softly on the cheek and then bashfully turned away.

Emmy noticed. "Are you blushing?" She hugged him. "You are so sweet."

Mrs. Hemingway stepped out of the kitchen. "Don't you two look adorable. Now let me see you, dear." Emmy stood up and spun around. "Smart, spunky, and sweet. Just like you."

Seravina quietly entered the living room wearing her long-pleated dress with her hands behind her back. "Salutations." Her long blond hair was in an elaborate braid starting on her right side and spiraling to the left with an unbraided tail.

Emmy stood up and grabbed her relative's hands. "You look so lovely."

"Thank you, niece. You also are beautiful."

Mrs. H said, "Do you like the fit? Spin around, please." She spun. "You look elegant and gorgeous." Seravina smiled and did a curtsey.

"Where is my noodle? Your carriage will be here at six thirty. Muchogusto will be your driver. Just to warn you, he only says two words."

Emmy questioned, "Mucho gusto?"

"Yes. How did you know?"

"Know what?"

"The words he says."

"The words who says?"

"Muchogusto!"

"It is usually a pleasure to speak to you, but what are the words the driver says?"

"Mucho gusto."

"And the driver's name is whom?"

"Muchogusto."

"So whom the driver comes over and says mucho gusto…"

Granny corrected Emmy, "No. Muchogusto is the driver."

"So who is whom?"

Seravina interrupted, "I believe it is *who* and not *whom*."

Emmy asked, "The driver is Who not Whom?"

"When you said *whom*, it should be *who*."

"So whom is Who. Who is the driver? Who, the driver only says mucho gusto."

"Yes. He says it every time."

"Everytime says it?"

"Yes. Mucho gusto every time."

"Everytime says mucho gusto?"

"No. Muchogusto says it."

"Everytime says what?"

"Mucho gusto."

Tood popped his head into the living room. "Muchogusto is here with the carriage. Just a warning, ladies. He only says *mucho gusto*."

The ladies smirked at each other and moved into the foyer, where Tood was waiting.

They froze in their tracks when they saw the junkman standing next to the sunlight window. Mrs. Hemingway quietly whistled a catcall.

Emmy said softly, "Hummina, hummina, hummina."

Seravina said breathlessly, "Oh my. Oh my, oh my." She fanned herself. "Did the temperature rise or is it just me?"

Emmy answered, fanning herself, "It's not just you, sister."

Seravina and Emmy each made a low growling sound at the same time.

Tood turned and smiled at them. He had shaved his facial scruff and slicked back his brown waves. He wore a black fedora on the back half of his head. He wore a black suit jacket with white pin-stripes, a thin gray tie attached to a snow-white shirt. His ebony belt and silver buckle held up midnight pleated trousers, which partially covered his two-tone black and gray leather Oxfords.

Emmy and Seravina sauntered over to him.

Emmy touched his right sleeve. "Well, look who shines like a new penny. You are quite the hepcat, big Dadeo. You are styling in your Zoot suit."

Seravina rubbed his left arm. "Your handsome countenance has been enhanced with this smart and clever attire. I like your hat." She lightly touched it.

Tood removed his hat, bowed, slid it down his arm, and tricked it back to his head. The young ladies cheered. "Thanks. You both look magnificent."

Mrs. H rolled her eyes at Tood. "All that practice finally paid off." She opened the door for them. "You better get going, dears. Be back before midnight, or the carriage turns back to a pumpkin."

Seravina asked, "Is that true?"

Emmy calmed her down. "She is just joking with us. I think."

Tood handed Granny his camera. "Would you mind?"

"Not at all, dear."

"I wish I had my phone. I would love a picture." Emmy commented. "I lost it when I came to Between."

"What is a phone?" Seravina wondered.

Tood answered, "It's a communication device with many compooter features."

"What is a compooter?"

"It is pronounced *computer*," Emmy corrected. "I'll explain later."

Tood extended his elbows to them. They grabbed his arms and looked at Mrs. H.

"Smile." The dwarf snapped several pictures. "You all look fantastic."

"Where is Woof?" asked Emmy.

"He is groomed and waiting in the carriage for us," Tood replied. "Let's go."

"Have a swinging good time," Granny said as they walked past her.

The trio entered the classic black closed carriage from the only door on the right and waved to Muchogusto. Tood held the door open and helped the ladies up the stairs. Two spotted mustangs, Ringo and Star, pulled the vehicle. The driver sat on the elevated seat with the reins in his hands. He wore an all-black suit with a white fedora.

THE DOORS BETWEEN

He greeted the party with a friendly smile. "Mucho gusto."

Tood sat next to Woof, while Seravina and Emmy sat across from them. Tood tapped the roof three times, and the carriage slowly surged forward. Woof nodded to the ladies and then looked out the window.

Emmy asked Tood, "Is Woof all right?"

"Yes. He doesn't like the motion of the carriage. He gets motion sickness."

Emmy reached over and rubbed his chest. "You got this, friend." Woof licked her hand.

"Maybe he is a little nervous about the contest."

Seravina asked, "What contest?"

Tood said, "Every year, they have a swing dance contest. Woof has entered every year but has not won. He is the best." Emmy raised her right eyebrow. "Really. Woof is mind-blowing, but his dance partners could not keep up." Woof sighed and looked at Emmy.

"Maybe he hasn't met the right girl yet." Emmy winked at Woof and Tood. "I'll be your dance partner, Woof. As long as I get at least one dance with Mr. Doorf."

Woof gave a happy bark and turned back to the window.

Seravina asked, "How long should it take to get there?"

Tood looked at his watch. "At this pace, about forty minutes."

"This is a lovely carriage. Family heirloom?" Seravina asked as she touched the walls and seat.

"Yes," Tood answered. "It has been refurbished several times, but the bones are the same. I've made some modifications and upgrades of my own. Emmy, did you notice the wheels?"

"No. Why?"

"They are Goodyear rubber tires. Ladies, do me a favor. Jump up and down with me. On the count of three. One, two, three." They bounced up and down in their seats.

The cabin moved up and down, but the carriage rolled on smoothly and quietly.

"Independent front and rear suspension," Emmy answered.

"Exactly. Smoothest carriage ride ever." He leaned back in his seat. "With this button here, I can speak to Mrs. Hemingway back at the house."

"You got a button for drinks and some grub?" Emmy scoffed.

Tood pressed the third one down and raised his eyebrows up and down. The floor between them opened, and a small table emerged with four bottles in an ice bucket and a covered snack bowl.

"Nice," Emmy said and grabbed a bottle. "What are the other buttons?"

"The second one is an intercom to the driver. The fourth one activates the music. I have a big collection. What do you think, Vina? Would you like to listen to something?"

Seravina said, "Impressive. Perhaps in a moment. I have a question about the music and dancing tonight."

"What's your question?" Tood replied.

"I'm not sure what to ask or what to expect. Will there be an orchestra?"

Tood sat up. "They are called musical bands. There are horns, drums, trumpets, clarinets, violins, violas, bass, guitars, flutes, piano, but not a full orchestra. They play fast-paced big-band swing music, but they also have slow songs and have many talented female and male singers. Some of the best musicians I have ever heard are in Between."

Seravina smiled. "Thank you." She mumbled, "Clear as mud. What about the dances?"

Emmy raised an eyebrow. "The best? Clearly, you're spinning your wheels. I happen to be an expert of swing music, and I can cut a rug like Fred and Ginger."

Woof turned, glanced at Tood, and then stared at Emmy.

Seravina asked, "Who are Fred Ginger? What is cut a rug?"

"Incredible swingers. It means to dance, boogie, bustin', movin', jump, jive, swing, move your feet to the beat, baby," Emmy explained.

"I am not an infant!" Seravina protested. Emmy rolled her eyes.

Tood asked, "Classic swing or modern swing boogie?"

THE DOORS BETWEEN

Emmy sat back in her seat. "Apples and oranges. It's all good fruit. Test the professor, Jack." She put her hands behind her back and crossed her legs.

"I think he asked about the music, not the fruit. You are not a professor. Why did you call him Jack?"

"It's the lingo of swing, sweet dollface. I was giving the old man some business. Bebop bebe, de dow diddle, digga digga digga, digga do."

"What are you saying? Did she answer my question?"

Tood laughed, and Woof howled. "She's scatting!"

"King Tut, let's get the tunes humming so Pollyanna can get with the groove and stop being a square," Emmy barked.

"Isn't scat bear dung?" Seravina gasped. "I am not a polygon. I think you insulted me."

Tood hit the music button, and Benny Goodman's "Flying Home" began playing.

"Out of sight, Dadeo. Swing it, baby." Emmy snapped to the beat.

"Where is that noise coming from? Is there an orchestra in the carriage?"

Emmy explained, "Yeah, dollface. Three witches from Oz used magical powers to trap a whole band inside these mini squares. Do you believe this chick? I have a bridge in Brooklyn I would like to sell ya."

Seravina answered, "I am not interested in a bridge, thank you. Witchcraft would explain the music and your strange behavior."

Emmy said, "Did you just insult one of the greatest musicians of all time, the professor, Benny Goodman?"

"Is that who is playing? It sounds like sheep, goats, cows, and rams loudly bleating during the summer heat. Tood, would you lower the volume, please?"

Emmy's face turned red. "Tood, turn it up! If Stringbean doesn't like it, she can cover her ears, or I'll send her back to the farm! She has flipped her lid."

"I'll just change it to more soothing music." Tood changed it to classical music.

"Are you calling me, Stringbean? Tomato face!"

"Tomato face! How about I cut you up and put you in a salad?"

Tood interjected, "Emmy. Seravina. Ladies. One of you switch seats with me."

"Gladly." Emmy moved next to Woof, and Tood sat next to Seravina.

The classical music was the only noise which broke up the strained silence.

Ten minutes later, Seravina broke the silence. "I am more accustomed to this style of music. I am sorry, Emmy. I should not have insulted your music."

Emmy replied, "You revved my engine, dollface. I'm sorry. I should not have insulted you. I got a little carried away with the jive attitude."

Tood asked, "Maybe you could teach Seravina to swing?"

"Cool beans!" Emmy smiled. "I could teach you the basic steps, if you would like. What dances do you know?"

Seravina said, "I would love it. I just need a little time." She thought for a moment. "Are you familiar with Branle? No. Pavane? Galliard? You must know Saltarello? No. Volta? No. My new favorite, so much action." She clapped her hands. "Gasper Sanz Canarios?"

Emmy looked at Tood, dumbfounded. "Are these pasta dishes or dances?"

Tood smirked. "Those are Renaissance dances. Very popular among the elves."

"Well, Auntie, at least you like to dance. If you want action, then I am going to introduce you to the Charleston, Lindy Hop, Texas Tommy, Louie Armstrong, Elvis Presley, and Chubby Checkers."

"Are they famous dances?"

"Some are dances, and some are singers who inspired dances."

Tood hit the second button. "Please go slower."

"Mucho gusto." The intercom sounded, and the carriage speed reduced to a crawl.

He hit the third button again, and the table disappeared back into the floor. "It's not a lot of room, but it will do."

Emmy jumped into the middle. "These are the basic steps. Once you get this, you can improvise the rest. Even some of your medieval moves?"

"Renaissance," Tood corrected.

"Tomato, tamato," Emmy continued. "Watch my feet. This is a rock step." She did it on her left and right foot. "Your turn." Emmy sat down.

Seravina stood in the middle and completed the rock steps.

"Do it again. Keep going," Emmy called out.

"What do I do with my hands?" Seravina asked, rocking back and forth.

"Put them at your side. When we add music, just sway with the beat. It will become more natural. Good. Sit for a moment." Emmy got back up. "This is a triple step. Now you try."

The elf princess did a continuous triple step.

"Great. Stop. Now we combine the rock step with a triple step. Watch. Rock step, triple step, rock step, triple step, rock step. Repeat. Your turn." Emmy sat down.

Seravina performed it flawlessly until the carriage hit a bump and she fell on Tood. "Sorry."

"No problem. You are doing great. Keep going."

Emmy called to the couple. "Okay, recess is over, kids. Junkman, play a slow swing jazz tune, maybe a ballad. Watch me as I rock step, triple step to the music."

This went on for the next forty-five minutes with Emmy introducing more basic moves like the box step and the two-step. The junkman slowly increased the tempo of the music and Seravina's speed.

A voice called from the intercom, "Mucho gusto."

Tood called back, "Thank you, Muchogusto." He turned to his friends. "We will be entering town in five minutes."

"How did you…never mind. But I didn't show her…" Emmy started.

"I will be fine. Thank you. I feel more comfortable," Seravina said.

"Are you sure?" Emmy asked.

"Yes. Don't worry, Professor. If I get stuck, I'll improvise. Tomato, tamato." She snapped her fingers and smiled.

"Potato, patato." Emmy grinned. She gave her a light punch on the arm. She hurt her hand. "Ow. You're starting to catch on, Stringbean."

CHAPTER 27

As in Water, Face Reflects Face; so a Man's Heart Reveals the Man

The young ladies looked out of the windows and saw the stone and brick buildings of Tween dimly illuminated flames from the streetlamps.

Seravina asked, "What is that glow coming from the center of town?"

Emmy replied, "It is this beautiful moving fountain. I saw it up close and personal the other night." She looked at Tood. He smiled.

"It is amazing." Seravina gazed at the structure and then bit her lower lip. "I feel like I have seen it before."

"This is your first time in Tween. It must be déjà vu," said Tood.

"Must be." Seravina was not so sure.

The carriage stopped in front of an old warehouse with a heavy metal door with a small rectangular slot near the top. The sign with bright red letters above the door read *Five Pennies*.

"This is our stop," Tood explained. "I need to explain some protocols before we go in. First, we are guests of Woof. He is the top dog here, literally. He comes here every week. Tweeners love him but barely tolerate me. We are with him." He had their undivided attention.

Emmy commented, "We are the Woof pack. Cool."

"Last, when we walk in, we walk behind him. We greet the patrons and head to his table before we go to the dance floor." He hit the roof three times.

They heard the driver climb down the carriage and open the door. He held out his hand to the ladies and helped them down. He announced, "Mucho gusto." Tood and Woof jumped down on their own. Muchogusto closed the door and climbed back to his seat. The carriage slowly meandered down the street.

Tood asked Woof, "What's the passphrase?"

Woof gave a short bark.

Tood walked up to the metal door and banged four times. The metal slot clanked open. Dark eyes glanced at the newcomers, and then a deep voice spoke. "It's a new dawn."

Tood replied, "It's a new day."

"It's a new life for me."

Tood replied, "And I'm feeling good."

"How ya doing, junkman? You's wailing later tonight?"

"Maybe, Benny. It's a surprise."

"My lips are sealed, boss. Is that the Woof? Come on in."

The slot closed with a bang, and the door creaked open. "Hooked on Swing" wafted through the hallway leading to the band and dance floor. Woof jumped inside.

"Always a pleasure, Woof man." Benny held the door open. Emmy went in after Woof and winked at Benny. "You brought some lookers this time." Benny winked at Seravina and then closed the door behind Tood. He ogled her and then moved to the front. "Excuse me." He walked them to the end of the hall.

"Please wait here. Red's coming. He will walk you to your table. See you on the dance floor, Tootsie." He walked past the group and winked again at the elf princess.

Seravina leaned forward and whispered in Emmy's ear, "That man winked at me twice and purposely brushed his hand lightly against my posterior."

Emmy looked back at Benny. "What a card. It means, dollface, he likes you."

"If he touches me again." She looked back at the bouncer and smiled. "I will break his hand."

"Cool your jets, sister," Emmy whispered. "Play it like ice."

"What?"

"Be cool. If you let him see it bothers you, he'll be a dog with a bone."

Seravina thought for a moment and then walked back to Benny. "Benny, right?"

"Yes, sweet cheeks." He smiled.

"Here's the thing, Benny. I'm here with the Woof. If he hears of you touching his fine young lady, then Woof won't be happy. You dig?"

Benny gulped. "I dig. Sorry, dollface."

Seravina patted him on the cheek. "No problem, bub." She walked back to Emmy.

Emmy asked, "What did you say to him?"

"I was playing it cool, sweet cheeks."

Emmy smiled. "We are going to have so much fun tonight." She grabbed her hand.

Red came around the corner. He was a tall man with blazing red hair, big smile, and a gray tuxedo. "Welcome to the Five Pennies. Mr. Woof, I'm sorry to say your booth is not ready yet. I sincerely apologize. It will be only a few minutes. Free drinks and food for the whole gang."

Woof barked. Tood interpreted, "Thanks. We will wait. What seems to be the problem?"

Red lowered his voice. "I don't like to speak ill of other patrons, but we had an incident with a certain Legion captain."

"Oh, really?" Emmy asked.

Red called over his shoulder, "Jimmy, Tommy, Dorsey, go help the cleanup in section four. Tell Ella and Peggy to bring drinks and appetizers to the front tables." He leaned in closer. "As a matter of fact, El Capitan paraded in here with a whole crowd of carnies, tearing up the joint, climbing on the walls, stringing up wires everywhere, and—"

Seravina interrupted, "I believe they were circus performers. Trapeze artists, to be precise."

The group turned toward her. "If you look in the rafters, there are colorful ribbons hanging from a tightrope." Seravina pointed up.

They all looked up and saw the tightrope and ribbons.

Red continued, "She's right. It was pandemonium. Then this large dame came in with—"

Seravina jumped in again. "An enormous grizzly bear." She pointed. "There are claw marks on the columns."

Red sassed her. "All righty, Sherlock. How about you tell us what happened?"

"Certainly. If you look over there." She pointed to a tarnished area of the floor. "The carnies got the bear drunk and spilled all sorts of alcohol, which removed some of the floor's finish. The bear went berserk and smashed into a lamp, which ignited fireworks. Notice the burn marks on the floor, ceiling, and on the far wall. If I'm not mistaken, your staff was able to get everyone out, including the bear, through the bay doors in the back. The bear was dragged out, leaving claw marks on the floor. Finally, as the captain and his gang left, someone threw a rock which shattered your globe chandelier. I found shards of chandelier glass on the floor. You replaced it this morning."

Red was speechless. He started clapping and then smiled. "That was flipping incredible. She is exactly right."

Emmy and Tood clapped and congratulated her.

"You really are Sherlock Holmes. You brainiac!" Emmy hugged her arm.

"Thanks." She squinted. "Who is Sherlock Holmes?"

"You. He was a great detective who used deductive reasoning to solve crimes," Tood explained. "I am so impressed."

Seravina blushed from all the attention.

A man in a black tuxedo approached the group. "The table is ready, boss."

"Wonderful." He turned to Woof. "This is Louie. He will take you to your table. I guess I have a little more cleanup to complete. Thanks to you, Ms. Holmes." He kissed her hand. "Have a great time, folks." He called to another waiter, "Armstrong, move that table to cover the spot on the floor."

"Follow me, please," Louie said.

They followed him to a front center booth next to the dance floor. Couples were dancing to the music on the wooden parquet floor. Sparkling lights trimmed the stage and around the band.

"Artie will be your waiter. You need anything, just ask," Louie said. "Have a wonderful time. Mr. Woof, happy to see you back for the Jump and Jive. My money's on you to win this year."

Emmy smiled. "Thanks. I'm his partner this year."

Louie looked her up and down. "Good luck, sweetheart. You are going to need it." He walked away, shaking his head.

"Tood, what did he mean I'm going to need it?" Emmy questioned.

"Nothing to worry about. It's just…"

"Just what?"

"Woof has been a little rough, no pun intended, with his dance partners."

"Define rough."

"Emmy, isn't the music great? Don't worry. I know he will be more careful with you."

"Spill it, Doorf, now."

"Okay, okay. I will give you the injury report for the last five years: broken arm, fractured ankles, dislocated shoulders, severe whiplash, and…what was the other one?"

Woof whimpered.

"Oh yeah. How could I forget. Head contusion and broken ribs." Tood chuckled. "His partner broke ribs when they spun out of control." He started crying. "And crashed into the head of a spectator." He snorted. "Four rows deep." Tood wiped tears from his eyes. "It's funny now, but…"

Emmy was not laughing. Tood's smile died. The house music of "In the Mood" could be heard.

Artie arrived carrying a try with glasses, a full pitcher of water, and a large bowl.

"Welcome to the Five Pennies. What can I get you fine folks?" He placed the glasses and bowl and filled them up.

"Three Shirley Temples, tater skins, and ale for the Woof," Tood barked and threw five gems on the tray.

"Yes, sir! Right away," Artie said and ran off to the kitchen.

Emmy started to protest. Tood raised a finger. "Trust me. You could not handle the hard stuff in Between. Remember the fudge, Emmy? Multiply it by ten for the booze."

"Seravina, are you feeling okay?" Emmy asked.

"I thought I saw someone I know. I guess it's déjà vu."

Tood asked, "Who?"

"See those two men standing by the bar?" Seravina pointed.

"They are Sergeant Popson and Corporal Chang," Tood muttered. "Oh no."

Popson and Chang noticed the pointing and came over to their table.

"Hey, Lieutenant Junk. I didn't think you and Woofy would show your stupid mugs around here again," Popson commented.

"Especially since you were both embarrassed so badly last year," Chang finished.

"What happened last year?" Emmy asked.

Popson explained, "This paisano didn't tell you! He and Woof were laughed off the floor. Actually dragged off by the staff and the coppers."

"What?"

Chang continued, "It was hilarious. In the middle of their routine, they started fighting. I mean knockdown, drag out, call the Legion brawl."

Emmy turned to Tood. "Why were you fighting?"

Tood quietly replied, "I went left instead of right…"

Popson continued, "Crash! Headfirst into each other in the middle of the floor. Ha! Good times! Ha!" He slapped Tood on the back. "Tood then crashed into the spectators."

Woof appeared directly in front of Popson and Chang and snarled. The instigators jumped back in fright.

"Easy, Big Dog. Just teasing. We'll settle this on the dance floor. Okay."

"Popson, Chang, do you recognize this young lady?" Tood pointed to Seravina. She waved to them.

Popson smiled and leaned against the booth. "Sorry, Green Eyes. I would never forget a beautiful lady."

Chang chimed in, "I remember you."

Seravina perked up. "You do?"

"Yes." He grabbed her hand and kissed it. "You were in my dreams last night."

Emmy spoke up. "Enough. Abbott and Costello, take the show on the road."

"Well, hello, Blue Eyes. Why don't you join me on the road? Away from these losers," Popson said.

"Beat it, Bert and Ernie. These roads are permanently closed. Take a hike."

Popson said, "See ya on the dance floor, sweetheart."

Chang said, "Catch ya later, dream girl." They both walked away laughing.

Emmy punched Tood in the arm. "You have been Woof's dance partner not just last year but every year, haven't you? Why didn't you just come out and say it?"

Seravina asked, "How did you know? Tood, you suffered all those injuries dancing? I don't know if I want to go on the floor."

Emmy explained, "I saw them once before almost starting World War III over another minor disagreement."

"Yes, I was, and I did. It's embarrassing losing every year to those jerks."

"Those jerks are going to win again if Woof and I don't get some practice!"

Artie arrived with the drinks and food. "Here you go, folks. Hot off the presses." He leaned close to Emmy. "Excuse me, miss?"

Emmy replied, "Yes, Artie?"

"Rumor has it you are the Woof's new dance partner. If it's true." He looked over his shoulder. "Odds are 20 to 1. To finish the first round."

Tood spit out his drink. "First round?"

The waiter continued, "Thirty-five to one for the second round, 100 to 1 for the third round."

Seravina asked, "How about winning outright?"

"At least 200 to 1."

Emmy spoke up. "I'll take that bet, Artie. Here's my gems."

"To win it all, dollface? Are you kidding?"

The confident dancer slid her purse to the waiter with a smile.

A miniature black book and pencil materialized in Artie's left hand. "All right, I'll put ya down. Name?"

"EC...Zinger." She grinned.

"Got it, EC Zinger. Funny." He accepted the currency, and then it vanished.

"Artie, you wanna get an inside track?" She leaned toward him.

"Me? No! I'm legit. The boys in the back just want a little info on the junkman's replacement. No offense, junkman."

"None taken." Tood grimaced.

She gave him a half smirk. "Artie, come here. Come closer. Don't be shy." She whispered in his ear, "I'm the best swinger you will ever see. But the Woof and I need a place to practice privately. You dig?"

Artie winked. "Thanks, miss. I'll get right on that." He rushed to the back.

"I hope you know what you're doing. These guys are sharks," Tood warned.

"Don't worry, Dadeo. I am a great white."

Tood asked Seravina, "Would you like to dance?"

"No, thank you. Maybe later."

"Emmy, care to dance?"

"I thought you would never ask." She put her hand in his, and they walked to the dance floor. The house orchestra started playing "Lover, Come Back to Me" as they got into dance position.

"I'll try not to break any of your bones," Emmy teased.

"Thanks. It is very kind of you, EC Zinger." They moved perfectly together to the music. "Are you sure about this bet?"

"Pops, the kid knows how to roll the dice. Trust me."

"I trust you completely. You just seem a little…"

"Different. Better. Cocky. When I woke up, I felt like a new Emmy. So much has happened to me in such a short time."

"I know." He gave her one and a half turns.

"I just figured, why should I live scared of the unknown? I just need to seize the day. Be myself. You know."

"Carpe diem."

"Tood, you are a fine dancer."

"Thanks. You are not bad, kid."

"I'm the best you'll ever see." She laughed and spun with him.

"You are almost as good as Jocelyn."

"You danced with my mom?"

"Who do you think taught Josie those moves?" Tood grinned and gave her a twirl.

"Seriously? I'm impressed. You were her swing partner. Why haven't you mentioned it before?" Emmy questioned.

"I don't know. It just came to me. You know, you are the spitting image of her."

"Yeah, play another record, old man." Emmy grinned.

"She could make me laugh with the funniest—"

"Puns. More like the corniest."

"I loved her laugh, especially—"

Emmy finished, "When she snorted like a pig!" She gave a little snort.

"She used to make the best blue—"

"Berry muffins. With the sugar on top!" Emmy laughed and then snorted.

"Like mother, like daughter," Tood commented. "How is your mother?"

Emmy opened her mouth to answer, but the song ended. While she and all the dancers applauded the orchestra, she shrugged her shoulders. Rock and Rye began.

"You ready for a little more swing, kiddo?" Tood asked.

"Always." They jumped and jived together.

Tood and Emmy returned to the table after the next song of "Flying Home." Halfway to the table, the next song, "The Twist," began playing.

Emmy rushed over to the table and grabbed Seravina's hand.

"Time to practice some of those moves, Stringbean."

"What? Now?" Seravina panicked.

"Yes!" Emmy pulled her up and dragged to the dance floor. "Just do what I do."

Woof howled at them as the band leader sang into the microphone.

"Come on, baby. Let's do the twist!"

Emmy and Tood did the Twist.

"Come on, baby, Let's do the twist."

Seravina watched, crossed her arms, and then turned to go back.

"Take me by my little hand and go like this."

Tood jumped in front of her and held out his hand. He smiled. She reluctantly placed her hand out. He spun her while doing the dance.

"E-yah, twist. Baby, baby, twist, Ooh yeah, just like this."

"Come on, little miss, and do the twist."

Seravina began to slowly twist to the music and grinned at her friends.

"My daddy is sleepin', and mama ain't around. Yeah, Daddy just sleepin, and Mama ain't around. We're gonna twista, twista, twista till we tear the house down."

"Round and round and round. Yeah, twist. Round and round and round. Twist, baby, twist. Round and round and round. Ooh yeah, baby, twist."

The dancing trio laughed and grooved to the rest of the song.

Woof howled again as they came back to the booth.

"Thanks, Woofy. I can't wait to see your moves," Emmy replied.

Seravina said, "That was enjoyable."

Tood teased, "It's called fun."

The princess remembered. "Oh, Artie said he would have a room with a view after the first singer performs." She drank some water.

"Fabulous," replied Emmy and reached for her cocktail.

The lights on the stage and the audience went dim, and the band curtain closed as a master of ceremony walked to the center microphone. A spotlight illuminated his tall frame and cast an extra-long shadow against the curtain.

"Welcome, one and all. Thank you for coming to First Timer Night at Five Pennies. I am Lawrence. On behalf of Red and the whole staff, I would like to thank you for showing up. You folks are paying the rent. All joking aside, yes, I believe it was a joke, Red. Don't forget to stay around for our annual Jump and Jive dance competition following the performers. I see the Woof is here, along with Popson, Chang, Fred, Ginger, Gene, and Dorothy. All contenders for the crown. All can sign up at the east bar. This year, the new artists and Jump and Jive will be broadcast live via radio throughout the whole land!" The audience cheered.

"Anywho, we have a great lineup of first-time performers from all over Between. This first young lady will steal your heart and your precious gems. I wish she was all mine. Let's give a warm Five Pennies welcome to Andrea Elfstone." He lowered the microphone and the stand onto the dance floor.

The spotlight faded to black. The stage curtain went up slowly. The band played a sultry introduction of "Your Heart is as Black as Night." The female singer swayed up to the microphone stand. A soft spotlight turned on and reflected off her shimmering long red dress.

"Your eyes may be whole, but the story I'm told. Is that your heart is as black as night."

"Lady Miner? Andrea," Tood said and leaned forward.

"Tood, do you know her?" Emmy asked.

He whispered, "She is on the city council. I met her the other night. Shh."

"Your lips may be sweet, such that I can't compete, but your heart is as black as night."

Seravina said, "She has a lovely voice and is pretty."

Tood wasn't listening to his friends. "She is fine."

"I don't know why you came along, at such a perfect time. But if I let you hang around, I'm bound to lose my mind. 'Cause your hands may be strong, but the feelings all wrong. Your heart is as black as night."

The house band played a melancholy riff with a clarinet solo.

"Wow," Tood whispered. The young ladies noticed.

"I don't know why you came along, at such a perfect time, but if I let you hang around, I'm bound to lose my mind. 'Cause your hands may be strong, but the feelings all wrong. Your heart is as black as night." Andrea paused. "Your heart is as black as night. Oh, your heart is as black. As night. Ah-ah, oh."

The spotlight faded. The audience cheered and clapped. Tood stood up, enthusiastically cheered, and whistled as the house lights came on. He turned to the Woof pack. "She was great."

Emmy and Seravina said with sarcasm, "Yeah, great."

Andrea took a bow and noticed Tood giving her a standing ovation and whistling. She gave him a little wave and a brilliant smile. She removed the mic from the stand. "I would like to dedicate this next song to a smart young man I just met. Swimming in the Nile." She winked at Tood, and the band played the intro. Tood sat down.

Emmy whispered to Seravina, "Look out, sister. I think we have another contender."

Seravina's eyes narrowed at Andrea. "I will rip her heart out."

Emmy said, "I like the enthusiasm. But remember, play it cool."

"Cool as an ice pick." The elf bent the steel fork in half.

"I know a little bit about a lot of things, but I don't know enough about you." Andrea moved toward the audience on the left. "Just when I think you're mine, you try a different line, and, baby, what can I do?"

"I read the latest news, no buttons on my shoes, but, baby, I'm confused about you. You get me in a spin, oh, what a stew I'm in.

'Cause I don't know enough about you." She moved to the center tables closer to Tood.

"Jack-of-all-trades, master of none, and isn't a shame. I'm sure that you'd be good for me if you'd only play my game." She walked past his table and moved to the right. "You know I went to school, and I'm nobody's fool. That is to say, until I met you! I know a little bit about a lot of things, but I don't know enough about you." The band played a soft bridge with a piano solo. She swayed back to the middle and stood in front of the Junkman. She pointed to him.

"You know I went to school, and I'm nobody's fool. That is to say, until I met you! I know a little bit about a lot of things, but I don't know enough about you." She seductively moved over to Tood and sat on his lap. "I know a little bit about biology and a little more about psychology. I'm a little gem in geology."

Tood snickered. Emmy had to grab Seravina.

"But I don't know enough about you." She stood up, took a step back, and spoke to Tood. "Can't wait until Friday, King Tut." She reached out her index finger and touched his nose. She sang again. "But I don't know enough about you." She moved back to her starting mark. "But I don't know enough about you."

The whole audience cheered wildly, except two young ladies in the center booth. Tood clapped slowly and sat down with his face blushing.

"Wow. She did incredible," Todd commented.

"So what's happening on Friday, King Tut?"

"You guys heard that?"

Seravina jumped in. "The whole building heard it, you buffoon."

"Hey, why all this venom on me? I was just listening to her sing."

Seravina said, "More like enthralled. Did you not understand her intentions? She sat on your lap!"

"Vina, it was part of the act. Emmy, you've seen shows before. Tell her."

"Sorry, cowboy. This is your own rodeo. But I am sure someone wants to know more about you."

"Seravina, Emmy, it was just a song. Woof, back me up."

Woof howled and gave a low sultry growl toward Andrea.

Emmy and Seravina gasped.

"Thanks for not helping, pal."

Lawrence, the MC, came back to the stage. "Wasn't she just great, kids? I told you. While we wait for the next act to set up, the band is going to play a few kicking tunes. Hit it, boys."

"Go Daddy O" jumped from the instruments.

Artie returned to the table with a second round of drinks. "Ms. Zinger and Mr. Woof, the room is ready. Please follow me."

Emmy and Woof followed the waiter to the back of the kitchen to a flight of stairs. "Up the stairs. Second door on the right. Should be what you need."

"Thanks, Artie." She kissed his cheek as she headed up the stairs. "You are a gem."

Woof licked his other cheek and ran up the stairs.

Artie smiled and called up the stairs, "I left some drinks and grub for ya. Swell kids."

Seravina and Tood sat awkwardly across from each other as the rousing music played. They sipped their drinks.

"Tood, you seem to be a fine dancer."

"Thanks. You know, Vina," Tood broke in. "Dancing is a lot like sparring. Moving back and forth, making sure you keep the right footwork, balance, and spacing between you and your partner. Except you are not trying to hit him with a weapon."

She leaned forward. "I'd feel more comfortable with a weapon in my hand."

Tood laughed. "I know you would."

"Tood, the music is fine. It's just moving too quickly for me. I want to dance, but I do not want to look like a fool."

"I have an idea. Be right back." He slid out of the booth. "Don't move."

"Wouldn't dream of it."

She smirked and watched Tood meander through the dancers and almost got hit a few times. "He could have walked around, the jester."

THE DOORS BETWEEN

He jumped on the stage and went to the maestro. He whispered something to him and slipped a few gems into the conductor's pocket. He gave Tood a thumbs-up. Tood jumped offstage and carefully navigated through the swingers.

He reached Seravina without injury. He sat next to the princess. "It's all set. The band is going to slow it way down. One of my favorites, 'My Old Flame.' I see the concern in your eyes." He stood back up and held out his right hand. "I will lead. You—"

"Follow." She put her left hand in his.

They said together, "To the ends of the earth." She stood next to him.

"Let's get into starting position for a swing two-step. Put your left hand on the side of my shoulder. My left hand will be on your shoulder blade. Place your right hand in mine up here. Are you fine?"

"I am fine." Seravina blushed. "This is very intimate."

He smiled. "Now bend your knees a little and lean slightly forward."

She leaned too much and fell on him. "Sorry."

"It's okay. Relax. Just a slight lean. Great. Now we sway back and forth in the hips."

Seravina rocked back and forth. "But the music is too fast."

"This is just practice. We slowly sway left and right. Good." He positioned her off set of him. "So when I step forward, you step backward. Step, touch. Step touch. Don't look at your feet. Look at me. I am starting with my left. You start with your right. Ready. Go. Step, touch, step, touch. Good. Again. Step, touch, step, touch. Look up, my lady. Your feet will be there. Good. Stop. Now we add sway, sway after the step, touch, step, touch. Ready?"

"No. My hands are perspiring." She wiped them on her dress.

"You are doing great," Tood encouraged. "Ready?"

They returned to the starting position. "Ready."

"Step, touch, step, touch, sway, sway. Good. Step, touch, eyes up, sway, sway. Now back. Step, touch, step, touch, sway, sway. Great. Stop. I think you're ready. The rest we will improvise."

Seravina said, "Tomato."

Tood replied, "Tamato."

The fast-paced song came to a climax, and the dancers and audience applauded. The maestro turned around and bowed. He walked up to the microphone. "Here is something for all you non-swingers. A request from the turtles and snails in the crowd."

The soft and low piano music was accompanied by a smooth trumpet.

"Ready?" Tood asked. They got into the starting position again.

"Yes." She smiled.

Tood counted to four. Then they moved together, stiff at first but gradually more relaxed and natural.

"Keep your eyes on me," Tood said. "You are a natural. Remember." She looked at him. "Don't try to hit me."

Seravina laughed out loud. After a few moments, she looked at her feet again.

Tood stopped. She kept moving and ran into him. "Sorry."

"Trust your feet. I must remove your vision."

"I am not wearing a mask."

"No mask. Come here." He stepped closer to the novice and pulled her close. "Can you see your feet?"

Her face turned red, and she gulped. "No." They were only inches apart. He smelled like the spring woods after a rainstorm.

"Good. Same steps. Keep your eyes on me. Ready?" Seravina nodded.

They stepped and swayed throughout the whole dance floor.

Tood said, "Your feet and you are doing well. Let's try a two-step with a twirl."

"What is a twirl?

"Look at that couple. It's a spin and a half on the first slow. Think you can do that?"

"I'll try."

He led her into a two-step. He whispered, "Fast, fast, slow, slow."

On the next sequence, he said, "Fast, fast, twirl, twirl."

She did a full spin and ended up facing Tood again.

"Almost. Let's try again. I'll slow it down. Now."

She twirled perfectly and was dancing next to him in a promenade.

They promenaded around the floor, with Tood leading her into several twirls and switches back to the swing two-step.

"Tood, can we twirl again?"

"Of course." He moved her into twirl, promenade, and then back again.

Neither had noticed the music had stopped, and they were the only couple left on the dance floor. He led her into another double twirl and then unexpectedly dipped her.

They stared deeply into each other's eyes. The audience cheered for their dance.

Tood lifted her upright, grinned, and took a bow. Seravina curtsied and walked off the floor with him.

"Tood, you are a great leader. Thanks for the dance."

"You made it easy, and you didn't step on my toes."

She laughed. "Not yet. I need some water and fresh air." She fanned herself.

"You did so well. I'll get the water. I will meet you in the courtyard."

She stepped on the brick pathway into the open-air courtyard garden. The night air was cool and refreshing. It had greenery and flowers on the outside, benches on all four sides, and a small fountain in the center. She sat on a round bench which encircled the fountain.

Tood arrived moments later with four bottles. She saw him and patted the seat next to her.

Seravina commented about the drinks, "Are you expecting a party?"

Tood smirked. "Just a party of two, my lady. Two are water, two are sarsaparilla, a local beverage."

"Water first, please." She received the water and drank it right away.

"Where's the fire?" Tood commented.

She finished the water with a satisfied "Ahhh. Just what I needed. Thank you."

"You are welcome. Would you like to try the sarsaparilla?"

"Please." She sipped it. "It tastes like the other soda pop." She drank more. "Less sweet, more earthy. I like it better." She took another drink.

"I am glad you do. It's one of my favorites. Sarsaparilla is actually a root used in the beverage."

She finished her bottle. "It was refreshing. Thank you." A little burp escaped. "Excuse me."

"All is forgiven, Vina." He quietly swigged his drink.

Seravina looked down. "Tood, I have not been completely honest with you."

Tood moved closer to her. "You really are trying to take over the world?"

Seravina peered up with tears. "No. It is stupid, really."

"You can tell me anything."

"In the barn, when we were sharing stories, I did not tell the truth. You see, I am so foolish. My instructor never kissed me."

"Did you want to kiss your instructor?" Tood asked.

"Good gracious! No! I made up the whole story about the kiss."

"It was very convincing."

"My teacher was an old man. He did report me to my father, and I did try to kill him, but I could not touch him."

"So why create this fiction?"

"I am sorry. I did not want to reveal the truth."

"What is the truth?"

"I have never been kissed on the lips. When I was younger, I made a vow to the Good to only kiss the man I knew was the right one for me. I had a few adequate suitors, but none were worthy. As I grew older, I became more involved in military campaigns than social gatherings and parties. The Good and my father had been so kind and patient with me. He trusted me to find the right man and almost never pushed his way on me."

"He knew his daughter well."

"My father set up a meeting for me to meet a young lord from Ponn. He knew I would like this one. I believed him." Tears glistened in her blue eyes. "He never said that about any of the other suitors." She gave a sad smile. "My uncle and I came to the king's chambers to get more information about the mysterious visitor. I was wearing a green gown, and I had yellow flowers in my hair. Before we knocked, we heard raised voices and then a struggle. The chamber door was locked. I heard my father scream in agony. We smashed the door into splinters."

Tood edged closer to her.

"Blood. Blood on the bed. Blood on the floor. My father colored crimson. Divadus stood there covered in gore, holding a blade. His accursed engraved knife crying red tears. The murderer leaped to the nearest window and escaped. In horror, we knelt before my father, but we could not stop the bleeding. I lifted him into my arms, and he recognized me. He smiled. With his dying breath, he said two things: 'He has the stone.' Then he turned to me and put his hand in my hair. 'You are more lovely than any flower.'" She sobbed and put her head down.

Tood put his hand on her knee and offered his monogrammed handkerchief.

She sweetly accepted, wiped her eyes, and blew her nose. She looked at him.

"Holding that in for a while?" he asked.

Seravina gave a sad laugh. "Could you tell?"

"Vina the Volcano." Tood smiled. She chuckled.

"Tood, I have another confession to make to you."

"Go ahead."

"All these images I've been seeing, I believe they are more than déjà vu. I think they are incomplete memories of events which took place before you found me in the cell."

"Seravina, whether they are memories or not…" Tood paused. "I never told you I retrieved you from the Arms cell."

"See what I mean? I don't know how I know that. I cannot remember. I am frightened of what I could have done to someone. I may have ruined a man's life."

"Who? Outside of Benny the Bouncer and Muchogusto, I am the only man you have met. Benny gave you a few winks, and Muchogusto touched your hand. You gave me a nice shot to the torso, but it hardly ruined my life."

Seravina was not convinced. "I guess. I feel like I lost pieces of a puzzle and cannot figure out the picture." She looked at Tood. "It was an excellent strike. You noticed the winks?" She grinned at him.

"Yes. Listen, you helped me restore my memories and the truth of what happened to your family and in Between. There is still a lot to process, but you have changed my life for good. Seravina, just getting to know you has made my life better. Not just better, fantastic."

"Thank you." She touched his hand and looked down. "You are so sweet to me. I've never met a person like you. I wish I had a friend of your worth back home."

"Your father was right about you."

She looked at him. "How so?"

He moved his hands gently to her warm cheeks. "You are more lovely than all the flowers." He moved in slowly and kissed her waiting and wanting full lips. She closed her surprised eyes and lingered in the delicious moment. Their lips parted, and Tood grinned. She opened her eyes and realized what had just happened. Seravina tenderly moved her right hand palm up to his left cheek. He lightly kissed her palm. She peered into his grayish silver eyes. She slowly moved her hand away.

Smack! She slapped the Doorf across the face. "How dare you take advantage of me! I just told you about my dead father! Who do you think you are?"

Tood backed away, rubbing his left cheek. "Ow! I thought—"

"You thought with your charming voice, sensuous dancing, and debonair ways you could steal my heart and kiss!" She raised her left hand and swiped, but Tood dodged it.

"Sensuous? Debonair? Charming? Me? I did not steal it. I thought you wanted…," Tood protested. He dodged another strike.

"Yes, you! You…jester. Then you gave me an exotic drink to lower my inhibitions. I will tell you what I want, when I want it! Not a second sooner." She turned away and folded her arms across her chest.

"It's nonalcoholic. My lady, Seravina, I do sincerely apologize. Vina, I acted rashly and—"

Before he could finish, the flustered princess turned, threw her arms around him, and gave a long wet kiss which melted his two-toned shoes.

She moved away and whispered, "Now, we should return to the table before the others worry." She softly touched his cheek. Tood just nodded. She stood up and glided away. Tood sat there in stunned and bewildered ecstasy. She looked over her shoulder and giggled at the shocked junkman.

She entered the dance hall and happily sat with Emmy and Woof. They were watching and listening to the latest first-time performer masterfully playing the accordion. They did not notice her arrival for several minutes.

"You did fantastic with your two-step with Tood," Emmy commented. "We saw you from the practice room. The twirling is fun, right?"

Seravina blushed. "Yes. The twirling was fun. He is fantastic." She sweetly sighed. "I mean the twirling was fantastic. Is there anything to drink? I'm parched."

While still looking at the stage, Emmy said, "The waiter should be back in a moment with water and some special punch. Woof claims it is delicious."

A few minutes later, Emmy stood up and applauded, and Woof howled when the act ended. "He was great. He made that accordion sing. Did they announce his name?" she asked Woof as the crowd gave the performer a standing ovation.

The canine yiped.

Seravina interpreted. "Wired Apple Yankee Witch? Does that mean something to you?"

Emmy repeated, "Wired Apple Yankee Witch?" She shrugged. "It doesn't matter. He was fantastic."

The waiter arrived with three glasses, a large bowl, a pitcher of water, the red house punch, and spicy penguin wings. The house band played "Misty."

"Thanks, Artie." Emmy asked, "Hey, do you know the name of the accordion player?"

"Nah, sorry. This is his first time here. He's a prima donna, is all I heard." The waiter poured two glasses and a bowl for Woof. Emmy and Seravina sipped the sweet concoction, but Woof finished it all.

"How was your practice?" The elf princess finished her first glass and poured another.

Emmy replied, "Smooth as butter."

When the band started "One Clock Jump," Seravina looked around but did not see Tood. "Have you seen Tood? I thought he was right behind me?" She finished her punch.

Emmy said, "You lost him! How could you!" Emmy sarcastically waved her finger at her. "He is a big boy. He'll find his way back. Hey, take it easy on the punch, Stringbean."

She scoffed. "This mild children's concoction. I have imbibed the strong drink from the Blasted Lands in victory over the tarachtans!" She slammed her fist on the table.

"Okay. Let's talk about that later. Just slow down your…consumption, princess."

The master of ceremony came back to the stage at the end of the song. "Ladies and all your grease balls out there, we have one final act and two songs before we remove all your lovely seats and tables. Why? To expand our dance floor for the annual Jump and Jive competition. This is also your last chance to sign up for the biggest hullabaloo in Tween. Wait. We are the only hullabaloo in Tween."

The crowd laughed.

Woof softly barked to Emmy.

"Don't worry, mighty hunter. We are all set. We're a lock."

He licked her cheek.

Seravina took another drink and nervously looked around but still could not find Tood. She finished another glass. "Where could he be?"

"Would you relax, Vina? He will be here."

Seravina stood up and cried out, "Tood! Where are you?"

Emmy pulled her down. "How much of that punch did you have?"

"Two or three glasses of pinch. I think." She giggled. "Do ya think Ima skunk?"

"No, you are drunk. No more for you."

"What about…what's his name? Toof. That big sweet guy is such a good kisser."

"Oh, boy. Don't worry, princess. Your knight will show up." Emmy whispered to Woof, "And I'll break his neck."

"I kissed him back, baby. I think I melted his boots."

"Great. Let's just watch this next act. It should be great. They usually save the best for last."

Tood stood backstage when the accordion player finally walked off. "Great job, Wired Apple. I have never heard anyone play so amazing."

"Thanks, kid. I got them warmed up for you. Knock 'em dead." He patted Tood's back and walked past.

"Thank you, Mr. Yankeewitch."

"Flipping burgers! They never get my name right!"

The crowd laughed at MC's latest joke. "So without another further ado, our last performer. I assure you, fine folks, this local band is far from junk. They are going to blow your socks off. Put your hands together for Standard Blues Deviation."

The stage lights went dark as the MC exited. The curtain lifted, and a spotlight went to the microphone in the center. A man stood there wearing a fedora with his head slightly tilted down. His pin-stripe black suit jacket was over his left shoulder.

Emmy said, "I like the name." She squinted and recognized the silhouette.

She turned to Seravina, who was not looking at the stage. "I found your knight."

"Where? I don't see him."

"Look up there."

Seravina peered at the spotlight just as the artist began to sing.

"Birds flying high," he sang a capella. "You know how I feel. Sun in the sky." He continued, "You know how I feel."

"Is that Tood?" Seravina yelled. Emmy hushed her.

"Breeze driftin' on by. You know how I feel. It's a new dawn. It's a new day. It's new life for me." The band started playing a blues riff. "And I'm feeling good. I'm feeling good."

Emmy said, "He is so good."

Seravina whispered, "I think I'm in love."

"Fish in the sea. You know how I feel. River running free. You know how I feel. Blossom on a tree. You know how I feel." He sang the chorus again. "It's a new dawn. It's a new day. Its's a new life for me. And I'm feeling good.

"Dragonfly out in the sun, you know what I mean. Don't you know? Butterflies all havin' fun. You know what I mean. Sleep in peace when day is done. That's what I mean.

"And this old world is a new world and a bold world for me. For me!" The band played the chorus and bridge more intensely.

"Stars gonna shine, you know how I feel. Scent of the pine, you know how I feel. Oh, freedom is mine, and I know how I feel. It's new dawn. It's new day. It's a new life. It's new dawn. It's new day. It's new life. It's a new dawn." He threw down his jacket. "It's new day. It's new life. It's a new life. For me. And I'm feeling good." The music slowed and quieted. "I'm feeling good. I feel so good. I feel so good." The spotlight faded to black as he moved back to his starting position.

The crowd roared in applause as they jumped to their feet. Emmy whistled along with several others. Woof and Seravina howled praises to the stage. The sparkling lights came back on, revealing Tood and his band bowing their thanks.

Tood came to the microphone. "Thank you. I would like to dedicate this next song to my friends, who came a long way to hear this junkman wail. Feel free to get loose with this rockabilly tune. The Good be with you." He turned to the band and counted down silently. Then he yell-sang into the mic with the band rocking.

"Do you know! Do you know! Do you know where you will go! Oww!"

The band played a loud jiving intro. "Get on up for this Rockabilly bandwagon," Tood called to the crowd.

Couples leaped to the dance floor. Emmy started clapping her hands and moving her feet. Woof howled and wagged his tail. Seravina snapped along to the upbeat music.

The princess said, "He is so good."

Emmy whispered, "I think I'm in love."

"If DC-10 ever fell on your head and you're laying in the ground, all messy and dead, or a Mack truck run over you, or you suddenly die in your Sunday pew. Do you know where you're gonna go?

"It can happen any day. It can happen anywhere. It can happen while you're nappin' in your easy chair. It can happen at home. It can happen at school. It can happen while you're scattin', like a scattin' fool. Do you know where you're gonna go? Come on!

"Do you know where you're gonna go? Do you know where you're gonna go? Do you know where you're gonna go? Straight to heaven or down the hole? Ouu! Yeah! Do you know where you will go! Oww!"

The whole audience swayed with the music as the dancers were swinging fast and loose. Tood did the Charleston onstage while the band wailed the chorus and bridge.

"Do you know where you're gonna go?" Tood pointed to the crowd.

They yelled back, "Where you gonna go!"

"Do you know where you're gonna go?"

"Where you gonna go!"

"Do you know where you're gonna go? Straight to heaven or down the hole? Ouu! Yeah! Do you know where you will go! Oww!" The band had another short solo.

"Do you know where you're gonna go?" Tood pointed again to the crowd.

They hollered back, "Where you gonna go!"

"Do you know where you're gonna go?"

"Where you gonna go!"

"Do you know where you're gonna go? Straight to heaven or down the hole.

A 747 fell out heaven. Fell through the roof of the 7-Eleven. You're working on a Slurpee. Things get hazy. Reach for a Twinkie.

Now you're pushing up daisies? Do you know where you gonna go? Come on!

"Do you know where you're gonna go?"

The audience and staff screamed back, "Where you gonna go!"

"Do you know where you're gonna go?"

"Where you gonna go!"

"Do you know where you're gonna go? Straight to heaven or down the hole. Last time!

"Do you know where you're gonna go?"

The audience and staff were frenzied. "Where you gonna go!"

"Do you know where you're gonna go?"

"Where you gonna go!"

"Do you know where you're gonna go? Straight to heaven or down the hole."

The music and singing abruptly ended. The deafening roar engulfed the band in a tsunami of enthusiastic appreciation in whistles, wolf calls, yelling, screams, and overzealous applause in a standing ovation.

The MC ran onstage, clapping his hands. "Wow! Let's hear it for Standard Blues Deviation!" The crowd roared again. "The junkman can wail and swing! Take a bow, fellas!" Tood and the band took a bow, and then the curtain slowly lowered down as the audience clamored for more. "Red, you gotta sign them up as a regular gig. Double wow. Well, ladies and germs, if you would kindly leave your tables and please head to the bars and courtyard. The staff needs just a little time to get the dance floor ready for the Jump and Jive competition."

As the audience and dancers moved off, Red could be heard giving orders to the staff. "Glen and Miller, find the junkman and have him meet me in my office. Mel and Lionel, make sure Cab and Calloway get the house band set up for the competition. Deano, find Sammy and Frank. They were taking care of a rodent problem. I need them at the bar. BOB! I hope you got the restroom cleaned up. Bingo Pal! Great, take Crosby with you and remove the trash. Artie, come here. How is Woof man? Peaches. Have Duke count the rocks from earlier in the night. Bix, get over here. Find Elvis. He's going onstage. What? He left the building! Great, someone bring me a Shirley Temple and a jelly roll. Larry, get Moe and send some curly fries to section four. Mark! Where are your brothers? They should have been here hours ago. They missed the coal train at the mines and are miles from Tween. Danny! Okay, okay, you can sing the coconut song during the next intermission. Virginia, bring mayo to the judges' table. They need it for their subs. Yes, yellow mustard too. Bill and Haley, make sure you get the comments card from the guests. Brian, forget the other drink. Bring me a gin and seltzer. Doris, what time is it? One day I will get a watch after Rosemary gets a clue. Come on, Ray and Charles. Let's get this floor ready. Five minutes, you Schlapinskis! Louie, do something, and don't call me boss. I'll be in my office."

Emmy, Seravina, and Woof met Tood as he walked down the stairs from the stage. Woof licked him, and the ladies gave him a warm embrace.

"Well, Mr. Dorf, you went beyond the moon. My head is spinning."

Seravina drank some more punch and said, "You are fantastic. How did you do that thingy with your voice?" She loudly whispered, "It was sexy. Marry me. Right now."

"How did she get another glass?" Emmy took the glass away.

"Hey! I was eating that."

"Drink a bit too much punch, my lady. I warned you."

"Yes, you did. You are so sweet." She pitched his chin. "You big barbaric buffoon. Give Mama a kiss." She reached up toward Tood but passed out in his arms.

"So that's what it looks like when you pass out. Freaky," Emmy commented.

"All competitors, please come to the stage front with your partners for final instructions. We will start in five minutes after the meeting," Lawrence announced.

"Go. I got her," Tood said while Seravina snored. "Woof and Emmy, just remember something."

Emmy and Woof stopped and looked back.

Seravina perked up for a second. "Go break their legs!" She went back to sleep.

Tood smiled. "Just win, baby!"

Emmy ran back and gave him a quick peck on the cheek. "You got it, junkman."

She and Woof ran to the stage.

CHAPTER 28

She Girds Herself with Strength and Strengthens Her Arms

"Jump Jive an' Wail" crackled from the radio speaker in the living room of the Doorf Estate. Mrs. Hemingway had been fanatically listening to the dance competition. They had broadcast the first-time performers at the start. She beamed with pride for Tood and his band. His singing voice surprised her. It differed from his normal speech. Popcorn debris and two empty bottles of sarsaparilla littered the coffee table, couch, and floor. In nervous anticipation of Emmy and Woof's final's dance, she sipped on another beverage.

"Welcome back to the Jump and Jive dance competition hosted by Five Pennies. I have been your announcer, Hobbs, with my distinguished colleague, Madman Higgins. If you are just joining the broadcast, you have missed out on so much swinging action. But it is not too late to get down here and see it for yourself."

Higgins replied, "Never too late to see an amazing display of power, grace, athleticism, and speed. Wow, pow, boom! These dancers are incredible."

Hobbs responded, "So right. The crowd had swelled from a few hundred to over a thousand Tweeners just to see a glimpse of these fine entertainers. Thank you so much for tuning in to the show. While the band is being reset for the last two couples, we decided to do a recap of the first two quarters."

"Rounds. Like boxing, Hobbs. It has been a dance fight since the beginning, especially between the last two sets of swingers. Pow, pow!"

"You are so right, Madman. Joe Popson and Iris Rivera, last year's champs, have been going step to step with their clear challengers, the Woof and EC Zinger.

"We know practically nothing about this newcomer, except *wow*! She's a looker, and she moves like a graceful tornado. Bam!"

"To give us some insight on the remaining dancers, we have two of our judges here in the booth. Welcome, Lady Mayor Jenny Kokinkus and Wired Apple Yankee Witch. Thanks for taking some time with us novices."

"Thank you," Jenny replied.

Wired Apple said, "It's actually pronounced—"

"Ms. Mayor, you are an accomplished swing dancer. What are the contestants going through right now?"

"Popson and Rivera have been here before and were successful. They have been brilliant. So they should be calm, but their competition has been out of this world."

"Could you elaborate?" Hobbs asked.

"Certainly." She cleared her throat. "We have seen the Woof in the past. Stupendous, but his partner could not keep up with his style."

Madman interjected, "You are referring to the junkman and the huge brawl between them. Zoom! Pow! But he sure can wail!"

"Exactly. Woof and Lieutenant Doorf would both try to lead, which always became problematic. EC Zinger, however, beautifully follows and leads in such perfect coordination. It's like they read each other's minds. I have never seen anything like it. They dance with no care and no pressure."

"Great analysis, Ms. Mayor. Maybe you should join us in the battleball booth?"

"Thanks. I would love it. Anytime."

Madman asked, "So, Mr. Yankee Witch, if that is your real name, how has the music affected the whole competition? Since you are the self-proclaimed musical expert."

"Well, Madman, the first round of music was used to trim the herd from the thirty couples competing. The judges narrowed it down to the top twelve by critiquing their technique, style, showmanship, coordination, and tempo."

"Interesting."

"In the second round, or walking the line, all the remaining dancers had the same fast swing music, but they only had one minute to impress the judges. Each couple would make three passes and show us their best moves. We picked the top four to move to the final round."

Hobbs said, "Now the contestants usually get to choose their own song in the finals. But not this time."

"Correct," Wired Apple continued. "Instead, each judge submitted their favorite swing number. Each couple drew a number from a hat. The numbers match the four songs. The dancers would not know which is their song until it plays. The first two couples performed respectively to 'Zoot Suit Riot' and 'Sing, Sing, Sing.' They did an adequate job. I submitted a recent original song I wrote. Popson and Rivera will dance to my song, 'Don't You Forget the Cheese.' The Woof and EC will dance to 'A Cool Cat in Town.' Now let's get back to my name…"

Hobbs jumped in, "The lights are flickering. Sorry, that's the signal for the judges to return and the start of the final dancers' performance. Thanks again for your time." The judges quickly left the booth.

"First up, Popson and Rivera. The dance floor lights are on. They have walked into the center of the floor. They are in their starting position," Hobbs commented.

"They look beautiful and confident. Wowwe zow!"

The house band gave a rousing swing introduction to "Don't You Forget the Cheese."

"Here we go!" Mrs. H squirmed on the couch. She heard the back screen door rattle. She moved to the locked door and peeked out the side window. Just darkness.

The radio blared, "Don't forget, don't, don't you forget. Don't you forget the cheese."

"Did you see that move? Boom! What's that called?"

"It must be my nerves or too much sarsaparilla," Granny commented. She sat back down.

"As me and the boys were going out the door, my baby had one thing more. Daddy, you know I love you more and more. But I don't wanna fight, and you wanna make this right. Just don't forget the cheese!"

A rattle came from the front door. Mrs. Hemingway turned to the front door. She reached under the coffee table and flipped a switch, and bright lights burst on around the entire exterior of the house.

"Don't forget, don't, don't forget. Don't you forget the cheese…"

Shadows and darkness quickly slinked back into the black of night. The front door slowly creaked open, and the business end of a double-barrel shotgun protruded forward as the dwarf creeped on the porch. She peered all round and gingerly stepped backward inside. She locked and bolted the door and kept the shotgun with her as she walked back to the couch.

"One more time! Don't you forget. Don't, don't forget the cheese…"

She sighed. "I must be on edge." She reached under the table and hit another switch. She listened for a moment and could hear Beethoven's Symphony No. 5 blaring on the outdoor surround sound system. "Now back to the show." She sat back in her chair.

"What a performance by Popson and Rivera! The crowd is going crazy!" Hobbs shouted. "That is one tough act to follow!"

"They were spinning and flying around the dance floor! Pow wow *zoom*! The crowd is still on their feet!"

THE DOORS BETWEEN

"The champs have stepped up to the challenge. Will the Woof pack give an outstanding answer? We will find out right after this break from our sponsor, Pepe's Grill!"

"Who has the best java in the land? Pepe's Grill! Pepe's Grill! Who can make a sandwich with one hand? Pepe's Grill! Pepe's Grill! Who cooks fresh pinguinos every day? Pepe's Grill! Pepe's Grill! Who guarantees the food or you don't pay? Pepe's Grill! Pepe's Grill! Pepe's Grill! A proud sponsor of the Jump and Jive and Battleball 300!"

"Welcome back to the Jump and Jive. We are finally down to our last couple. Do they have what it takes to defeat the champs, Popson and Rivera?" Hobbs said.

Higgins responded, "If they are better than the champs, I will eat my fedora! Boom! Without any further ado, Woof and EC Zinger!"

Hobbs said, "All the lights have dimmed. The spotlight is in the middle of the floor. Where are the dancers? The music is about to start. The drums and singer started, *meeoww*."

A swoosh echoed through the radio speakers. "EC has just materialized in the spotlight. 'A COOL...CAT...IN TOWN. *Play it nice.*'"

"She is solo dancing. What is that move called?" Higgins asked.

"Spin it, baby."

"Fishtails into Tabby the Cat. Leg, knee, and hip movement are perfect."

"It's late at night while the dogs are sleeping."

"Woof just appeared next to her doing the same moves. Wow!"

"Now they are doing a Charleston with a big kick. They moved flawlessly into a Big Apple Swing out and then full break swing out."

"She leaving the Cape, and the wheels are turning."

"Did she just slide over his back? Zow! Now the Woof just slid off her back!"

"Stepping on ice, but the temperature is rising."

"They are matched perfectly. SuzieQ, Apple Jack, tranky doo. Seamless."

"She steps in the club and walls are burning!"

"They are on fire! Call the fire pump!"

"There's a cool cat in town, never settles down, she loves chasing the dogs around."

"These swing outs into various individual moves and spins are blazing and incredibly smooth."

"There's a new kid around, and she knows she is bound to be the leader of the whole rat pack, and she won't wait until the return of the facts."

"Is there a move these two don't know? Go! Kid! Go!" Hobbs cheered.

"There's a cool cat in town, never going down. One day she's even headed for the crown! A...cool...cat...in...town. Swing it, boys."

The saxophone and trumpet solos blared. Smoke billowed from Ms. H's radio.

"Hobbs! Hobbs, did you see that!"

"EC just spun around Woof seven times in row and landed on beat, right into a sweet boogie stomp."

"Hobbs, I am calling that move the EC Tornado! Zoom!"

Mrs. Hemingway sniffed the air. "Is the oven on?"

"I don't know what to say. Wow! You better start eating that hat!"

"A cool cat. I dig what you're doing. A cool cat in town," the sultry voice cooed.

"The crowd is on their feet. The cheers are deafening! These kids are having the time of their—"

Flames burst around the radio as the broadcast stopped. Granny yelped and ran over to the kitchen. She returned with a small red fire extinguisher and put out the untimely blaze. She unplugged the device and then kicked it across the room.

"Are you kidding me! Piece of junk. I am going to bed." She stomped on it again, grabbed the shotgun, and left the room, grumbling about technology. She could still hear Beethoven playing outside on a loop. She opened the basement door and walked down the stairs. "The one time I needed to use it, the blasted thing catches fire."

CHAPTER 29

Do Not Boast about Tomorrow, for You Do Not Know What a Day May Bring Forth

Emmy, Seravina, Tood, and Woof slept in after their outstanding night on the town. They arrived at the estate after midnight. Mrs. H had been up with the birds and handling her daily activities. She cleaned up the mess in the living room. She prepared a hearty breakfast of flapjacks, savory meats, fruit bowls, and of course, coffee for the party crew. Tood woke up on his normal schedule of 8:00 a.m. He shuffled and stumbled into the kitchen to infuse caffeine into his bloodstream. Mrs. H sat at the island, sipping her fragrant tea. He kissed her on the head and then grabbed a giant mug with painted ladybugs. He poured the black elixir into his mug and floated three sugar cubes. He stirred it twice and brought it to his lips.

"Good morning. I assume you all had a wonderful swinging time, dear," Granny said softly.

"Yes, thank you. Good morning, Mother. Emmy is an incredible dancer. I had to teach Seravina a few moves, but she was a natural," Tood commented and sipped some more.

"Some moves, dear. Interesting. Did Woof showboat again?"

"Of course. He and Emmy won the Jump and Jive. They were sensational together. They did moves I had never imagined. Why did you say interesting?"

"I am not blind, son. I see how you glance at her. Her eyes glow at just a peek of you. That's quite a shiner on your cheek."

Tood grabbed a vibrant red apple and two pancakes with his other hand. He kissed her on the cheek. "I will be in the basement if you need me. Anything to report?"

"Nothing yet, dear." She blew him a kiss. "You should sing more often."

He caught the imaginary kiss and sang "Feeling Good" as he left the room.

About two hours later, Seravina, Woof, and Emmy hobbled down the stairs. Seravina wore Tood's red robe. Emmy had a quilt draped around her shoulders and the dance trophy in her arms. Woof immediately went outside and did not return. The princesses meandered to the kitchen and were greeted with delightful breakfast aromas and a warm dwarf hug. Emmy triumphantly placed the trophy on the kitchen table. They eagerly ate the food. Emmy finished her meal with black coffee. Seravina concluded hers with herbal tea.

They both asked simultaneously, "Where's Tood?"

"He was in the basement," Granny said. "But I believe now he is at the front door. I believe congratulations are in order."

They both answered, "Thank you."

Tood walked into the kitchen from the dining room. He held an open envelope and was reading an official Tween document.

He looked up. "Good morning, ladies! I hope you had a great sleep."

Seravina replied first, "Divine." She blushed and then used the teacup as cover.

"I have this weird kink in my neck, but it was worth it." Emmy kissed the trophy and rubbed her neck. "I haven't swung like that in a year."

"What do you have there, dear? It looks important," the caretaker asked.

"I have been summoned to Tween by the mayor." He handed it to Mrs. H. "Captain Chico and Mrs. Miller have gone missing. Apparently, after a riotous mob, there was a house fire. I am currently in charge of the Legion and the investigation. I have to go right away."

"Is there not a superior officer over the captain?" Seravina asked.

"Yes. Colonel Miller. His wife is missing."

"Anything I can do?" Emmy asked.

"Yes. Come with me."

"To Tween? Really?"

"Yes, really, champ. I will need another set of eyes and someone I can trust. You said you were an investigator."

Emmy protested, "I am…but…but what am I going to wear?"

Seravina interjected, "Tood, may I accompany you as well?"

"Not this time. I'm sorry, my lady," Tood apologized and touched her cheek. "You are not yet acclimated to Tween traditions and speech. Soon." He gently touched her elbow and winked at her. She gave him a slight smile.

Tood turned to Emmy. "Mrs. Hemingway can help you dress appropriately. Will you come with me?"

"Yes. I'll go," Emmy responded.

"Great. Would you call Woof home? He responds well to your sweet voice," Tood said and walked to his bedroom to get ready. He closed the door.

"Come along, dear. We must get you dressed properly." Granny took Emmy by the hand. "I have just the thing for you."

Mrs. Hemingway pushed a wooden diamond on the wall next to the torture room. The wooden panel slid to the right and disappeared into the wall. She dragged Emmy into a wardrobe room. It was an enormous walk-in closet with garments, dresses, skirts, etc. on hangers on the right. Shoes, boots, sandals, heels, sneakers, etc. in small cubbies on the left. There were lady fashions from multiple eras of human history. Emmy's mouth hung open at the sheer volume of the room and clothing options.

"Dear, close your mouth. You will catch a chick-hen," Granny commented.

Emmy closed her mouth. "Has this room always been here? It's enormous."

Granny said, "Yes, dear." She walked to the back of the room. A beautiful classic nineteenth-century indigo dress trimmed in white lace lay on a headless mannequin. "Here it is."

"It is quite elegant," Seravina commented from the doorway of the wardrobe. "It will coordinate nicely with her sweet voice, blue eyes, and ebony hair."

"Thank you. I thought so too," Granny replied. "I worked on it while you were sleeping."

Emmy touched the fine texture of the lace. "You made this? For me? Oh, Granny!" Emmy's eyes misted as she hugged her granny. "Thank you. It is gorgeous. I've never had a dress like this."

"You're welcome, dear. Now no blubbering. Go around the corner and get your clothes off and I'll help you get ready."

"I will procure an appropriate hat and scarf for this ensemble, niece."

Emmy smiled and went around the corner. "Thanks, Auntie. Hey, what is this thing?"

"Auntie," Seravina muttered. "Mrs. Hemingway," she called and looked through the clothes.

"Yes, dear?" Mrs. H poked her head out.

"I have misjudged your fashion sense. Please accept my humble apologies."

"Of course, dear." She took a step toward the elf and whispered, "I may need your assistance in helping Emmy get dressed. She has never worn a corset."

"Is she a barbarian?" Seravina teased.

"Apparently." Mrs. H chuckled and announced, "But she is our little savage."

"I can hear you," Emmy called from around the corner. "I am not a…ahh!" She struggled with the undergarment and stumbled and fell to the floor.

"Just relax, niece." Seravina walked over and peeked around the corner's edge. "I know how to deal with the uncivilized."

Emmy snapped, "Wearing this thing is barbaric. Ever hear of a bra?"

The princess shook her head at Emmy. "Bra? Never heard of him. Good heavens, girl, you have it inside out and backward. Were you raised by primitives? Take it off completely."

Tood stepped out of his bedroom fully dressed in his Legion uniform. He placed the helmet under his left arm and closed the door. He went to the kitchen and grabbed a picnic basket. He stored apples, bread, bottles of RC Cola, and some roasted penguins into it.

He called out to the living room, "Are you almost ready?"

Seravina replied, "She will meet you in the foyer."

Tood gathered the basket and went to the front door to wait. He examined his watch. "Almost eleven," he muttered. He went back to his room and grabbed his satchel and wrapped it around his left shoulder. He put on his helmet. He looked out the front window into the cloudless sky.

Emmy stepped into the foyer and cleared her throat. "I'm ready." The Hemingway original flowed smoothly down to her shins. She wore a matching small blue bonnet and a faded pink and beige scarf with tiny white roses. She wore comfortable toffee front-laced knee-high boots. She held a small leather purse which coordinated well with the outfit.

Tood's jaw dropped. "You look…amazing. A perfect Between society lady."

"Thank you, kind sir," Emmy said in her best British accent. "I clean up quite well."

Tood rolled his eyes. "Cute. Just talk normal."

"Okay." She slightly frowned.

Tood called out, "Thank you, ladies. We are leaving now. We will be back as soon as possible."

Mrs. H responded, "You're welcome, dear."

Tood stuck out his right elbow and opened the door. "Let us be off, miss."

She put her hand out and smiled. "Of course, kind sir."

They walked out the door and headed to the Ruins. "Are you nervous?" Tood asked.

Emmy replied, "A little. What does it feel like to magically travel?"

Tood answered, "It's like…no one has ever asked me before. It's like…it's like stepping through a small waterfall but not getting wet."

"Oh," she pondered.

"Emmy," Tood started. "As a lieutenant, I can have a personal assistant. In Tween, you will be my assistant, Ms. Castillo. I don't know exactly what to expect there. It could get dangerous."

"Danger is my middle name," she teased.

Tood smiled. "Thanks for getting ready so quickly. You look wonderful."

"No problem. Thank you. Granny and Vina helped immensely. It's Ms. EC Zinger," she corrected.

"You're right." Tood grinned. "Just hold on tight, Ms. Zinger." She gripped his arm. With their next steps, they vanished into the blue sky.

CHAPTER 30

As a Dog Returns to His Own Vomit, so a Fool Repeats His Folly

Woof sniffed the air before he drank from the pool at the base of Little Smackover Falls on the east side of Between. He had completed about half his patrol to stop for a drink just south of the Battlegrond. He had taken a southern route from the estate to the Village of Waydownz. His friends in the village provided him with a hearty morning meal. From the village, he traveled through the southern Felds to Flatgap. They congratulated him on his victory in the dance. He demonstrated a few moves. The eastern Felds of harvested fruit and nut trees were clear as he made his way north to Little Smackover Falls. The sun had already begun its descent into the west. He thought of Emmy and sighed. She would love it here. He loved dancing with her.

He had smelled something irregular as he approached the waterfall but could not pinpoint its location. He finished his drink and laid down on the banks of River Drayne. He scanned the area and closed his eyes. His exceptional hearing picked up a small flock of penguins waddling toward him on the right. There it was again. *Waddle, waddle, shuffle, slide.* Normally, penguins would walk. *Waddle, waddle, shuffle, shuffle.* The flocks usually avoided him, but this group was following him. He heard it again, but it sped up and changed. *Waddle, waddle, slide, slide.*

He opened his eyes and saw the birds marching only two hundred yards away. A rather large figure hunched behind the penguins, urging them forward. He smelled decay and death emanating from them. He listened, and the cadence changed again. *Waddle, slide, slide, slide.* At a hundred yards, Woof stood and observed the flightless birds, encircling him. This caused him to back up to the water's edge. There was no more waddle. *Slide, slide, slide, slide.*

At thirty yards, he could see the water avians no longer had their white chest. They were all black, bumpy, and each had four tentacles. At twenty yards, Woof tried to give an explosive growling bark, but instead, he yelled, "Halt!" The monsters halted their advance.

A hissing sound came from the largest penguin. "Sentientss beingsss. Howss nicesss."

The creature raised up to its normal six-foot height. It was wearing a gold chain with a precious stone pendant. Its tentacles curiously moved back and forth. "Thisss willss bees goodsss fors usss. Whosss ares youss?"

"I am Woof, king of the Firrest and protector of Between. Leave now, or you will be destroyed, tarachtan," Woof commanded.

"Hes knowsss usss, but wees notss hearsss of Woofsss," the leader hissed. "Bettersss youss joinsss usss. Yesss? Weess sentsss tooss killss allss."

"Who sent you? I want to know who I will soon be following. Did he give you that pretty chain?" Woof questioned. "How do you walk about in the sunlight?"

The tarachtan gave a hideous laugh. "Youss asksss goodsss thingsss. Yesss, mastersss givesss usss goldsss stonesss. Sunsss nooss hurtsss usss. Youss wantss chainsss tooss? Youss toosss wantss killsss allsss?"

Woof replied, "Yes, I want to kill." He eyed the entire group. "All of you. I shall rip that chain off your dead salty corpse."

The man-spider cackled with an evil glee. "Youss aress sssurroundssss. Weess shalls seeesss whosss killsss whosss. Attackssss!"

Three penguin-spiders on the left struck at the canis majoris with their stingers, but Woof disappeared and then reappeared behind them and ripped off their heads in a single bite.

"Killsss itsss! Killsss itsss!" the tarachtan screamed in anger.

The next four penguins on the right spat at him, but Woof teleported away behind the leader. The penguins spat again, but on their leader instead, blinding it. Woof laughed and then ripped off the tarachtan's left arm and right leg. Woof dodged a wild punch before traveling behind the spitters. He beheaded them with a swipe of his giant paw.

"Fleesss! Fleeess!" the hobbled tarachtan yelled to the five remaining penguin-spiders. "Getsss awaysss!" They slowly slid away in various directions.

In seconds, the fleeing penguins' heads were sliced off. Woof had used his tail as a sword to finish off his foes.

"Stupidsss birdsss," the man-spider complained and slapped his own head in disgust. He hissed as he tried to crawl away. "Usss shouldsss hasss usesss monkeysss."

Woof grabbed the tarachtan's leg with his teeth, hoisted him in the air, and slammed him to the ground. The creature screamed in agony.

Woof threatened the beast. "If you tell me what I need to know, I shall make your death quick and painless."

"Youss nottss stoppss usss allsss. Mastersss hasss greatsss powerss."

Woof picked him and slammed him again. The tarachtan pitifully wailed from the attack.

"Did you travel here in linens, wrapped up in a bundle?"

"Yesss, usss didsss," it replied in confusion.

"Where is the bundle?" Woof growled.

"Byss waterss fallss. Whyss needsss sheetsssss? Nooss magicssss."

"Thank you. Don't move." Woof sniffed the air in the direction of the waterfall. He disappeared and then reappeared with the linens in his mouth. He dropped the linens and then retrieved two spider-penguin heads. He placed the heads in the linen and wrapped them up. He walked up to the creature.

"Youss eatsss thosess birdsss? Youssss strangesss. Woofsss isss…"

"Now for your quick and painless death." Before the creature could protest or attack, Woof snatched the necklace off its neck.

Instantly, the tarachtan and the remaining heads and bodies of penguin-spiders turned into salt pillars. He slipped the necklace around his neck. It clinked against Emmy's gift. He picked up the bundle with his mouth.

He sniffed the air. It was Emmy and Tood. They were somewhere in the city. He could not wait for them to return home. He had to warn them. He also had to finish his patrol to make sure nothing else had invaded Between. He howled his frustration. He decided to finish his patrol, notify the dwarf, and then find Tood and Emmy.

He stopped his teleportation when he heard a sweet whisper. It was her. Emmy said his name. He changed his mind and direction and sprinted toward the Battleball Stadium and Tween.

CHAPTER 31

Better a Dry Morsel with Quietness than a House Full of Feasting with Strife.

Tood and Emmy emerged from under the Bridge Between and walked north to the southern entrance of Tween. Emmy was surprised at how comfortable she felt in her new outfit. Emmy did not know much about architecture, but she had visited Colonial Williamsburg in Virginia on a freshman college trip. The city of Tween had the same feel as Williamsburg and old Main Street of Charleston, South Carolina. She and her mom stayed in Charleston numerous times.

The people on the streets seemed friendly. The men tipped their caps to her and Tood, and the women did a slight curtsy. The children were drawn to Tood like a magnet. They waved at him, threw balls to him, brought him snacks, and asked him endless questions as they walked through Freeside to the mayor's office.

"Tood, find any good junk? What did you find? Can I have it? Who is this? Is this your girlfriend? What's her name? Is she the Jump and Jive champ? Show us some moves, lady! Is Tood a good kisser? You want some water? Where is Mrs. Hemingway? Can she bring us more snacks? Where are you going, Tood? Is your girlfriend going to help you? See ya, Tood. Bring us some good junk next time."

"That was quite an inquisition," Emmy commented. "You handled them like a trained politician. You kept your answers brief and on point. They always like that?"

"Sometimes," Tood answered. "They were especially excited about the lovely visitor from another world. They twice asked if you were my girlfriend, champ."

"I noticed, Lieutenant. So how often do you bring your girlfriends to this side of town?"

Tood blushed and stammered.

"Did I just make you blush? How cute," Emmy teased.

Tood regained his composure. "Just ten, I think. Maybe twenty. There have been so many girlfriends. I can't remember them all."

"Right," Emmy sarcastically replied. "I do have a more serious question."

"Go ahead."

"The tape of Captain Chico. How did you make it? It was decent quality video production. Do you have cameras in Between?"

Tood stopped walking. He scanned the street. "Emmy, put your arms on my shoulders." She listened. "Now brush my left shoulder and pretend something is there." She brushed his left shoulder. "Look at the top of the lamp on the left. Look about three feet up and three feet to the left on the next building."

Emmy scanned the region, but it was fuzzy at first. Emmy brushed his shoulders again and then looked again. This time, it was crystal clear, and she noticed a tiny bird statue with a nut-shaped miniature camera in its mouth. She smiled.

POOF! Camera powder exploded and flashed as smoke engulfed them. Emmy and Tood coughed as the cameraman waved his arms and cleared the smoke.

"Sorry, Lieutenant," the photographer apologized, "Just getting a photo for the *Daily Muck*."

"No problem, Carl." Tood coughed. "Just give us a warning next time."

"Sure, Lieutenant. I just like to catch people in the moment. You two were having a moment."

Emmy blurted out, "No, no, no. No. We were not having a moment. We had a moment. A couple nice moments, but—"

Tood cleared his throat.

Emmy slowly finished, "But not now."

Carl pulled out a small notepad and asked, "And who are you, miss?"

Tood responded, "She is Emmy Zinger, my new Arms assistant."

Carl continued, "Ah. The new swing champion. Congrats. Did you know the Five Pennies is under investigation for illegal gambling? Any comments?"

Emmy opened her mouth, shut it quickly, and politely grinned.

"Any statements you would like to make about the riot and the missing leaders?"

Tood replied professionally, "No comment currently. This is an ongoing investigation, and we will be doing all we can to help and protect our citizens."

"Can you provide any clarity on the cause of the mob? Some have suggested it was caused by Captain Chico, so he could run away with Mrs. Miller. Any ideas, Lieutenant?" Carl badgered Tood.

"The mayor and the Legion will fully investigate all leads and get to the bottom of the situation. We have to get to a meeting with the mayor."

Carl continued, "I see you both are wearing gold rings. Do you both endorse the new gold fashion craze hitting the streets of Tween?"

"No comment. No more questions, Carl." Tood walked briskly away with Emmy in tow.

"Tood, did he say gold fashion craze?" she whispered.

"Nice to meet you, Ms. Zinger," Carl called after them. Emmy waved.

"We should not talk about it now. We are almost there."

"You said it would be a summer breeze, not a craze!" Emmy fumed.

Tood reassured her, "Don't worry. It is just a passing fad."

"That guy is persistent. Who is he?"

"Carl Tuckerson. He is the chief editor and reporter for the *Daily Muck*, our largest newspaper. The town just got radio broadcasting, and he does the Tween news by the same name. It's mostly gossip, opinions, and some news," Tood explained.

Emmy wondered, "He seems familiar to me."

"Here we are." Tood and Emmy walked to the foot of the stairs to the mayor's house.

Guard Baron, stationed there, saluted Tood. Tood nodded and went up the stairs with Emmy. He rang the doorbell. Reggie came to the door with a friendly smile.

"Lieutenant Tut, it is a pleasure to see again." Reggie smirked. "Come in, sir."

"Thank you. Reggie, this is Emmy Zinger, my assistant."

He gave her a bow. "The pleasure is all mine. Any friend of the lieutenant is a friend of mine."

Emmy gave him a curtsy. "Good be with you, sir. I didn't say I was his friend."

"Good bless you, miss. She is a feisty one, isn't she, Lieutenant Doorf?"

Tood grinned. "No comment."

"Come this way, sir. They are waiting for you in the study, like before." They followed Reggie down the hall. He opened the door and announced them.

"Lieutenant Doorf of Arms and his assistant, Ms. Zinger," Reggie proclaimed.

"Lieutenant, welcome back to my home," Mayor Kokinkus announced. "Have a seat. Ms. Zinger, is it? Please have a seat also." He and the rest of the council members, minus Mrs. Miller, were seated around a round table with highback chairs. "You are an excellent dancer. Wonderful job last night. Thanks for coming so quickly. I hope you have been briefed."

"Thank you," Emmy replied.

"I heard about the mob, the fire, and our missing leaders, Captain Chico and Mrs. Miller," Tood explained.

The mayor replied, "The colonel has asked not to be a part of the investigation for obvious reasons."

Emmy asked, "What obvious reasons?"

Colonel Miller cleared his throat. His eyes were red and haggard. "When I returned home after the meeting, Mrs. Miller left me a note for me in the study." He produced the letter. "She wrote she was in love with Captain Chico and was running away with him last night. I was heartbroken. My love had left me. I drank all night and passed out in my study."

Tood took the letter. He and Emmy read it silently.

Emmy spoke, "Colonel, I'm sorry this happened to you. Please don't get upset when I ask this next question. Are you sure this is her handwriting?"

"What do you mean? It looks exactly like her writing style. Someone else sent me this note besides my wife?"

"Possibly," Tood explained. "Ms. Zinger just wants to make sure it is authentic."

Jenny said, "I have a note sent by Mrs. Miller last month. Would that verify it?"

"Yes," replied Emmy. Jenny left the room.

"When I woke up in the morning, my servants told me about the mob and the fire. Guard Baron then reported to me that Captain Chico and Mrs. Miller were missing."

Jenny returned with the note and handed it to Emmy.

"Thanks." Emmy put both notes in her purse. "We will examine them later."

The colonel spoke up, "I did not want my emotions to get in the way of a search. I have organized the guards in search parties, but they will be reporting to you. I have asked any citizen with information about the mob or the missing persons to report to Arms."

"Ms. Zinger and I will head there right away." Tood and Emmy stood up.

"Tood, please sit down," Andrea responded. "By the way, great singing last night."

He blushed. "Thank you. You did amazing."

Emmy cleared her throat.

"Thanks." Andrea blushed. "I am sorry to say the council cannot help you in any way in the investigation. Each one of us has been compromised by Captain Chico or Mrs. Miller or the mob."

Tood and Emmy sat back down. "What do you mean compromised?"

Ms. Mayor spoke up first. "I was leading the mob against the captain. But we did not burn down his house. His house was on fire before we returned from the stadium."

Emmy asked, "Why would you lead a mob against your fiancé, Ms. Mayor?"

"Please call me Jenny," Jenny answered. "Because that two-timing sleazeball was cheating on me for months."

Tood asked, "How did you find out?"

Jenny burst, "You mean how did the whole town find out? You see, I went to see Jak at our secret rendezvous at 10:00 p.m., right after our council meeting. I was running a little late and arrived approximately at 10:05 p.m. There I saw Mrs. Banker. She was waiting there along with a few other women."

"It is true. I was there to see Jak," Mrs. Banker admitted.

Jenny continued, "When we realized the reason we all were waiting for Captain Chico, we all became furious. More and more women arrived every minute, each with a secret love story about Captain Chico. We were all so angry and disgusted to have been treated so rudely. I guess I became more vocal than all the rest and became the leader of the mob. The Legion guards tried to disperse us, but we were too enraged and grew larger. We marched with torches on Arms and waited for the coward to come out. He fled out the back door, and we thought he went to the stadium."

Tood observed, "So you went to the stadium and did not find him there. What did you do?"

"We sat together." Jenny teared up. "Cried, talked, and eventually calmed down. Mrs. Banker helped me disperse the ladies. All of them promised us they would go home. The fire started after we had been at the stadium."

Emmy questioned, "Who do you think started the fire?"

Andrea answered, "That's an easy one. I did. I burned down Chico's house."

Tood looked with concern at her. "Andrea? Why?"

"Chico and I also had a secret romantic relationship. After our council meeting, I went looking for him and found him at the City Sphere Fountain. I ended the relationship completely. He appeared so sad and remorseful. I walked away from him, but then I had second thoughts, so I turned around and went back to the fountain. I remained in the shadows when I overheard him speaking out loud. He mocked me and laughed out loud about running away with me."

"You must have been upset," Emmy consoled her.

"I was furious. I was just a plaything to him. I ran back to my apartment. I grabbed a torch and went to his house. I was going to throw it through the window, but they were boarded. I tried the front door, but it was locked. I climbed the back fence and entered through the back door. I went to the bedroom and threw the torch on his bed. Flames quickly engulfed the bed and jumped to the floor and walls. I only wanted to destroy his bed, but it got out of control. I had to flee to escape the flames. I ran all the way home."

"Were you hurt?" Tood asked Andrea.

Andrea looked at Tood. "My hair and dress were singed, but I am okay. Thanks."

Emmy cleared her throat again.

Tood coughed. "Mr. Banker, what about you?"

"I don't believe I am ready to disclose that," Mr. Banker started.

Mrs. Banker finished, "He embezzled funds from the bank. Chico found out and had been blackmailing him ever since."

Emmy asked, "How did Chico find out about that?"

Mrs. Banker stated, "I told him." All the leaders gasped. "Not directly, of course. The captain could be clever and very persuasive."

Mr. Banker grabbed his wife by hand, and they went to the farthest corner.

Tood looked at the mayor. "What did Captain Chico have on you, sir?"

Mayor stood and went to the fireplace and placed his right hand on the mantle. "Gambling debts on battleball games. Chico said he would clear it all up if I..."

Emmy asked, "If you what, sir?"

Mayor Kokinkus put his head down. "If I promised...if I promised to give..." He teared up and looked at Jenny. "I promised to give Jenny to him in marriage."

"You what?" Jenny stood up and fumed. "Like I'm a commodity to be traded."

"Jenny, I'm so sorry. Chico threatened to send men after me. I was scared. I was expecting to pay him off or give him a new position, but he just asked me to not get in the way."

"You were willing to hand me over to a man who just threatened you instead of standing up for your position, your family, and your own daughter!" Jenny screamed and ran out the room. Andrea waved to Tood and chased after Jenny. The mayor fell to his knees and began weeping.

Tood looked at Emmy. "We need to get to Arms." He addressed the leaders. "You all have a lot of things to clean up. Thank you for the information. We will get back to you when we have more information." They stood up and left the study.

Reggie met them in the hallway. "Well, that was a quick one, sir. You really rattled their cages."

"Apparently," Tood answered and stopped in the hallway. "Reggie, make sure you look after the mayor and Jenny. They will need your help to make amends with each other."

"I will do my best, Lieutenant." Reggie put his hand out to shake. "Who do you think held this family together for so long?"

Tood shook his hand. "I know you will. We will see ourselves out. Thanks."

"Fine, sir. Happy hunting." Reggie went back to the study.

"This is unbelievable," Tood said to Emmy as they exited the front door.

"I know," Emmy replied. "It was like a soap opera. I barely had time to take notes."

"Not what I meant. Humans are humans for good and bad. I meant Captain Chico has more power in this town than I thought. All of them had been manipulated, coerced, blackmailed, lied to, and controlled by our captain. He has been the mastermind running the whole town. We have to find Mrs. Miller before Chico returns."

Emmy asked, "You don't think they ran off together?"

"Not a chance," Tood replied. "He ran off by himself and left her here to suffer. If he would not run away with Andrea, he would not run off with anyone else."

"You seem pretty sure."

"I know Chico."

"Do you know Ms. Miner as well? You like her, don't you?"

"I don't see how that is related to the case."

"It could cloud your judgment. She just admitted to burning a house to the ground."

"Yeah, but…" Tood stopped in the street next to Arms. "You are right. I must remain objective. Thanks, Emmy."

"No problem. I hope you can get used to it."

"Used to what?"

"Saying, 'You are right.' It sounds so good when you say it. Say it again, please."

"You are right?"

Emmy corrected, "Not a question. More a matter of indisputable fact." She grinned.

Tood rolled his eyes. "We are here, Ms. Zinger. I suggest you interview half the crowd, and I will take the rest."

"Of course, Lieutenant. I am at your beck and call." Emmy saluted. They turned the corner together and faced a crowd of at least three hundred men, women, and children.

CHAPTER 32

My Son Eat Honey because It Is Good and the Honeycomb Which Is Sweet to Your Taste

The Legion had set up two desks outside of Arms for the Tweeners per the colonel's orders. One was for any information of the riot, and the other line for any information on Mrs. Miller and Captain Chico. When Tood asked the crowd to form two lines, nearly half the citizens left. The group which left thought the tables were set up to sell battleball tickers.

After two hours of endless interviews, conspiracy theories, wild stories, frivolous notes, and moronic questions, no significant information or leads had been discovered. The various Legion search parties had also neither found anything nor anyone. Emmy and Tood

THE DOORS BETWEEN

decided to take a break in the captain's office for lunch. Tood assigned two guards to conduct some interviews for half an hour until they returned.

"Do I have to listen to one more report about too many flies in the stables?" Emmy complained as she closed the office door. "I mean, come one, people. Flies are always in a stable, right?"

"I know. It was every fifth person that would complain about the flies." Tood rubbed his right hand through his hair and sat down at the desk. "I hope this is helping. Did you find out anything new or useful?"

Emmy picked up the food basket off the floor and put it on the desk. "Not really. I mean, I learned lots of stories about Captain Chico and all his affairs." She picked up a drumstick and savored the bite. "I know this is penguin, but it is so good. I wonder how Woof is doing."

"He'll find us if there is anything to report." He also picked up a drumstick. "I also heard lots of stories of Captain Chico, but only a few about Mrs. Miller." Tood chose an apple and tossed it in the air. "You know what I think is strange?"

Emmy caught the apple. "Tood, I find this whole thing bizarre. Two days ago, I didn't know this whole world even existed." She tossed the apple back to him.

"Yeah, I get that." Tood took a bite and ignored her comment. "But it's how all these women from all over town are having a relationship and meeting Chico in the same place. Yet there was never a conflict before yesterday evening. This is a small town. Word gets around quickly."

Emmy took another bite and reached for an RC Cola. "It's like they were oblivious of any other woman's interest in Chico." She drank some soda. "They act hypnotized."

"Or under a spell?" Tood stopped chewing and sat in Chico's chair. "What if Chico has some use of magic and has used it to manipulate people to do his bidding?"

"He didn't affect me," Emmy nonchalantly commented and grabbed a carrot.

"What? Are you serious? I believe you said something about him not meeting the right girl yet," Tood commented.

"Did I? I...I don't remember." She blushed and stammered and bit into her carrot.

"Sure." He suddenly thought of something. "Emmy, I need to ask you something about your mother."

"I know. Last night, you asked me, and I never responded. It is just hard to share what happened to her."

"What do you mean?"

"After my grandfather died...she...she had a nervous breakdown. My mom went clinically insane. She would talk nonsense for hours in the house and on the streets. She became a danger to herself, others, and me."

"I'm sorry. I didn't know. What happened?" Tood stood up and went to the window.

"I called the police when she threatened a neighbor and myself. It was the hardest thing I had to do. I had to sign papers to have my mother institutionalized. She told me she would never forgive me or speak to me. I have not spoken or seen her for three years."

"Emmy, thanks for telling me. This may sound odd, but can you remember any of the nonsense your mom spoke to you?"

Emmy sat down on the corner of the desk. She closed her eyes. "She would repeat, 'I have to go home. I must get between the doors. I have to find the doors. Where is the door between? Where is your father? I must find your father. Between door is home. I want to go home.'" She opened her tear-filled eyes. Tood stood before her.

"Emmy, look at me," he whispered. "Your mom is not crazy."

She wiped the tears away. "What? What do you mean?"

"Don't you see? She was trying to go home. Home to Between. She was trying to get home. Here." They embraced in sweet silence.

Three loud intruding knocks broke the quiet. Emmy and Tood jumped and then chuckled.

"Who is it?" Tood asked.

"It is Guard Baron, sir. You have a visitor waiting in line."

"Who is it?"

"It is an extremely large dog holding some smelly sheets in its mouth," the guard replied. "A citizen recognized the canine as your dog, Woof."

Tood called out, "Send him into Arms right away."

"Yes, sir!"

Emmy opened the office door as Woof bound through the front doorway. Baron had held the door open and then closed it once Woof was inside.

Emmy hugged her friend before they went into the office together.

"Tood, look. He has a gold necklace just like mine." She shut the office door, and Woof gently placed the linens down on the desk.

"So, old friend, good to see you," Todd started. "What have you found?"

Woof lifted his left front paw to his mouth and cleared his throat. "Emmy and Tood, don't freak out."

Emmy and Tood freaked out because Woof was not barking but speaking in clear sentences.

"Tood! Is Woof speaking words?"

"What? I heard him too!"

"I can hear you. I am not deaf," Woof commented. "I have some vital intel to report."

"This is not the voice I thought he would have. Is it Australian?" Tood replied.

"Yes. Me neither." Emmy rubbed Woof's head. "I thought it would be deeper and gravelly, more Eastern European."

Woof moved away from Emmy. "Stop that for now. Listen, we have a serious problem."

Tood commented, "Look how his face and eyes scrunched up when he said serious problem."

Emmy said, "You are so cute, my mighty hunter." She tried to hug him again.

This time, Woof teleported away to the other side of the room and snarled. "Tarachtans! Are in Between! I just killed a whole brood by Little Smackover Falls! Open the linens, Tood. See for yourselves. We are all in danger."

Tood opened the linens and closed it quickly. "Take me there right now. Emmy, lock the door. We will be right back." He put his hand on Woof. "I'm ready." They teleported away. *Swoosh*.

Emmy locked the door, and when she turned around, they were gone. "I'll just wait here then."

She moved behind the desk and plopped down in the chair. *Squeak*. She spun around three times. No squeak. An annoying squeak roared when she leaned back. She sat upright. No squeak. She leaned back again. Squeak. She placed her boots on the desk and crossed her legs. No squeak. Almost automatically, her hands lounged behind her head, and her eyes rested. She opened one eye and sat upright again. She decided to search the desk.

She opened the top drawer but found only pencils, pens, and a letter opener. She went to the second drawer and found some empty files and a love note from Ms. Miner. She tugged on the third drawer, but it would not open.

She got the letter opener and pried the drawer open. She discovered a file labeled "Doorf, Tood." It had a list of Tood's character traits, including strengths and weaknesses. It also had various black-and-white pictures of Tood throughout the city. There was a picture of Woof and Mrs. Hemingway. Chico also had her picture with a question mark. She removed at least ten files with the city leaders' names on them. She emptied the drawer.

She thought it looked too shallow for the perceived depth. She felt along the sides and *click*! The bottom popped slightly ajar, revealing a secret compartment. "Bingo."

An ornate hand-carved wooden box lay inside the hiding place. Emmy removed it and placed it on the desk. Emmy hesitated and stared at the box.

"Opening this box would be a serious privacy violation. On the other hand, it could provide clues about Captain Chico." She decided to open it.

She placed her hands on the sides of the box.

Swoosh. Tood and Woof reappeared in the office. Emmy jumped in the air.

"Flipping burgers!" she screamed. Tood and Woof were startled by Emmy.

"Emmy, are you all right?" Woof spoke.

"Yes, thank you. I'm fine. I found this inside his desk."

"What is it?" Tood asked.

"I believe it's Chico's treasure box. I had one when I was young. I kept my valuable stuff in an old cigar box. I don't remember why my mom had a cigar box. She didn't smoke."

Tood stared at the box. "Emmy, Woof and I must go back to the estate. There are tarachtans, and they are heading there. You will be safer here. Seravina and Granny are in grave…" Tood rubbed his right hand along the left edge of the box. The box popped open.

"Hey! I was about to do that when you poofed in and nearly scared me out of my corset."

Woof apologized, "Sorry." She gently rubbed his head and ears.

Tood removed an item wrapped in a handkerchief, a smaller wooden box, a wooden toy horse, a dried-out flower, a metal airplane, a black hair comb, a pack of bubble gum, a piece of folded parchment, a faded Polaroid picture, and a small yellow envelope with a card inside.

Tood opened the handkerchief and discovered a dried honeycomb.

Woof sniffed it. "This is from Bee Cave," he explained.

"This is a World War II British fighter plane." Emmy examined the toy and placed it down. She picked up the black comb. *Unbreakable* was etched on it. "Picture Day. When I was in grade school, we would be given this type of comb for Picture Day."

Tood picked up the parchment and unfolded it. "This is an advanced certificate of completion from Cutoff University."

Emmy picked up the Polaroid. "This must be his mother. He looks like her." She gently put it down. She recognized the yellow envelope. It read, "Nathaniel Green Elementary School."

"Tood, this is where I went to school." She pulled out the card. She read it out loud. "Second Grade. Teacher: Mrs. Joceyln Castillo. Student: Ramon Jak Chico. My mother taught him. How is this possible?"

Tood opened the small wooden box with the initials RJC. He slowly raised a gold chain necklace attached to an emerald stone amulet.

CHAPTER 33

For Her House Leads to Death and Her Paths to the Dead

After Tood and Emmy left, Seravina went to her room and got dressed for the day. Vina briefly explored the upstairs rooms and noticed the pull-down attic. She quietly pulled the string and guided the retractable ladder to the floor. She climbed it to the top. Fluorescent lights glowed as she stepped onto the landing. A thick black cable ran from the attic floor to the rafters and then outside to the rooftop. Small dust-covered wooden crates randomly littered the loft's floor. Natural light emitted from a beautiful bay window on the right. She noticed large male footprints, which had started to fill with dust, leading to and from the window. The princess followed the tracks.

They led her to a dustless blue cloth tarp covering something large on miniature wheels. She pulled the tarp to reveal a massive refracting telescope. It had the same dimensions as the one in her palace observatory. She carefully wheeled the delicate equipment from the shadows into the window's light. Vina peered out the window and spotted a target. She precisely pointed the telescope toward a distant building. She gently placed her face close to the eyepiece. She made a slight adjustment to clarify the vision. She saw Tood's servants coming in and out of a barn. She touched a button, and the view magnified the barn door. The workers carried various metal items, including a silver saber with a wooden handle.

"Marvelous," she whispered and grinned. She returned the telescope to its original position and softly covered it up. She retreated in silence from the attic and closed it up. She wiped her soiled hands on the back of her jeans.

She came down the main spiral staircase, humming "Feeling Good." She wore pedestrian blue jeans, a long-sleeved purple Henley, and her walking boots. She notified Mrs. Hemingway of her intentions of finishing the tour of the grounds and visiting a large outbuilding. The caretaker explained it was called the junk shop. She just asked Vina to stay within the walls of the estate. The royal visitor agreed.

Seravina exited from the front door. She stepped off the front porch on a brick path. A wonderful bouquet of floral aromas gently tickled her nose. She breathed it all in and then sneezed once. She tried it again. This time, no sneezing. She walked down the path and recognized the smell of her favorite but could not spot it. Rosebushes on her left, rows of tulips and daffodils on the right. She saw a grouping of lilies, which were orange and yellow, like a flame. Next to them, but hidden under the leaves, the object of her affections, the Elvush Grandiose, a purple and yellow lily, commonly called the elf lily. She lightly whistled "You Are My Sunshine."

The princess carefully picked one of her lovelies and inhaled the sweet aroma. Instantly, memories of the palace gardens flooded her. When she was a child, she loved walking with her mother and father among the floras. Her father would always pick two elf lilies, one for her beautiful mother and one for her. He would kindly place them behind their ears. One time, Seravina had placed the flower behind his ear. She could still hear his hearty laughter. She slowly raised up, grinned, and neatly arranged the lily behind her right ear.

She went to the front gate and decided to visit the junk shop instead of the battleball field. She could not quite understand how a sport based on battle has no blood or death. The princess followed the bricks toward a large dark roofed shack with green-gray siding. She passed two male workers, who tipped their hats as they passed. She smiled and nodded toward them. She hummed the song in the sunshine with the birds, katydids, and crickets. Clanging and banging from the shop became louder as she approached.

Clang, bang.

Father had taken her to the royal swordsmith after her first successful hunt. He had promised her a new blade. He did not mention she would be going to the forge every day to learn the forging process. He also did not notify her of her daily hammering of the metal in a sweaty inferno.

Bang, clang!

He failed to inform her she would be creating her own weapon with only minor help from the sword master. He did tell her all the great and noble weapons of the realm had been forged through great trials, blood, and tears. She had created four magnificent blades. She never had a chance to tell him how much she cherished every smoke-filled, oil-soaked, blistered finger moment.

Clang! Bang!

Seravina eagerly stood at the doors of the clamorous junk shop. She was about to open the right door but stopped and listened.

Silence. No clang, no bang. No birds. No crickets.

She stepped back from the doors.

Silence.

She leaned forward to the door and listened to the peaceless silence.

She heard a faint sucking and a slurping noise. She heard another then another. Her superior ears heard seven distinct disturbing sounds. Seravina tiptoed backward from the doors to the brick path. She silently turned and glided up the path toward the estate house. Halfway there, she frantically sprinted to the front door. The elf lily detached from her hair and floated to the brick path. She scrambled inside and locked the door.

"Mrs. Hemingway!" she screamed. "The estate has been invaded! Where are the weapons?"

The dwarf scampered into the foyer with a meat cleaver in her hand. "Fire and the pit! What is going on?"

Seravina reported, "There are at least seven tarachtans inside the junk shop. They will be heading this way shortly. I'm sorry, but your laborers are dead. I need weapons. You must mount any defenses immediately."

The caretaker nodded and said, "There are Legion swords in Tood's bedroom. I will lock the back door and meet you in the basement."

Seravina calmly rushed into the bedroom and found two sheathed swords mounted on the wall. She grabbed them both and departed down the stairs.

"Over here, dear," Granny called from the mirror. "I need your help to set the defenses." She removed a panel of the mirror wall, and three rusty metal levers appeared. A dusty sign in red-orange letters read *Emergency Only*. Seravina moved to the open panel. "You turn the top one to the left while I turn the bottom one to the right. Then we both push the middle one. On my count, dear. One, two, three!"

They grunted and pulled the first levers into position. They both placed their hands on the middle one. "Ready? Let's push." They strained with all their might, but it would not budge. They collapsed against the immovable object.

Seravina said, "Let me try something." She stepped back from the wall and held out her hands. Two electric orbs formed. She walked to the lever and pushed with the orbs pulsating in her hands. "Time to push, dwarf!" The dwarf and the elf grunted and strained, and the lever began to move slowly and then sprang into place. Grinding wheels, spinning gears, and an electric hum could be heard activating the security throughout the house.

"What is happening?" Seravina asked.

"We call it the Iron Dome, dear," Mrs. H explained. "It is like armor covering the entire house, including the roof, the windows, and the doors. It also raises the outside walls another fifteen feet and initiates automatic turrets. That should hold them for a bit. We are safe for now. Let's see where the enemy is."

THE DOORS BETWEEN

The caretaker walked over to the panel where Tood had gathered the quarterstaffs. She pulled a small crooked dagger, and the wall opened to a secret room. The lights turned on as Mrs. H moved to a wall covered in nineteen-inch darkened windows from the floor to the ceiling.

"Are these magic mirrors to see the outside world?" Seravina asked as she touched the glass.

"In a manner of speaking, dear. Please step back. It can be quite luminous."

Mrs. Hemingway pulled out a keyboard and typed in a password. The wall windows gave a soft glow, and then pictures of various Between places became vivid and clear.

Seravina scanned the screens. "I see Emmy and Tood. They are so tiny. They are sitting at desks. Emmy! Tood! We need your help! We are being attacked!" She tapped the monitor. "Come in all haste! Emmy! Tood! I do not think they can hear me. I will yell louder."

"Not necessary, dear. They cannot hear you."

"Are they prisoners in the magic box?"

"No, they are not prisoners." Mrs. Hemingway sighed. "We have magical birds which fly throughout Between and show us moving visions from their eyes."

"Amazing," Seravina awed. "I am glad they are not prisoners. I was going to smash them out." She grimaced. "Can you show us our perimeter and the junk shop?"

Mrs. H typed a sequence into the keyboard.

The televisions blinked, and a new set of pictures filled the screen. Dread and fear filled the ladies. Hundreds of small and large tarachtans climbed in droves over the massive outer walls and destroyed some of the turrets. Like an enraged colony of giant black ants, they scrambled and decimated all in their path. Four screen pictures disappeared, and white and black dots appeared.

"Is it snowing now?"

"No, dear. The enemy has destroyed the magical birds."

"With snow? Highly irregular for tarachtans." She turned back to the screens.

Mrs. H observed, "They have stopped moving. They are on top of the estate walls. What are they waiting for?"

Seravina knew. "Orders. They were sent to trap us here." She ran toward the stairs.

"Wait. Where are you going?" Mrs. H called after her.

"To parley. To ask them what they want."

The caretaker moved out of the video room. "Not like that. I have made something special for you."

"For me? Thank you. It isn't more Between peasant clothing?" Seravina scoffed. "I need nothing but my wits and this sword."

"How about some armor and a helmet?" The dwarf opened another secret compartment, and a black and red bodysuit emerged on a mannequin.

"Yes, of course. But...what is that beauty?" Seravina approached it.

Mrs. H grinned. "It is called body armor. It strong, light, flexible, and can be worn under your clothes. It is impervious to fire, water, cold, wood, heat, rocks, bullets, arrows, spears, swords. It protects from the neck to your toes. I stitched Emmy's dress and corset from this material. Its only weakness is the slow plunge of a knife. No slow strikes on the battlefield. Go ahead. Hit it, dear."

Immediately, Seravina removed one of the swords from its sheath. She took one step back and jumped into the air. On the way down, the princess smashed the sword into the suit with all her might. The suited mannequin shot across the room like a frightened jackrabbit and bounced off the wall.

Seravina walked over to the toppled dummy. She examined the suit and smiled. She picked up the mannequin. "Not a mark. That should have severed its arm. Where may I change my clothes?"

The caretaker pointed to the back right corner. "Just press the mirror on the left side. I will try to contact Tood and Emmy while you dress."

"Thank you. My whole army would be invincible should they be clothed in this body armor," Seravina proudly proclaimed. "It is so soft."

"You're welcome, dear. The only invincible army is Good's and His Son on Judgment Day."

"Today is not that day, my fair dwarf. We will win the day."

Mrs. Hemingway grinned and then went to the monitor desk to retrieve a walkie-talkie. "Tood, come in. Over." She waited a minute and repeated, but still with no response. She looked at the screens. The dark sea of creatures waited on the estate walls and would not approach the house. "Tood, come in. Over." This time, she mashed the signal button on the walkie in three long sounds, then three short bursts, and finally, three long sounds again. No response. She grabbed the keyboard and changed screens to Tween. Tood and Emmy were not at the desks. "Where are they?"

Bam! Bam! Bam! What sounded like large metallic objects had been hurled and struck the shielded front door.

Granny switched the view back to the estate. A tarachtan was holding a black flag and waving it back and forth. "What in Good's holy name are they doing?"

Bam! Bam! Bam! Three more objects smashed into the house.

Seravina had quietly slipped behind Mrs. H. "I believe they want a parley."

The elder dwarf jumped in the air, dropping the walkie and keyboard. "Don't do that." She caught her breath. "How does it fit? Do you like it?"

"Words cannot express the gratitude, the admiration, and—"

Bam! Bam! Bam!

Seravina's new suit comfortably contoured her body and still gave her great flexibility. The red sections of the suit on her arms, legs, and torso were beautiful and menacing. She wore black combat boots and had both swords fastened properly, one on each hip.

Bam! Bam! Bam!

"I shall parley with this beast to give us time. I shall not do anything foolish," Seravina said and moved to the stairs.

"Wait. You will need this." Mrs. H handed her a modified hockey helmet. It was a shiny black helmet with a black visor and a galloping red horse on each side. "The visor can be lifted up, but it is bulletproof."

"Wonderful." Seravina covered her head. It fit perfectly. "I love the stallions. What is a bullet?"

Bam! Bam! Bam!

"Oh, dear. It is…it is a miniature lead arrow which travels at a great velocity when it is fired from a gun."

"Fascinating." Seravina lifted the visor and asked, "What is a gun?"

Mrs. Hemingway took a deep breath. "It is a metallic weapon which shoots the bullets."

"Good to know. See you in a bit." The elf closed the visor and bounded up the stairs.

Bam! Bam! Bam!

A muffled voice came from the floor. Granny scrambled to the sound.

"Mama Bear, come in. Over. I received your signal. Over." Tood's voice echoed in the basement.

The caretaker snatched the walkie from the floor. "I'm here, dear. Over. Do we have a surprise for you. Over."

Seravina went to the front door and opened it slightly. Shattered, broken, and dusty human and animal skulls littered the front porch. She yelled in a deep voice to the tarachtan holding the flag. "What do you want, beast?"

The leader held up his blackened bumpy hand, and the other creatures stopped throwing the skulls. "We wishes toos parleys. Whos ares yous?"

Seravina answered, "I am Sir Redhorse. A valiant knight of Between. I speak for the master of this house. Speak now. Who are you, and what is your business here?"

"Redhorses? IIss speaks fors mys masters. Yous mays calls mees Death, ifs yous doos nots gives uss elfs," the leader spoke.

"Death. Your name suits you. What happens if we turn over the elf? Safe passage?"

Death's wicked laugh echoed around the walls as it rippled throughout the black mass of tarachtans. "Safes passages! Yess, yous wills have passages to the fires and the pits. Turns elfs overs now, or yous wills joins yours friends ons porchess."

Seravina placed her right hand on the chin of the helmet. "Interesting proposal. However, since we are in parley, I have a counteroffer. If your best warrior can defeat me in hand-to-hand combat, we all shall surrender and do what you wish. But if I defeat your warrior, then your whole dark army departs with your lives. Unless you are fearful."

Death scratched his head and sneered, "Ha ha ha! Redhorses likess toos gambles with Death? I agrees with yours terms. Steps forths froms the porches, and wees shalls sends outs ours champions."

Seravina closed the door and stepped out from the porch into the light of the courtyard. The creatures on the walls booed, hissed, and threw skulls at her.

Death called out to the horde, "Sends forths! The Rakken!"

The monsters cheered as something enormous moved from beyond the wall.

"Rakken! Rakken! Rakken! Rakken! Rakken!"

Seravina crossed her arms and pulled out the swords in one clean motion. The metal rang true throughout the yard as the champion stomped closer.

The Rakken leaped over the wall and landed fifty feet away from Seravina. It was only slightly taller than her, but twice as wide. All its muscles bulged and rippled as it flexed and eyed her viciously. "Ares yous thee bugs I was calls to swats? A red horse flys?"

"I thought you would be bigger. Did the sunlight shrink you?" Seravina insulted him.

"Rakken hass presents fors red ponys. A familys members." He tossed a dehydrated horse's skull at her feet. "Looks likes yous mothers." The dark champion laughed.

Seravina drove a sword into the dry soil, leaned on it, and casually crossed her arms and legs. "Since we are speaking of family, the elf told me about the Rakkens." She looked at the nails on her right hand. "I was told the Rakkens sold their souls to the devil himself in exchange for the elfin crown."

"It's iss trues, red cow. Soons we shalls ascends thrones ands rules alls elves and mens!" Rakken roared, and the horde cackled.

Seravina looked at the nails on her left hand. "Is it true you have been hiding for years, in fear of the elf princess? Didn't she wipe out your entire family and place a bounty on your head?"

"Rakken nots hides! Nots fears punys princesss! Rakken destroys heirs to thrones! Enough talks, red goat. Wees fights, you dies."

"Fine." She stood up and pulled the sword from the ground. "Would you like to know the bounty given to man or elf for your demise?"

"Golds, jewels, lands, no one's cares," Rakken roared and removed his wicked battle-axes from his back.

"I care. For it is the reason I fight today. The reward for your destruction would be the princess's hand in marriage. I will have my reward."

"Yous speaks too muchs, red camels! I's goings to cuts off your tongues!"

Seravina sneaked a glance to the house door. Still closed.

She shut her eyes. The beast rushed toward her. His first thunderous step with his right foot reverberated in slow motion. She could hear the axe blades slicing through the warm air. She listened to his nostrils flare as he screamed a battle cry. She perceived a slight quiver in the left ventricle of his racing heart.

She dodged right at the last second as the axes slammed into the ground. She countered with a slash, which the beast blocked with his left axe. They moved to and fro, clashing and clanging sword to axe. Seravina realized for the first time she was dancing with the monster. Back and forth, side to side, face-to-face, move after move, she flowed gracefully into both offensive and defensive positions. She grinned. The beast could not touch her. She inflicted pain and wounded him with each landing strike. She laughed, and the Rakken roared in pain. Were they now singing? The dark champion stumbled to the ground. He wheezed and coughed up dark green blood.

"Are you winded, beast? Do you need a respite?" Seravina taunted. "I shall give you eternal rest."

The Rakken wiped his mouth and spat at the elf. He bellowed in defiance and pounced as quick as a hunting puma. The alert princess took a half step back and dropped the sword in her right hand. She reared back her right arm and leaped toward her foe. She punched the charging enemy on the left side of his chest.

Both axes flew out of his hands as the Rakken clutched his heart. His limp body rocketed backward in an arch. He slammed into the ground with a backbreaking thud. A dust cloud emerged from the fallen tarachtan. A momentary silence engulfed the hideous spectators. Then the horde on the wall hissed and threw assorted debris at her.

She landed unscathed and peeked at the door. It was slightly open. "Time to finish this dance, Rakken."

Rakken scrambled to his feet, clutching his chest, breathing heavily. "Whose are yous?"

She removed her helmet. Her blond hair floated in a slight breeze and traveled down her back.

"I am the Red Horse of the Apocalypse. I AM WAR!"

With malice, the tarachtans had recognized her. Death and the horde immediately bombarded Seravina with hundreds of skulls at once. Seravina's head was struck several times. The hits spun her, and she crashed to the ground. She lay helpless and unconscious before her enemies.

Rakken approached her, limping and dragging one battle-ax. The beast screamed in victory, and the black mass yelled back in defiance of the elf princess. He raised his weapon to deliver the death knell.

Swoosh. The elf princess simply disappeared before the Rakken's eyes. Instead, a curly-haired man wearing a western poncho with strange shiny goggles stood before him. He had a forked staff in one hand and a silver sword in the other. The stranger gave a precise strike to the Rakken's heart with the staff. Rakken doubled over and dropped the weapon. With a singular slash, the stranger removed the beast's head from the blackened body.

The salt pile remains of the Rakken spirited away as the stranger dashed to the door. The tarachtan army hurled an array of weapons and artillery at the fleeing man. The goggled stranger dove inside the doorway. The black mass screamed and chased the attacker. He quickly slammed it shut and locked it on the pursuing enemies.

Tood removed his goggles and ran to the basement. He triple bolted the basement door. Mrs. Hemingway had Seravina in her lap. She had cleaned the elf's head wounds. "How is Ms. War doing?"

"She is breathing but still unconscious." Mrs. H put a cold compress on her head. "Dear, she was quite brave."

He kneeled next to Seravina. "I know. I wish she had just waited until we arrived." He softly touched her cheek. "She looked like she was dancing on air as she fought." Her eyes slowly blinked open.

"Tood, I knew you would…" Seravina cleared her throat. "What took you so long?"

Mrs. Hemingway helped her sit upright. "Dear, what is the last thing you remember?"

Seravina's eyes filled with confusion. "What do you mean? I just put this incredible suit on. I am about to confront the tarachtans. Why does my head hurt? Tood! It's you. I knew you would come. What took so long?"

Tood looked her in the eyes. He put his index finger in front of her and moved it back and forth. She followed his finger for a moment then closed her eyes and put her hands on her temples. "Ouch! Why does my head hurt so much?" She opened her eyes. "Tood, It's you. I knew you would come. What took you so long?"

"Dear, it's all right now. Hush now and rest your head on Granny."

"But I have to face the tarachtans in my new fancy suit."

"That can wait, dear. You rest." She put the compress back on.

"I will." She closed her eyes. "I am so glad Tood is here. What took him so long?"

Tood walked over to Woof, who had been watching the monitors. "She has an extreme concussion. She might never remember the battle with the Rakken."

Woof said, "I'm sorry. She is a mighty warrior. She will heal. Tood, do you see a problem on the screens?"

"Yes. We have about three minutes before the monsters breach the Iron Dome."

THE DOORS BETWEEN

"The forces are disproportionate." He pointed to the estate. "All the tarachtans are here in chaos and battle, but Tween is peaceful and calm," Woof corrected him.

"Misdirection. We are focused here, while the real target is…" Woof finished, "Emmy."

Tood grabbed the keyboard and then threw it down. "I should have seen it sooner." He looked at screens. He saw Emmy running down a street with a guard. "There she is! Where is she going?"

The best friends noticed a mangled tarachtan following her.

Woof said, "I will go now. She is in danger."

"Wait!" Tood called. "You can't teleport out yet. The electromagnetic field around the house and walls are too strong. It is almost done charging to full capacity."

"Electric field for what?" Woof asked.

"For the only other thing able to destroy tarachtans. It's 1.21 gigawatts," Tood answered.

"You mean?" Woof grinned.

"A bolt of lightning." Tood looked at his watch.

He covered the caretaker and Seravina in a rubber blanket. A deafening electrical buzz could be heard. He placed a rubber blanket over himself and Woof. He glanced at his watch, which glowed in the dark, and then at Woof. "In about ten seconds, you are going to see some serious sh—" The basement went black as the charge reached its apex.

Electricity surged from a large iron rod atop the metal-encased house and connected to the outer walls. In a perfectly rectangular circuit, the power crackled, surged, and jumped throughout the dark army. Echoing screams bellowed from the black horde as the lightning bolts ripped them apart.

Zap!
Zizzle!
Zam!

All the tarachtans on the house, inside and outside the walls, were zapped, electrocuted, and obliterated from Between.

CHAPTER 34

A Friend Loves at All Times, and a Brother Is Born for Adversity

Emmy and Tood decided she would be safer in Tween protected by the Legion. Tood and Woof would leave from the front door of Arms and teleport when it was clear. Tood had radioed Mrs. Hemingway about the tarachtans, but she and Seravina had already been attacked. They were barricaded in the house and awaiting the enemy's next assault. Tood took the gold necklace and asked Emmy to place everything back carefully. Woof and Tood left and promised to be back as soon as possible.

She replaced all the items back into the wooden box. She returned the box into the secret compartment. She ate a bit more food. Suddenly, she took out her journal and started writing at a break-pencil pace.

Emmy returned to the desk and interviewed at least ten more citizens, half of which complained about the flies. She did learn Captain Chico had been seen traveling by horse to escape the mob.

His horse's name was Spitfire. Lady Miller and the captain had a relationship for years and worked closely together during the council meetings. Lady Miller had her own horse named Dandy, and she would often ride out to the mills. She also learned Lady Miller had always wanted children and taught toddler-age children. She was a wedding planner and known for having an eye for details.

"Excuse me, guard. Where are the stables?" Emmy inquired.

"There are down the street and to the left, Ms. Zinger. You can't miss it 'cause of all the flies." He chuckled.

Emmy smiled. "Thanks. Could you escort me down there, please? I am not very familiar with Tween."

"Yes, of course, Ms. Zinger. I was just making a little joke about the flies."

"No problem." Emmy smiled. "It was funny. What's your name, soldier?"

"Dennis. Guard Willim Dennis, miss. My friends call me Will. I saw you the other night swinging. You are awesome."

"Thanks. You are sweet. Well, Will, I am ready when you are." Emmy stood up.

As Dennis stood up, Corporal Chang came around the corner. "Dennis, where are you going?" He winked at Emmy.

"Corporal Chang." Will saluted. "I was going to escort Ms. Zinger to the stables, per her request."

"Really? Were you relieved of duty?"

"No, sir."

"Dennis, you remain here and finish the interviews, and I will escort Ms. Zinger to the stables," Chang ordered and stuck out his elbow. "Are you ready, Ms. Zinger?"

"Yes. Thank you, Corporal." She placed her hand on his elbow. "Thank you, Will. My name is Emmy, by the way."

"Anytime, Emmy." He gave a gentleman's bow.

Chang and Emmy walked down the street out of sight of Arms. Chang turned right at the next corner.

"The guard said the stables were on the left," Emmy noticed.

"We are taking the long way around to my favorite pub. I thought a beautiful woman could use proper refreshments after all those boring interviews. I hope you don't mind." Chang grinned.

"That sounds nice. Thank you. Just one drink, and then please bring me to the stables."

"Of course, Ms. Emmy." They walked a few hundred feet in silence. "I have heard rumors that you are the girlfriend of Lieutenant Junk. I mean Doorf."

Emmy laughed. "Word travels fast. No. I am his cousin from Waydownz."

"Oh, I see. Kissing cousins, perhaps."

Emmy did not laugh.

Chang gave an odd smirk. "Waydownz is pretty far aways. How did you get to heres?"

Emmy began to feel uncomfortable. "I walked some." She paused. "But I really got here because of a magical necklace with a green stone. Then I hitched a ride on a dragon."

Chang acknowledged her and then gave a hideous laugh. "Dragons! There are no dragons heres. Yous funny."

They passed a sign that read 50/50 Club. "I think we passed it," Emmy announced.

"Thats says clubs, not pubs," Chang replied, irritated. "Justs around the next corners. Great drinks." He walked faster and pulled Emmy.

*****

Guard Dennis had just finished his last interview with a large circus woman holding the leash to a friendly grizzly. "Thanks again. We have all your information. We will contact you if we need anything else. Have a great day."

The woman and the grizzly waved as they sauntered away.

Dennis breathed a sigh of relief and leaned back in his chair. He saw two riders approaching Arms. He recognized Sargent Popson but rubbed his eyes when he saw Corporal Chang riding next to him.

Dennis left the desk and went to Chang. "Sir, did Ms. Zinger find the stables?"

Chang was perplexed. "What in the Drift are you talking about?"

Dennis replied, "Sir, you were here not ten minutes ago, and you escorted Ms. Zinger to the stables."

Popson spoke up. "Dennis, he has been with me this entire time. We just came back from patrol of the mines. What is this all about?"

"Hopefully, nothing, sir." Dennis asked Chang, "Sir, do you have a twin brother?"

Chang replied, "No. I have a younger brother, but he is only ten."

Dennis apologized. "Sorry, sir. I must have mistaken the corporal for someone else. I have finished the last interview. May I go, sir?"

Popson answered, "Yes. But first, where is Ms. Zinger?"

Dennis ran in the direction of the stables. "I'm going to find her," he called back and drew his Legion-issue steel sword.

"Strange," Chang reflected as he dismounted. "I thought I saw a cousin of mine this morning, but he lives by Little Smackover." He shrugged his shoulders. "Was I that strange when I joined the Legion?"

"Yes." Popson laughed. "Stranger! You told me your grandmother was an elf."

"I said she had pointy ears," Chang corrected. "Like an elf. I had a dream about an elf the other night."

"Let me guess. Did the elf have white hair, smooth creamy skin, a gold necklace, a killer body, and piercing green eyes?" Popson asked and laughed.

"Como tu? ¡Es exactamente verdad!" Chang exclaimed.

"Yo soy?" Popson replied.

"Muy interesante," Chang pondered.

*****

Chang pushed Emmy into a brick wall down an empty alley. She stumbled and fell to the ground. His breathing was labored and hissed his demands. "Stays there. Us iss waiting for drinksss to arrives."

Emmy replied, "I think I don't want a drink anymore." She brushed herself off and stood up. "Who are we waiting for?"

"Master's signals. Now hushess befores I closes your mouths for goodsss." He easily pushed her back down. She remained seated.

"How exactly did you get here, Chang? Do you have a pretty necklace too, or did you ride a dragon?"

"Yess, master's gives me pretty golds to comes gets yous. Now quiets almost timesss." He peered down the alley away from her. "Dragons comings. Don't worries."

He eagerly turned back around and faced Emmy. He held two bubbling and steaming crystal chalices. "Drinks! We drinks this, ands we sees the masters togethers."

"I definitely do not want that drink. Especially not from a vessel with a pestle."

"This noos vessels from pestles. This iss chalices from palaces."

"Are you sure it's not a flagon with a dragon or a vessel with a pestle or maybe a hobbit's goblet?"

"Noos flagons withs pestles, nors vessels with dragons, no goblets hobbit's. It's palaces from chalices!"

"Did you mean a flagon with a dragon, a vessel with a pestle, a hobbit's goblet, and a chalice from the palace?"

"Yesss! Onlys chalices froms palaces!"

"Oh. I never drink from a chalice from the palace. I only drink from a vessel with a pestle. Maybe a flagon with a dragon. I sipped a hobbit's goblet. Once I had a glass with an ass. Sometimes I wash down a cup with pups, but my favorite is a mug with a bug." Emmy rattled off and gave her best winsome smile. "Mayhaps, do you have a mug with a bug?"

Chang's perplexed face changed into an evil grin. "Yous funnys. Likes to plays gamess. Whethers or nots mug with bugs, cups with pups, glasses with asses, hobbit's goblets, flagons with dragons, or vessels with pestles, you wills drinks from chalices from palaces. Ors I breakss youss scrawny neckss."

THE DOORS BETWEEN

"Breaks my necks? Well, why didn't you say so in the first place? I don't need a mug with a bug, a cup with a pup, a glass with an ass, a hobbit's goblet, a flagon with a dragon, or a vessel with a pestle. Hand me the chalice from the palace." She reached out her hand to receive the cup. When he released the chalice, she removed her hand, and it shattered on the cobble. The liquid disappeared into the street. "Oops, I broke the chalice from the palace. Sorry."

An enraged Chang threw his glass against the wall, and with one kick, he sent Emmy flying to the darkest part of the alley. A wicked scream of fury echoed in her ears. Chang heaved for several minutes until he calmed down. "Nows, I haves toos snaps yours irritatings necks. Comes heres."

Emmy searched the ground with her hands and felt a wet metal pipe. She gripped it and hid it behind her as she slowly stood up. "I am sorry about the drinks. I know you worked so hard to find me, and I have ruined it. I did not mean to upset you. You are just doing a job for the master. Your master must think you are special to send you to get me and he gave you a necklace. May I see your pretty necklace? I want to compare it to mine. See." She carefully stepped closer to Chang and pulled out her necklace from under her collar.

He turned around with an excited smile. "Oouuss! Its iss pretties." Chang looked down and reached under his shirt. "Sees, mines pretties toos."

When he looked up, Emmy smashed his face with a home run pipe swing. Chang's head tilted to one side, and he crumbled to the ground.

"Three-time, tri-county softball champ!" She spit on the ground. She ran back down the alley and went back past the 50/50 Club. Emmy looked back, but there was no pursuit yet. When she turned the next corner, she ran directly into a guard. They both jumped back in surprise.

"Emmy, why do you have a pipe?"

"Chang attacked me. He might be chasing me. Will, why do you have your sword drawn? Could you take me to the stables now?"

"I was looking for you. Yes, follow me," Will replied. They ran around the next corner and then walked fast. "What happened?"

"Chang started speaking strangely, dragged me down an alley, and threw me to the ground. He tried to force me to drink a potion. He wanted to take me to his master," Emmy said. "Your sword?"

"The real Chang showed up at Arms, so I thought you might be in trouble." He looked behind them, but still no pursuit.

"Thanks. I am. Will, that thing is not Chang. It is a man-spider thing. A tarantula man? The only way to kill it is to chop off his head or sunlight."

"A tarachtan? From the fairy tales?" He shook his head.

"Fairy tales?"

"It's based on a children's story. A large spider climbs up a house to attack the kids while they sleep. It gets washed out by a storm. When the sun rises, it dries up everything and drives the spider into hiding. The tarachtan continues its climb in the dark to kill the children."

"The itsy-bitsy spider?"

"It's not small according to the story. If you don't do it's bidding, it sucks the life out of you. I could sing it."

"A charming nursery rhyme. No," Emmy sassed.

"Okay. Let's say I believe you. It is walking around in the sunlight."

Emmy stopped walking. "Will, it is wearing a necklace with a green amulet. Remove the necklace while it's in sunlight and it turns—"

"Into a pillar of salt. I know the fable," Will finished in unbelief.

When he looked back, he witnessed Chang slowly hobbling and sliding down the street toward them. Darkness shadowed half of Chang's face, his spider eyes bled green down his face onto his uniform, and two wicked tentacles protruded from his back. Will's eyes bulged as his shaking hands pointed to the advancing monster. Emmy looked and gasped.

The tarachtan hissed and screamed at her, "Emmys! Thats wass notts nicesss! Emmys! I wass onlys goings to snapss necks. Buts nows goings to rips outs hearts!"

Emmy jumped in front of Will and commanded the beast, "Halt! Creature of darkness! I know magic, and one more step and I shall unleash it upon you."

Chang halted and asked, "Emmys knows magicss?"

Will leaned over to Emmy. "What are you doing?"

"Magic. I hope," she whispered and closed her eyes. She put her hands out in front of her. The creature stepped back. Emmy felt the sparks in her hands and sensed the electric balls forming in her hands. Emmy opened her eyes and saw a softball-size electric orb in each hand.

"Stop! Go back to your master. One more step and I will hurl these at you!" Emmy threatened. Chang stumbled and slowly retreated.

"I think he is moving back," Will commented. "Those look so amazing."

"I know, right?" Emmy said and lost her concentration. "No, no, no, no, *no*! Come back!" The orbs slipped through her fingers, gently rolled down the cobblestones, and sunk into the ground two steps in front of Chang.

The tarachtan bellowed a wicked bloodcurdling laugh. Emmy and Will jumped in fright and ran from the haunting cackle. "I isss goings toos enjoyss thiss killss."

Chang stepped forward and felt a low rumble. Two large boulders exploded from the ground, smashing the creature and rocketing him into the air. Emmy looked back to see the explosion of rocks and debris.

"What was that?" Will reacted.

Emmy grinned. "Magics."

Emmy and Will ran all the way to stables. Despite the numerous flies, they entered. The guard locked and bolted the door.

Emmy asked, "Which stall is Captain Chico's?"

"I'll show you." Will led her to the farthest stall on the left. "Here it is."

She took out her notebook from her waistcoat and began writing feverishly.

"Emmy, that thing knows we would be coming here. We have to either keep running or fight." He swatted the flies away.

"I know." She kept writing and leaned against the wall. "Do me a favor and look in Chico's stall under some hay. If I look, I may freak out and pass out."

"Sure, I'll look." He stepped into the stall. Hundreds of flies buzzed him. "What am I looking for?"

"Anything out of the ordinary," Emmy answered. She wrote faster.

"Everything looks in place. Except for all the flies." He moved farther in. "Wait. I see a handle. Pretty small like a knife handle. Want me to pull it?"

"No! Just move some of the hay around it. What do you see?"

"It looks like a dress. It's not just a dress! It's a body!" Will scrambled out of the stall and closed the door. "Who is that?"

"I believe it was Lady Miller. Someone murdered her and hid the body here. Probably to implicate Captain Chico. Lady Miller also had a stall here. You will find her travel bags in the stall with her horse." Emmy wrote it all down in her notebook. "Go look."

Will crossed over to the other side, looked in the stall, and reported back. "The horse is gone, but the bags were there. What does that mean?"

Emmy wrote it down. "I don't know yet."

The stable doors ferociously rattled. An evil voice echoed in the stalls and frightened the horses. "Emmys. Emmys, I ams heres to killss yous. Emmys, Emmys."

"Will." Emmy looked him in the eye. "No matter what happens to me, you must keep this notebook safe and only give it to Lieutenant Doorf or his dog, Woof. You can trust them. Tell them everything you saw."

"His dog?"

"Promise me, Will."

He took the notebook and hid it inside his Legion jacket. "I promise."

The stable doors burst open, and Chang slowly slid toward Emmy and Will. The creature had only one human arm left, no human face, and the Legion uniform in tatters. It held a four-pronged pitchfork, and all its tentacles were menacingly out.

"Noos mores tricks, Emmysss. Rocks hurts usss badss. Buts I hasss yous trapsss. Times toos sees the masters." The tentacles closed the doors and secured it.

Will jumped in front of Emmy. "Come no further, beast." He pointed his sword at Chang. "I have sounded the alarm, and more guards will be coming."

"Yous sounds noos alarms. Theres noos alarms. Gets outs of mines ways!"

Chang leaped and thrust the pitchfork at Will. He blocked it with his sword. Will countered with a slash to its head. Chang dodged it and thrust again. Will successfully blocked the pitchfork but did not expect the heavy left swipe from the tentacles. It smashed Will into the air, and he crashed against the stable wall. He did not get up.

"Nows its justs mees and yous." He pointed the pitchfork at Emmy.

"Oh my! Is that the master behind you?" Emmy exclaimed.

Chang turned his head. Emmy attempted to strike him again with the pipe. Three tentacles grabbed her arm in midswing and removed the weapon. Chang turned back around. "Noos mores tricks. Times to dies, Emmyss."

He slowly pushed the pitchfork into her lovely dress just below her ribs. The black tentacles whipped her face and shredded the blue garment. When he reached her skin, she winced. Blood trickled down on the middle fork. The monster sneered.

"Wait! Please wait!" she cried out. "May I have some last words?"

The creature stopped pushing. "Screams, cries, words, no cares, no ones hears."

She whispered something inaudible.

"Whats? Can'ts hears youss."

She mumbled.

"Whats?" the creature screamed.

"She said, 'Watch out.'"

"Ohs. Thanks yous. Watches outs? Fors—"

Will slashed the beast's head off. It tumbled to the ground and dissolved into salt as it rolled into the sunlight. The tentacles instinctively grabbed the pitchfork and maliciously thrust it into Emmy's stomach before they fell limply to the floor. Will removed the necklace with the tip of his sword, and the body slowly changed into a salt pile.

Emmy fell backward with the pitchfork inside her. In horror, Will tried to catch her, but she smacked the ground with a hollow thud and moan.

Will ran to her side and propped her up. Her eyes were closed with tears in the corners. "Emmy, oh no! No! No! No. I am so sorry."

She opened one eye. "Will, is it gone?"

"Yes, we destroyed it. You were so brave. You did magic."

"So cool, right?" She gave a little cough. "I really like this dress. I didn't need this accessory." Emmy smiled, and a little blood dribbled out. She closed her eye. "Will, tell my family I…"

Will felt her last breath expel from her lungs. He rubbed her hair and cried for his new friend. A moment later, she disappeared from his arms, and the pitchfork clattered to the floor. He frantically searched the hay, but she had vanished. He wept.

Two minutes later, a quiet swoosh disturbed the stale air. A deep voice came from the shadows. "What happened here, guard?"

Will sobbed. "We fought the creature…Ms. Zinger and I. Emmy and I fought a tarachtan, and we destroyed it."

"Where is Emmy?" Woof stepped out of the darkness.

"That thing plunged a pitchfork into her…I was too late. She is gone," Will cried.

"Did her body disappear after she…"

"Yes." Will wiped his eyes and noticed the giant canine. "You must be Woof."

"I am. What is your name, brave warrior?" Woof walked over to him.

"Will Dennis, sir."

Woof bowed his head before the guard. "Sir Will Dennis, you must come with me. Grab your sword and put your hand on my coat," Woof encouraged.

THE DOORS BETWEEN

Will grabbed his sword, stood, and sheathed it. He put his left hand on Woof's thick fur. "Where are we going?"

Woof said, "To friends."

Swoosh! They vanished from the fly-infested stables.

CHAPTER 35

Treasures of Wickedness Profit Nothing

Chico opened his eyes when the barn door swung open. The sunlight blinded him, so he quickly turned over in his blanket. He heard tiny, little footsteps creep into the barn. He heard a gasp and a quick run out the building. The whole structure shook when the barn door slammed shut. Dust and hay fluttered down upon the sleepy captain.

"Well, someone did not know I was in here." He yawned and then stretched. "Not bad for a barn." He sat up and scanned the area. Spitfire was in the closest stall to him, along with his saddle and satchel. He stood up and stretched his back as he walked over to his horse. Spitfire whined. Chico rubbed his neck and chest and produced an apple from his bag. The horse eagerly enjoyed the snack. Chico grabbed another apple and bit it. "So what are the plans for today?" Chico said to himself and took another bite.

The barn door slowly opened and closed. "Jak? Jak? Are you awake?"

THE DOORS BETWEEN

"Neil, I'm over here by the horses," Chico replied.

Chico turned around and waited for Neil to walk over to him. His brother carried a steaming red mug with the Arms emblem on the side. He still had a slight limp in his left leg.

"You must leave today. You said one day, and now it is the beginning of day three. I've heard rumors about you, a riot, and a fire in Tween." He handed Chico the mug, and he accepted it.

"Good morning to you too, brother. I see your leg gives you some trouble." He breathed in the rich aroma and sipped the java. "This is good coffee. I hope the rumors were juicy."

"They said you led a rebellion against the mayor. You caused this limp. I'm not your real brother."

"Not a bad idea. I could be mayor." He took another drink. "Our foster mother would say otherwise. You are the closest thing I have to a brother. I do recall saving your life."

"Because you put me in danger." Neil took a breath. "You mean the mother who passed away last year and you didn't come to the funeral."

"Sorry. Neil, I apologized for that. I didn't receive the notice until after the championship game."

"Jak, you sent me a note and a basket of fruit. I haven't seen you in five years."

Chico turned to his horse and touched his mane. "I've been busy with Legion and Tween business."

"You make time for your precious Arms but not your own family?" Neil spouted.

"So we are family again?"

"Jak, this is the kind of circular reasoning which made you run away in the first place."

"For the record, I did not run away. I joined the Legion and started a new life."

"This new life which excluded me and everyone else in Cutoff. Mom was hurt, and you didn't care."

"She was not my mother, but she was a fine person to take me in. I have to find out the truth."

"I can't believe you are still holding on to that fantasy of yours. 'I'm from another world.' You never came to grips, which all the other orphans did. Our parents abandoned us."

Chico turned around and rushed up to Neil's face. "My real mom did not abandon me. I was taken from her. I left here to find answers and find her."

Neil did not back down. "Did you find her, Jak? Did you find the city of Charlene, West Carolina, in your United Sates?"

"It's 1212 Winding Way, Charlotte, North Carolina, United States," Chico corrected, almost like a prayer.

"Whatever."

"Not yet, but I'm close. You know the Doorf?"

"The junkman? Not personally. Why?"

"He knows something about my world. I know it. I have proof!"

"Like the postman, the university professor, your so-called grandfather, and—"

"False leads," Chico claimed. "I do have proof."

"Jak, he is the junkman. He and the junkers collects garbage and waste all around Between. That is all. There is no conspiracy. There is no other world. This is only the world we have. Try to live in it." Neil tried to put his arm on Jak's shoulder.

Chico stepped away and into the stall. "Great advice. I'll do that. Thanks for your hospitality and food. I won't be bothering you anymore." He took one last drink and handed the mug back. He turned his back. He placed a faded yellow blanket on his horse. "I have a game today. First game of the new season. You should bring the family to the stadium." He put the saddle on Spitfire. "You can stay at my house. I can get you great seats and VIP passes."

Neil walked to the barn door. "Maybe one day, we will get out there. It would be great to see you in action. I'll listen to the game on the radio. It has been good to see you. Come to the front door before you leave. Please."

Chico nodded and finished saddling the horse and walked him to the front of the house.

Neil stood there with his wife and their four-year-old son. "This is Lisa, my wife. And this bundle of fun is Jack, your nephew."

THE DOORS BETWEEN

"It is nice to meet you. You have a good man there. Treat him right," Jak said. He reached into his satchel and pulled out a small bag. He tossed it to Neil. He jumped into the saddle and pointed to the youngster. "Keep out of trouble, young man. Thanks for everything."

Neil came over to the horse. "You can stay another day, brother. Lisa just started making breakfast."

"No thanks, brother. Neil, you were right. I need to get back to my world and try to live in it. The Good bless you."

"You are always welcome," Lisa said and nudged Neil. "Here is a snack for the road." She handed him a small burlap bag. "Next time, you can sleep in the house."

"Next time we meet, you all can sleep in my house," Jak replied.

"The Good be with you, Uncle!" Little Jack exclaimed.

Chico smiled and rode away back through town. He headed east back toward Tween but took the southern route past the Drift, the pasture lands. Spitfire enjoyed the leisurely walk near the meadows where he was born. It was quiet and serene. Maybe another day in Cutoff would have been fine. He opened the snack bag and removed a sticky item. He bit into a large warm cinnamon roll. He sighed and enjoyed every morsel.

The captain rubbed Spitfire's neck and spoke to his companion. "It would be pleasant to be around the family. Neil seems like a good father. If he could do it, then maybe. Just maybe. You know I have a kid on the way. Start a family. Family." He shook his head. "I have to get back to my family. My mother."

He was almost to the Bridge Between when he spotted two Legion guards on horses trotting toward him. As they got closer, he recognized them.

"Popson and Chang!" Chico called out. "Has everything cooled down in Tween?"

"Not really, sir," Popson answered. "We were sent to escort you directly to Arms."

"Who sent you?"

Chang explained, "Well, a citizen spotted you on the Driveaway near the Church of Good. The mayor and Lieutenant Doorf asked us to keep you safe."

"Keep me safe? Why have you been looking for me? I sent a letter to Colonel Miller that I was taking a few personal days. I put it in the postbox before I left."

Chang and Popson looked at each other when he mentioned Colonel Miller.

"Captain, it is not safe for you on the streets. We need to hurry and get you back to Arms," Popson whispered.

"You are under orders not to tell me anything," Chico realized. "The mayor and Lieutenant Junk will explain everything."

"Yes, sir. But believe me, sir," Chang interjected. "We are on your side."

"Maybe the only two in Tween," Popson shared. "But on your side, Cap."

"Thanks," Chico replied. "Off to Arms we go."

They trotted past the southern entrance of Tween and headed to the Mills entrance. A large angry crowd of men and women were blocking the gateway. They galloped north around the Driveaway and entered the Arms gateway. They could see the enraged crowd running down the streets toward them. Chang grabbed their horses' reins and blocked the doorway from the pursuit. Chico and Popson quickly dismounted and ran to the Arms front door. Chico and Popson burst through the door and then slammed it. The captain bolted it tight. The mayor and Tood were waiting in the foyer next to the cell.

"Mayor. Lieutenant Junk. What have you done to my town? Why is another mob after me?" yelled Chico.

Before the captain moved another inch, Tood had placed tight iron shackles on his wrists and ankles.

"Ouch!" Chico cried out. "How did you do that so quickly? What is going on?"

Mayor Kokinkus cleared his throat. "Captain Jak Chico, you are under arrest for—"

"I'm under arrest!" Chico snapped. "For being chased out of town by a mob of women? Suspension, maybe, for dereliction of duty, but arrested? Come on, Mayor. What is going on?"

Tood stepped toward Chico.

"Don't you come near me again, junkman. I will kill you," Chico threatened. The mayor nervously stepped back.

"Captain, please step into the cell, or I will be forced to put you there," Tood explained in a grim voice.

Popson pleaded, "Please, Captain. Go into the cell. Peaceably."

Chico deadeyed the mayor and Tood but listened to Popson. He shuffled his way into the cell. Popson closed and locked the cell.

Chico rattled his chains against the metal bars. "To fire and the pit, would someone please tell me what is going on?"

The mayor started again, "Captain Jak Chico, you are under arrest for the murder of Lady Miller. Your duties as captain have been suspended. A counselor can be provided before the arraignment. Everything you say or do can be used against you in the court of law."

"You will remain in custody here until you are arraigned, and a trial date has been set before Judge Jeremiah Stonebraker, Speaker of the House of Vote," Tood finished.

"I should have stayed in Cutoff," Chico muttered to himself and put his head down.

CHAPTER 36

As Cold Water to a Weary Soul, so Is Good News from a Far Country

The Battle of the Tarachtans was over, and the Doorf Estate stood in shambles. The strong walls were burnt and lay in ruins. The once lush and beautiful garden, vegetables, flowers, and bushes were charred and smoking. Instead of a peaceful pond, steam pillowed away from scorched earth. The metal casing around the house was torn and beaten. Tiny electric sparks chased each other around the windows and along the roof. The front door had been smashed and lay in splinters. Salty debris dusted all the porch and foyer, including the spiral staircase. The thick dust covered all the pictures, paintings, and furniture. Silence and remorse blanketed the once vibrant home.

Tood, Woof, and Will sat still in the living room chairs. Seravina wore a bandage around the left side of her head. She sat on the couch with a weeping Mrs. Hemingway. Seravina had her arm around the caretaker.

"I can't believe...she is...just gone," Mrs. H cried out in agony. "Why? Why is my Emmy gone?" The room echoed her feelings but remained silent.

She gained some composure, but with tears, she pleaded, "Tood, there's got to be...something...anything...how about the gold necklace? Could...couldn't we use it somehow? Don't just sit there! Do something!"

Tood whispered but did not move, "Mother, Mother, I miss her too. But we don't know how the necklaces work or where one would travel to. We don't know if she is dead, alive, injured, or floating somewhere near Jupiter." He slammed his fist in the wall, creating a small crater. Tears dropped to the dusty floor. "I just don't know what to do."

Woof sadly howled and then paced over to Tood. The junkman embraced and wept into the silvery coat. A quiet dread hovered over the group of friends.

Distant thunder rumbled from miles aways. *Tink, tink.* A few raindrops hit the metallic roof. *Tink, tink, tink, tink, tink.* The tinks resonated quickly into an orchestra of water pouring over the estate. Within moments, the deluge ceased, and the storm passed. Soft twitters and bird whistles could be heard coming from the back porch.

"I volunteer!" Seravina and Will announced at the same time.

"For what?" Tood snapped. "There is no mission. There is nothing we can do! Will, you and I must return to Tween to solve this murder. Thanks to Emmy's notes, we have some clues. Seravina, my lady, your head injury will take at least a few days to heal, even with the potion."

Will replied, "I just thought I have the tarachtan's necklace. He was going to take Emmy to his master."

"So we kill you and also send you to this master? To a person who is powerful, cunning, and ruthless? Where? We don't know if it's a prison, a palace, a ship, or a house. We are not killing anyone to send them to the unknown."

"Sir Will and Lady Seravina," Woof said. "Your hearts are in the right place, but my friend is correct. We can only gather more intel, be patient, and stand strong for each other."

Granny wept loudly and hugged Seravina.

A loud avian chirp echoed from the hallway, startling the group.

"What is that? An ostrich?" Seravina asked.

"I think it's a bird trapped in the house," Tood commented.

The creature rang out again, exactly the same.

Woof said, "That is not a real bird. All birds change their pitch, frequency, and volume between calls."

It rang out again.

Will stood up and walked down the hallway toward Tood's bedroom.

It rang again.

"I've found something. It's under debris and dust. Should I pick it up?"

"If it's not a dead bird, go ahead, dear," Granny called out.

Will entered the living room cleaning one side of a small flat rectangular shape.

"It was a flat black box making all that noise." He dusted off the other side, and the box glowed. No one else noticed.

"Cool, light." He rubbed it again. Words and numbers appeared with the light. He read it to himself. "Passcode. Hey, what is a passcode?"

Tood had been staring out the back windows. "It's a password, but using numbers, in a sequence of four digits."

Will sat down on a chair. "Thanks." He rubbed the other side of the box. Letters dirtied with soot appeared when he removed the scum. "What is Emmy's favorite number?"

Seravina recalled, "She said her team number was 12."

Will hit the box twice. "No. When is her birthday?"

Granny called out, "December 12."

"No. What year was she born?"

"It's 2000, Will. Why are you asking these questions?" Tood asked, rubbing his temples.

Will answered, "Emmy's box has a passcode, and I'm trying to figure it out. No. 'Final attempt.' What does that mean?"

Tood replied, "It means if you fail to give the correct code again, the device will lock." He looked at Will. "Don't try any other numbers. What did you guess already?"

Will said, "I tried 1221, 1212, 1220. Why?"

"Try 1200."

"Okay." Will typed it in. "Great! It worked." The light changed. Will read the screen. "You have a message." He handed the device to Tood.

Tood stood, wiped his tears, and read it aloud:

"Hey, KT and the wolfpack. Sorry about not reaching out sooner. I have been so busy on my vaca at my new favorite place between the beach and the cape. Love it! Y'all would love it here. Please take some time off and visit. Mom and I will be here awhile. I fear I will never come home to the Queen City. I met the mayor, and he is the king of bungabunga. LOL! But there are acres of sites to see and walk. There is an arcade called the Palace, and I won a giant pink baby bear. LOL! So much fun! It's much better than last year's dump. Just north of New Amsterdam. OMG, let Coach and Hunter know how much I miss them, but I've kept up my training. ECZ. The new uniform is shredded, sorry. Let Stringbean know she has not won the bet and keep practicing her new moves. Bill, thanks for all your help with the insect problem. You rock! Tell Cap to keep his chin up, and I know he is innocent. My mom has acted like a new person in the surf and sand. Dry hair is my problem even with the humidity. Conditioning, am I right? I would love y'all to visit and escape from the north. This paradise has no spiders so far and is so much fun in the sun. KT, don't forget what our buddy General Akbar said about the final frontier. See ya soon. Love ya. ;)"

Granny asked, "What does that mean? I am confused."

"Am I Hunter? Who is this Bill?" questioned Woof.

"Who is it from?" Seravina asked.

Tood read it again to himself. He smiled from ear to ear.

"EC Zinger."

The End

EPILOGUE

The morning sun briefly pierced through the overcast sky. The sunshine cast eerie shadows through Spanish moss dangling just above the murky waters. Zydeco music drifted happily across the giant lily pads. The junkers living just south of the bog played their instruments at the same time every day. The weeping willows, slimy pines, brackish elms, bruised reeds, delicate cattails, and sleepy cypress trees swayed to the music and shifting winds. The slough serenade announced the coming of the marsh monarch. Green meaty frogs, red-tailed lizards, and sweet-tasting turtles leaped and disappeared from their logs as the quagmire queen patrolled the southern part of her reign. All the swampland fish, silver snakes, and brown water moccasins made way for their mighty deadly dictator. The wasps, flies, gnats, cicadas, crickets, water bugs, and even the mosquitoes became silent in reverence of the bayou's behemoth. The flamingos, gulls, pelicans, falcons, and herons bowed low in the mud and paid homage to the fifty-five-foot-long and four-feet-wide massive reptilian royalty.

The music drifted away as she moved slowly to the sloppy north. She liked the junkers' name for her, the Wamp queen, but other humans called her the Wamp monster. The Doorf man had always honored their contract and alliance. The Doorf had never been late with the monthly tribute, but tonight was the second day of the full moon. He had until midnight.

She felt the uneven ripples of a boat paddling just east. Who would dare defy the ordinance and trespass into her kingdom? She overheard voices and splashing. With stealth, the queen moved to intercept the interlopers. She could see three dark creatures on a skid, humanlike but with tentacles, talking and complaining about her bayou.

"Ifs the masters says its heres, wees goes here toos gets its. Wees the onlys ones lefts froms Doorf's houses. Nows shuts yours mouthes ands paddles," the ugly one commanded.

The short one complained, "Glads wees dids arrives lates. Lots of sparks. Buts wees travel alls night, ands wees nots finds nothings. Justs weeds, frogs, ands stupids muddies waters. Nos treasure, nos jewels, nos linens." It splashed the water and stopped paddling.

The tall one replied, "Wees finds lots and lots of buggss. Whats theys eats whens theys donts eats us?" It swatted and missed horseflies buzzing around the trio.

The ugly one tried to hush them. "*Sssssh!* Bees quiets. Bees quiets. Donts yous remembers whats the masters says abouts the swamps monsters? Massives crocodiless whichs drowns yous ands eats yous holes." He whispered, "Bees quiets! Wees ares closes. Iss feels its."

How dare they call me a mere crocodile, the behemoth thought. *The Doorf is their master. The disrespect! They would pay dearly for this insult and intrusion.*

The silence lasted only for a minute.

The short one started, "Theres iss nos stupids crocs heres. I ams toos tireds toos keeps goings. Let's rests ons thats islands overs theres." He pointed to a tiny isle with mangroves.

The tall one said, "Agrees! Wees takes a votes. Alls in favors of rests on islands, raises yous paddles." The crew lifted their oars over their heads.

The ugly one compromised, "Okays, okays, as longs as yous shuts upps."

They quietly maneuvered the boat to their rest stop. They moored the boat and stepped on dry land.

"Donts goes fars. Stays togethers and gets somes frogs fors mees too. Ims starvings. Ims the leaders," the ugly one announced and began sniffing around.

"Yess, sirss," the short and tall one replied together. They laid on the ground and closed all their eight eyes. They rested their arms behind their heads. Within moments, they were asleep.

Seven minutes later, the short one heard a muffled sound and light splash of the muddy waters. He opened one eye.

"Wheres stupids goes offs? I hopes he finds goods frogs ors juicy turtles." He killed a mosquito on his leg with a tentacle. "I hates its heres." His heavy lids closed in slumber.

A bloodcurdling scream echoed from the far side of the island. The short one jumped to his feet in fear.

"It's the leaders. Iss comings!" He sprinted toward the sound through the mangroves. He stumbled over a soiled white log. His tentacles accidentally ripped open several layers of its soft bark. He flew over the bundle and crashed headfirst into a waist-deep mud puddle. The bog slop covered his body completely.

He was about to complain but felt the ground quake and branches snap. Whatever was moving was quickly coming closer. He heard a loud reptilian hiss, which sent shivers down his body. He slid back into the sledge. A deep threatening voice came from the creature stomping ten feet away.

"I know you are here, short one. Your friends are dead! I drowned one, and the other dissolved when I ripped off his head. This is my swamp. My kingdom you have unlawfully invaded. I am the Wamp queen. If you are hearing my sweet voice, it was a surprise to me too. I must have swallowed one of those necklaces your friends were wearing. It smelled of magic. Did the Doorf send you to kill me? Pretty poor attempt."

The monarch waited for a response. When none came, she whipped her massive tail and shattered a tree right above the last tarachtan. The debris floated down upon the muddy isle.

"You can't hide for long, shorty. I will find you, and I will destroy you. The Doorf will pay for this incursion. By the way, I am not an ignorant crocodile. I am the mother of alligators! I am your worst nightmare!"

The resilient queen smashed another tree before sliding back into the murkiness. A sharp branch fell upon the white log and ripped several more layers.

The tarachtan listened for the final splash of the queen's tail into the slime. He reluctantly lifted his head and scanned the area with his eight orbs. Stillness. He counted to ten and rose to his knees. Silence. He waited another ten and stood to his feet. Quiet.

The monster had moved on for now, but she would be back. He removed himself from the hole, dripping with mud. He silently spun around and noticed the massive white log which had saved his life. It no longer appeared to be a white tree but a giant humanoid shape. It wasn't a tree or a log but torn white linens. It was the treasure they had been seeking.

An evil grin formed around its muddy mouth. "Iss founds its. Iss gets alls rewards."

He kneeled next to the soiled white bundle and removed the branches and leaves covering it. He placed his ear next to the open section and listened. "Steadys hearts. Master will be so—"

A large purple hand with black pointy nails burst from the opening and encompassed the tarachtan's entire head. The fingers squeezed the muddy skull like an overripe orange. The captive wriggled and struggled to break free, but to no avail. Before his life became extinguished, he heard one word.

"OOGERRR!"

ACKNOWLEDGEMENTS

To the only Good Creator, Great Author,
and Eternal Savior of my soul.

To my Mommy and Poppy, whose sacrifice and love gave me hope.

To my bride, Terry, for her incredible love, patience, and support.

To Vicente for being my meek and funny inspiration.

To my grand cheerleaders, Gabby and Gianni!

To K.K. for her artistic skills and curious ears.

To my first reader and best editor, Isabella.

A la mejor familia loca: Y, Y, N, D, K, J, A!

To COVID Christmas: The Between spark.

ABOUT THE AUTHOR

I thrived and survived as the youngest child of eight in a Puerto Rican family, living in Fort Hunter, New York, a small town far away from Brooklyn. I meandered in middle school of the brave. I crusaded through high school and scaled the heights of higher education at Clarks Summit University, Pennsylvania. I encountered my beautiful wife, Terry, in Millersburg, Ohio. I won her heart in a Skyview gazebo. My wife and I, with our four inspirational children and grandson, love, cook, dance, and sing in Charlotte, North Carolina. I currently mold the minds of middle school scholars at Concord Academy. I love the Lord, my family, swing music, and treasuring all sorts of junk.

Printed in the USA
CPSIA information can be obtained
at www.ICGtesting.com
LVHW051749121123
763661LV00067B/2334